Healing Hearts

by

C. B. Clark

Healing Hearts

Contact Information: info@thewildrosepress.com

Cover Art by *Debbie Taylor*

The Wild Rose Press, Inc.
PO Box 708
Adams Basin, NY 14410-0708
Visit us at www.thewildrosepress.com

Publishing History
First Yellow Rose Edition, 2020
Print ISBN 978-1-5092-3014-3
Digital ISBN 978-1-5092-3015-0

Published in the United States of America

The back of his neck itched. *"You're* Stella King?" *Of course she was. Who else would be waiting here at this time of night?* Once again, he glanced at the photograph clenched in his hand—gray curls, thick glasses, sixty years old. *That* was the Stella King he'd hired. The itching amped up to a full-out assault.

She stood and held out her hand. "Nice to meet you, Dawson."

He stumbled back another step, his worst fears confirmed. This gorgeous woman was the nanny he'd hired to look after Deirdre.

Her light-blue wool sweater did nothing to hide the full, rounded mounds of her breasts. Her legs looked a mile long in the white denim, skintight, designer jeans tucked into a pair of knee-high, high-heeled, black leather boots. Her perfume wafted on the evening breeze, a heady mix of spring flowers and something subtle but decidedly feminine.

He struggled to swallow, but his throat was parched, his tongue as dry as old leather against the roof of his mouth.

Silence stretched between them. An owl hooted from a nearby tree, crickets chirped in the tall grass lining the ditch, and still he didn't move.

She frowned and dropped her hand.

Praise for C. B. Clark

HEALING HEARTS is award-winning author C. B. Clark's sixth novel published by The Wild Rose Press. *BITTER LEGACY, BROKEN TRUST,* and *SECRET BETRAYAL* are out in Audible.

~*~

"*BROKEN TRUST* was an amazing mystery. I read this book in a few hours because I couldn't put it down."
~PRG's Reviewers' Choice Award 2018

~*~

"*BROKEN TRUST* was such a great book full of so many twists and turns from beginning to end."

~Rebecca A.

~*~

"Are you looking for a romantic suspense story that is going to have you clinging to the edge of your seat? *BROKEN TRUST* by C. B. Clark is one of those incredible suspense-filled books."

~Reviews by Crystal

Dedication

For Brooklyn—
may all your wishes come true under the rainbow trees

Chapter 1

Damn it! He should be home in bed instead of driving on this godforsaken, sorry excuse for a road in the middle of the night.

A dark shape darted out of the thick bank of pine trees and sprang onto the road. A pair of eyes glowed in the glare of his approaching headlights.

Dawson Wheeler cranked hard on the steering wheel, avoiding the deer by inches.

The animal, white tail flashing like a flag, bounded into the ditch and vanished into the forest.

He released a breath he hadn't been aware he was holding and eased his foot off the accelerator. Crashing into a deer or moose wouldn't make this day any better. He rolled down his window and inhaled the sweet-smelling, rain-washed air. The sky had cleared after the morning's rain shower, and a thin sliver of moon cast a faint glow over the dark wilderness, the trees silhouetted against the velvety sky. In the distance, a dusting of fresh snow glimmered on the jagged peaks of the Coastal Mountains.

Why had he agreed to this crazy idea? He had enough to do at the ranch without having to babysit some pampered know-it-all, especially with that damn mine business hanging over his head.

He slowed as he approached Spirit Falls. The bus stop was nothing but a widening of the road with an old wooden bench set amidst weeds and wildflowers. Glancing at his wristwatch, he grimaced. Mack Hicken, the cantankerous old bus driver who'd driven the route between Hosten and Spirit Falls for what seemed like forever, prided himself on keeping to his schedule in spite of flat tires, knee-deep snowdrifts, and mud-filled ruts.

The bus would have dropped any passengers off an hour ago, but not a single man-made light broke the darkness. The rain and accompanying high winds had delayed Dawson, but the person he was there to pick up should still be waiting. Where would she go? It wasn't as if a coffee shop was open down the road, or that she could catch a ride in a passing vehicle.

Traffic was sparse on the old logging road at this time of night. Spirit Falls' heyday had fizzled with the bust in the lumber market, and most folk had moved on long ago. The town consisted of a few boarded-up buildings and a broken gas pump. Jim Svenson ran a small general store for locals, but Jim's daughter had just had twins, and the proud grandpa had taken an extended vacation to Hosten to meet his new grandsons.

The woman Dawson had come more than a hundred kilometers to pick up must have taken one glance at the desolate emptiness of Spirit Falls and refused to get off the bus. She was probably on her way back to the bright lights of Hosten right now. If she'd bailed, that meant he was off the hook.

Smiling for the first time that day, he pressed down on the gas pedal and sped away from the bus stop. A flicker of white on the shoulder ahead caught his eye, and he slammed on the brakes. The truck skidded to a stop, his seatbelt digging into his shoulder. Catching his breath, he peered through the mud-spattered windshield.

A woman sat perched atop an oversized suitcase. Long, wavy strands of golden hair glowed in the sweep of light cast by his headlights and formed a halo around a face that wouldn't be out of place on the cover of a fashion magazine. Her full lips lifted in a tentative smile, and she waved.

He frowned and tugged the photograph of the woman he was supposed to meet from his coat pocket and squinted in the glow of the dash lights. The lined, grandmotherly face beamed at him. He glanced at the gorgeous blonde watching him from the roadside. A sinking feeling settled deep in his gut. He removed his cowboy hat, ran his fingers through his hair, and tossed the hat onto the passenger seat. Maybe she was waiting for someone else.

Maybe.

He turned off the motor and opened the truck door and stepped out. "Sorry about that." He waved at his truck. "I didn't see you sitting there." He shifted closer, and her beauty struck him like a punch to the gut. He reeled back. "Ev...everything all right, miss?" His mouth dried, and his tongue fumbled over the words. "Do...do you need some help?"

She blinked, the sweep of her long dark eyelashes brushing her cheeks. "Thank heavens you're finally here. The bus driver dropped me off an hour ago. I thought I was going to have to spend the night on the side of the road."

"Good thing I came by then. I'm Dawson Wheeler from the Circle 5 over by Checheko Lake. I run cattle...Black Angus. They're the best you can find in these parts—all grass-fed, prime, on-the-hoof beef, and—" He gritted his teeth to stop his rambling. *What color were her eyes?* Impossible to tell in the glare from the headlights, but he guessed they were blue.

"Hello, Dawson. I'm Stella King."

The back of his neck itched. *"You're* Stella King?" *Of course she was. Who else would be waiting here at this time of night?* Once again, he glanced at the photograph clenched in his hand—gray curls, thick glasses, sixty years old. *That* was the Stella King he'd hired. The itching amped up to a full-out assault.

She stood and held out her hand. "Nice to meet you, Dawson."

He stumbled back another step, his worst fears confirmed. This gorgeous woman was the nanny he'd hired to look after Deirdre.

Her light-blue wool sweater did nothing to hide the full, rounded mounds of her breasts. Her legs looked a mile long in the white denim, skintight, designer jeans tucked into a pair of knee-high, high-heeled, black leather boots. Her perfume wafted on the evening breeze, a heady mix of spring flowers and something subtle but decidedly feminine.

He struggled to swallow, but his throat was parched, his tongue as dry as old leather against the roof of his mouth.

Silence stretched between them. An owl hooted from a nearby tree, crickets chirped in the tall grass lining the ditch, and still he didn't move.

She frowned and dropped her hand.

"I…uh…er…I wasn't expecting, um…" Sucking in a deep breath, he tried again. "Look, there's been a mistake. I was expecting someone a little—" He coughed and searched for the right words. "—well, someone a little older." He held out the crumpled photograph. "The photograph the agency sent—"

"Oh, that. They told me there'd been a mix-up. Apparently, the company sent you the wrong picture."

Her laugh floated through the air like a melody.

"But as you can see—" She fished in her oversized, black leather purse, pulled out a rhinestone-studded, pink wallet, and flipped it open, flashing him her driver's license. "—I am indeed Stella King, the woman you hired."

He studied the identification, but no matter how many times he read the details, the facts didn't change. "But, you're too young. You—"

She cut him off again. "I'm thirty-two, Mr. Wheeler. Surely that's old enough to be a nanny to a five-year-old."

Dawson tunneled his fingers through his unruly mass of dark curls. "You don't understand. The Circle 5's a working ranch, Ms. King. There's just me, Deirdre, and Alf, and the boys around most of the time. Sometimes weeks go by when we don't see another person." He paused and waited for her to understand what he was trying to tell her.

Her brows arched. "Yes?"

He ground his teeth. Why was she making this so difficult? "Don't you see?" Her unwillingness to understand the consequences of an attractive woman on an isolated ranch irritated him. He shuddered at the upset her presence would cause in the smooth running of the ranch. His gaze traveled over her again. His pulse raced, and he cursed under his breath. He hated losing control, but from the second he'd spotted her blonde hair shining in his headlights, he felt as if he were spinning out on a patch of black ice.

"No, Mr. Wheeler, I'm afraid I don't see." Her voice was full of starch.

"A woman alone, surrounded by a pack of lonely men…" He trailed off at the fire sparking in her eyes. *Blue. Her eyes were blue.*

She planted her hands on her slim hips. "I travelled for God knows how many hours on that ancient wreck of a bus, breathed in clouds of diesel and road dust, bruised every inch of my body from plunging into mile-deep potholes—all because I understood a job was waiting for me. And now you're telling me the job no longer exists?"

Bruised every inch of my body. He blew out a ragged breath. *Every inch?* He forced himself to focus. "Of course, I'll reimburse you for your time and inconvenience."

"What are you afraid of, Mr. Wheeler—me, or yourself? Because I can assure you the last thing I'm interested in is romance. You and your men will be quite safe."

He eyed her boots. How the hell did she expect to walk anywhere off the pavement in those heels? He opened his mouth to tell her he wasn't hiring her no matter what, but then he noticed the subtle signs of strain he'd missed earlier.

Her face was a pale mask. Dark circles rimmed her eyes, and an all-too-familiar haunting sadness lurked in the vivid blue depths.

The next words out of his mouth stunned him. "All right, Ms. King. The job's yours if you want it. I hope you realize what you're getting yourself into. Now, come on, we've got a long trip ahead of us." Ignoring the warning bells clanging inside his head, he grabbed her bag, hefting the bulky suitcase, and tossed it into the back of the pickup.

****

Stella bit back a groan as the truck hit yet another pothole, tightening the restraining strap of her seat belt with each bone-jarring lurch. Her body ached from ten long hours riding the bus. Her eyes, gritty from a combination of exhaustion and the ever-present dust hanging in the air, stung. She'd kill for a long soak in a hot bath and a cold glass of white wine, but that wasn't about to happen. Not any time soon. She stole a glance at the intriguing man beside her.

Under the concealing shadow of his brown-felt cowboy hat, he looked to be in his mid-thirties. His face was rugged with strong bones and a firm jawline. His eyes, visible in the reflected glow from the dashboard lights, were a deep brown, almost black. Dark stubble covered the lower part of a face bronzed by the many hours he must spend outdoors facing the elements. Thick, black hair teased the collar of his frayed, plaid shirt.

He'd come close to refusing to give her the job. Maybe that wouldn't have been a bad thing, but she'd sublet her condo in Vancouver, stored her furniture, and taken a leave of absence from her job. She needed a refuge, a fresh start, time to heal. Dawson Wheeler and the Circle 5 Ranch were supposed to be her sanctuary. Now she wasn't so sure.

The slowing of the vehicle drew her out of her thoughts.

He steered the truck off the rough gravel road and

onto a narrow, winding track that tunneled between thick stands of coniferous trees. The engine throbbed as the truck crawled along the bumpy trail. Branches scraped the sides of the vehicle. He drove into a small clearing, then braked, and switched off the engine. The headlights faded and died. Darkness settled over the truck like a thick cloak.

"Why are we stopped here?" She peered through the cracked windshield at the surrounding night and shuddered. Never had she been in a place so devoid of light, but as her eyes adjusted to the darkness, features took shape—trees, rocks, more trees. Moonlight shone like a pale band of silver illuminating the ripples on what looked like a large lake. She leaned forward and stared through the windshield up at the sky. Millions of stars dotted the inky blackness.

"Look—" He huffed out a breath. "—this is as far as we can go tonight. It's dark and I'm bushed. We'll head to the ranch tomorrow at first light."

Was he serious? They were spending the night there? In the truck? Shoving a stray curl behind her ear, she studied the dark shapes of the looming trees, the cold night sky, the unsettling darkness, and shivered. A piercing howl rent the air, raising the hairs on the back of her neck. "What was that?"

"Sounds like a wolf."

"A…a wolf?" She fumbled in her purse for her cell phone and switched on the light app. The interior of the cab lit up, revealing his stark features.

His lip curled in a smirk. "You're not in the city, Ms. King. Out here, there are lots of wild animals. If you stick around, you're gonna encounter wolves, bears, moose, deer, even a cougar if you're lucky."

Lucky? She rubbed the goose bumps on her arms. "But—"

He cut her off. "There aren't many people here, and places are pretty far apart. We can't hop in a taxi or ride a subway." He expelled another loud sigh. "Try and get some sleep. You've got a long day ahead of you tomorrow. Deirdre's excited to meet you."

"Deirdre's your daughter, right?" She leaped at this crack in his icy exterior, hoping to find out more about the man and his family. The information the agency sent had been light on details.

He nodded.

"I'm looking forward to meeting her too. What's she like?"

He scrubbed his jaw, the rasp of whiskers loud in the close confines. "She's five." He shrugged as if that said it all.

"No, I mean, what's she really like? What sort of things does she enjoy doing?"

He was silent so long she feared he wasn't going to answer, but then he cleared his throat.

"Dee loves everything. She has so much energy it's enough to drive you crazy. She's like a little dynamo who'll run you ragged one minute and break your heart the next. You should see her—"

He stopped, rubbed his chin again, and crossed one booted foot over the other. "Look, it's late. I don't know about you, but I'm beat. I've been up since the crack of dawn. Now, please turn that damn light off, and let's get some sleep. We'll talk in the morning." Without another word, he pushed his seat back into a reclining position and stretched out his long legs. In the next heartbeat, his eyes closed.

"What are you doing?"

One eyelid popped open. "Trying to sleep."

The anger she'd struggled to keep banked burst free. "Look, Mr. Wheeler...er...Dawson...this is ridiculous. I'm not spending the night in this truck. Take me to a hotel. I'll stay there. You can pick me up in the morning."

Both of his eyes were open, and he was watching her. "A hotel?"

She nodded.

"You want to stay in a hotel tonight?"

Again she nodded, though with less certainty.

The corners of his mouth twitched. "Good luck with that. The nearest hotel is a good two-hour drive, but then again, not many folks would call Crabb's Corner a hotel, it's...more of a road stop. Betty has some bunk beds in the back room she rents out to the guys on the road crews. Bathroom's down the hall, but the coffee's good."

Her heart sank. What had she gotten herself into? "Two hours, you say?"

"Yep."

"And there's no place closer?"

"Nope."

"So I'm stuck here in the cab of this truck the rest of the night in the middle of nowhere? With you."

"Yep." He lowered the brim of his hat over his eyes.

Great, just great.

"If I were you, I'd get some sleep."

Eerie howling filled the night, and she shuddered and hunched into her seat.

"There's a blanket and a pillow on the back seat if

you're cold." His deep voice reached her out of the darkness. "And a thermos of coffee on the floor by your feet."

Coffee.

The word blazed like a neon light. She fumbled at her feet and found a hard metal cylinder. Holding the thermos on her lap, she unscrewed the cap. The earthy smell of roasted coffee drifted out of the thermos.

"Sorry. I forgot cups. You'll have to use the top of the thermos."

She poured coffee from the thermos into the small metal cap and set the thermos on the floorboards. The coffee was hot, and fragrant steam warmed her face. The first sip was like heaven, the second even better. By the time she'd drained the cup, her anger had eased, and the strain of the long day's travel took its toll.

She'd boarded the plane at the Vancouver Airport early in the morning, and after a two-hour flight, landed in the bustling city of Hosten—if you could call a town of twenty thousand people bustling.

The bus trip was ten hours of agony through kilometers of forested hills and grasslands. They'd passed small towns, most just road stops with a gas station and convenience store, and arrived in Spirit Falls as the sun was setting. That was a rude awakening. As far as she could tell, the *town* consisted of four boarded-up buildings, a rusted old pickup truck, and a ditch littered with empty beer cans and plastic water bottles.

After the bus chugged away in a noxious cloud of diesel exhaust and road dust, she'd waited for her new employer to show up. As the minutes ticked by, her fears she'd made a huge mistake increased. But then

Dawson Wheeler had skidded to a stop in his mud-spattered, red, four-wheel-drive pickup and his abrasive attitude, and the long day just got worse.

She yawned, her body aching for sleep, and slid a glance at the man beside her.

His long, lean, muscular body was relaxed, his breathing slow and steady.

The wolf howled again, joined by another haunting cry.

A shudder rippled through her. She twisted around and leaned over the back of the seat and grabbed the blanket and a pillow lying on the back seat. The blanket was soft brown wool and smelled like wood smoke. She lodged the small pillow behind her head and tugged the blanket up to her shoulders. Settling back in the seat, she switched off her phone light and forced her eyelids closed. She shifted, squirming to adjust her bottom on the hard seat.

A coyote's yipping drifted in through the partially open driver's window. An owl hooted. Some sort of creature barked like a dog, followed by a threatening growl.

She gulped and pressed the light app and shone the beam of light on her new boss.

His chest rose and fell with frustrating regularity.

Once again, she turned off the light and set her phone on the console. Tugging the blanket up to her neck, she peered through the windshield at the surrounding darkness. What was that he'd said about cougars and bears? Had he been trying to frighten her so she'd beg him to take her back to the bus stop? If so, his efforts were futile. Nothing he did or said would change her mind. She'd come a long way to reach the

Circle 5 Ranch, and she'd be damned if she'd quit before she even started. Bottom line—she needed this job, not the paycheck, but the salvation the work itself provided.

She yawned, and in spite of her frustration and anger, the rigors of the day took their toll. Soon she succumbed to sleep.

Chapter 2

"Have a good sleep?"

Stella blinked in the sunlight streaming through the bug-spattered windshield. Groaning, she sat up and rubbed the tight muscles in the small of her back.

Dawson Wheeler leaned in the open driver's door, his dark eyes gleaming.

Was he serious? She'd squirmed all night struggling to find a spot where the metal latch of the seat belt didn't dig into her hip or the hard plastic armrest didn't numb her shoulder. "Great, thanks." She didn't bother to hide her sarcasm.

"Better have another cup of that coffee. Sounds like you could use some." He grinned again. A matching set of dimples popped out on his lean, beard-roughened cheeks.

Why, he's a hunk. The startling thought blazed through her.

In the next breath, his mouth tightened, and the lines of his face realigned into their usual forbidding harshness. "Time to get moving. I don't know about you folks in Vancouver, but we don't keep banker's hours in the Chilcotin." He spun around and strode away.

She glanced at her watch. *Banker's hours?* It wasn't even six o'clock. She fished in her large, black leather bag for her brush and ran the bristles through her tangled hair. Using a couple of tissues, she wiped the previous day's dust from her face.

She squirmed on the seat and grimaced. Damn. She had to use the bathroom.

Peering through the windshield, she studied her surroundings. The small clearing had been hacked out of the thick coniferous forest. Narrow shafts of bright sunlight streaked through the branches of the surrounding towering evergreen trees. A wooden dock extended twenty feet into the cobalt-blue waters of a large lake.

That was all.

No buildings. No toilet. No handy washroom with running water and privacy.

Nothing but trees and more trees.

A small airplane floating on two pontoons was tied to the end of the dock. Dawson Wheeler stood on one pontoon, his legs braced against the rocking motion, loading her suitcase into the plane.

Her heart stuttered, and all thought of relieving herself vanished.

They were going to fly? *In that?* The small plane looked like a child's toy with its single propeller on the nose and fragile-looking struts attached to the two flimsy wings.

No way!

Her hand shook as she wiped her face with another tissue. Slinging her purse over her shoulder, she climbed out of the truck.

The long grass was wet with dew. A rich, loamy scent of damp earth and green plants infused the fresh air. A mosquito landed on her arm, and she swatted the annoying insect. A high-pitched whine filled her ears as a cloud of the hungry bugs attacked. She slapped and waved her arms, but for every bug she squashed, ten more appeared. Scurrying across the small clearing in a frantic rush to escape the voracious horde, she stumbled over a root and staggered a few steps before righting herself.

"Ms. King? Are you ready to go?"

She startled at the sound of his deep voice. "Ouch!" She slapped her neck and then her arm. "Are the bugs always this bad?"

"No." He grinned, and the devastating dimples flashed. "Sometimes they're a lot worse." He jerked his thumb over his shoulder toward the lake. "Your suitcase is stowed on board. If you're ready, we should go. In these parts you never know how long the weather will hold."

She gulped and studied the plane. "We...we're flying to your ranch?"

"Either we fly or it's a two-day pack trip on horses or ATVs. There aren't any roads to the Circle 5." His mouth tightened. "Not yet anyway."

The tiny plane bobbed like a cork on the water. She wiped her damp palms on her jeans. "Where...where's the pilot?"

"You're looking at him."

"*You're* flying the plane?" Her mouth dried. "I...I thought you were a rancher."

"I'm a man of many talents." The corners of his mouth quirked. "I can take you back to the bus stop if you'd like."

She read the challenge in his dark, piercing eyes. He wanted her to refuse to fly. Her cowardice gave him the perfect opportunity to be rid of her.

Water lapped against the dock pilings, squirrels chittered in the trees, and the air was filled with the incessant whine of mosquitoes. White fluffy clouds scudded in the pale-blue sky. A flock of ducks spiraled down and landed on the lake with a flurry of splashes and quacking.

Sweat dampened her sweater and trickled between her breasts.

"Well?" He crossed his arms over his broad chest and drummed his fingers on his arms. "Your choice."

The silence between them hummed.

She wiped her damp palms on her pants again. Two choices faced her—call it quits and return to Vancouver and all the darkness and pain, or get on the plane and start a new life. She swallowed and lifted her chin. "Let's go." She prayed he didn't hear the tremor in her voice.

"Okay, then." A smile played about his well-sculpted lips. "We have an hour flight. You might want to use the…er…facilities before we take off."

The urge to pee returned with a vengeance. "Where's the bathroom?"

His grin widened, and he pointed at the surrounding forest. "Pick a tree, any tree."

"What? Are you serious? There's no bathroom?"

"Welcome to the great outdoors." He chuckled and turned and strode along the dock to the plane, calling over his shoulder, "Watch out for the bears."

Anger fired her blood, and she glared at his back, wishing he'd trip on the uneven planks and fall into the water. What was she doing in this godforsaken place? The last time she'd been out of the city, it had been to attend a company picnic at a local resort that boasted a heated pool, hot tub, indoor plumbing, and a five-star restaurant.

She swiped a mosquito off her arm and studied the towering trees, the thick undergrowth, and the menacing shadows and shuddered. No way was she peeing in there. No way.

Her traitorous body had a different idea, and the urge to urinate became overwhelming. Cursing her new employer under her breath, she stomped across the clearing and into the trees. The sun's light dimmed under the thick canopy of branches, and she stumbled over hidden rocks and tree roots. Wild rose bushes scratched her hands and grabbed at her clothing.

She ducked behind a tree, praying its massive trunk would hide her from any prying eyes, and undid the clasp on her jeans and crouched.

Relief.

A branch snapped somewhere behind her.

Heart pounding, she jumped to her feet and tugged up her pants and fled, not stopping until she reached the clearing. Her hands shook as she struggled to do up the snap on her jeans. Was that a bear? A cougar? She swallowed, her mouth dry.

A squirrel scolded her from a branch overhead, his high-pitched chatter sounding as if he were laughing at her skittishness.

Rummaging in her purse, she found a small bottle of hand sanitizer and squirted the gel on her hands and rubbed. She glanced at Dawson, hoping he hadn't witnessed her panicked flight from the forest.

He had his back to her and was busy loading boxes into the plane.

The plane!

She'd forgotten all about it, but there it was, looking just as fragile and unsafe as when she'd first spotted it. How could she have told him she'd fly to his ranch? What had she been thinking? But did she have a choice? She wanted—no, she needed—this job. It was supposed to be her lifeline, a way back from the painful darkness.

She sucked in a deep breath. *Okay.* She could do this.

Her knees shook as she shuffled down the narrow, wobbly dock to the floating airplane. She peered through the open plane door into the tiny, crowded interior. Her heart skittered. A dozen stories of horrific plane crashes reeled through her mind like a late-night horror movie.

Inhaling a shaky breath, she stepped onto a bobbing pontoon and grasped the metal handles at the sides of the open door. Her knuckles whitened, and her breath hitched in and out in ragged pants. Her heart beat so fast she feared it would explode.

Calm down.

Thousands of people flew every minute of every day. They didn't crash. She could do this. Of course she could. Her mind was made up, but her body had other thoughts, and her muscles refused to obey. She hung frozen, gripping the handles, suspended above the inky blue water.

"Let me help." Dawson's warm breath fanned her face. "Okay?"

She met his gaze, expecting his mocking grin, but compassion shone in his dark eyes. Her throat was too tight to form words and she nodded.

He wrapped his strong arms around her hips. "It's

19

okay. I've got you. You can let go now."

The warmth of his body seeped through her jeans. His scent, a hint of leather, wood smoke, and something spicy, surrounded her. Goose bumps broke out on her arms, and she shivered. She uncurled her cramping fingers and eased her hands off the handles.

He lifted her and hauled her up the ladder and into the belly of the plane and plopped her on the passenger seat. "Buckle up." Slamming the door closed and setting the lock, he settled on the pilot's seat.

Heart hammering in her chest, her breath escaping in rapid pants, she fumbled with the seatbelt, but her fingers were numb, and she dropped the strap.

He leaned over and placed his hand over hers and guided the latch into the clasp.

She sucked in a breath at the searing heat of his touch, but froze when the roar of the powerful engine reverberated through the cockpit.

Clenching her hands, she dug her fingernails into the skin on her palms. She welcomed the pain. The discomfort distracted her from the fact they were racing across the glistening water. She squeezed her eyes shut against the rushing blur and covered her ears in a futile attempt to block out the high-pitched whine of the straining engine.

She was thrust against the back of her seat as the tiny plane lifted off the surface of the lake and soared into the air. She refused to look as the plane leveled off, and the engine settled into a steady roar. Sucking in great gulps of air, she fought against her rising panic.

You're okay. You're okay. The silent mantra repeated over and over.

The sonorous drone of the plane was oddly

calming, and her heart slowed its frantic pace. Okay, maybe she'd take a peek. Wide-open blue sky surrounded her, reminding her of the peril. Sucking in a breath, she squeezed her eyes closed again. She was better off with her eyes sealed against the frightening reality of flying hundreds of feet above the ground in this matchbox of a plane.

****

Dawson glanced at his passenger for the umpteenth time since take off.

A thin, white line rimmed her tightly compressed lips. A furrow creased her smooth forehead. Her hands were clutched on her lap, her knuckles white. She held herself stiff and erect like a soldier facing a firing squad, though her legs trembled.

He placed his hand on her leg in an attempt to ease her incessant shaking, but at the warmth of her slim thigh beneath his palm, he yanked his hand away as if he'd been burned and gripped the controls.

This was Alf's fault. Just wait until he got hold of the interfering old curmudgeon. Dawson had been opposed to hiring a nanny for Deirdre. He couldn't stomach the idea of someone stepping in where Anna should be, but Alf had persisted, until finally Dawson had caved. When that old man set his mind on something, he was like a raging bull. There was no deterring him.

He shot Stella another glance. She was terrified. He'd known the second she looked at the plane that she was frightened of flying. Hell, her fear had been impossible to miss. Her face had turned the color of Alf's oatmeal, and her large, expressive eyes darkened with terror.

Dawson had leapt at the opportunity her fear of flying provided. If she refused to get in the plane, he had the perfect excuse to take her back to the bus stop. But she'd surprised him with her courage. She was a quivering mess, but she allowed him to help her into the plane, and now they were in the air.

He stared through the windshield at the scene below, and his heart swelled with pride. Jagged, snowcapped mountains gleamed in the distance. A carpet of thick evergreen forest interspersed by a myriad of gleaming, jewel-like lakes and glistening rivers stretched as far as the eye could see. There wasn't any sign of human interference with nature's rugged beauty; no roads cut through the thick forest; no scars of logging clear cuts, nor mining operations. Nothing but pristine wilderness.

At least not yet.

He'd grown up on this land. Oh, he'd lived other places—big cities and small—but this part of the country was the place he called home. The wild, rugged wilderness of the Chilcotin Plateau in central British Columbia challenged him. The land gave him strength. For the past four years the ranch had provided a much-needed refuge.

Checheko Lake loomed on the horizon, and in a few seconds they flew over the large clearing marking the Circle 5 homestead. The neatly laid-out log buildings of the ranch house, barn, and outbuildings passed below. The horses in the corral kicked their heels and galloped in circles as he guided the plane lower, circling the ranch house.

A tiny figure burst out of the house and raced across the clearing toward the lake.

He grinned, a familiar rush of warmth filling his heart, as Deirdre scrambled down the steep bank to the wharf. Even though he'd only been gone overnight, he missed her. She'd begged him to take her with him, but he'd wanted some time alone with the new nanny to establish the ground rules.

He grimaced.

He sure as hell hadn't followed his plan. Not by a long shot. Stella King's youthful beauty had unsettled him so much he hadn't mentioned anything about guidelines. No matter. He'd explain the conditions of her employment as soon as they arrived. If they were going to survive the long months ahead, he'd have to set out rules. His rules.

A headache threatened as he imagined the reactions of his men to the arrival of the all-too-attractive Ms. King. He'd have to instill the fear of God into them to get them to behave around her. He couldn't afford to have the smooth running of the ranch disrupted, not for anything. Especially not now when so much was at stake.

He circled back around. Checheko Lake lay directly ahead, and he shifted his mind to the intricacies of landing the light plane on the gleaming water.

****

Stella expelled her breath in a whoosh, unclenched her aching hands, and pried open her eyes.

The plane was skimming across a lake.

Relief washed over her. They hadn't plummeted to the earth in a fiery ball. The sun glistened on the lake, turning its waters a deep azure blue. A breathtaking vista of rugged, snowcapped peaks towering over endless acres of green coniferous forest was visible through the water-spotted windshield. A huge, two-story log house sat atop a rise overlooking the lake. The brilliant morning light reflected off several large windows that must offer the inhabitants an unbelievable view of the lake and surrounding valley.

Dawson Wheeler pressed buttons and flipped switches on the console and steered the plane toward a large wooden dock.

A small figure waved from the dock. The child was dressed in a colorful combination of bright pink coveralls and an aqua-blue T-shirt. Her hair blazed in the morning light and took on a life of its own. The mop of fiery red hair stood out from her face in wild, twisted strands.

Dawson steered the plane alongside the dock.

The little girl raced toward them, two enormous, shaggy, black dogs barking at her heels.

Dawson slipped off his headphones, unclipped his safety harness, rose from his seat, threw open the door of the plane, and leaped onto the swaying dock. No sooner had his feet landed than the child launched into his arms. Staggering under the impact, he gripped her in an exuberant hug.

The dogs ran in frenzied circles around the pair, barking, their tails wagging.

The little girl wrapped her arms around her father's neck and clung.

Dawson grinned, showing even, white teeth. His rugged face softened as he chuckled at something his daughter said. The joyful sound echoed in the still morning air.

Tears stung Stella's eyes, and pain wrenched deep in her belly. She turned away from the happy scene.

With clumsy fingers, she fumbled with her seat belt clasp and clambered out of the plane.

The excited chatter of the child and Dawson's gruff, affectionate responses created fresh pain. Stella hurried past them along the wobbly dock to the shore, desperate to escape this poignant reminder of her devastating loss. Tears burned her eyes. She'd been certain she could handle this job, but if just watching the child and her father was agony, how was she ever going to be the little girl's nanny?

"Ms. King, wait a moment. I'd like you to meet my daughter."

She wiped her damp cheeks with the sleeve of her sweater before she wheeled around and faced them. Pasting a bright smile on her face, she kneeled down to the child's level. "Hello. You must be Deirdre. I'm Stella."

Bright-blue eyes stared out of a small, pale face. Freckles dotted Deirdre's nose and peppered her cheeks.

Stella held her smile under Deirdre's penetrating gaze as the child took her measure.

Deirdre grinned, exposing a row of white teeth from which two were noticeably absent. "You're not old," she lisped. "Daddy said you'd have gray hair, thick glasses, and lots and lots of wrinkles. It's true, isn't it, Daddy? I heard you telling Alf."

"Did he?" Stella cast a glance at Dawson and almost smiled at the discomfort flushing his rugged features.

"He said no city lady would want to come way out here. He said you couldn't handle the ranch. But he's wrong, isn't he? You're gonna stay, right?"

Dawson shifted from one boot-clad foot to the other, looking even more uncomfortable.

Stella couldn't help but take pleasure in his embarrassment. Good to witness the arrogant rancher cut down to size by his pint-sized daughter. "Your father has some pretty crazy ideas."

He quirked an eyebrow, and for a heartbeat, their gazes locked.

She sucked in a ragged breath, stunned at the piercing intensity in the dark depths of his eyes. Her mouth was desert dry, and she licked her parched lips, but froze when his gaze settled on her mouth. Liquid heat flooded her veins.

"Stella?"

Stella dragged her gaze from Dawson. "What is it, Deirdre?" She struggled to focus, refusing to acknowledge the bewildering feelings being near Dawson evoked.

"Do you like to play dolls?" Beneath her childish excitement lurked a swirl of dark emotions, hinting at the loneliness she must experience every day living on this isolated ranch.

Where was her mother? The information packet she'd received from the hiring agency, hadn't mentioned a wife, but Dawson wore a plain gold wedding band on the fourth finger of his left hand so he must be married. Odd his wife hadn't come to greet them. Was she away somewhere? Or was he divorced? But then, why the ring?

She shook her head. Her employer's marital status was none of her business. Thrusting away all thoughts of Deirdre's handsome father, she smiled at the child. "I love dolls. We're going to be the best of friends. I just know it."

The girl's elfin face lit up. "You're staying?"

"Of course." She dared not look at Dawson. He'd made no secret he didn't want her there. The trill of excitement that had flared like a meteor between her and Dawson wouldn't happen again. Her life was complicated enough without adding an affair with her married boss into the mix. She'd stay as far from him as possible and focus on this wondrous child.

She smoothed her hand over Deirdre's vibrant mass of red curls. "How did you ever get to be so pretty? I don't think I've ever seen such a lovely shade of hair."

Deirdre giggled. "Alf says my hair looks like a rusty old nail, but he's teasing. Mommy's hair was just like mine, and everyone says Mommy was real pretty."

Was? Stella glanced at Dawson, but he looked away.

One of the enormous, wiggling, tail-wagging dogs jumped up to greet her, its two front paws landing on her chest.

She stumbled back a step.

"Shas! Down," Dawson ordered.

The big dog dropped to all fours, but sat at her feet, tail wagging and panting.

"It's okay. I like dogs." She patted the velvety dark head and scratched behind his floppy ears. "Hello, Shas."

The tail wagging sped up a notch.

"His name means bear. Daddy named him that because he looks just like a bear." Deirdre giggled and pointed at the second mountain of a dog busy sniffing Stella's boots. "That's Sneakers. He's got white on his paws like he's wearing sneakers." She giggled again.

Upon hearing his name, Sneakers' ears pricked, and he barked, his pink tongue lolling, a long string of drool dangling.

"Come on, Dee, let's show Ms. King her room." Taking the child's small hand in his much larger one, Dawson towed Deirdre behind as he headed toward the collection of buildings on the bluff, leaving Stella and the dogs to follow. "I'll send one of the men for your suitcase."

A rocky path led up the hill to the clearing. Stella stumbled over rocks and exposed roots, wishing she'd worn sturdier shoes. She'd known the knee-high, black leather boots weren't practical for walking in the country, but they'd been on sale, and she hadn't been able to resist. It had been so long since she'd treated herself. Besides, they made her legs look good. At least that's what the salesgirl had insisted.

Panting from the climb, she paused at the top to take in her surroundings. The ranch house dominated the large clearing. The sprawling, two-story log building was an imposing structure, but suited the rugged, wilderness setting. A thin spiral of smoke trailed from a river-stone chimney. A deep, covered porch extended across the front of the building. Several white wicker chairs with dark-green and crimson cushions were set on the porch. She imagined sitting on one of the comfortable-looking chairs and enjoying the sunset's vibrant colors as they reflected on the still waters of the lake below.

The tart fragrance of pine trees, earth, and sun-warmed water was so different from the automobile-exhaust stench of the city. The silence unsettled her.

The sighing of the breeze as it caught the branches of the nearby trees, and the relentless buzzing of insects were the only sounds that broke the morning's stillness.

A screen door banged open, and a small wiry man stomped across the porch. He wore a sweat-stained, red cap, snug-fitting, faded blue jeans, and a plaid shirt rolled up at the sleeves, exposing sinewy, tanned arms. He removed his cap and scratched his thinning gray hair. "Well, it's about time." He swaggered to the edge of the verandah. "I was starting to think you were never gonna get here."

Pinned under his intense scrutiny, but sensing the importance of his approval, Stella didn't turn away.

"We had a late start," said Dawson. "Seems some people like to sleep in."

She scowled and did a slow burn. If he'd wanted an earlier start, he should have woken her sooner. All too aware of Deirdre and the assessing older man watching this byplay, she fought to suppress her irritation. She stepped onto the porch and extended her hand toward the little man. "Hi, I'm Stella."

His bright-blue eyes, set in a weathered face, stared at her for several long seconds before he clasped her hand in his.

The wiry strength of his grip surprised her.

"Alf. Pleased to meetcha." He surveyed her once again and chuckled. "Well, well, well. These next months are gonna be mighty interesting."

Behind her, Dawson snorted. "Deirdre, show Ms. King to her room. I need to check on that sick bull."

Alf released her hand and faced Dawson. The warm smile faded. "Before you head off to the barn, Dawson, there's something you should know."

Dawson's eyes narrowed, and his body stiffened. "What is it?"

Alf tugged a red-checkered cloth handkerchief from his back pocket and wiped his glistening brow. "One of the men found a dead cow in the back pasture."

"Wolves?"

The bandy-legged man shook his head. "Animal had been shot."

The lines bracketing Dawson's mouth deepened. "Hunters?"

Alf shrugged. "Not sure, but that's the third one this month. I notified the cops, but they're busy dealing with an incident at Crabb's Corner, so it'll be some time before they get out this way."

A pulse in Dawson's rigid jaw ticked. Without another word, he stomped off toward a large, metal-roofed, log building on the far side of the clearing.

The two dogs raced ahead, barking.

Stella turned to Alf. "What's going on?"

He jammed his cap on his head and pasted a smile on his leathery face. "Nothing for you to worry about."

Deirdre grabbed her hand and tugged. "Come on, Stella. Let's go. Wait 'til you see your room. I helped Alf fix it up. Didn't I, Alf?" Deirdre's small body vibrated as she danced from one foot to the other, but beneath the excited chatter, wariness dulled her bright eyes. It didn't take an expert to see she was starved for attention.

Dawson had said no other women or children lived on the Circle 5. The ranch was in the middle of nowhere, and the nearest civilization—if you could call Spirit Falls civilized—was kilometers away. She smiled down at Deirdre and squeezed her small hand. "Okay, let's go. Show me around, Dee." She paused. "May I call you Dee?"

Grinning, Deirdre nodded and dragged Stella into the house.

"Now, Dee, don't you go and tire Stella out on her first day," Alf called after them. "You mind, now. Lunch is almost ready. I have hot soup and sandwiches, and I made chocolate chip—" The screen door banged shut, cutting off the rest of his words.

Deirdre placed a finger over her lips, and with a cheeky, gap-toothed grin, tiptoed over to a large wooden table and snatched two cookies from a cooling rack. Eyes twinkling, she handed one cookie to Stella and crunched into the other.

Even though she knew she should be setting a stern tone for the rambunctious child, Stella couldn't hold back a giggle. Time enough for establishing rules later. For now, the important thing was to bond with Deirdre.

She studied the delicious-looking treat. When was the last time she'd indulged in a cookie? The past year, food had tasted like sawdust and wasn't worth the bother. She sampled a tentative bite. Her eyes widened as a burst of rich milk chocolate and sweet butter exploded on her tongue. She nibbled another mouthful.

"They're good, aren't they?" Deirdre beamed. "Alf made them." She chomped into her own cookie, and spoke around a mouthful of crumbs. "They're my favoritist." Her whisper was loud. "Alf's the bestest cook in the whole world."

"Darn right I am, missy." Alf's voice carried from the porch through the screen door. "Don't you forget it. And don't eat any more of those cookies before lunch. You hear?"

Both Stella and Deirdre giggled.

Stella wiped cookie crumbs from her sweater and studied the homey kitchen. Bright, late-morning sunshine streamed through two large picture windows. A cheery fire crackled in a river-stone fireplace. A massive, gleaming, oak table, surrounded by a dozen mismatched wooden chairs, dominated the room. Delicious aromas emanated from an enormous pot simmering on a top-of-the-line, stainless steel, industrial-size propane stove. A matching, double-door fridge was against one wall.

"Come on, Stella. Come see my room." Deirdre dashed out of the kitchen.

Chewing the last of her cookie, Stella followed. If these first minutes were any indication, her stay at the Circle 5 wouldn't be boring.

The ranch house was large. Each spacious room was furnished with an ad hoc jumble of overstuffed, comfortable-looking furniture, rough pine tables, and paintings of snowcapped mountains and thick, verdant forests. Braided rugs covered the scuffed hardwood floors, adding vibrant splashes of color.

By contrast, Deirdre's bedroom definitely belonged to a young girl. White, frilly, lace curtains hung on the large window, and a pink-satin bedspread dotted with images of fairytale princesses in flowing pastel ball gowns, covered the single bed. A tufted, white headboard and matching canopy completed the princess theme.

Dolls of every shape and size lay scattered on the desk, the dresser, the bed, and a bench below the window. Picture books lined a wooden shelf along one wall. Board games, puzzle boxes, and a myriad of art supplies were stacked on a child-size white, pine table in the corner. Posters of horses and cartoon princesses lined the walls.

A framed photograph of a pretty, smiling young woman sat on the small bedside table, but before Stella could ask about the woman in the picture, a bell clanged.

Dee huffed out a breath. "We gotta go. That's the lunch bell. Alf doesn't like it if we're late." She raced out of the room and scampered down the stairs.

Stella hurried after her. She was going to have her hands full keeping up with Deirdre and all that boundless energy.

Alf sat on a wooden rocking chair before the fire, drinking a cup of coffee and reading a newspaper, a gray cat curled on his lap. Both the cat and Alf looked up at their entrance.

After studying her with bright, unblinking, golden eyes, the cat yawned, laid its head on Alf's lap, and went back to sleep.

"There you are." Alf rested a veined hand on the cat and smiled a greeting. "We don't stand on ceremony here. Lunch is on the table. Sit down and help yourself. The guys are out working, so it's just us today."

Deirdre plopped down on a chair and grabbed a sandwich. She guzzled a glass of milk, leaving a white milk mustache on her lip, and then dug into the sandwich, chewing with her mouth open.

Stella bit back a reprimand at Deirdre's eating habits. Lessons in manners were going to be high on the priority list. She pulled out a chair and sat before a bowl of steaming soup. The mouthwatering aromas of rich, meaty broth teeming with vegetables and a hint of tarragon and garlic filled the air.

"Well, what do you think?" Alf asked.

"The house is great." She swallowed the mouthful of soup. "And this soup is delicious."

The corners of his eyes crinkled. "That's not what I meant."

"No?"

He arched a single brow, and a knowing look settled over his craggy, sunburned face.

Heat surged up her neck as she discerned his meaning. He wanted to know what she thought of Dawson. She focused on her soup. "I have no idea what you're talking about."

"Oh, I think you do. Yes, I do. I may be old, but I'm not blind. No siree."

"Stella, are you finished? I want to show you the barn." Deirdre bounced on her chair, her tiny body in perpetual motion.

"Now, Dee," Alf said, "don't you rush Stella. There's plenty of light in the day yet."

Glad for the chance to escape the man's sharp gaze, Stella spooned up the last morsel of soup and wiped her mouth with a cloth napkin. "The soup was delicious, Alf. Thank you."

"I do what I can." He scooped the cat in his arms and stood. "Go on. Get out of here, you two."

"Stella, come on. Let's go see the horses. There's Caspar, Whiskey, and Trotter, and Mabel, and… Well, you'll see. We got lots." She grabbed Stella's hand and dragged her outside to the corral where she spent the next hour explaining the individual quirks of each horse as if she were describing her best friends.

The sun was setting by the time they returned to

the house. Deirdre ran ahead while Stella paused to admire the view from the porch. As she'd suspected, the deck offered an unrestricted, sweeping vista of pink-streaked sky reflecting a rosy hue on the snow-covered distant peaks and transforming the lake into molten lava. A flock of birds rose like a cloud and swooped over the lake. A loon's haunting call echoed across the valley.

She inhaled the tart tang of evergreen mixed with the pungent aroma of wood smoke. It had been a long time since she'd appreciated the beauty of her surroundings, a long time spent immersed in darkness and sorrow. The ever-present tears stung her eyes.

"Pretty, isn't it?"

She spun to meet Dawson's inscrutable gaze. "Mr. Wheeler, you…you startled me."

"Don't let the beauty fool you, Ms. King. This is a harsh land." His lips curled in a sardonic sneer. "If you're going to survive here, you'll have to be more aware of your surroundings. Next time it could be a cougar sneaking up on you."

It was on the tip of her tongue to snap that no cougar in its right mind would sneak up on this porch with two dogs guarding the house, but one glance at the sly gleam in his eyes, and she sealed her mouth. He was baiting her. She wouldn't play his game, but she couldn't resist a dig. "I'll take my chances with the cougars."

A laugh burst out, and he grinned.

Almost against her will, her lips curved in an answering smile. What was it about him? He drove her to anger one minute and had her grinning like a fool the next. Again, a flash of something nebulous sparked in the air between them. Mesmerized by the searing heat of his gaze, she stood frozen, her breath quickening as he lowered his head.

His warm breath fanned her cheeks.

Her heart fluttered like a moth against an irresistible light source, and a frisson of desire trilled along her spine.

"Supper's ready." His husky whisper rumbled against her ear.

She blinked. "Supper?" She lurched back from the heat emanating from his large body.

An unreadable expression flitted across his rugged face. He opened the door and gestured. "After you, ma'am."

Embarrassed at her unbridled response to his male magnetism, she strode past him, taking great pains to ensure she didn't brush against him.

Chapter 3

Seven strangers sat around the kitchen table, each man's gaze riveted on her.

She stumbled under the onslaught of their blatant curiosity, but forced a smile to her stiff lips. "Hello. You fellows must be the ranch hands I've heard so much about. I'm Stella King, Dee's new nanny. Looks like we'll be working together for the next while."

Though the men ranged in ages from just out of adolescence to middle-aged, they were of a similar type—whipcord lean with wiry muscles honed by years of hard labor. Their weathered faces, visible under an assortment of sweat-stained caps and dust-covered cowboy hats, were wreathed in welcoming grins, their eyes bright with interest.

Alf coughed loudly, and the men shoved back their chairs, whipped off their hats, and stood.

One young man, his dark hair drawn back in a short ponytail, and his acne-scarred cheeks flushed red, nearly knocked over his chair in his rush to shake her hand. "Brett Connors, ma'am." His large, callused hand gripped hers. "Pleased to meet you."

The next man to step forward was older than the others, but his smile was as welcoming. His receding red hair revealed patches of freckled, sunburned scalp. The angry red line of a jagged raised scar cut across his cheek from the outer corner of one eye to his grizzled upper lip. "I'm Jim McClennan, Ms. King. Welcome to the Circle 5." He eyed her up and down. "It's been a long time since we've seen the likes of you 'round these parts."

Dawson muttered a curse, and Jim's grin faded as he beat a quick retreat and sank back on his chair.

One by one, the other men stood and introduced themselves. Bob, Pierre, Jean-Luc, Samuel, Alphonse...their names ran together in a blur. All the men were friendly and welcomed her to the ranch, but Dawson's persistent glare placed a damper over their enthusiasm.

As the meal progressed, the men's nervousness disappeared, and she enjoyed their good-natured banter as they teased and poked fun at each other. Several times she even laughed out loud. Something she hadn't done in months.

Dawson's brooding presence hung over the hilarity like a threatening black cloud. His stony silence didn't go unnoticed by his men.

She caught the frequent wary looks they shot at him. *What was his problem?* He should be pleased she interacted with his men so well—happy they'd accepted her. Hadn't he been worried about her arrival disrupting the smooth running of the ranch? The hairs on the back of her neck tingled, and she slid a glance his way.

His eyes were shuttered, his mouth tightened, and he jerked away when she caught his eye.

She focused on the delicious meal. Baked ham, scalloped potatoes, creamed carrots, corn on the cob, and coleslaw. Homemade pecan pie for dessert completed the feast. She finished chewing the last bite of flaky piecrust and set down her fork. "Thank you for supper, Alf. The food was delicious." She patted her flat stomach. "If I keep eating like this, I'll weigh a ton."

The old man's lined face reddened. "Why, this spread's nothing special."

Bob, one of the more voluble ranch hands, guffawed. "Who are you kidding, old man? We haven't eaten food this fine in ages."

Alf glared. "And you won't be eating food like this again if you don't stop flapping your gums."

She was surprised at how quickly the younger man backed down in the face of Alf's sharp retort. The other men respected the feisty cook despite his small stature and advanced age.

Dawson spoke for the first time since the meal started. "I want to talk to you men in my study. Now."

He'd spoken quietly, but the men laid down their forks and scrambled to their feet. One by one, they bade her goodnight and disappeared through the door into the hall.

Dawson pushed back his chair. "Time for bed, Dee. Ms. King will get you settled. I'll be up later to say goodnight."

"Awww, Daddy, do I have to?" Deirdre's lower lip jutted. "This is Stella's first night. Can't I stay up and watch a movie with her?"

"Deirdre." His voice was stern. "You don't call adults by their first name. You know better. Her name is Ms. King."

Deirdre's heart-shaped face paled, and her lower lip trembled. "But she said I could." She swung toward Stella. "Isn't that right, Stella? You said I could."

"Dee!" Dawson's dark brows furrowed. "Don't

argue."

"Deirdre's right." Stella launched in, anger flaring. "I told her to call me Stella." Dawson was the boss. How he chose to run his ranch was none of her concern, but how he treated his daughter most definitely was. She clasped Deirdre's small, cold hand in hers and squeezed. "We're going to be the best of friends. Isn't that right, Dee? And friends call each other by their first names."

Dawson narrowed his eyes, and his mouth tightened. A pulse ticked in his jaw, and two red patches bloomed on his rugged cheeks.

Stella braced for his outburst.

"We'll discuss this later, *Ms. King.*" He shoved back his chair and stomped out of the room, leaving a thunderous silence in his wake.

Stella blew out a ragged breath, not sure if she'd won this round or not. Fixing a bright smile on her face, she patted Dee's hand. "How about a story before bed?"

The little girl's eyes lit up, and she leaped from her chair and ran to Stella and wrapped her thin arms around Stella's waist. "Can we read *Black Beauty*? Please? It's the bestest-ever story."

"You bet." Warmth filled Stella at the excitement shining in the child's expressive blue eyes. "But first, you have to have a bath like your father said. Go upstairs and get ready. I'll be up in a few minutes."

Deirdre raced off, leaving Alf and Stella alone in the large kitchen.

Stella began clearing the dishes from the table, but halted when Alf tapped her arm.

"Leave 'em be. Go see to the child."

"But you did all the cooking. Helping with the

dishes is the least I can do."

The creases at the corners of his eyes deepened, and he nodded. "I knew hiring you was the right thing." He gathered plates and cutlery and strode across the room to the sink and placed the dirty dishes in the soapy water. "Go on. See to Deirdre. She needs you."

Shrugging off his cryptic comment, she strode out of the kitchen and sought out her rambunctious charge.

An hour later, she sat on the edge of Deirdre's bed.

Dee's cheeks were rosy and flushed from her bath. Her red hair lay in damp spirals across the pillow; her pink lips were pursed. Her eyelids twitched as she dreamed.

Stella smoothed her hand over the blankets, and a familiar scent wafted in the air, eliciting a sharp stab of pain. She inhaled again, breathing in the distinctive sweet smell of a child. Memories flooded her, memories too painful to bear. Too tired to fight the onslaught, for the second time that day, she sank into the grief of the past. Tears overflowed her eyes and trickled down her cheeks.

A cough startled her. Without turning toward the open door, she knew who stood watching. She blinked back the rush of tears and swiped at her damp cheeks.

"We need to talk." The air of authority rang clear in Dawson's brisk voice.

Wiping her damp eyes again, she followed him out of the darkened bedroom, along the hall, and down the stairs. She slowed, lagging behind his tall, broad-shouldered frame. This was it. This was when he fired her for standing up to him in the kitchen.

An image of Deirdre's pale, elfin face rose before her. Well, let him try. The child was lonely. She needed her new nanny, needed a friend. Dawson could rant all he wanted. His anger wouldn't make any difference. Stella would do the same again if doing so meant Deirdre's happiness.

He halted before an open door and motioned for her to enter the room beyond.

Head held high, loins girded for battle, she marched into the room. A lamp on the desk and the fire crackling in a small fireplace lent the room a warm ambience.

A large black, shaggy dog—Shas?—lay stretched before the fire. His tail thumped the floor in greeting.

The other dog was curled in a ball on one end of a chocolate-brown leather couch. A snore erupted, and deep in sleep, he didn't acknowledge her entrance.

A reclining leather chair was behind a large wooden desk with a laptop computer set on its gleaming surface. Books on ranching, local history, veterinary medicine, and a selection of best-selling thrillers lined the shelves along the walls.

Dawson pointed to the couch. "Sit."

Heat flared in her cheeks. Did he think she was one of his dogs, and if he uttered a command, she'd obey? "I'd rather stand."

The furrow between his brows deepened, but he shrugged. "Suit yourself." He stalked behind the desk, tugged open a drawer, and held up a half-filled liquor bottle. "Want a drink?"

"Why not?" She didn't normally drink, but the alcohol might give her courage for the impending confrontation.

He filled two glasses with amber-colored liquid.

On the wall above the couch, a large photograph,

framed in oak, showed a beautiful, auburn-haired woman holding an infant in her arms. Stella edged closer to the portrait. Tendrils of fine red hair escaped the baby's crocheted pink cap. Deirdre. The woman holding her must be Dee's mother. The same woman smiled in the photograph on Dee's bedside table.

The loud clunk of a bottle plunked on a hard surface broke through her thoughts. She tore her gaze from the photograph.

Dawson handed her a glass of liquor and leaned his hips against the desk, a drink in his hand, his face stormy.

"The photograph's lovely." She gulped. "Dee's so cute with her red hair, and your wife is beautiful."

"She was." He raised his glass and drank a long swallow. "She passed four years ago."

"Oh...oh, I'm so sorry." A wave of sympathy washed over her. "How—" She inhaled a shaky breath. "—how did it happen?"

"It was a long time ago."

His clipped tone made it clear he didn't want to talk about his wife's death. His strong, tanned throat worked as he swallowed another slug of whiskey. A tuft of enticing dark hair peeked above the open collar of his faded denim work shirt.

He raised his glass again and tossed off the contents. Grabbing the bottle, he refilled his drink. His hand shook, and a splash of liquor slopped on the desk.

"Look, Mr. Wheeler, I'm really sorry about your wife—"

"Call me Dawson. We're *friends*, right?" His sarcasm was evident. He raised his glass in the air. "Here's to your new job at the Circle 5, Stella." He drank, swallowing more than half the contents.

She blinked. "Wait a minute. You're…you're not firing me?" She sank onto the couch beside the slumbering dog.

"Not yet."

"Thanks, I think."

"Why are you here? Why the Circle 5? And why a nanny? I read your resume. You're way overqualified."

She shrugged. "I needed a job."

"Plenty of jobs in the city."

Her uneasiness grew under his probing. "I…I wanted a change. I thought I'd enjoy the country."

His dark gaze burned into hers. "There's something you aren't telling me, something you're keeping secret. Why is that, I wonder?" He shoved away from the desk and crossed the room, lowering himself onto the couch beside her.

Inches separated them. Heat emanated from his large, masculine body.

"I have to be honest with you, Stella. I wasn't in favor of hiring a nanny. Deirdre and I have been fine without one for years." He sipped his drink. "Alf can be pretty insistent when he gets an idea into his head."

"Your daughter's a wonderful child, but she's lonely. She misses her mother."

He brushed his fingers through his hair, rumpling the glossy curls. "She doesn't remember her mother. Dee was only one when my wife…she passed, and we moved here."

Her heart softened at the sorrow lacing his voice. All too well she imagined how difficult life must have been after his wife died, leaving him with an infant. Reacting to the pain etched across his face, she placed her hand on his arm, offering unspoken comfort.

He tensed, the muscles bunching beneath her hand.

In the next breath, he erupted off the couch, his face hard, his eyes shards of ice. "I'd appreciate it if you kept your hands to yourself. I don't want any misunderstanding. This is a business arrangement, nothing more. I hired you to do a job. I fully expect you to carry out your duties as instructed."

Her face flamed. "I...I—"

"I don't want your pity either." A thin white line rimmed his sealed lips.

"I can't imagine why someone as bitter as you would need it." Her mouth snapped shut on the cruel words. She regretted her outburst, but his baseless assumption she was flirting propelled her over the edge, and she couldn't stop. "I can assure you, Mr. Wheeler, it won't happen again."

"You're damn right it won't. I've changed my mind. You're leaving in the morning." He picked up his drink and guzzled the remains.

"You're firing me?" She leaped to her feet and planted her hands on her hips.

"You're damn right I am."

"But, I've just started. I..." Her voice trailed off in the face of his fierce glower. This job was her chance to start over. No way she was going to let this arrogant son of a bitch go back on his word. "Why are you so afraid?" She moved a step closer. "What exactly is it you think will happen if I stay?"

His eyes narrowed and his nostrils flared. He inhaled a deep breath, and after several beats, he nodded. "All right. We'll try this arrangement for three weeks and see how it goes. But at the end of three weeks, if the situation hasn't worked out, you won't object when I take you back to Spirit Falls."

Relief surged through her. "Agreed." She turned to leave, but his cold voice stopped her.

"Oh, and Ms. King, you'll stay away from the men."

"You'd better believe it. I'll stay well away from *all* the men." Satisfied she'd had the last word, she quickened her pace, and head held high, sailed out of the room.

****

Dawson poured himself another drink and rubbed a hand across his aching eyes. Was it his third or fourth? Hell, he'd lost track. Whatever, it was too much. He'd have a headache in the morning, but the buzz was worth the pain. He wanted to drink enough alcohol to deaden the all-too-vivid memory of Stella's soft, warm touch.

She hadn't been there a day, and the ranch was in an uproar. He glowered as he recalled the evening meal, when his usually competent ranch hands fell all over themselves in their attempts to impress the new nanny. Their actions would have been laughable if it weren't obvious their fascination with her was going to affect their work.

He swigged another big swallow of scotch. He'd read the men the riot act and laid out the ground rules for their behavior toward Stella. He'd been harsher than he probably should have been. After all, most of them had worked for him for years. They didn't deserve to have him leaping all over them because they were attracted to a beautiful woman. Any man not in his grave would react the same. Hell, look at the ass he'd made of himself. No teenage boy could have behaved more foolishly.

All day as he'd gone about his chores, he couldn't erase the enticing image of her long, shiny, blonde hair, creamy-smooth skin, and kiss-me lips. And then there was her body. Hell, no wonder he hadn't been able to concentrate. He'd been so caught up in the shape of her ass he'd almost been kicked in the head by the cantankerous old bull he was tending.

Because of her, he'd broken his word to Dee and hadn't given his daughter a good night kiss like he always did. Always. Every single night. Except tonight.

He should never have given in to Alf's nagging and hired her. Worse, he'd agreed to let her stay for three weeks. But who could blame him? The glint of sadness lurking in the azure depths of her eyes, the tearstains on her cheeks, and the certainty she needed this job, had weakened his resolve.

He was right about one thing, though. She was hiding something. Why else would a fine-looking, smart woman like her want to hide away on a ranch in the wilds of the Chilcotin Plateau?

He stumbled and grabbed the edge of the desk. Damn. He'd better sober up. He had serious issues to deal with. The ranch had lost three cows in the past weeks. Each animal had been shot and left to rot. It was hunting season, but his property was posted as a no-hunting zone. His gut told him the killings were deliberate. The dead cattle weren't from a hunter's stray bullet.

He scrubbed his face again as his unease grew. The dead cattle weren't the only unexplained acts happening on the ranch. The previous week an irrigation pump had been smashed, the week before, someone had cut the high-pasture fence and two of his prime breeding bulls escaped.

And then there was that damn mine. Were all those events connected?

His head pounded as he struggled to think, to work out the angles, but the alcohol had fogged his brain. Yawning, he set his glass on the desk and whistled to the two sleeping dogs.

They rose, stretched, and padded on silent paws after him as he staggered from the office and down the hall to his bedroom.

Not bothering to undress, he kicked off his boots and fell back across the king-size bed.

Sneakers bounded up beside him, licked his face with a long wet tongue, and spun around three times before plopping down on Dawson's leg.

Shas settled on the padded dog bed on the floor at the foot of the bed.

He rubbed Sneakers' silky coat, grateful for the dog's warm presence and unconditional love. No matter what sort of an ass he made of himself, the dogs loved him.

Sneakers snuggled closer and rested his big head on Dawson's stomach.

The room reeled, and he slammed his eyes closed. He'd had too much to drink, and yet not nearly enough. Alf was after him to quit, but no matter what promises of sobriety he made, nearly every evening after Deirdre was in bed, when he was alone in his den, the bottle of scotch called to him like a cheap whore. The lure of escape from the pain of his loss and aching loneliness was too strong. Before he knew it, he'd poured one drink, then two, and three, until more often than not, he staggered to bed and passed out.

He swiped a hand over his face, the rasp of two days' growth of beard loud in the quiet bedroom. Opening his eyes, he stared at the shifting shadows on the ceiling. That night's drinking hadn't been brought on by loneliness or grief. The finger of blame could be pointed squarely at one person—Stella King.

Her image flickered across the shadows.

Sneakers' back legs kicked and jerked as he chased rabbits in the throes of a dream.

What was it about the damn woman that transformed him into a backwoods curmudgeon? He wasn't usually such a jerk. His eyelids grew heavy and closed as exhaustion, combined with copious amounts of alcohol, took effect. Within seconds, he drifted off to sleep.

Chapter 4

Stella woke with a start.

Deirdre stood beside the bed, her red hair a vivid tangle, emphasizing the paleness of her heart-shaped face.

"Good morning, Dee." Stella yawned and sat up against the pillows. "You're up bright and early."

Deirdre stared in watchful silence.

"Cat got your tongue?"

"I thought you were dead."

"Wha...what?" A shiver laced through her.

"Alf says dead people look like they're sleeping."

Stella's laugh died in her throat at the solemn expression on Deirdre's wan face and the worried look in her expressive eyes. "Come here." She patted the space on the bed beside her.

Deirdre climbed onto the bed and laid her head on Stella's shoulder.

An ache started deep in Stella's heart. "Have you seen any dead people, honey?"

Deirdre shook her head. "Have you?"

An image too horrible to contemplate flashed through Stella's mind, but before the stab of agony overwhelmed her, she swallowed back the lump in her throat.

Deirdre's forehead creased in a frown. "You're sad. Why?"

Stella wiped her tears with the sleeve of her nightgown and pasted a bright smile on her face. "It's all right, honey. I'm fine."

"Daddy's sad sometimes. He misses Mommy. I miss her, too."

"Do you remember her?" Hadn't Dawson said Deirdre was a one-year-old when her mother died? She couldn't possibly have any memories of her.

"Daddy has lots and lots of pictures. I look at them all the time. Mommy was pretty like a princess. Daddy says she was the prettiest girl in the whole wide world." The child's face fell. "Everyone has a mommy. My friends in town have mommies. Even the kids in movies and story books have mommies."

The lump in her throat was so thick Stella could barely speak. "Oh, honey."

"I know…" Deirdre scrunched on her knees facing Stella, her eyes bright. "*You* can be my mommy."

An all-too-familiar pressure filled Stella's chest. "You have a mommy. She's still here—" She placed her palm on Deirdre's chest. "—in your heart. She loves you very much, and she knows what a wonderful little girl you are."

"That's what Daddy says."

"Well, your daddy's right." She released a shaky breath. "You're a lucky girl. You have a daddy who loves you to the moon and back."

A smile flickered at the edges of Deirdre's rosebud mouth. "That's from my picture book, the one Daddy reads to me sometimes." She played with a red curl, twining it around her tiny fingers. "Alf loves me too. And Alphonse, and Jean-Luc, and the rest of the guys."

"See? You're lucky. You're surrounded by people

who love you."

"But they're not mommies." The tiny voice was muffled. "I want a mommy."

"Oh, Dee." Emotion welled in her throat, and she hugged the girl's thin frame.

Deirdre squirmed, breaking free. "Do you have rainbow trees where you come from, Stella?"

"Rainbow trees?"

Deirdre's head bobbed, her red curls dancing. "They're trees that are bent over a path in the forest." She bounced on the bed in her earnestness. "Alf told me if you stand under a rainbow tree and make a wish, your wish'll come true.

"I wish for the same thing every time." She grinned and bounded off the bed, skipped across the room, and twirled in a pirouette. "But I can't tell you what my wish is. Alf says if I tell, my wish won't come true."

Stella's heart stuttered. It wasn't hard to guess Dee's wish. Maybe one day her fervent hope for a mommy would come true, and Dawson would remarry. Yeah, and maybe pigs would fly. No woman would put up with the arrogant, bitter rancher, no matter how handsome he was.

Dee attempted a cartwheel and crashed to the floor with a thud, landing on her bottom. "Do you know how to do cartwheels, Stella? Can you show me?" The solemn waif vanished, replaced by an effervescent dynamo.

"What time is it?" Judging by the bright light streaming into the room, the hour was late. After her unsettling confrontation with Dawson the previous night, she'd tossed and turned for hours. The gray light of morning had seeped through the curtains before she'd finally fallen asleep.

Deirdre shrugged. "I can't tell time, but the little hand on the clock in the kitchen was on the number ten." She stood on her tiptoes and spun, her red curls swirling in a gleaming mass. "I wanted to wake you a long, long time ago, but Alf wouldn't let me. He said you needed your sleep."

"Remind me to thank Alf." Stella picked up her watch from the bedside table and glanced at the time. Yikes! Climbing out of bed, she grimaced as her muscles protested. She stretched her back and groaned. Every bump, lurch, and bone-shattering shudder of her long, tortuous journey by bus over the pothole-filled gravel road was etched into her aching body. She looked longingly at the comfortable bed. If only she could crawl back under the covers and spend the day recovering. But Deirdre was waiting, a hopeful expression on her freckled face. Stella ruffled the girl's tangled curls. "Well, what shall we do today?"

"Everything. I want to do everything."

Stella bit back a groan, but the child's enthusiasm was catching. "Where should we begin?"

"Let's play dolls first. I've got lots and lots of baby dolls. They have clothes, and pretend bottles, and diapers, and everything. After, we can go see the horses, and Blackie has a new litter of kittens, and—"

"Whoa." Stella held up her hand. "Let me get dressed and eat some breakfast, and then we'll get started on your list."

"I'll set up my dolls." Deirdre scampered out of the room.

The rest of the morning flew by in a whirl of activity as Stella struggled to keep up with the energetic child. By the time Alf called them to lunch, she was more than ready for a break. The constant activity, and Deirdre's boundless enthusiasm took her mind off her own troubles. For the first time in a long while, she'd laughed out loud at the antics of a child.

Dawson didn't show up for the noonday meal, nor did he appear at supper. No one commented on his absence.

For her part, Stella was relieved not to have to face him, especially after the previous night. He'd had the temerity to inform her she was on a three-week trial. Well, she liked challenges. If he hoped she'd give him an opportunity to prove she couldn't handle this job, he'd better think again. She hadn't made it through four years of undergraduate school and three more of law school, finishing top of her class, from a lack of determination.

Dawson Wheeler was arrogant and irritating. Sure, he was good-looking in a rugged sort of way, and his well-developed biceps were pretty hot, but she wasn't interested in a relationship, not now, maybe not ever. She was there for one reason, and one reason only—to escape Vancouver and the haunting memories lurking on every corner.

The advertisement on the *Vancouver Times* job posting website seeking a nanny for a five-year-old at a remote cattle ranch in the Chilcotin had sounded like the perfect solution. What could be farther from downtown Vancouver than the Chilcotin Plateau? Hundreds of kilometers of sparsely inhabited forest and mountains separated the two locations.

Arriving in the Chilcotin was like stepping into an earlier century. Dawson's ranch had electricity, but the power was generated by a combination of solar and wind power, backed up by two large diesel generators located in a nearby shed. They had a satellite dish for television and another for the Internet, but no cell service. All phone calls had to be made on the radiotelephone in Dawson's office or the satellite phone only used for emergencies.

Being away from the frenetic energy of the city was the balm she needed to heal. She grimaced. At least the idea of working as a nanny on the remote wilderness ranch had seemed like the perfect plan until she met her employer.

But she had to think of Deirdre. The child was starved for companionship. She needed Stella, and Stella needed her. And so she'd remain at the Circle 5, in spite of Dawson Wheeler and his autocratic dictates.

The evening flew by as Deirdre led Stella from one activity to another. She'd begged Stella to read one more story, asked for yet another drink of water, had gone to the bathroom twice, until she'd lost the battle and closed her heavy eyelids. Now the little dynamo was finally asleep.

Stella brushed back a stray curl from Deirdre's forehead and tiptoed out of the room, leaving the door ajar so she'd hear if Deirdre woke in the night. A yawn escaped, and she leaned against the wall in the hallway, too weary to advance another step. Keeping up with Deirdre was a challenge, but her exhaustion wasn't from the child's constant activity. She'd enjoyed Dee's chatter and infectious giggles, but the strain of holding back the ever-present flood of grief threatening to engulf her wore her down.

Deirdre's every giggle, every silly, corny joke,

every pout, reminded her of all she'd lost. Her shoulders shook, her knees wobbled, and she sagged to the floor. Memories, sharp and agonizing, swirled. The pine-paneled walls of the ranch house dissolved, and she was back in her spacious home in North Vancouver.

She'd just found out she was pregnant. The new life she carried in her womb was a promise of joy for her and Nicholas, one she hoped would heal the gulf between them. She'd spent countless happy hours crocheting blankets for the baby and preparing the nursery, her heart filled with dreams of the life growing within her.

Keegan's birth had been an uneventful delivery, and the baby boy arrived in the world screaming and red-faced. Even wrinkled like a wizened old man, he was more perfect than she could have imagined. Her heart swelled with joy when he opened his tiny puckered mouth and let out a loud wail of protest at being thrust into a world of light and cold.

From the moment she and Keegan returned home from the hospital, her life was idyllic. She spent her days nursing her precious baby, changing his diapers, bathing him, holding him, and loving him.

Nicholas transformed from a busy, driven executive to a doting father. He came home early to be with Keegan. How many times had she come upon father and son, rocking in the nursery chair, Nicholas cradling Keegan and crooning a soothing lullaby?

A sob escaped, and she jammed her fist in her mouth to stifle the sound as memories of that nightmare day thirteen months ago when her world imploded, swamped her.

She blinked against the blast of sun streaming

through the filmy curtains covering the bedroom window. Breathing in the peaceful stillness, she relished the quiet, so rare since Keegan's arrival.

Her breasts, engorged with milk, throbbed. Fingers of unease crawled along her spine. She peered at the bedside clock.

Nine o'clock.

Keegan was usually awake and squalling hungrily long before now.

Leaping out of bed, she rushed along the hallway to Keegan's room. She paused on the threshold.

The room beyond was dim and silent.

Heart pounding, she pushed open the partially closed door and stumbled on leaden feet toward the crib.

Keegan lay on his back, his tiny body swaddled in the blue flannel blanket with the baby penguin design, just as she'd placed him the night before when she crept in to give him a kiss after she returned from the party.

She clapped her palm over her mouth stifling a moan. Her heart stuttered. An icy chill filled her veins.

"Stella?"

Unbearable pain crushed her, and she fought the strong hands grasping her arms and lifting her to her feet. "No!"

"What's wrong? Is it Deirdre? Is my daughter okay?"

The grip on her arms tightened, dragging her out of the horror of the past.

"Stella?" Dawson's voice held a sharp note of command. "Has something happened to Deirdre?"

"I...I..."

He shook her, forcing her to look at him. "What's

wrong?"

The razor-sharp talons of the nightmare released their grip, but not the pain. The wrenching agony was sharp and poignant, as it was every minute of every day since that nightmare morning thirteen months ago. She blinked at Dawson. "Deirdre?" She shook her head. "No…no, she's fine."

The strained white lines on his handsome features smoothed, and his fingers relaxed their steely hold. He dug a handkerchief from the back pocket of his jeans and shoved the red-patterned cotton cloth into her hand. "What's wrong, then? Why are you crying?"

Biting her lip to stop the trembling, she swiped her streaming eyes with the handkerchief and stumbled back a step. "I…" Words failed, and she spun to flee, desperate to escape his piercing gaze.

"Stella, wait, don't go." He grasped her arm.

"Please. I…I'm tired." She tugged against his restraining hand, but he held tight.

Cupping her chin, he lifted her head. "Tell me what's wrong. Why are you crying?"

She kept her gaze fixed on his strong, tanned neck, refusing to meet his eyes.

"Stella, please tell me. Did Dee do something to upset you? Did one of the men?"

The warm huskiness in his voice unnerved her, and against her will, she looked at him and sucked in a ragged breath. The signs were all-too-evident. His ebony eyes were filled with haunting shadows. The aching well of grief, the heartache, the never-ending sense of loss sucked the soul out of a person and marked you for life.

"You know what it's like to lose someone you

love." Her voice was a hoarse whisper.

The sharp angles of his face softened, the taut line of his jaw easing. He brushed a tear from her cheek, the tips of his callused fingers gentle.

Their gazes locked.

"Daddy, is that you?" Deirdre's high-pitched voice, calling from her bedroom, broke the connection.

His eyes shuttered, and he dropped her arm as if her skin burned.

"Daddy?"

"Go to bed, Stella. Get some sleep." He about-faced and strode down the hall to Deirdre's room.

She stared after him, her brow furrowed. He switched his emotions on and off like a faucet. She'd come to the Circle 5 seeking salvation, hoping this wild land and the company of strangers, people who didn't know her tragic story, people whose eyes weren't filled with pity, would help her heal. Now there she was...day two, and already she'd dissolved into a bucket of tears in front of her employer.

How in Heaven's name would she survive the next months?

Chapter 5

The next evening after she'd settled Deirdre in bed, Stella found Alf in the kitchen washing dishes in the large, stainless steel sink. "Let me help." She removed a drying towel from the drawer and picked up a wet plate from the draining rack.

"Thanks, Stella, I'd appreciate some help." He wiped his shiny forehead with the back of a soapy hand. "It's been a long day."

"You work too hard." She placed the dried dish in the cupboard.

"What are you saying?" He pinned her with a hard gaze. "You think I'm too old for this?"

She opened her mouth to apologize but stopped at the twinkle in his eye. "You're not ready to be put out to pasture. Not yet anyway."

He chuckled. "That's for damn sure. Got a few more miles left on these old bones, I guaran-damn-tee you."

Her laugh burst out. She picked up another plate and spoke the question that had lurked in her head all day. "Where's Dawson? He wasn't at lunch or supper again today. Has he gone somewhere?" *Or is he avoiding me?* The words remained unspoken, but after their awkward confrontation last night, was it possible that Dawson was hiding from her?

The ranch hands had all been at supper, but

Dawson's chair at the head of the table had sat empty, his absence like a coiled snake in the room. No one spoke of it, but it was all she could think of. After exposing her fragile emotions the night before, she'd dreaded facing him, but not seeing him was worse.

"I don't know what's up with that boy. He's usually as regular as clockwork at meals. He has a mighty big appetite, but these last couple of days..." A cloud settled over Alf's features, dousing his smile, and he shrugged. "Anyway, today's different. He's up in the high pasture. Rode out before dawn this morning." The lines in his face deepened. "Another dead cow."

"Someone's killing your cows? Who would do that?"

"Damned if I know, but Dawson's furious. Those cattle are worth a heck of a lot of money."

"He went up there alone? Is that safe?"

"Don't you worry about him. He can look after himself. It's the son of a bitch who's been shooting our stock who'd better watch out. If Dawson gets hold of him—" He shook his head, his face grim. "Well, let's just say, I wouldn't want to be him."

She shuddered. "Is he always so angry and bitter?"

Alf stopped scrubbing a pot and stared out the window. "He has a lot on his plate right now." He huffed out a breath and met her gaze. "He didn't use to be like this. But ever since Anna died, he's been lost. He's angry at the world."

His Adam's apple bobbed in his thin throat. "And then there's his drinking..." His voice trailed off, and he picked up the dishcloth and scoured the bottom of the pot. "Never mind. You don't need to hear all this."

His drinking? Dawson had a problem with alcohol?

He'd downed several glasses of scotch the night she arrived, but that was a long way from a drinking problem. Did he drink to drown his sorrows?

After Keegan died, she'd sought out the bottle for escape, but the brief respite offered by booze didn't last, and the next morning the pain was even sharper, so she'd quit. "You said he has a lot on his plate right now. Are you just talking about the dead cows? Or is there more?"

"That's part of what's bothering him, but there's a lot more at stake."

"What's that?" She was prying, but the more she learned about her moody employer, the better she could understand him.

"Ever since those damn mining folk have been coming around, Dawson's been on edge." He sank his hands up to the elbows in the soapy water and scrubbed a steel-wool pad over another food-encrusted pot. "As if he'd sit back and let those arrogant buggers stroll in here like they own the damn place." He scrubbed harder, grunting with the effort. "No damn way, not Dawson Wheeler. Not my boy. He loves this land too much. We all do."

"What…what mining people?"

"Those men who've been traipsing all over the Circle 5 these past three months." He wiped a soapy hand over his forehead, leaving a smear of bubbles. "Those slimy bastards. They talked all nice and civil until we cottoned on to what they were up to."

A knot in her gut tightened. "What are they up to?"

"Seems they have the notion to develop a copper mine on Circle 5 land." His eyes flashed fire. "Can you believe their gall? They want to rip this place apart."

"Do you know what company they represent?" She winced at the squeak in her voice.

He shrugged. "Hell if I know." He pointed with his chin at a pine hutch on the far side of the room. "I've got one of their cards over there somewhere."

On leaden feet she stumbled over to the hutch. Sifting through a stack of bills and store flyers, she found a small, cream-colored card embossed with plain black lettering and an all-too-familiar logo. The glass she was drying slipped from her hands and crashed on the hardwood floor. "Oh, dear. I'm so sorry." Face burning, gut clenching, she crouched and picked up the scattered shards of glass.

"Mind or you'll cut yourself." He dried his hands on the apron at his waist and hurried to a closet. Opening the door, he removed a broom and dustpan. "Here, use this."

Once she'd swept the tiny pieces of glass into the dustpan, she emptied the pan over the garbage.

"You okay, Stella? You're awful pale all of a sudden." Alf watched her intently.

She faked a yawn. "I...I'm just tired. It's been a long day."

Alf's face softened. "I'll bet. Dee could tire out a whirling dervish. She's one busy little gal."

Her fingers tightened around the card, creasing the edges. She dropped it on the stack of mail.

"It's been a long while since I've seen that little gal so happy." He untied the apron around his waist, and set it on the counter. "I know this place isn't what you're used to, but I sure as crackin' hope you plan to stick around. Dee's taken a real liking to you. I wouldn't want to see her hurt."

She couldn't meet his gaze.

"You sure you're okay?"

Not certain if words could fit around the fist-sized lump in her throat, she swallowed and nodded.

"Look, we're as good as done." Alf patted her shoulder. "You head off to bed. I'll finish up here."

Too guilt-ridden and exhausted to argue, she mumbled her thanks and plodded out of the kitchen and dragged up the stairs. After she brushed her teeth, she donned her nightgown and crawled into bed, burrowing beneath the covers. She didn't think she'd sleep, and she expected to lie awake tossing and turning, stewing over the ramifications of what she'd learned, but as soon as her head hit the pillow, her eyes closed, and she fell into a deep sleep.

Three hours later she awoke, heart pounding, eyes swollen and gritty from tears. Nightmare images of Keegan swaddled in white satin in his tiny white coffin filled her mind. She punched the damp pillow and tossed it on the floor. Throwing back the covers, she climbed out of bed.

Wallowing in self-pity wouldn't bring back Keegan. He was gone...forever. Her stomach spasmed as pain lanced through her along with the overwhelming desire to wind back time and slow it down so she could savor those all-too-few precious moments with him.

Guilt was an acid eating her soul, destroying it piece by piece. She should have died instead of Keegan. She'd wanted to die, prayed for death, but was too much of a coward to do the deed. And so she lived...if her daily existence for the past thirteen months could be called living. One unrelenting, lonely, bleak day followed another. Each second, each minute, each hour, drove her closer to her goal—the day her heart stopped beating, and she joined Keegan.

Since her arrival at the Circle 5, the all-consuming burden of guilt had eased, as smile by smile, giggle by giggle, the unstoppable force of Deirdre Wheeler crept into her shattered heart. A watery smile broke through her tears, and she wiped her damp face. Hard to live in a gray, ghostly world haunted by her dead son when Deirdre looked at her with such hope and joy.

Deciding a cup of warm milk would help her sleep, she crept along the dark hallway and down the stairs. Other than the creaks and groans of the log beams settling in the cooling night air, the house was quiet. She shivered and rubbed at the goose bumps on her arms, wishing she'd worn her robe over her thin cotton nightgown.

The kitchen was warm and smelled of the delicious venison stew Alf had prepared for supper. An almost-full moon bathed the room in pale gray-blue light, and she navigated her way to the refrigerator without turning on the lights. She poured milk into a small pot and ignited the flame beneath the burner on the propane stove. In minutes, the milk was bubbling, and she poured the steaming liquid into a cup. Raising the cup to her lips, she sipped.

"Couldn't sleep?"

She choked on a mouthful of hot milk. Coughing and sputtering, she wheeled around.

Dawson lounged in one of the rocking chairs beside the fireplace. The remains of the evening fire smoldered in the grate and cast a reddish-gold glow across his rugged features.

"I…I didn't know you were back."

He slumped in the chair, his long legs stretched before him toward the fire, warming his wool-sock-clad feet. "I got in an hour ago." He scrubbed his hand over his dark-stubbled jaw and yawned. Laying his head against the cushioned back of the rocking chair, he closed his eyes.

"You look tired." She hugged her arms across her chest. "Was it a long ride?"

His eyes snapped open.

The infernal flush of heat seared her cheeks. "Alf said you rode up to the high pasture today to check on some dead cows."

His upper lip curled. "Cattle or beef stock. Never cows."

"What?"

"We raise *cattle* on the Circle 5 for beef. You know, the stuff you buy in the meat section of the grocery store."

"I know where meat comes from," she snapped. "You think you have me pegged, don't you? As far as you're concerned, I'm a big city woman whose sole goal is to disrupt the running of your precious ranch." She planted her hands on her hips. The dam had been breached. Nothing would stop the angry torrent. "What could I possibly know about ranching? All I'm capable of is shopping in the local mall or sipping wine spritzers in a glitzy hotel lounge." She glared. "Am I right?"

He chuckled, the sound rich and masculine. "Okay, you got me. I get it. I shouldn't judge you."

She nodded, feeling as if she'd scored a point in a game where she didn't know the rules. She sipped her milk. Hopefully he didn't notice the trembling in her hand.

"Alf tells me you're doing a good job." He rubbed the back of his neck. "Deirdre likes you."

"Damned with faint praise."

"I didn't mean that. I..." He paused and ran long fingers through his hair. "I wanted to thank you."

She searched for the barb hidden in his unexpected praise, but sincerity shone in his tired eyes. Her heart lurched, and she smiled. "She's a great kid."

"Yeah, she sure is." He yawned again, and his eyes drifted closed. Lines of exhaustion etched across his forehead, and dark smudges underlined his eyes. His chest rose and fell in a slow, steady rhythm.

"Would you like some warm milk?" She kept her voice a mere whisper in case he was sleeping. "There's more in the pot."

He opened his eyes, the dark irises probing. His gaze strayed to her mouth.

She took a staggered inhale.

Time stood still, and the world stopped revolving.

His lips curved in a slow, sultry smile. "A hot toddy would be real nice, Stella. Thanks." His voice was a warm caress.

She blinked, fighting to catch her breath. "A...hot drink. Okay, I...I can do that."

"Even better if you add a dollop or two of whiskey."

She scurried to the stove, still struggling for breath, needing distance, space, air. "I'll...I'll just be a minute." She fumbled, her fingers clumsy, as she set her cup on the counter and opened one cupboard after another, searching for whiskey.

"Upper left cabinet by the stove." His deep voice

flowed across the dim kitchen.

She opened the cupboard he'd indicated and found a bottle of rye whiskey sitting on the top shelf. Standing on tiptoes, she stretched for the bottle, all the while aware of his gaze raking over her. She yanked down the bottle, filled a mug with hot milk, and poured in a generous portion of whiskey, cursing under her breath when a splash of hot liquid slopped onto the counter. Clasping the mug in two hands, she edged closer, her bare feet whispering over the cold floorboards.

His eyes were closed, the lines scoring his usually harsh features softened. A snore escaped his lips.

She inched closer, drawn to him as if to a magnet, and set the hot toddy on the small pine table beside his chair.

The burning coals in the fireplace created enough ambient light to reveal the ravages of grief on his handsome face that even sleep didn't erase. His tanned hands, loosely clasped, rested on his flat stomach. His fingers were long, the large knuckles chapped, the skin reddened and rough. The ragged white ridge of an old wound scored the back of one hand amid a sprinkling of fine black hairs. A plain gold band ringed one finger.

His wedding ring.

She pressed her hand to her throat and swallowed hard at this evidence of his enduring love for his deceased wife. All those years, and he hadn't removed his ring.

He shifted, sinking lower in the chair and crossing one sock-covered foot over the other, emitting another soft snuffle. His head sagged sideways, and a glossy lock of hair slipped across his forehead.

She brushed back the wayward curl and lingered,

caressing the silken softness so at odds with the man himself.

"Don't mind me." Alf stood in the doorway, his eyes twinkling with a devilish gleam as his gaze shifted between her and the sleeping Dawson. His bushy gray brows quirked. "I left my pipe here somewhere, but I suppose I can get it some other time."

She snatched her hand back. Heat flared in her cheeks. "I couldn't sleep." She pointed at the steaming cup on the table beside Dawson. "I...I made some warm milk."

The corners of Alf's mouth twitched. "Right."

"No, really. I woke up and couldn't get back to sleep, and I wanted some warm milk. I don't know why, but a warm drink helps me sleep, and then I saw Dawson, and he looked so tired. He asked me to make him a hot toddy so I—" His quiet chuckle stopped her babbling.

He strolled into the kitchen and nodded toward Dawson. "Must be a mighty powerful concoction. He looks done in."

Dawson emitted a loud snort and continued snoring.

"I'm going to bed." She swept by the old man, in a rush to escape to the sanctuary of her room. His quiet chuckles followed her like the hounds of hell as she flew up the stairs.

****

Dawson rubbed the sleep from his eyes. Streaks of bright morning sunshine shone through the large kitchen windows, stabbing his eyes and piercing his brain. He sat up, wincing as his cramped muscles complained. Rubbing the knot in the back of his neck, he cursed and eased his stiff body out of the tight confines of the old wooden rocking chair.

He stared at the cup of cold milk on the table beside his chair, and his gut twisted. He'd fallen asleep in the god-awful, uncomfortable chair instead of his king-size bed. One minute he'd been resting by the fire in the dark kitchen before heading to bed, and in the next breath, Stella was in front of him wearing a white nightgown that did nothing to hide her curves.

He rubbed his hands over his cheeks, grimacing at the loud rasp of stubble. God, he was tired. These past few days had been damn hard—dead cattle, vandalism, the ever-present threat of the mining company employees searching his land for minerals, to say nothing of Stella's arrival.

As if the torrential rain in the afternoon wasn't bad enough, he'd found the dead animals. His blood had boiled at the wanton waste. The cattle had been shot, and their bodies left for the coyotes. He'd followed the tracks of an ATV for hours, but under the onslaught of rain, the trail petered out, and he lost them.

When he finally arrived home, he'd run smack into the one person he didn't want to see, the one person guaranteed to ruin an already crappy day. And then he'd made a fool of himself by falling asleep.

"Mornin'."

Alf's cheerful greeting cut into his sour thoughts. He grunted in response.

"Well, you're sure in a good mood this morning." Alf bustled around the kitchen, grinding coffee beans, banging pots, opening and closing cupboards, and running water in the sink.

Dawson stretched and rubbed the small of his back.

"Coffee ready yet?"

Alf pointed to the coffee pot starting to perk on the gas range. "Just about." He studied Dawson. "Your sour mood have anything to do with our new nanny?"

"Of course not." He lowered his head so Alf wouldn't detect his lie.

"Right."

Ignoring Alf's laconic disbelief, he rubbed his aching muscles. His sore back and cantankerous mood were Stella King's fault. From the moment he set eyes on her, his world had flipped upside down. With her shiny fall of golden hair, mile-long legs, and nicely rounded ass, she was an eyeful.

But it wasn't her good looks that explained his unsettling reaction to her being on the ranch. If that were the case he'd head into town for a weekend and find some willing, no-strings-attached, female companionship to ease his tension.

Nope, nothing that simple.

The air of a wounded animal surrounded Stella and tugged at something buried deep inside him. He had a desperate desire to erase the sadness lurking within her luminous blue eyes. And that scared the shit out of him.

Instead of sending one of his men to investigate the dead cattle, he'd ridden off into the high pasture alone, hoping the rugged beauty of the surrounding mountains and the strenuous work would clear his head. He rubbed a knot in his shoulder. His plan had flopped. Big time. He'd thought of her all day long.

After he'd rubbed Rocky down and settled the big stallion in his stall in the barn, Dawson had entered the quiet kitchen and sat down before the fire for a few minutes to warm up prior to heading to bed. How was he to know she'd waltz into the kitchen in the middle of the night wearing a slip of a nightgown? The sight of her bare toes with their painted pink nails, and slim ankles peeking from beneath the almost-transparent white gown stirred his blood more than if she'd been dressed in a string bikini.

Too exhausted to rein in his body's unbridled reaction, instead of fleeing to his bedroom like he should have, he'd stayed and drunk his fill of her lithe body as she'd moved around the kitchen preparing his hot toddy.

And then he'd fallen asleep. Go figure.

"Dawson?"

He blinked at Alf. "What?"

"Whoa. Don't cut my head off just 'cause you're in a bad mood."

"Sorry. I'm beat and sleeping in that damn chair didn't help." He yawned and kneaded the pads of his fingers into his left shoulder.

Alf harrumphed. "Coffee's ready." He poured coffee into a mug and handed Dawson the steaming cup. "Drink up. You look like you've been trampled by a herd of wild cattle."

Dawson lifted his cup and inhaled the sharp tang of coffee made strong and dark, the way he liked. In desperate need of a caffeine jolt, he gulped the burning liquid, wincing as it scalded his mouth.

"I was telling you about the two mining fellas Alphonse ran into in the southwest quarter section yesterday."

"What?" His tiredness vanished. "Are you kidding me?"

"Wish I was, but Alphonse saw them clear as day.

He asked them outright what they were doing on private property, but they showed him a bunch of legal papers. Said they had permission to be on the Circle 5." The metal coffee pot clanged, as Alf slammed it down on the burner. "Weren't much Alphonse could do, but he sure as hell was fired up when he told me. It was all I could do to stop him grabbing his rifle and heading back out there."

"Damn." A headache throbbed low and steady behind Dawson's eyes. He dug the pads of his thumbs into his temples. The same scenario had played out all too often over the past months. Geologists working for a large mining conglomerate surveyed his land, drilling core samples, searching for minerals buried in the ground, trespassing.

"It ain't right. A man's land is a man's land." Alf plunked a large, cast-iron frying pan on the counter. "What about that lawyer fella you talked to? Can't he do nothing?"

"He wasn't any help. All he did was cost me a pile of money and tell me there's nothing I can do." A month ago, he'd contacted a lawyer in Vancouver, but the man told Dawson the geologists had every right to trespass and look for whatever minerals lay under the soil. Apparently, he only owned the surface of his land, not what was buried beneath. Who the hell knew?

"You're gonna do something, aren't you? You're not gonna let them destroy the ranch."

Dawson chewed on his bottom lip. With 150,000 acres and five thousand head of Black Angus cattle, the Circle 5 was the biggest operating ranch in the region. It had been his father's ranch and his father's before him. He hoped one day Deirdre would run the ranch.

His dream was what made all the long hours and hard work worthwhile. At least, that had been his hope until traces of gold and copper were discovered beneath the green grass and forested hills.

If the proposed mine was approved, all his plans would go to hell. Money was involved. Big money. Some of the cash flow from the development of a mine would come his way, but with the wealth came destruction. Fertile green land ruined, forests cut down, lakes and rivers polluted, all for a few dollars in the bank.

He drained the last of his coffee. "I'll tell you one thing, Alf. That mine isn't going to happen. Not on Circle 5 land; not while I'm alive. I'll fight it with everything I've got and then some." He marched over to the sink and rinsed his cup under the tap. "You can take that to the bank."

Chapter 6

A loud, authoritative knock sounded on her bedroom door.

"Come in."

The door swung open and Dawson stood in the doorway. His gaze swept the room and settled on the suitcase on her bed. His mouth tightened. "What's this?"

"I'm all packed. Just let me say goodbye to Dee and Alf, and then we can leave."

"Just where do you think you're going?"

"Back to Vancouver." *Where did he think?*

"Why are you doing this?"

"Why are *you* making this so difficult? This is what you've wanted since the beginning." She'd tossed and turned all night, reliving every second of their intimate encounter in the dark kitchen, trying to figure out why it disturbed her so much.

Nothing had happened, nothing improper was said, but, as the cold light of early morning filtered through the gauzy window curtains, the truth hit her. She was attracted to him. More than attracted. Much more. With the shocking realization dawned her determination to leave. She was there to help Deirdre, not have an affair with the child's damaged and grieving father. "This isn't working out."

"Why not?" He jammed his hands in the front

pockets of his faded jeans.

She blew out a breath. *Really? Was he going to make her say it?* The attraction between them was almost visceral. And it wasn't just her. She'd seen the male interest darken his eyes.

"I thought we agreed you'd try the job for three weeks." One dark brow arched. "What's changed? If Deirdre's done or said something that upset you, I can talk to her, and we'll sort this out."

"It's not Dee. She's great." She twined a curl around her fingers and shuffled her feet. "You don't remember last night? In the kitchen?"

His rugged face flushed, but his gaze held steady. "I was pretty tired, but I'm certain nothing…er…nothing untoward happened, and I usually have a pretty good memory for things like that."

"I thought…" Her words trailed off in the face of his confusion.

He crossed his arms over his chest and leaned his long, lean body against the doorframe. His tanned biceps flexed beneath his rolled-up shirtsleeves, and his faded jeans tightened over his muscular thighs. "About last night…" His gaze bore into hers.

"Ye…yes?" She twisted the hem of her shirt into a knot.

"I apologize for falling asleep."

"You were exhausted."

He nodded and a dark curl fell over his forehead, the same lock of hair she'd fondled, testing its unexpected softness.

Heat rushed up her neck.

"I was tired, but that's no excuse." A flicker of something—of what?—lit his dark eyes. "Is that why you're leaving, because I fell asleep?"

"What?" She shook her head. "This isn't about you falling asleep."

"Well, then what *is* this about? Because from where I'm standing, I don't get it. One minute you're determined to stay, and the next you're chomping at the bit to leave."

The curl caught in the long eyelashes of his right eye. Her fingers twitched, itching to brush back the stray lock.

As if reading her mind, he swiped his hand over his face, sweeping the curl off his forehead. Two long strides, and he stood over her. "Are you going tell me what's going on? Because right now, I'm at a loss as to why you're leaving. I thought you wanted this job."

"I do."

"Well, then, what's going on?"

She stood, wanting to meet him eye to eye, or as close to it as her five-feet-six inches could get her to his more than six-foot height. "Last night, I realized there's an...an attraction between us."

"An attraction? Really?" He stepped closer and his boots brushed the toes of her shoes.

The scent of coffee, leather, and something masculine eddied in the air between them.

He trailed a callused finger along her arm. "We're both adults. We can control ourselves." He grinned, flashing white, even teeth. "At least, I can."

She reeled back, rubbing her arm where he'd touched, her skin tingling.

"Anyway," he continued, seemingly unfazed by her reaction. "We have to think of Deirdre. She's what's important. You're good for her. She likes you. It would be difficult for her if you were to leave so soon." He blew out a breath. "In spite of your struggle to control your...er...your desire for me, I'm prepared to let you stay." The corners of his mouth twitched, and his eyes sparkled.

"*You're* prepared to let me stay?" She grabbed the dresser to stop from smacking the smug look off his too-handsome face.

He nodded, his eyes suddenly wary.

"You're a piece of work, you know that?"

"I'm just saying, there's no reason for you to leave. I promise I won't do anything—" He arched one dark eyebrow. "—improper."

She grabbed the handle of her suitcase and jerked the heavy bag onto the floor. It landed with a thud. "Your arrogant attitude is exactly why I'm leaving." She yanked up the extendible handle and wheeled the suitcase behind her as she marched around the bed toward the door.

He grabbed her elbow, stopping her. "Look, I was teasing. Can't we talk about this? You know, two mature adults discussing what's best for a five-year-old."

His fingers on her arm burned, and she jerked away. "Mature adult? *You?* You can't be serious." Her voice rose as she spit out the words, fuming.

"Look—" He jammed his hands in his front pockets. "—I'm not any good at this. I'm sorry. I'd like you to stay. Please. For Deirdre."

She shifted from one foot to the other. Part of her wanted to flee, to escape the inevitable, but another, more primal part, urged her to stay. And then there was Dee. The young girl's heart would break if Stella went home. But with Deirdre came Dawson and all the complications being around him entailed. She blew out a breath—the battle was already lost. "Okay."

His mouth curled in a tentative smile. "Okay? You'll stay?"

"Yes, but only for a few more weeks."

He opened his mouth to speak.

She held up her hand. "Deirdre needs companionship. I won't leave her in the lurch. She's had enough heartbreak. Once you find a replacement nanny, I'm outta here."

His smile expanded into a cheeky grin. "You've got a deal." He shifted closer.

Once again his scent surrounded her. She tried not to breathe and struggled to recall why she was angry. He opened his mouth, and she focused on his lips. Like a moth to a flame, and just as doomed, she shuffled forward until the heat from his body washed over her. He caressed her cheek, the rasp of his fingers igniting shivers along her spine.

"Stella, I—"

"Why were you shouting?" Deirdre stood in the open doorway, her lower lip trembling, her robin's-egg blue eyes glistening with tears.

Stella sprang back. "Dee."

"I heard you," Deirdre said. "Stella was using a big voice. We're not allowed to use big voices in the house. You said so, Daddy. It's the rule."

"Come here, honey." He knelt on the floor and gathered her in his arms. "There's no need to be upset."

She lurched back from his embrace and looked at Stella with accusing eyes. "Don't be mad at my daddy."

"Shhhh." Dawson's big hands rubbed soothing

circles on Deirdre's narrow back. "Stella's not mad." He stared at her meaningfully. "You're not angry with me, are you, Stella?"

Stella swallowed under the combined weight of their penetrating gazes. "Your daddy and I had a...we had a...a disagreement. It was nothing. There's no need for you to worry."

Deirdre wiped her eyes with the tail of her dad's plaid shirt. She pointed at the suitcase. "You're going away." She faced her father. "Daddy, don't let Stella leave. Please. Make her stay. I'll be good. I promise. I'll be the bestest little girl in the whole world."

"That's up to Stella."

Stella fought to swallow over the lump in her throat. How could she hurt this precious child? Boxed into a corner, she smiled at Deirdre. She'd regret her decision later. "I'm not going anywhere, Dee. I'm staying right here with you."

"And Daddy too, right? You'll stay here with me and Daddy?"

Stella nodded at Deirdre. "Daddy, too."

"Yippee." Deirdre broke free of her father's embrace and leaped into Stella's arms.

Stella staggered back, falling onto the bed, Deirdre clasped to her chest. Her heart swelled as Dee's small, warm body clung. Over the riot of red curls, she met Dawson's gaze.

A smug smile wreathed his rugged face.

Deirdre grabbed her hand and tugged, hauling her from the bed. "Come on. Alf's making banana pancakes." She placed her other small hand in her father's and dragged both adults out of the room and down the hall.

Stella's mind whirled as she stumbled along. Why had she agreed to stay? After what happened—or more importantly, didn't happen—last night in the kitchen? Was she looking for trouble?

Deirdre tugged her and Dawson into the kitchen and into a wall of mouthwatering aromas. "I found them, Alf. They were in Stella's bedroom."

The ranch hands, seated around the table drinking coffee, swiveled as if a single unit and gaped. Their sharp-eyed gazes shifted between one pair of joined hands to the next and back again.

No one spoke.

Sparks snapped and flames crackled in the fireplace. The steady ticking of the clock mounted on the wall was loud in the strained silence.

All too aware of the picture the three of them made, Stella slid a glance at Dawson.

His eyes were shuttered, his mouth set in a thin, forbidding line.

Deirdre released their hands and scampered toward the table and climbed onto a chair.

"What are you all staring at?" Dawson growled at the men and stomped over to his chair at the head of the big oval table and sat down.

As if his words broke a spell, the men resumed slurping coffee.

Stella made her way to an empty seat, but before she pulled out her chair, the scrape of wood on the hardwood floor filled the room as the ranch hands scrambled to their feet.

"Mornin', Miz King," they chorused in unison.

She smiled at their old-fashioned courtesy, mumbled good morning, and sank onto her chair.

The men sat.

Alf bustled over with plates piled high with pancakes, rashers of bacon, and mounds of fluffy scrambled eggs. He set a plate before Dawson, one before Deirdre, and another before Stella, and stood back beaming. "If I do say so myself, these are the best darn pancakes in the Chilcotin."

She looked at the plateful of food and winced. At home, she either skipped breakfast or grabbed a piece of toast and munched on it as she drove to work. This was more food than she ate in a day, let alone at one sitting.

"Go on. Take a bite. Let me know what you think," Alf urged.

The food smelled wonderful. She lifted her fork, cut a mouthful of pancake, dipped it in a small pool of maple syrup, and popped it in her mouth. The pancake, delicately flavored with banana and vanilla, was fluffy on the inside and crisp on the surface. She grinned. "It's scrumptious, Alf."

"I told you," said Deirdre, her mouth full of pancake.

Alf beamed and swung around and bustled to the stove where he heaped more food on plates and handed them out to the ranch hands.

Stella chewed another mouthful of pancake. The food was delicious, and suddenly she was starving. Gradually, she became aware a silence had settled over the table. She glanced up.

The men's gazes were fixed on her, wide grins on their sunburned faces.

She finished chewing and dabbed her mouth with her napkin. "What?"

Bob grinned, revealing a gold filling in the back of his mouth. "I never met a woman your size who could plow through her grub so fast."

The men waited, watching her reaction to Bob's teasing.

Her face flamed, but she chuckled. "Well, then you've never seen me eat an apple-and-almond cheese tart from Sherman's Deli. Now, that's a sight."

They roared with laughter, and the tension in the room dissipated. Everyone relaxed.

Everyone, except Dawson. He sat rigid in his chair, his gaze fixed on his plate, his food untouched.

Why is he so angry? Stella rubbed the knot in the back of her neck. Did it bother him the men accepted her? Or was he upset because for once he'd let his guard down and allowed his feelings to show?

"Want some coffee, Stella?" Alf hovered over her, an old fashioned, large metal coffee pot in his hand.

She held up her cup. "Thanks, Alf."

Bob cleared his throat and waited until everyone quieted. "You won't believe this story, Miz King. It's a real doozy."

"Call me Stella, please," she said for what had to be the hundredth time.

He slid a glance toward Dawson and gulped, his Adam's apple bobbing in his throat. "Okay…Stella."

Dawson's coffee cup clattered on the table.

Bob blanched.

"Tell me what happened, Bob." She ignored Dawson's glower. "I could do with a good story."

"Yeah, go ahead, Bob," Alf said. "We all wanna hear, don't we, Dawson?"

Dawson's brow furrowed, and he grunted.

"See?" Alf nodded at Bob.

Bob coughed and cleared his throat. "Well, a few years back, a bunch of us boys were at the Anaheim Lake Stampede. We'd spent the better part of the afternoon in the beer garden and were three sheets to the wind. Jean-Luc here—" He jerked his thumb at Jean-Luc.

Jean-Luc's face flamed beneath his thick black beard.

"Well, he went and signed up for the bull riding even though he ain't never been on a bull before. He's from Quebec. No bulls there, leastwise, none like the wild ones 'round these parts. Ain't I right?" He chuckled and swatted Jean-Luc on the shoulder. "It was a sight to see, let me tell ya. Poor old Jean-Luc wasn't on the bull more'n a tick before he flew off like he'd been shot from a cannon."

The men guffawed, and Stella joined in their good-natured laughter.

Alf wiped tears from his eyes. "It was two weeks before he could walk straight, let alone climb back on a horse. I was sure Dawson was going to send him packing."

More laughter ensued.

The legs of a wooden chair slammed on the floor, sounding like the crack of a gunshot.

The laughter stopped.

Dawson stood, hands on his hips, scowling. "Don't you men have work to do?"

The men's faces froze into expressionless masks. They mumbled goodbyes, shoved back their chairs, and hustled out of the kitchen.

"Daddy? What's wrong?" Deirdre's voice was a

thin squeak. "You look mad."

He ignored her as he glared at Stella.

She returned his gaze with a steady one of her own. *Damned if he'd intimidate her.*

"Daddy?"

"Shhhhh." Alf patted the child's hand. "Quiet now. Why don't you run up and clean your room? Last I looked, the place was a holy mess."

"But you promised." She leaped up and ran to Dawson. "You didn't forget, did you? You can't take back a promise. You can't." Her words ended on a wail. Tears flooded her eyes and spilled down her pale, freckled cheeks.

Dawson's jaw worked as he gritted his teeth. He blew out a long, ragged breath and stroked Deirdre's fiery hair, smoothing the wayward curls. "No, Dee, I didn't forget."

"Yes," she shouted, her tears forgotten.

Stella bit back a smile at this blatant evidence of the little girl's ability to wrap her father around her tiny finger.

"Just you wait, Stella. You're gonna love it." Deirdre clapped her hands and bounced on her toes.

"Love what?" A frisson of unease trilled down her spine. She looked from daughter to father, at the excited anticipation on the face of one, the bitter resignation on the other. Her trepidation grew.

"Didn't Deirdre tell you?" A pulse in his jaw ticked a rapid tattoo.

"Tell me what?"

"Daddy's gonna take you riding." Deirdre's face glowed.

"Riding?"

The little girl nodded.

"Why, Ms. King, surely you aren't afraid of riding horses too, are you?"

Heat flooded her face at his not-so-subtle reference to her fear of flying. "Of course not. I love to ride." At least she didn't have to lie. She'd taken horseback riding lessons as a child and used to go riding every weekend. At least she had until—she shook her head, cutting off the painful memory.

"I promised Deirdre I'd take you riding today; show you a bit of the ranch."

"I picked out your horse," piped the little girl. "Daddy said I could." She skipped over to Stella and threw her arms around her waist. "His name's Caspar, and he's the bestest horse on the whole entire ranch."

Stella allowed the exuberant troublemaker to drag her out of her chair, across the kitchen to the door, and outside to the corral.

How bad could this be? The words rang through her head in a frantic refrain.

Chapter 7

Stella urged her horse into a canter, controlling the spirited animal with practiced ease.

Dawson followed her progress around the arena as she ran the ten-year-old gelding through its paces. Her slim thighs clad in skintight, designer, faded blue jeans—purposely ripped at the knees, for God's sake—gripped the horse's flanks, her lithe body at one with the animal's fluid movements.

He ground down on his back teeth. This was his fault. He should have let her go. But what choice did he have? Every time he looked into Dee's eyes, his heart melted. He'd do anything to make his daughter happy, anything to make up for the loss of her mother. If keeping Stella King at the ranch put a smile on Dee's face and a light in her eyes, he'd do his damnedest to convince the woman to stay.

No matter the cost.

Breakfast had been a goddamn circus. His men, usually a sleepy, taciturn group in the morning before they swilled their minimum three cups of Alf's high-octane brew, gushed like a bunch of schoolboys over the new girl in class. Hell, they'd salivated like a pack of starving dogs with a slab of double-A prime rib at the prospect of showing off for Stella.

From the first second he'd laid eyes on the new nanny, he'd known how the men would react. But he hadn't counted on how much their shenanigans would bother him. At one point during breakfast he'd had to grab onto the edge of his chair to stop from leaping over the table and punching some sense into Bob.

Stella hadn't helped.

The musical trills of her laughter filled the kitchen, each note poking like a sharp stick in his gut. The story Bob told wasn't *that* funny. She'd never laughed at anything *he'd* said. He kicked the hard packed dirt with the toe of his boot. Hell, he'd hardly seen her smile.

A shriek of high-pitched giggles caught his attention.

Dee was laughing at the antics of Stella's horse as it pranced around the corral, head held high, tail swishing like a plume, as if it had won the blue ribbon in the show ring. Dee glowed with happiness. In that moment, she looked so much like her mother it felt like the ground was falling away beneath his feet.

His heart swelled. Stella's presence was good for Dee. *That's* why he'd stopped Stella from leaving. He'd done it for Dee…always for Dee.

But he couldn't help the sinking certainty he'd made one hell of a big mistake, especially after the unsettling events that morning. Walking into the kitchen, the three of them with their hands joined together like a family, had been a betrayal. For the briefest heartbeat, he'd been happy, and had allowed a fantasy to form where they really were a family. He rubbed the gold wedding band. It wouldn't happen again. He'd make damn sure of it.

Again, his gaze was drawn to the woman on the white horse. Her golden hair curled in wild disarray around her flushed face; her lips were full and inviting.

The glow from the morning sun transformed her eyes to a brilliant blue.

He bit back a groan. Who the hell was he kidding? He wanted to kiss her, just like he'd ached to the previous night in the moonlit kitchen. He would have too, if he hadn't fallen asleep before he had the chance to make a damn fool of himself. Instead, he'd woken up to Alf crashing and banging around the kitchen.

The old codger had taken Dawson aside after he'd had his coffee and warned him of Stella's vulnerability. As if he hadn't seen that for himself. She wore her sorrow like a heavy cloak, dulling her eyes and bringing tears when she thought no one was looking.

He'd gone to her room fully intending to apologize for his boorish behavior, but the second he'd seen her suitcase on the bed, all thought of asking forgiveness fled, and his pride took over. The next minute they were shooting barbs at each other.

The minute after that, he had her in his arms. She smelled so damn good. He'd almost moaned aloud at the velvety-soft, smooth skin under the rough pads of his fingers. If Dee hadn't come running into the room, he'd have kissed Stella, and not a friend-zone kiss either.

Not even close.

He'd have nuzzled her, skimmed his tongue over her sweet lips, tracing their shape and texture, and when she opened for him, he'd have stroked her tongue with his until they were both panting and wanting more.

Right there. Right then.

"Am I doing something wrong?" Stella's soft voice broke into his torrid thoughts.

"What?"

"The way you're frowning, I figured I must be doing something wrong."

A man could get lost in the deep pools of her eyes. He cleared his throat, struggling to swallow. Sweat broke out on his forehead. Damn. He was no better than his men.

"Dawson? Are you okay?"

His irritation mounted. She knew damn well she'd ridden the horse well, but he wasn't going to tell her. "Riding in an arena is entirely different than riding across open country." He took perverse pleasure in the glint of anger sparking in her sapphire eyes.

They glared at each other until her horse nickered.

"Where are you taking Stella, Daddy?" Deirdre ran up and hugged him around his knees.

"Taking me?" Stella's brows arched.

His stomach tightened. Damn. He was hoping Dee would be satisfied watching Stella ride Caspar around the corral. He didn't want to take her for a ride. *At least, not on a horse.* He gritted his teeth until they ached. *Down, boy. Not going to happen. Not now, not ever.*

He opened his mouth, an excuse on his lips, but hesitated.

Dee's small, trusting face glowed with the surety he'd make good on his promise.

He muttered a curse under his breath and forced a smile. "Where do you think I should take her?"

She didn't hesitate. "Tor's Ridge."

He cringed. "Tor's Ridge is a long ride, especially for someone who hasn't been on a horse for awhile."

"Please, Daddy?"

He looked into his daughter's eyes. His heart turned to mush as a sinking dread washed over him.

Reluctantly, he nodded.

"Yipee." She pumped her tiny fist. "Oh, Stella, you'll love Tor's Ridge. Daddy says it's the prettiest view in the whole Chilcotin."

Stella swung toward him. "We're going for a ride…together?"

He nodded, a headache forming behind his eyes. Tor's Ridge was a good six-hour ride there and back. No way could he spend an entire day alone with her. Not without making a fool of himself. Again, he was tempted to tell her they weren't going riding after all, but one look at Deirdre's excited face froze the words in his throat. "I'll saddle Rocky."

****

"What about Deirdre's horse?" Stella called to his retreating back.

"I'm not going."

"What?"

"I'm staying here with Alf. Just you and Daddy are going." Deirdre beamed.

"But—"

"You and Daddy will ride faster without me. Daddy says I'm too little to gallop."

Before she could ask how far Tor's Ridge was, Deirdre ran off after her father.

Caspar neighed and tossed his head.

She rubbed a soothing hand along his satiny neck, understanding the poor animal's trepidation. The way Dawson looked at her with his piercing dark eyes set her on edge. She shuddered as she recalled how he'd watched her riding in the ring, a fierce frown on his face.

A whinny caught her attention.

Dawson sat astride a massive stallion the color of ripe prairie wheat, its flowing mane shining molten gold in the morning sun. His bearing was one of supreme confidence in his ability to control the powerful animal. With his dark-plaid shirt, sheepskin vest, worn, faded jeans, and brown-felt cowboy hat, he looked like a vision from a bygone era.

Her heart fluttered.

"Ready?"

The coldness of his tone dispelled her fantasy. "I can't go." She hoped he didn't hear the quaver in her voice.

"Why not?"

"I…I have a headache."

"You have a headache? And you can't go? Gee, that's too bad."

Her flush deepened at his phony regret. Would it have been so awful to take her riding?

"We'll have to do this another time." His tone of voice made clear there wouldn't be another time.

Deirdre ran up to them. "You have to go, Stella. I made Daddy promise he'd take you. Please?"

One look into Dee's trusting eyes, and she crumpled. She wasn't any better than Dawson when it came to resisting the child. She pasted a smile on her face. "Okay, I'll go."

"Yipee!" Deirdre jigged a little dance and clapped her hands. "You're the bestest."

A few short hours later, she regretted her decision.

Dawson hadn't uttered a word since they'd ridden away from the barn.

Her horse was well trained and kept pace at a steady trot behind the stallion, but her body ached from the endless bouncing across the uneven ground. She was already looking forward to a hot bath when they finally returned to the ranch.

At least the scenery was captivating. Each bend in the trail provided a new vista worthy of a picture postcard. They'd forded shallow streams, ridden alongside pristine lakes with crystal-clear water sparkling under the warm sunshine, and trotted across stretches of grassland with vibrant splashes of late-season wildflowers blooming amidst the sea of rippling gold.

She gripped the leather horn and leaned back in the saddle as Caspar dropped into a small dip and climbed up the other side cresting a rolling hill.

The Chilcotin Mountains, their peaks coated with a fresh mantle of snow, gleamed in the distance. Evergreen forest stretched as far as the eye could see. She breathed in the pungent aroma of pine and the sweet scents of clover mixed with wild roses and purple lupins. No wonder Dawson loved this stunning, rugged, untamed wilderness. So much like the man himself.

She shifted, trying in vain to find a comfortable position on the unforgiving leather saddle. Her horse-riding skills may have returned, but no amount of skill made up for her lack of practice. Caspar stumbled over a rut, and she winced. He was a great horse with a smooth gait, but her bottom was used to sitting on a padded desk chair, not a hard saddle.

She followed Dawson and his stallion across a meadow through purple and yellow wildflowers and a sea of tall, yellow grasses. Seed coats disturbed by their passing floated in the air and hitchhiked on the short hairs on Caspar's flanks.

Dawson rode like he'd been born on a horse. His fluidity of motion made man and horse seem as one. When they started out, his face had been a closed mask, his mouth tight, body bristling with underlying anger. But as the ride progressed, the lines bracketing his mouth and furrowing his brow softened, and the stiff set of his shoulders loosened.

She'd even caught him smiling. Once.

"What the hell?" Dawson reined in his horse and leaped to the ground. He sprinted across the meadow, leaving Rocky to graze. His stream of angry curses carried across the expanse of dried grass.

She nudged her horse ahead.

Dawson had stopped by a group of wooden stakes pounded into the ground. A strip of neon-pink flagging tape tied to each stake fluttered in the breeze. The stakes marked out a rough rectangle. Two parallel, rutted tracks cut deep into the soft earth and led away from the marked area and disappeared into the nearby forest.

Dawson, his face flushed red, dark eyes flashing, grabbed a stake and ripped it out of the ground. His shirtsleeves were shoved over his elbows and ropey veins bulged across his tanned forearms. He snapped the wood between his hands and threw the pieces aside, and yanked another one out, and another, not stopping until all the stakes lay shattered on the ground.

"What is it? What's wrong?" She clambered off her horse, ignoring the protesting twinges in her thighs. She studied the scattered pile of broken stakes. Words and numbers were written in black on the pink strips. A twinge of unease stirred in her belly.

She picked up a broken stake and examined the

plastic tape. Her heart stuttered as she read the familiar words written in black felt pen across the neon pink—Imperial Monarch Resources. She sucked in a breath and dropped the stake. "Dawson, what's going on?" she asked again, but she knew. Oh, she knew.

"What the hell do you think's going on?"

She staggered back from the outrage sparking in his dark eyes.

He inhaled several deep breaths. "Look, I'm sorry." He removed his hat and swiped his damp forehead with the back of his hand. "The—" He pointed at the jumble of broken stakes. "—damn mining company's been at it again."

"They're surveying your land?"

He grimaced as if he'd tasted something sour. "Looking for copper and gold deposits. Seems they have every right to conduct their surveys and test drills." He kicked a piece of broken stake, sending it sailing several feet.

"I can't stop them because I don't own the mineral rights to my own land. They can waltz on here riding their ATVs and chewing up the pasture any time they want. There's not a damn thing I can do about it." He met her gaze. "Can you believe that?"

She shook her head, but she was lying. She'd witnessed the same scenario play out time and time again. Ice trickled down her spine. He was angry with her now; she didn't want to see what would happen if he found out she'd taken a leave of absence from the very mining company surveying his land. "Have they found anything?"

"Damned if I know. One of their managers flew in to see me a month or so ago." He kicked a clod of dirt, and a cloud of dust rose in the air. "He was pretty closemouthed about the whole thing, but Mildred Crubbs, who runs the general store over in Smoky River, told me she'd heard the mining company was going ahead with their plans to develop a copper mine somewhere in this area."

He swatted at a fly. "I'll be damned if I'll let them build a mine on my land. I've seen the damage. Look at that Stony Mountain mine up in the Cariboo. The tailings pond breached and poured seventeen million cubic meters of poisonous chemical crap into the surrounding lakes and rivers. The area was pristine. It'll never be the same again." He blew out a ragged breath.

"Not all mining companies are like Stony Mountain." She couldn't meet his gaze. "Some companies care about the environment. I've heard Imperial Monarch is one of the good ones."

He snorted. "Yeah and I've got some beachfront property in the middle of the bloody desert to sell you."

"The government has strict environmental policies that mining companies have to follow. Besides, think of all the jobs. An operating mine would be a real boon to this area."

His eyes narrowed. "You sound like one of them. What's your stake in all this?"

She ducked her head, hiding behind the fall of her hair. "I'm just saying, there are two sides to this."

He harrumphed.

A flock of small birds swooped low over the grass and landed in the top branches of a tall willow, chirping an afternoon chorus.

Caspar shook his head, dislodging flies and jangling the reins.

The wind rustled through the sea of grass, flattening it in waves, and tangled her hair. "You love this land, don't you?" she finally asked to break the strained silence.

He bent and tugged up a hunk of grass and held out the roots clumped with dark soil. "This is some of the richest, most fertile soil you'll find anywhere. That's why my grandfather bought this land, why my father stayed, and why I'm here. The wealth of this land isn't in the minerals hidden underneath." He set his cowboy hat back on his head and blew out a breath.

Another echoing silence stretched between them.

What could she say? If Imperial Monarch found copper on the Circle 5, they'd be eager to develop a mine on the property and extract the ore. The price of copper was high. That was all the more incentive to dig the valuable mineral out of the ground and ship the ore overseas.

But the mine wasn't a done deal. Not yet. Maybe never. Before a mine could go ahead, years of environmental assessments, archaeological surveys, and court appeals would have to take place. Most mining proposals died before a shovel made a dent in the ground.

"I'm sorry." His voice was a rough rasp. "I didn't mean to give you a lecture. This has nothing to do with you. You're only here for a few months. What do you care?"

The question was rhetorical, but before she thought better of it, she said, "Because I do. This land is unique and worth protecting. But we still need mines. We use the minerals miners dig out of the ground to make cars, computers, cell phones, and any number of objects."

He swatted at a buzzing fly.

She forced a chuckle. "Sorry. I guess it was my turn to lecture." She tried to see into his eyes, but his face was shadowed under the brim of his hat.

"You live in the city. This mine, if it's developed, is right in my backyard. They'll cut down *my* trees, pollute *my* water, and dig up *my* land." His jaw was set, the ever-present pulse ticking as if a time bomb.

She opened her mouth but stopped at the fierce expression on his face. Arguing would get her nowhere. Besides, he was right. In a few weeks, she'd return to Vancouver and resume her job, the Circle 5 a distant memory.

"Let's get out of here." He covered the distance to his horse in three long strides and leaped onto the saddle. Grabbing Rocky's reins, he guided the golden stallion toward the trail into the forest. "Come on."

Chapter 8

Dawson's shoulders were stiff, his body rigid, as he urged his mount into a fast trot and vanished into the forest shadows.

Stella hurried to her horse, untied the reins, and clambered on, wincing at the stabbing pain as her bottom bumped on the unforgiving saddle.

He was angry.

She didn't blame him. He loved this land. Despite her comments supporting mining, she was well aware of the industry's dark side. No matter how closely a mine followed the environmental guidelines set out by the government, damage to the land was inevitable.

Caspar nickered a warning, and she ducked, narrowly avoiding poking out her eye on a low-hanging branch.

They left the trees, forded a narrow stream, and climbed a winding trail up a rocky hill. The path was steep and littered with loose scree, dwarf juniper bushes, and kinnikinnick. She tightened her thighs around Caspar's flanks as he stumbled over the sharp rocks. Pain radiated through her thighs and backside with each jarring jolt.

Caspar, chest heaving and sweat dampening his flanks, climbed the last few feet, and they crested the ridge.

She blew out a breath of relief and urged the tired

horse across a grassy meadow to a trickling stream. Swinging her leg over the saddle, she lowered herself to the ground. Her legs wobbled, and she grabbed her saddle for support.

Dawson dismounted with casual grace, unaffected by the long, arduous ride. "Looks like you're hurting."

"I'm fine." The lie slipped from her lips.

Caspar chose that moment to decide he was thirsty, and the big animal sidled away, heading for the creek.

She yelped as her support deserted her. Her legs buckled, and she would have slid to the ground if Dawson didn't lunge and grab her around the waist.

"You little fool." He scooped her into his arms.

"I'm fine. Really. I just need a minute." A rush of warmth enveloped her at his enticing scent of leather, soap, and horse.

Ignoring her protests, he strode across the small clearing, carrying her as if she weighed little more than Deirdre. He set her on the ground so her back rested against the rough bark of a large pine tree and crossed to his horse and removed a small nylon pack tied to the saddle.

Squatting beside her, he opened the sack and lifted out a metal thermos, unscrewed the top, and poured steaming liquid into a cup. "Drink this."

She wrinkled her nose at the bitter aroma.

"Come on. It'll make you feel better."

Her fingers brushed his as she grasped the cup, and a jolt of awareness shot through her.

"Go on. Drink."

She sipped and immediately, soothing heat licked a trail down her throat and settled in her belly. Her muscles relaxed, her aches eased, and a warm lethargy settled over her. "What is this?"

"An old remedy of Alf's. You don't want to know what's in it." He grinned, revealing a startling flash of even white teeth. A matching set of dimples danced in his lean cheeks. The lines radiating from the corners of his eyes deepened, and his face transformed from merely handsome to outright gorgeous.

She gaped, unable to look away, her heart thudding.

"Have some more." He refilled her cup.

Their eyes met, their gazes locking.

Silver lights sparked in his coal-black irises. His long dark eyelashes framed his expressive eyes.

"I'm sorry." His voice was a rough husk.

"It's not your fault. You couldn't have known riding a horse would make me so sore."

"I should have figured it out. You haven't ridden in a long time. You're not saddle hardened." He plucked a blade of grass and stuck it between his lips. "But that's not what I meant. I'm sorry for what I said this morning. In your bedroom." He stared into the distance. "Believe it or not, I'm not always a jerk." He tossed the piece of grass aside and blew out a breath. "You've done wonders with Deirdre. She adores you. I appreciate that."

She flushed at his unexpected praise. "I did my share of provoking." She smiled and held out her hand. "Truce?"

An answering smile spread across his face. "Deal." His grip was firm, his callused palm warm against hers.

Hands joined, time stood still.

Caspar's whinny broke the spell, and Dawson tugged his hand free.

Her hand tingled as if charged with an electric current, and she resisted the urge to look at her palm to see if her skin was red.

"Wait until you see the feast Alf packed." Shooting to his feet, he strode with his long, easy gait toward the horses. He removed their saddles and rubbed their sweaty coats with a rag he tugged from his saddlebag. Tethering the horses to a small tree, he let them graze on the lush green grass blanketing the clearing. His plaid cotton shirt stretched across his broad shoulders. The sleeves were rolled up past his elbows. His faded jeans hung low on his slim hips.

She averted her gaze before he caught her drooling.

Lugging another small nylon pack, he returned to her side. Their shoulders brushed as he lowered himself beside her.

A shock rocketed through her at the fleeting contact.

He fished in the sack, withdrew a checkered cloth and placed it on the ground. Digging into the pack once again, he drew out one delicacy after another. The tantalizing aroma of fried chicken filled the air. A tub of potato salad, homemade buns, and a selection of delicious-looking cakes completed the meal.

"Alf did all this?"

"He's a man of many talents." A teasing light twinkled in his dark eyes. "Besides, he's seen how you can put away the food."

"Good thing there's lots, then. I'm starving." She matched his grin with one of her own.

Chuckling, he dug into the food.

They ate in companionable silence. After they finished, he packed the remains of their lunch into the bag and settled against the tree trunk.

His shoulder rested against hers, and heat from his body seeped through the sleeve of her cotton blouse, filling her with a sense of peace and contentment.

The stream sparkled in the afternoon sunshine as the water gurgled and splashed against moss-covered rocks. A multicolored array of wildflowers dotted the lush grass like jewels on a green velvet cloth. Gold-and-black-spotted butterflies flitted from one vibrant petal to another. The breeze whispered in the evergreen boughs, bees droned, birds tweeted, and a squirrel chittered. The air was redolent of pine needles, growing plants, and warm, fertile earth.

"It's so pretty here."

"I'm glad you like it. This is one of my favorite places." He yawned and tugged the brim of his hat lower and closed his eyes. His chest rose and fell in a slow, steady cadence.

Her eyelids grew heavy, and she too closed her eyes and dozed.

When she awoke, the spot beside her was empty. A patch of flattened grass at the base of the tree was proof she hadn't dreamed the moment of warm companionship. She searched the clearing.

He was saddling the horses. As if sensing her gaze, he turned and smiled a slow, lazy grin. "Finally up? I thought I was going to have to play the prince and kiss you awake."

A desire for him to do just that flashed through her. Her cheeks burned. "What...what time is it?"

"Time we headed back."

She struggled to her feet, wincing as her sore muscles protested. Her legs wobbled, but by the time he led over her horse, she was able to walk without limping. A shudder rippled through her at the sight of the hard leather saddle. She dreaded the agony of sitting on the unforgiving perch for the next several hours as they negotiated the rough track back to the ranch house.

He must have seen the dismay in her eyes because his face softened. "We'll take it slow going back." He supported her foot with his clasped hands while she climbed onto her saddle.

She bit back a groan as her bruised bottom made contact with the hard leather.

"Will you be okay?"

She forced a reassuring smile. "I'll be fine." *I hope.*

He grasped Caspar's reins and led the two of them to the edge of the clearing. "You have to see this before we leave." He pointed into the distance. "You can't come to Tor's Ridge without seeing the view."

She sucked in a breath. The ridge offered a panoramic vista of dense, evergreen forests and a patchwork of azure lakes. A glistening river snaked across the valley. The late afternoon sun gilded the distant mountains with muted, golden light. "Wow. It's beautiful."

"I've always loved this view. It reminds me why I live here."

"Can we see your ranch?"

He waved his arm. "This is all Circle 5 land, everything for as far as your eye can see." The pride in his voice revealed the depth of his love for the rugged land.

"Incredible."

"I hope I can keep the land this way." His jaw tightened. "I want Deirdre to stand here and see this, and her children, and her children's children."

"It's something, all right," she murmured, unsure whether she was referring to the wild land or the intriguing man beside her.

****

She urged Caspar into a lope. Gale force winds howled through the trees and tore at her hair. Icy fingers seeped through her thin shirt, raising goose bumps. The storm had appeared out of nowhere. One minute she and Dawson were enjoying the warm rays of the late afternoon sun, and the next, the wind freshened, and dark menacing clouds obscured the sun.

The stench of ozone filled the air, and a bolt of lightning blasted into a tree, setting it ablaze. A booming clap of thunder followed, and the earth shuddered.

Caspar flattened his ears and reared, his front hooves pawing the air.

She yanked the reins, fighting to control the frightened animal.

Another clap of thunder trumpeted through the valley as the heavens opened, and sheets of freezing rain pelted down. The drops stung where they hit the exposed skin on her hands and face. She couldn't see more than a few meters in any direction.

Where was Dawson? At the first distant thunderclap, his high-strung stallion had broken into a panicked gallop and raced into the trees. He was a skilled rider, but even the most experienced horsemen were sometimes bucked off their horses.

Caspar, prancing and straining against her tight hold on the reins, raised his head and whinnied. His ears pricked, and he snorted as a dark shape appeared out of the gloom.

Stella exhaled a breath she hadn't been aware she was holding when Rocky trotted out of the trees.

Dawson sat atop the big horse. He'd lost his hat, and his hair was flattened to his head. Rainwater sluiced off his hair and ran in rivulets down his face. His sodden clothes revealed the taut muscles in his arms and shoulders as he fought to control the skittish stallion. He guided his horse closer and leaned across the narrow space separating their nervous mounts and shouted over the storm's fury, "Looks like the storm's here to stay. We have to find shelter. There's a cabin not far from here." He grabbed Caspar's reins from her numb fingers. "I'll lead. Follow me."

By the time a ramshackle wooden building loomed through the sheets of rain, her clothes were soaked through, her hair hung in thick, wet ropes, and icy water dripped down the back of her neck.

One side of the shack's rusted, corrugated metal roof extended several feet, and Dawson urged his horse under the protective overhang.

Caspar sidled beside the stallion.

Dismounting, Dawson tied the horses' leads to a hitching rail and helped her climb off Caspar. He clasped her hand and together they ran up the warped wooden steps. Without knocking, he twisted the latch, opened the door, and led her into the cabin.

The air inside was frigid and smelled of damp rot, wood smoke, and rancid bacon grease, but they were out of the wind and the onslaught of icy rain. Thin gray light from two rain-streaked, small windows set high in the unpainted wood walls revealed the rustic interior. A card table with two metal chairs, a rickety-looking wooden chair, an old wood stove, and a narrow bed covered by a patchwork quilt filled the tiny room. A tattered rag rug covered the bare wooden floor. Stacks of pocket books, their pages yellowed, corners curling from the damp, lay on a shelf beside the bed.

A rough wooden plank was nailed along one wall, and a collection of mismatched dishes, blackened pots, a cast-iron frying pan, and a plastic washbasin sat on its vinyl-covered surface. Sealed metal containers, she suspected were to keep the food inside safe from hungry rats and mice, were set on a wooden box under the shelf.

Several pairs of jeans, a faded denim shirt, two plaid flannel shirts, and a pair of white cotton, one-piece, long johns hung from nails hammered into the wall beside the bed. A sweat-stained cap and a gray wool scarf hung by the door. An old pair of scuffed cowboy boots lay on the floor.

Dawson pointed at the chair in front of the metal wood stove. "Sit down. I'll have a fire going in a minute."

Water dripped off her face and hair. Her body shook, her teeth chattering in an endless refrain. "Who…whose cabin is this?"

Crouching before the stove, he lit a match and set the flame to a neat pile of kindling and newspaper on the grate. A whiff of sulfur and smoke filled the damp air, and within minutes, a fire crackled and popped, promising warmth. He added some logs to the fire and sat back on his heels. "Henry Rivers lives here."

"Won't he mind we're using his place?"

He shook his head. "Henry's lived on the ranch since I was a kid. He showed up out of the blue one day and moved into this old shack. He never bothered anyone, so Dad let him stay."

"He lives here? In the winter?" She shuddered and edged closer to the heat.

"Henry…well, Henry's a different sort of guy. He traps, hunts, and keeps to himself most of the time." He pointed to where a chessboard with black and white chess pieces was set up on a small table. "When I was a kid, I used to ride out here. Henry taught me to play chess. He's pretty good. I never beat him, though I sure as hell tried."

"Where is he now? Is he out in the storm?"

"I don't know. Doesn't look like he's been here for a few days. His old four-wheeler is gone, so maybe he went into Hosten for supplies." The soft orange light from the flames flickered over his rugged features. "Look, you're freezing. Let me help you."

"N…n…no. I…I'm ok…okay." Her teeth chattered so much she could barely get the words out.

"You little fool." He lifted her foot and tugged off her wet boot and set it aside. Removing her sodden sock, he rubbed her frozen toes between his hands.

The warmth of his large, work-roughened hands kneaded life into her cold foot. "Thank you." Her voice was a whisper.

"Anytime." He finished with that foot, then removed her other boot and lifted her foot onto his lap and massaged her cold toes.

Too soon—much too soon—he lowered her feet to the floor. He grasped her hands and helped her stand as he drew her closer to the fire. "Let me help with your clothes." His long, tanned fingers fumbled with the tiny pearl buttons on her sweater.

She stiffened. "What...what are you doing?"

"Easy now." His voice was deep, and low, and soft, as if calming a skittish horse. "I'm just helping. You have to get out of these wet clothes."

"But—"

"Look, this isn't a seduction. I'm trying to help. If you don't get warm, you risk hypothermia. Your hands are shaking too much to fiddle with all these buttons."

She searched for the artifice beneath his words, but saw none. A fresh bout of bone-breaking shivers rippled through her. Her wet clothes clung to her skin like an icepack. "O...kay...kay."

He undid the rest of her buttons and helped her shrug out of the sodden garment. Next, he worked on the buttons on her shirt, slipping each button through a buttonhole until her shirt gaped, revealing the white lace cups of her bra.

He kept his gaze fixed on a spot over her left shoulder while he tugged her arms free of the wet blouse and hung it on a chair beside her sweater. Setting to work on her soaked jeans, he unsnapped the button at her waist, lowered the zipper, and tugged the wet denim over her hips and thighs.

As if in a daze, she stepped out of her pants. Clad in her bra and panties, she hovered over the wood stove, dancing from one bare foot to the other in an effort to get warm.

"Put this on." He wrapped a heavy, patchwork quilt around her shoulders, tightening the soft wool beneath her chin. "It'll keep you warm."

The blanket reeked of mildew, but the thick, padded fabric was dry and warm. She snugged it tighter.

"Take the rest off."

"What?"

"Your bra and panties are wet too."

She stared. He expected her to get naked? Here? In front of him?

"This is no time for modesty." His eyes narrowed. "Or do you want me to help you?"

She fought for breath. He wasn't kidding. He was perfectly prepared to remove her bra and panties if she didn't take them off herself. Alarm bells clanged in her head. This was dangerous territory, but he was right. Her wet undergarments kept the chill in. She needed to take them off.

Turning her back, and keeping the quilt wrapped tight, she undid the clasp on her bra and slid the straps off her shoulders. Next, she shimmied out of her damp panties. She set her sodden underwear on the seat of the chair with her other clothes. Clutching the quilt to her breast, cheeks burning, she huddled close to the stove.

He tossed another log on the blazing fire. "I should check on the horses. I'll be back in a minute." Opening the door to a blast of frigid air, he stepped into the storm.

Rain pounded on the metal roof, and fierce gusts shook the tiny shack, rattling the windows. In spite of the storm, the fire's heat spread through the small room, dispelling the damp, and the cabin was almost cozy.

Too cozy.

What was she doing naked in the middle of a raging tempest with Dawson Wheeler? Well, okay, she wasn't exactly naked. She was covered from her neck to her toes by a thick blanket, but there was no disputing the fact they were alone. Her stomach tightened. She needed to leave. Now. Before she did something stupid, something she'd regret.

The cabin door flew open and Dawson stepped inside in a swirl of wet, frigid air. He shrugged out of his vest and hung it on a nail. Water dripped off his hair onto the collar of his shirt. "It's a bitch out there." He shuffled closer to the fire, rubbing his hands together and holding them over the stovetop.

"You're soaked. You should get out of those wet clothes." Her face flamed. *Really?* Had she really told him to get naked? What the heck was she thinking? That was the problem. She wasn't thinking. Her reptilian brain had kicked in, and all she thought of was how desirable he was, even soaking wet, especially soaking wet.

A smile tugged the corners of his mouth. "Whatever the lady wants." He ripped open the snaps and shrugged out of his shirt, revealing smooth, bronzed skin over firm muscles.

A wave of heat flooded her. She'd seen gym rats lifting weights and flexing their over-developed biceps, but Dawson's taut body was altogether a different kettle of fish. His tight abs hadn't been formed in a gym, but honed by years of hard physical labor. His body tapered from broad shoulders to slim hips. A sprinkling of fine dark hair covered his chest and flat stomach. An intriguing line of hair vanished beneath the waistband of his low-slung jeans.

"Better turn around if you want to protect your maidenly virtue." His thumbs hooked the waistband of his wet jeans.

She gaped, breath frozen, unable to move. A snap and the grating rasp of his zipper jerked her out of her immobility. Face flaming, she spun and faced the stove. His chuckle added fire to the furnace heating her cheeks.

The rustle of damp cloth on wet skin filled the cabin as he removed the remainder of his clothing.

She stared at the fire, her back rigid, heart racing as images of a naked Dawson rocketed through her.

"It's safe. I'm decent. You can turn around now."

She hesitated, but risked a peek over her shoulder.

A brightly decorated blanket covered his broad shoulders, allowing a glimpse of curling, black chest hair. The blanket hung to his knees, revealing strong calf muscles and long narrow feet with high arches. His jeans and shirt hung on a chair back. His boots and a pair of wool socks lay on the floor. No boxer shorts, no briefs, no underwear at all.

She gulped.

As if reading her mind, he grinned a cheeky grin. "Commando."

"Wha…what?"

His eyes twinkled. "I always go commando."

She sucked in a sharp breath.

"Just in case you were wondering."

"I…I wasn't."

He chuckled.

She focused on the flames flickering on the old metal grate. The heat from the roaring fire seeped through the quilt, but the inferno inside her burned hotter.

Silence settled between them, broken by the crackling and sparking of the fire and the rain pounding on the tin roof.

She slid him a glance and stared, transfixed.

His cheeks were flushed, his hair a mass of tangled, damp curls. He stared into the fire. The flickering light revealed his dark eyes, rimmed by thick lashes, and strong cheekbones. The blanket gaped, revealing a sprinkling of dark hair growing in a vee shape across his chest and down his tapering torso, disappearing beneath a fold in the blanket. The band of gold on his finger gleamed as he clutched the blanket.

That jolted her out of her lustful thoughts like a dousing of ice water. Was he thinking of his wife? Was that why he looked so desolate? That photograph in his office, and the one in Deirdre's bedroom, showed a smiling, auburn-haired woman. Sad to think she'd died so young, leaving behind a grieving husband and baby. The fact he wore his wedding ring after so many years was a testament to the depth of his love and loss.

All too well she knew the toll grief wrenched from a person's soul. Keegan's death had nearly destroyed her. She'd never recover from the anguish, but after many agonizing months, she was beginning to remember the loving, happy moments rather than focusing on the terrible sorrow of his death. She had Deirdre to thank. The child's boundless enthusiasm, and her openness to love forced Stella to look beyond her loss. A smile flickered across her face. Amazing how deeply she cared for Dee in such a short time.

"Penny for your thoughts." Dawson's voice was a low rumble, barely audible over the pelting rain.

"I was thinking of Deirdre. She's a wonderful little girl."

"Yeah, she is." A frown furrowed his brow. "I worry about her. The ranch is so isolated. She should be with kids her age."

The intimacy of the storm and the cozy, warm cabin gave her the courage to ask a question that had rattled through her brain since she'd arrived at the ranch. "What—" She swallowed. "—what happened? How did your...your wife die?"

He was silent for so long she was afraid he wouldn't answer.

He twisted his wedding ring around his finger as if the ghost of his wife haunted him. His wounded dark eyes fastened on her. "Why do you want to know?"

"I'm sorry. You don't have to tell me. This is none of my business."

"No, it's okay." He scrubbed his hands over his damp hair. "We were living in Toronto. Anna didn't like the ranch...too remote and rugged." He spun the gold band around and around. "She couldn't live more than five minutes from the nearest outlet mall. Man, did that woman love shopping." He smiled and the blanket slipped lower, exposing his finely chiseled chest. Lost in his memories of the past, he didn't seem to notice.

"That was before Deirdre was born." He stopped fidgeting with his ring. "After Dee's birth, Anna...well, she changed." He scrubbed his hands over his face.

When he lowered them, the raw pain in his glistening eyes stabbed like a knife to her heart.

"I...I thought she was getting better, or I would never have left her. She asked me to go to the store and pick up diapers." He swallowed, and his Adam's apple bobbed in his strong throat. "I found her." His face contracted in pain. "She was in the bathtub. She'd slit her wrists. Deirdre was crying in her crib.

"After the funeral, I...I fell apart. I was a wreck. One day, a few months after it happened, Alf showed up. A week later, I sold the house, packed all our possessions, and Dee and I moved back to the Chilcotin. My dad was ready to retire, and I took over the ranch." His eyes were red and moist. "Been the three of us ever since."

Moved to tears, she swung away. "I'm so sorry."

"It was a long time ago. I've moved on."

She snapped her head around. "Bullshit."

"What?" He stumbled back a step.

"You heard me. If nothing else, be honest with yourself." Her heart raced as she called him out on his lie. No way had he moved on. The man was swamped with grief. "I know how you feel...the sadness, the loss. The worst is the guilt." She met his gaze. "You know what I mean. Why are you alive when the person you love isn't? What could you have done differently?"

His dark gaze searched hers. "Who did you lose?"

The painful lump in her throat thickened, and she blinked in a futile effort to dispel the tears pooling in her eyes. "My...my son." Her voice was a whisper. "My baby. He was only a few months old."

"Oh, man." He folded her in his strong arms and cradled her head into his broad shoulder, stroking her hair. "I'm sorry. So sorry."

She burst into tears.

Chapter 9

The fire was burning low when her tears dried and they drew apart.

Dawson lifted a corner of his blanket where it had pooled on his lap and dabbed her wet cheeks. The moment trembled with unspoken words. He traced the shape of her lower lip with the pad of his callused thumb. "I've wanted to kiss you all day."

Her heart thumped.

Curving his palm beneath her jaw, he tilted her face and captured her mouth with his lips. The kiss deepened as he crushed his mouth against hers.

Her lips parted, allowing ragged breaths to escape as a flare of heat ignited low in her belly.

Sliding his hands under her damp hair behind her neck, he drew her forward until her body was flush against his.

She caressed the smooth skin at the back of his neck. Her fingers twined through his silky, black curls, and she stroked his broad shoulders, thrilling at the play of well-honed muscles under her eager hands.

His tongue brushed hers in a sensual foray as the kiss deepened. He pulled back and his heated gaze met hers. "Are you okay with this?"

Her swollen lips trembled. She wanted this. Wanted his touch, his taste. More than anything, she wanted him. Her body vibrated with need. So why was a lump clogging her throat? Why was she hesitating? "I…I don't know. I don't think this is a good idea."

A log shifted on the grate. Rain drummed on the roof, and the windows rattled in a blast of wind.

"Okay. No problem." His movements were stiff and jerky as he released her and grabbed his jeans. The blanket dropped to the floor.

A blaze of heat seared her as she stared at the flex of lean muscles as he tugged on the wet denim. The man was built. "Dawson." His name escaped in a throaty whisper.

He zipped up his fly. "What is it?"

She wanted to tell him she needed him, wanted him, but the words stuck in her throat. "Nothing." She tugged the quilt tighter and hunched into its musty folds. "Nothing at all."

His eyes shuttered as he shrugged into his shirt. The damp cotton clung to his body. He didn't fasten the snaps, and the shirt gaped, revealing an enticing glimpse of soft, dark hair. Spreading the blanket on the floor near the fireplace, he flopped on his back, crossed his arms over his chest, and closed his eyes.

Her heart lodged in her throat. "What…what are you doing?"

"Trying to sleep."

"What?"

"We can't go anywhere in this storm. Best we can do is hunker down here for the night and head home in the morning."

The rain pelted against the window, and a steady plunk of water dripped from a hole in the roof into a pot. She shivered. "We're sleeping here?" As if to mock her, a loud clap of thunder reverberated through the cabin. She huddled deeper into the blanket.

The corners of his mouth twitched. "What's the matter, princess? Isn't this up to your usual standards?"

She bit her tongue, refusing to be baited. "You're going to sleep on the floor?"

His eyes opened and snapped to hers. He hitched a brow. "Unless you're offering to share the bed?"

Images of the two of them sharing the narrow bed, his body nestled with hers, legs entwined, his warm breath sweeping her flashed before her. "I...I don't know."

His mouth quirked. "I didn't think so. Now go to sleep. We have a long ride ahead of us tomorrow." His eyes closed again.

She scampered over to the bed, threw back the cover, and slid between the musty sheets. Shadows flickered on the ceiling's open rafters.

Over the raging storm and the crackle and pop of the fire, Dawson's slow, steady breathing filled the tiny shack.

The man was a machine. How could he sleep with the pounding rain, shrieking wind, and rumbling thunder?

She flipped on her side, struggling to find a comfortable spot on the thin, lumpy mattress. Her body thrummed from his sensuous kisses. She rolled onto her other side. If she closed her eyes, she tasted him, felt the rasp of his fingers caressing her skin, the warmth of his body.

Mixed in with the visceral ache was relief their kisses hadn't led further. She'd come to the Chilcotin to heal, not to have a fling with her boss. The last thing she needed was to fall in love with Dawson Wheeler, a man suffering from his own bottomless well of grief. A man too damaged for a relationship. A man in love with his long-dead wife.

There was no longer a choice. She had to leave the Circle 5. The sooner the better. When he looked at her with his heavy-lidded, passion-glazed, dark eyes, she was lost. If she stayed, it wouldn't be long before she succumbed. And where would that lead?

To a broken heart.

She turned on her back, closed her eyes, and ordered her mind to shut down and her body to relax. But like everything else in her life, her traitorous body didn't obey, and she tossed and turned for hours.

She must have dozed at some point, because she awoke to sunlight streaming through the grimy windows. Clutching the blankets to her breasts, she sat up against the pillow. The cabin was empty. Dawson must be outside checking on the horses. She swung her legs off the bed and scurried to the chair where her clothes were folded in a neat pile. The floor was cold on her bare feet. Goose bumps crawled across her naked flesh. The heavy tread of footsteps on the porch outside sent her scrambling back to the bed. She dove under the covers.

The door opened and Dawson stepped inside. A blast of cold, damp air filled the cabin. "Good. You're awake. Better get dressed." His voice was devoid of emotion, as if only a few short hours ago they hadn't been locked in each other's arms. "The storm's passed. Alf and Dee will be wondering where we are." Without waiting for her to respond, he strode out of the shack, slamming the solid wood door behind him.

She frowned. Something sure had his goat. Was he

cranky from trying to sleep on the cold, hard floor? Regretting their passionate kisses? Or upset he'd revealed too much about his wife's senseless death and his overwhelming guilt?

She climbed out of bed and struggled into her dry clothes. So they'd kissed. So his touch had set her senses on fire and flipped her world upside down. The kisses hadn't meant anything. Not to her.

Really? Nothing?

The traitorous thought scuttled through her mind, and with it flooded a deep-seated, all-out panic. This was exactly the complication she didn't need in her life. Leaving the ranch was the right choice, the sensible choice. She had to get far from Dawson Wheeler and the Circle 5 as soon as possible. Before it was too late. Before she did something she'd regret.

But what about Deirdre? She'd promised Dee she'd stay. How was she going to tell the precious child she was leaving? The burning in her stomach flamed to a raging inferno.

****

With a yank, Dawson tightened the cinch on Caspar's saddle.

The horse cocked its head, and his soft dark eyes regarded Dawson with silent reproach.

He rubbed Caspar's neck. "Sorry, old boy." His gut knotted as he recalled the hurt in Stella's luminous blue eyes when he'd snapped at her. He hadn't meant to be so harsh, but one look at her sleep-tousled hair and lips puffy from his kisses, and images of the previous night rose before him...the silken softness of her smooth skin...the taste of her sweet lips...

It had nearly killed him when she said no to his

advances, and it had taken all his strength of will to release her and back away. He'd spent the night tossing and turning on the cold, unforgiving floor, his body taut with need, his mind replaying every second of the blissful moments he held her in his arms.

He'd awakened with a pounding headache, and the gut-wrenching certainty he'd made a terrible mistake. Sure, she was sexy and beautiful, and every man's wet dream, but he had no right to touch her, let alone kiss her. She worked for him, for one thing. He was her boss. Worse, she was wounded, suffering from the death of her infant son, and like a jerk, he'd taken advantage of her vulnerability.

As if the situation wasn't bad enough, he'd made things worse by taking his frustration and anger at himself out on her. *Not cool, man. Definitely not cool.*

He tightened his grip on Caspar's mane.

The horse whinnied in protest.

He released his hold. "Sorry, boy." *Get hold of yourself.* The past night was a momentary lapse in judgment, a result of the storm and being in close confines with a desirable woman.

She'd wanted him as much as he ached for her. At least, she had, until her soft, pliant body stiffened like stone, and she turned away. She'd done him a favor. Hell, he should be thanking her. Imagine the consequences if they'd given into their passion. He shuddered. He'd dodged a bullet all right.

Caspar reared his head and butted him in the face.

"What the hell?" He rubbed his aching chin. "What was that for?"

The horse opened his mouth and whickered, exposing large, yellowed teeth, looking for all the world like he was laughing.

Dawson ran a soothing hand along the horse's neck. "You're right, boy. I deserved that. I'm a goddamn fool."

The cabin door opened and Stella stepped onto the tiny porch. She stomped over to Caspar, snatched the reins from Dawson's hand, and without waiting for his help, shoved her boot in the stirrup, and mounted the horse.

The bright morning light revealed her pale face and the dark circles under her eyes. She didn't look like she'd had much sleep either. "I'll see you back at the ranch." Gathering the reins in one hand, she spurred her horse, and Caspar trotted across the clearing and into the forest.

With a curse, he leaped on his horse and cantered after her. When he caught up, he nudged Rocky, and the stallion lunged past Caspar and took over the lead.

They rode through a forest of mature pine trees and out onto open grassland. After the wild storm, the clouds had vanished, and the sky was a crystalline blue. A gentle breeze ruffled the feathery heads of the ripening prairie grasses. The morning sun was warm on his shoulders, and he relaxed into the gentle sway of Rocky's smooth gait and breathed in the fresh air. It was one of those rare autumn days in the Chilcotin when summer reclaimed the land.

As much as he fought to keep his mind blank, he couldn't stop thinking of the woman riding behind. He didn't understand the anger gnawing at his gut. Every time he looked at her, his fury rose anew. He wasn't sure whom he was angrier at—himself for wanting her so damn much, or her for being so desirable.

He ran his hand over his unshaven cheeks. The last thing he wanted was an affair under his own roof. He had Deirdre to think of. His first instincts had been correct—the sooner Stella left the Circle 5, the better.

They rode for another hour before he reined in his horse and stopped beside a small stream. They were almost back at the house, and he wanted to inform Stella of his decision before they faced Deirdre, Alf, and the rest of the men. They had to settle this thing between them once and for all. Dismounting, he allowed his horse to graze in the lush grass as he waited.

She rode up and reined in her horse. Her brow furrowed. "Why are we stopping here?"

"We need to talk." He ran his fingers through his hair, wishing he hadn't lost his hat in the storm.

She slid off her horse and stood watching him with wounded eyes, making him feel even more like a jerk. Her long hair was a tangled mass floating in a golden cloud around her face. Her lips were swollen, her chin red from where his whiskers had rubbed her sensitive skin.

He swallowed. He wanted her. God help him. In spite of everything, in spite of his determination to send her packing, he wanted her. He gritted his jaw, grinding his molars until they ached. Kissing her was a mistake; a mistake he had to correct even if it killed him. "Last night...what happened between us..." He inhaled another lungful of air. "What we did...I didn't mean to...I shouldn't have...I hope you weren't..." *Damn!* This was hard.

She watched him with her big blue eyes.

He gulped and tried again. "I've been thinking it

would be better if you left. I know we agreed to a three-week trial, but this isn't working." He cleared his throat. "I think you'll agree what happened last night was wrong. It can't happen again. I'll fly you out tomorrow morning, and you can catch the bus to Hosten. Of course, I'll reimburse you for your expenses. I'll pay you the same amount as if you'd stayed the full three weeks."

Coldness seeped into her eyes, turning them as hard and brittle as shards of ice. She shot him a withering look. "Good."

He braced for her to say more, to accuse him of taking advantage of her, to blast him with a torrent of angry recriminations. "Good?"

"I agree. The sooner I leave the better."

His scowl deepened. She agreed? She wanted to leave? From the sound of things, she couldn't wait to get away. He should be glad she was taking his decision so well, but her cold, unemotional response jabbed like a burr. "So just like that, you're leaving?" He forced a laugh, but the sound resembled more a wail than a laugh.

His pent-up frustration unleashed, and he proceeded to make even more of a fool of himself. "You've always had a fantasy to make out with a cowboy? Is that it? Is that why you're here? Now you've ticked that one off your bucket list, you can go back to the city and the suits you usually suck face with?" His chest heaved as if he'd been running, and his head ached with a fierce pounding making it hard to think.

"Go to hell." Her eyes flashed anger. Matching red patches flared in her pale cheeks.

"Believe me, lady, I've been there."

They glared at each other.

A crow's raucous caw mocked them from the branches of a pine tree. The wind whipped her golden hair like a flag. The smells of sweet clover, dried grasses, and the rich, earthy tang of fall hung in the air.

He sucked in deep breaths, fighting to cool his fury. He was being unreasonable, but he couldn't stop the train wreck. "We're agreed, then. You're leaving." Forlorn and weighed down with an unnamed sadness, he remounted his horse. "Come on. We're almost at the house. I'll tell Dee you're going."

Chapter 10

Hot rage detonated through her like an explosion, and she grabbed the saddle horn and heaved up on the horse, ignoring the twinges of pain in her butt as she plopped down on the unforgiving saddle. "Come on, boy." She spurred Caspar's side. "Show me what you can do."

Caspar broke from a trot to a gallop in three long strides and sped off like a shot.

She leaned over his neck and hung on. They flew over the ground and raced past Dawson and his stallion. If she hadn't been clinging to the saddle horn, she'd have flipped Dawson the finger as she sped past.

The speed sent a jolt of adrenaline through her veins. Her heart pounded along with the horse's hooves over the ground. The wind ripped at her hair. Her eyes watered, and she squinted against the blast of air as they galloped through the tall grass and over a small rise. She risked a glance behind and smirked.

Dawson and his fancy stallion were a distant blob on the horizon.

Take that, *cowboy*.

They pounded down the other side of the hill. Caspar stumbled on the loose rocks, but righted his footing and raced on.

She leaned over the pommel and clung to his neck. Each stride, each jolt of hooves, struck like a fist pummeling her stomach. Why was she so angry? Dawson was right. She had to leave. He was only saying what she'd already decided. But he'd seemed so determined to get rid of her, as if he couldn't wait for her to be gone. Had the kisses they'd shared meant nothing?

And what about Deirdre? She'd be upset. Upset? The little girl would be devastated. But she was young. She'd get over it. Maybe the next nanny Dawson hired wouldn't be so weak. Tears filled her eyes, blinding her and streaming down her face.

Caspar snorted, and his ears flattened. He reared on his hind legs, his front hooves pawing the air.

A raucous cawing sounded, and with a wild flapping of wings, a flock of crows rose from the ground in a frenzied black cloud.

She fought to hang on, but Caspar bucked again, his big, muscular body twisting. In the next heartbeat, she lost her grip and launched in the air, screaming as the ground rushed at her. Her scream cut off as she slammed into the hard dirt.

She lay flat on her back, stunned, gasping for breath. The world reeled, and she squeezed her eyes shut until the ground stopped moving. The thud of pounding hoofbeats faded into the distance, and she opened her eyes and sat up.

Caspar galloped away, trailing clumps of mud.

Probing the back of her head, she winced. A bump the size of a golf ball was swelling from where she'd smacked her head on the ground. She flexed her legs and arms, but other than a few aches and pains, she was intact. Brushing back her hair, she wiped sweat and mud off her face.

A loud flutter of wings rent the air, and three huge black crows landed on the ground in front of her.

A bald eagle swooped in, and the crows squawked in protest and flew up into the branches of the nearby trees. The eagle pecked at a mound of tattered fabric.

What was that? Someone's garbage? Out here?

Her stomach clenched as she eased to her knees and pushed to her feet. Swaying, her legs rubbery, she edged closer. Her nostrils flared at the sickly sweet stench. She reeled back, stomach churning as the horrible reality of what she was looking at hit. Bile rushed up her throat. Gagging, she fell to her knees, and spewed vomit onto the muddy soil.

The thud of hoofbeats thundered across the meadow. Dawson leaped off his horse and raced to her side. "Are you okay?" With gentle hands, he lifted her to her feet. "You're as pale as a ghost. What's wrong? Where's Caspar? Did he buck you off? Are you hurt?"

Dripping sweat, stomach clenching, she swiped her arm over her mouth, grimacing at the acrid taste.

He cupped his hands on her shoulders. "Stella, answer me. Are you okay?"

She swallowed another bout of nausea and pointed a shaky finger.

He released his grip and strode toward the object on the ground, shooing the screeching eagle from its feast.

The crows cawed, watching from the branches of a copse of tall poplar trees like grotesque gargoyles.

She couldn't look, wouldn't look, but in spite of her resolve, she spun at the sound of Dawson's curse.

He stood over the dead thing, his face white and rigid.

"Is—" She gulped. "—is it…" Her throat closed and the words stuck.

"Yep."

A chill shuddered through her. "Are you…sure?"

"Yep." His voice was hard. "My guess is he's been here a few days. That's why the birds figure he's carrion."

She swallowed another bout of bile. "That…that's a *person*?" Even though she'd seen the body, she couldn't believe it. How could that pile of discolored rags and rotting flesh be a human being?

"Yep." He squatted beside the body.

"Wha…what…what happened? Can you tell?"

He didn't respond.

The breeze changed direction, and the foul odor settled over her like a fetid cloud. She retched, stomach heaving.

He strode back and drew her into his arms, melding her against his warm, strong body. "Easy. Breathe through your mouth. It's not so bad if you plug your nose."

Her breathing slowed as his deep-timbred, calm voice washed over her like a soothing balm. Following his instructions, she breathed through her mouth, keeping her nose plugged. It helped, not much, but the overwhelming stench of decay and rot eased. She slipped out of his arms. "What happened?"

His eyes were cold and hard. "Looks like someone shot him."

"What?" Her heart raced so fast she feared it would burst free of her chest. "Someone shot him? As…as in…murder?"

"I don't know. Probably a hunting accident." His

face was grim. "We need to get back to the ranch and alert the authorities. They'll want to check this out." He whistled for his horse.

The big animal, ears erect, eyes wide, nostrils flaring, trotted toward him.

"Easy, boy." Dawson ran a soothing hand down the horse's neck. "Nothing to be afraid of. Easy."

The big stallion stilled, though its ears remained upright.

Dawson glanced over. "Come on. We'll ride together."

"We're leaving him here?"

"No choice."

"But we can't just leave him." She pointed to the watching birds of prey. Their razor-sharp beaks and talons were designed for tearing flesh from bone. "They'll…they'll…" Her voice trailed to a whisper.

He reached in the nylon sack on his saddle and pulled out the blanket they'd had their picnic on and spread the blanket over the body. "We can't do anything else for him now." His mouth, rimmed by a thin white line, tightened.

"How…how long before the police get here?" A cloud scudded across the sun, casting the meadow into a gloomy twilight. Menacing shadows loomed in the dense stand of trees. She shuddered. A cold gust of wind whipped her hair around her face, and a numbing coldness gripped her heart.

He looked at the sky and shrugged. "Weather's good. They won't have any problems flying. Once we notify them, they should arrive in a couple of hours." Cupping his hands together, he gestured for her to put the toe of her boot on his palms and climb onto Rocky's saddle. "Come on."

****

The ride to the ranch house took an eternity. A pulse pounded in Dawson's temples, beating in time with Rocky's steady trot. A man was dead, shot through the back, and left in the open like a hunk of discarded meat.

He was a hunter and used to the damage caused by a bullet from a rifle, but this wasn't a deer or a moose. This was a man, a human being. His guts had heaved at the gaping entry wound in the man's back, the gouts of dried blood and gore on the earth, the stench. Even now the smell of death clung to them.

Accidents happened in hunting season. Every year the news had a story about some poor fool who accidentally shot himself or his friend instead of the deer he was aiming for. Dawson's gut knotted. Something wasn't right. This wasn't an accident. No one had reported the shooting. Had whoever killed his cattle also shot the poor man? The knot tightened. Was some trigger-happy killer hanging around the Circle 5? He studied the surrounding hills. Were they being watched?

He tightened his arms around Stella's waist and drew her closer. Her back was molded to his chest, her thighs bracketed by his. Under normal circumstances, he'd enjoy the softness of her curves and the brush of her silken hair, but nothing about this nightmare was normal.

The tightness in his gut eased when he spied the metal roof of the barn shining in the sun.

Deirdre and the two dogs were waiting by the corral when they rode into the clearing. She squealed

131

and raced toward them, the dogs prancing at her feet, barking and yipping. "Daddy! Stella! You're back."

Warmth rushed over him at the sight of her flushed face and ear-to-ear grin. "Hey, honey."

"Did you get wet in the storm? Alf said you must have found shelter. That's why you didn't come home yesterday." Dee danced from foot to foot. "We were scared when Caspar came back this morning. Did the lightning spook him? He doesn't like storms. I don't either. They scare me. Do they scare you, Stella? Were you scared? Where's your hat, Daddy? Did it blow off in the storm?" The words flew out of her mouth in an excited jumble.

"Whoa. Slow down, honey." He helped Stella off the horse.

Deirdre launched her tiny body at Stella. "I missed you."

Stella stumbled back a step under the onslaught, but caught the child in her arms and nuzzled her cheek. "I missed you, too, Dee."

Dee peered at Stella with her all-too-perceptive eyes. "What's wrong?"

"Nothing." Stella slid him a desperate glance.

"You've been crying. Your face is all blotchy."

"No, I…"

"Eeew. What's that smell?" Deirdre plugged her fingers over her nose and backed away.

"Let Stella have a bath and clean up." He slipped off the horse and ruffled Dee's riot of red curls. "You can help me in the barn. Rocky needs a good rubdown."

She beamed at her father, and scampered toward the barn, followed by the barking dogs.

He scrubbed the whiskers on his face. "You go and

wash up. I'll tell her you're leaving."

"What about…" Stella chewed on her bottom lip. "What about the body? Aren't you going to call the police?"

"I will, but first I want to talk to Deirdre. Your leaving is going to be hard on her. I don't want her to hear about it from anyone but me." His gut twisted at the play of emotions across her expressive face—hurt, anger, and something he couldn't identify. Every cell in his body yearned to hold her, to once again caress her soft curves and kiss her sweet lips. He blew out a breath. And that was why she had to go. "It's for the best." The second the words escaped his mouth, he wondered who he was trying to convince—Stella or himself.

She nodded and hurried across the clearing as if fleeing the devil himself. She brushed past Alf on the porch without a word and ran into the house. The screen door slammed behind her.

The old man stomped down the steps and crossed the yard. "About time you came home." The lines in his face were set and his eyes accusing. "Have a good time?"

Heat seared along Dawson's neck. If only Alf knew just how good a time he'd had. So good, the all-too-vivid memories of what happened in the cabin left him shaking. He schooled his expression and grabbed Rocky's reins. "We waited out the storm at Henry's place."

"How's he doing?"

Dawson ignored his question. If Alf knew he and Stella had spent the night alone, the old man's anger would escalate.

Alf's eyes narrowed. "Did something happen? She looked mighty upset."

"We found something up by Rosie's Creek. That's why Caspar ran off."

"What have those damn trespassing miners done now?"

"We found a body."

"A body? What the hell?"

"Looks like he was shot."

"Shot?"

"In the back and left for the crows." His gut clenched as an image of the bloated corpse rose before him. The flesh around the wound had been ripped and torn by animals, exposing bone, cartilage, and bloody strands of muscle. Some wild creature had gnawed the poor man's hand, and a finger was missing.

"Anyone we know?"

"Never seen him before."

"It's hunting season. Could have been a hunting accident."

"Could be."

"But you don't think so."

He met Alf's sharp gaze. "Man didn't look like a hunter. He didn't have a rifle."

"What aren't you telling me?"

"Survey stakes and a roll of flagging tape were on the ground beside him."

"Shit!" Alf spat on the dirt. "You're kidding me."

Dawson rubbed his damp palms on his thighs. "I wish I were."

"Shit." Another gob of phlegm hit the ground. "What are you gonna do?"

"Call the authorities. Let them figure this out." He

blew out a breath. "There's something I wanted to talk to Dee about, but I guess it'll have to wait." He held out the reins. "Will you take Rocky to the barn and check on Dee? I'll go and make the call." He rubbed his chin. "Oh, and Alf, keep this quiet. I don't want Dee knowing about this."

"Sure thing." Alf grabbed the reins and with his bandy-legged gait, led the big horse toward the barn.

Like a condemned prisoner heading for the firing squad, Dawson plodded toward the house. If his suspicions were right, and the dead man had worked for Imperial Monarch, all hell was about to break loose. Once he made the call to the police, investigators would descend on the ranch in droves, questioning everyone.

Chapter 11

Stella couldn't think of a time she'd been more exhausted. All she wanted to do was crawl into bed and sleep, but the stench of death clung to her clothes and hair and permeated her skin. She twisted the tap, and hot water streamed into the tub. She poured an entire bottle of rose-scented bath oil into the steaming water.

Floral-scented steam filled the small, tiled bathroom as she struggled out of her dirty clothes and tossed them aside. She tested the water with her toe and climbed into the tub and sank up to her neck in hot water. Muscles she hadn't known existed, ached. Her head throbbed, and her eyes were scratchy and dry.

A vision of the bloated corpse rose before her, and she moaned and squeezed her eyes shut. She couldn't stop thinking of the man who'd lost his life. Was Dawson right? Had the poor man been murdered? Even under the near-scalding heat of the bath water, she shivered, and goose bumps prickled along her arms.

The police were on their way. She'd never practiced criminal law, but she knew enough to know even accidental deaths had to be thoroughly investigated, the crime scene secured, all potential witnesses questioned, and an autopsy performed. But after the questions ended and the investigators left, she too would leave.

I think it's for the best.

Dawson's calm, unemotional words ran through her mind, each syllable stabbing like a knife to her gut. He wanted her to leave the Circle 5. Even after the past night, *especially* after the past night. She refused to cry. What was the point?

From their first meeting, an attraction had flared, an attraction that intensified with each ensuing encounter. Placing the two of them alone together in the isolated cabin, surrounded by pounding rain and fierce winds, created the perfect storm. The scenario had played out like someone's idea of a bad joke.

The pads of her fingers were wrinkled like prunes when she finally stepped out of the bathtub and onto the bathmat. After drying herself with a fluffy, white towel, she tugged on clean clothes. A hint of decay and rot lingered in the steamy air, and she doused herself with rosewater spray cologne. Better to smell like a flower garden than death. She'd probably have to burn the clothes she'd worn that day.

She stepped into the bedroom.

The door to the hall burst open, and Deirdre stormed in. Two red splotches stained her pale, freckled cheeks. "You're leaving!" Her chin trembled. Tears welled in her eyes.

"Dee—"

"Daddy said you're leaving." Deirdre looked at her with pleading eyes. "Is it true? Are you really going away?"

Stella attempted to take her in her arms.

Deirdre jerked away. "Tell me."

Her stomach churned at the raw pain on Deirdre's face, but she nodded.

"You said you wouldn't leave. You promised." Her

eyes flashed with fury. "You lied! I hate you. I hate you." Dee flew at her, her tiny fists flailing, striking Stella's cheek, her arms, and her chest.

Stella remained immobile, allowing Deirdre to vent her hurt and anger, knowing she deserved it. She'd promised the little girl she'd stay, but that was before the soul-shattering events at the cabin and the implosion with Dawson that followed. Her heart clenched, twisting like it had been ripped asunder.

The force of Deirdre's blows lost power, and she dissolved in Stella's arms as sobs wracked her tiny frame.

Stella crooned and rocked the distraught child, rubbing soothing circles over her narrow back. Her muscles cramped and her knees ached, but she continued to hold Deirdre close as she whispered calming words. She looked up at the sound of a footstep.

Dawson stood in the open doorway, his dark eyes filled with shadows. He opened his mouth as if to speak, but his lips tightened into a thin line. Shoulders drooping, he turned and plodded away, his tread heavy on the hall's wooden floor.

Deirdre's sobs lessened, and her labored breathing eased. Her tiny body relaxed as she fell asleep in Stella's arms.

She carried the sleeping child down the hall to her bedroom, laid her on the pink, frilly bedspread, and covered her with a quilt. Smoothing a stray lock of hair from Deirdre's damp forehead, she blinked back tears. In the short time she'd been at the ranch, she'd grown to love the little girl. And now she'd broken the child's heart.

She blew out a ragged breath. The young were resilient. In time, Deirdre's memories of Stella would dim, and she'd forget. Her own guilt and feelings of loss would take much longer to heal. She kissed Dee's smooth, warm forehead and shuffled out of the room.

Alf leaned against the wall, blocking her escape. His arms were crossed over his thin chest, his eyes penetrating.

She swiped at the tears on her face. She'd hoped to evade the old man until the morning, but from the determined expression on his lined face, a confrontation was unavoidable. "I just put Deirdre to bed."

He nodded his grizzled head. "I expect she's pretty upset."

"She's sleeping now."

"I hear you're leaving. Why?"

"Dawson wants me to go."

"And you believe that?" He continued to watch her as if searching for some hidden truth.

"Look, it's been a long day. I'm going to bed. Let me know when the police arrive." She brushed past him, but halted at his quiet words.

"I never took you for a coward."

"Wha...what?"

"I figured you'd fight for what you wanted."

She didn't bother to pretend she didn't know what he was talking about. "I can't fight for a lost cause."

"He needs you."

A bitter laugh burst from her lips. "Dawson? He doesn't need anybody. As long as he has his ranch and the memory of his dead wife, he'll be happy."

"What about Dee? Don't you care about her?"

His words stung, and she blinked back a fresh spate

139

of tears. "Of course I care. But she'll be okay. In a week, she won't remember my name." Tears clogged her throat, threatening to choke her. She pushed past him and rushed down the hall to her room and threw herself on the bed, giving in to heaving sobs.

She awoke drenched in perspiration. A headache pounded behind her left eye. She rubbed her aching temple with the pads of her fingers. The darkness in the room was broken by the cold light of the moon shining through the window. Giving up all pretext of sleep, she stumbled into the bathroom and splashed cold water on her tear-swollen face and dressed in jeans and a sweater.

The police would arrive soon. Hours earlier, Alf had knocked on her door and told her that mechanical problems with the RCMP helicopter had delayed their arrival. As the person who discovered the body, they'd want to question her. But after the authorities completed their investigation, she'd ask Dawson to fly her back to Spirit River where she'd catch the bus and return to Vancouver.

Fighting back a yawn, she rubbed her scratchy eyes. Her headache pounded like a jackhammer in her brain. Every muscle in her body ached like she'd gone a round in a boxing ring and come out the loser. She yawned again. If she hoped to make it through the next strained hours, she needed coffee, and she needed it now.

She slipped out of her room and tiptoed along the hall and down the stairs to the kitchen. The last thing she wanted was another run-in with Alf, or worse, Dawson. Not until she had coffee. After a couple of cups of strong, black brew, she'd be better prepared to face their disappointment and anger.

Moonlight streamed in through the large windows and painted the kitchen in a cold, blue light, leaving the corners of the large room in shadows. She fumbled for the light switch, but froze at a rhythmic squeaking.

The faint glow from the smoldering embers sparking in the fireplace revealed Dawson rocking in the chair beside the fire. His hat was tilted low over his eyes, and his broad shoulders drooped as he stared into the coals.

Did the man never sleep?

She turned to slink away.

The creaking of the rocking chair stopped. "You're up early."

She sighed. So much for escape. "I couldn't sleep."

"You too, huh?"

She retraced her steps, halting by the big propane stove, careful to keep several feet between them. "When do you think the police will arrive?"

"Soon as it gets light, I expect. They're flying in by helicopter from Hosten."

"I'd better make coffee." She picked up the heavy metal coffeepot and carried it to the sink and turned on the tap. Once the pot was filled with water, she set the pot on the counter and searched in the cupboard for the can of coffee beans. "It's going to be a long morning."

"Are you packed?"

She set the coffee can on the counter and grabbed the pot. With her back to him, she nodded, though she hadn't needed to pack. She hadn't unpacked from the day before. "Don't worry. I'm all set. I'll be out of your hair before you know it." Even to her own ears, her voice sounded stilted. "As soon as the police finish their investigation, I'll be ready to go."

The squeak of the rocking chair increased to a furious pace.

She gripped the handle, her knuckles white, nails scoring the metal, and lifted the heavy pot, placed it on the burner, and ignited the flame. She risked a peek over her shoulder.

If possible, his face was even stonier, his mouth a sealed line, his jaw rigid, the furious back and forth of the rocking chair a testament to his distress.

An unexpected wave of empathy washed over her. The previous day they'd found a decomposing body, and the police were on their way to investigate. His daughter was upstairs in her room having cried herself to sleep. "I…er…I'm sorry it had to end this way."

"Are you?" He shoved his hat back with his thumb. His eyes sparked with anger. "Are you really? Because from where I'm sitting, it looks like you can't get away from here fast enough."

She reeled back. "What are you talking about? *You* told me to leave." True, she'd agreed with him, but what choice did she have? He was the boss.

He erupted from the chair, setting it rocking like a wild bronco and stalked toward her, not stopping until his boots brushed the toes of her shoes. His penetrating gaze pinned her.

"Wha…what are you doing?" Her voice was a notch above a whisper. The heat from his body was like facing a blast furnace.

His eyes softened to a smoky gray. "Something I'm going to regret, but God help me, I can't seem to stop myself."

And just like that, the world tilted on its axis, and

the ever-present attraction between them flared to life.

Her heart raced as her blood pounded in her ears in a deafening roar.

He cupped the back of her head and drew her close.

His warm breath fanned her face as his scent—something woodsy and leather—enveloped her in a heady fog.

With agonizing slowness, he lowered his head and claimed her mouth.

Desire spiraled through her. Forgotten were his heartless words, her doubts and worries. In their place—yearning, passion, need.

The heavy tread of footsteps on the porch and the loud screech as the back door swung open broke through her erotic haze.

He muttered an oath and jerked away.

She swayed, bereft at the abrupt loss of the exquisite sensation of his lips on hers.

"Mornin' all." Alf bustled into the kitchen. "Sorry I'm late. Damn alarm didn't go off. Don't fret. I'll have a nice hot breakfast cooking in no time. Those RCMP boys will likely be starving when they get here." He halted in his rush across the kitchen, as if just noticing the strained silence. His button-bright eyes in their sea of wrinkles stared between Dawson and her.

Blushing, she looked away from his questioning gaze. "I...I put the coffee on." She slid a glance at Dawson.

His face was unruffled and calm, revealing no evidence of their passionate embrace.

"Thanks." Alf marched over to the counter and hefted the large, cast-iron frying pan and set it on the stove. With a flick of his wrist, he ignited the propane burner and switched the blue, flickering flame to high. He crossed to the fridge and removed two cartons of eggs. His motions were fluid, with little wasted movement, honed by years of practice. He cracked an egg into the sizzling pan and glanced over his shoulder. "I expect you're anxious to leave, Stella."

"Yes, I'm looking forward to seeing the city." She hoped neither he nor Dawson detected the lie. "Vancouver's an exciting place. It certainly has a lot more going for it than the Chilcotin, though I'll miss Deirdre, and you too, Alf." She glanced at Dawson to see if her barb hit its mark.

His rigid face showed no reaction other than a tightening of his jaw.

The thunderous roar of an approaching helicopter boomed overhead.

"They're here." Dawson stomped out of the kitchen, slamming the door behind him.

Chapter 12

Breakfast was a nightmare. The ranch hands sat in their usual places at the big, oval table, and two Royal Canadian Mounted Police investigating officers squeezed in beside Stella. Deirdre wasn't up yet, and Dawson's place at the head of the table was empty. He'd taken the two other investigators, who'd arrived on the large police helicopter, to the accident scene to see the body.

Alf bustled at the stove, filling plates with scrambled eggs and rashers of bacon, and refilling coffee cups.

The uniformed police officers were an all-too-vivid reminder of the man whose lifeless body lay in the meadow. They'd announced their intention to question everyone on the ranch as soon as they finished breakfast. The conversation was sparse, the air filled with tension as everyone focused on eating.

She stared at her untouched plate, and her stomach roiled at the greasy smell of the thick slabs of back bacon.

The door burst open and Dawson, a grim look on his rugged face, strode into the kitchen. Without acknowledging anyone, he sat at his spot at the table.

Alf hurried over with a steaming plate piled high with food and set it before him.

With a grunt of thanks, he started shoveling eggs

into his mouth.

The men cast furtive glances at one another.

Bob slurped his coffee. "So, what did the cops say, Dawson? Was it an accident? I mean, it would have to be, wouldn't it? It's not like we have killers running around the Chilcotin."

Dawson stopped shoveling eggs and wiped his mouth with a napkin. "Ask Sergeant Murphy. He's the one in charge."

All gazes turned toward the RCMP officer. He frowned and his thick gray eyebrows dipped in a vee over his bulbous nose. "I'm not going to speculate until the investigators conduct a thorough examination of the scene, and the coroner examines the body." He pinned each person with a sharp gaze. "I don't want any of you to talk about this, not to each other, not to your best friend, not even to your mother. I'll interview each of you, one at a time."

"You can use my office," Dawson offered.

Murphy nodded. "One more thing. No one leaves the ranch until we complete our preliminary investigation." His gaze settled on Stella as if he knew of her plans to leave. "That goes for *all* of you."

She gulped.

He dabbed his lips with his napkin and shoved back his chair and stood. "From what I understand, Ms. King, you found the body."

"Ye…yes."

"Right, then. I'll take your statement first."

Her stomach flip-flopped as she set down her cup and stood on wobbly legs.

An hour later, she staggered out of Dawson's office, palms damp, headache blasting, and feeling as if she'd been wrung dry.

Sergeant Murphy had asked her to repeat the events leading up to her finding the body.

He recorded the interview with a small, digital recorder.

She'd described the sudden storm and how she and Dawson had spent the night in the old cabin. When he raised his shaggy eyebrows, she hastened to explain she'd slept on the bed while Dawson had lain on the floor. Her face flamed at his knowing smirk.

When he finished his probing questions, he thanked her and told her unless something unexpected showed up in the initial examination of the victim, she was free to leave as soon as the body was airlifted back to Hosten.

The morning had been so hectic she hadn't had a chance to think of the torrid kiss she'd shared with Dawson in the cozy kitchen. She ran her fingers over her mouth. Her lips were swollen and tender. If she closed her eyes, the imprint of his hard body, his tongue teasing, his taste mingling with hers, was fixed in her soul.

She clenched her fists. *Stop!* The command razed through her. She was leaving…Dawson, Deirdre, the Circle 5…everything. That's what she wanted—to return to Vancouver. Isn't that what she'd said? Better shopping, new shoes, the mall. Away from Dawson. She strode into the kitchen and poured yet another cup of coffee from the pot bubbling on the stove.

The door opened and Dawson and one of the Mounties, who'd ridden out on the ranch's quads to examine the body, strode into the warm kitchen. The police officer's face was grim. He wore a bulletproof vest over his gray, uniform shirt. His dark-blue trousers had a wide yellow strip down each pant leg. His belt rode low on his lean hips, weighed down by a gun, baton, pepper spray, and a set of handcuffs. He slipped off his uniform cap and hung it by the door. "Where's Sergeant Murphy?"

"In the office." She pointed into the hall. "He's talking to Jim."

He nodded and strode out of the kitchen.

She swung to Dawson. "What's going on? What did they find?"

Dawson removed his hat and ran a hand over his tangled hair. His eyes were hollow, his face a pale mask. "It's not good." Without another word, he followed the officer.

She pressed her hand to her chest, trying to slow her heart's rapid pounding.

Jim strode into the kitchen and sank on a chair. He scrubbed his scarred face with his hands. "Can I get some of that coffee, Stella?"

"Sure." She poured the steaming brew into a mug and handed him the cup.

He nodded his thanks.

"What's going on?" She picked up a tea towel and twisted the damp cloth into knots. Her body hummed with an overdose of caffeine and nerves.

"The cops are calling in the coroner."

"The coroner?" Her heart skipped a beat. "I thought it was a hunting accident."

He slurped a mouthful of coffee and scrubbed his hand over his freckled scalp. Tendrils of rust-colored hair stood out like dandelion fuzz. "I dunno about that, but none of them look any too happy."

The back door opened, and Alf hurried into the kitchen, his craggy face wan. "Dawson back yet?"

"Got here about ten minutes ago," Jim said.

Alf's gaze swung to her. "Deirdre awake?"

She shook her head. "She's still sleeping. I guess she was tired."

"A broken heart'll do that to you." He peered at the battered watch on his sinewy arm. "Still, you'd think she'd be up by now. She must have heard the helicopter arrive."

A trill of alarm rippled along her spine. Alf was right. With all the comings and goings this morning, the child should have awakened hours ago.

Before she could voice her concern, Dawson marched into the room, followed by three Mounties. The fierce scowls on their faces cast all thought of Deirdre out of her mind.

"You all better have a seat." Sergeant Murphy's stern voice brooked no argument. His steely gaze settled on Alf. "Call in the rest of the men."

Alf rushed out of the room.

"Stella—" Dawson's voice was flat. "—would you please pour us some coffee?"

She retraced her steps to the stove and retrieved the coffee pot and several mugs. Setting cups and the coffee pot on a tray, she carried the loaded tray back to the table and placed it before the somber men.

The door opened, and Alf bustled into the kitchen, the ranch hands shuffling at his heels.

Once they were all seated and each man had a cup of coffee, Sergeant Murphy spoke. "The coroner and the major crime scene investigation team are on their way."

Her gasp echoed in the large kitchen. She shot a glance at Dawson.

His jaw was clenched tight, that infernal pulse ticking like a metronome.

"Why…why did you call the crime scene investigators?" she asked.

A deafening silence ensued. No one met her gaze. They were suddenly all fascinated by the contents of their coffee cups.

Sergeant Murphy cleared his throat. "There's not much of a question as to the cause of the victim's death. From what my officers observed, he was out in the open and wearing an orange fluorescent safety vest. Not likely a hunter mistook him for a moose or deer. He was shot in the back with a high-powered rifle. Looks like he died instantly." His mouth tightened. "We're looking at murder."

"Murder?" Her voice squeaked.

"Looks that way."

"But who—"

Dawson slammed his cup on the table with a thud. Coffee slopped onto the wood. "The Sergeant believes I'm the prime suspect."

She fell back as if he'd struck her. "You?"

An uneasy silence filled the kitchen.

The steady ticking of the clock on the wall and the men's heavy breathing grated on her ears.

Sergeant Murphy pushed back his chair and stood. "I want to talk to you in your office, Dawson. Give me a few minutes to make some calls and then join me." He headed toward the door to the hall, but stopped and swung back, eying the people sitting at the table. "No one is to leave this ranch until I say so. Corporal

Pearson will be here if you remember something you haven't already told me. Any detail, no matter how small, could be important." He nodded and strode out of the room.

The silence thickened, coiling like a living thing, rearing above them, threatening to strike.

Brett, his acne-scarred cheeks flushed red, shoved his chair back and rose to his feet. "I've got chores to do."

"You're free to go about your work. Just don't go beyond the perimeter of the house and barn," Corporal Pearson said.

As if released from jail, the men leaped to their feet with a clatter and bang of chairs and raced for the door. In seconds they'd disappeared, leaving Stella, Alf, Dawson, and the corporal behind.

Alf shoved back his chair and stood. "I'd better check on Deirdre."

"I'll go." Stella slid a glance at Dawson. His rugged features were blank, but his dark eyes revealed his inner anguish. She lurched to her feet, desperate to leave the kitchen and all the unsettling, dark undercurrents.

"Let Alf tend to her." Dawson's acid voice cut like a knife. "She has to get used to you not being here."

Keeping her head lowered, she hid her hurt with a fall of hair and grabbed a handful of dirty cups and stumbled over to the sink.

****

Dawson downed the cold dregs of his coffee and rubbed his hand over his burning gut. Too much caffeine on an empty stomach. He checked his watch and grimaced. The day was just getting started, and already it promised to be a bitch. Why did the sergeant want to talk to him again? What more could Dawson add to the detailed statement he'd already given?

He was a suspect, probably the prime one. Not a surprise. He hadn't hidden the fact he was opposed to the proposed mine. On more than one occasion, he'd chased mining company employees off his property, sometimes with a rifle in his hands. The situation looked bad. His sole hope was once the coroner determined the victim's time of death, he'd have an alibi.

Stella banged cups and pots as she washed dishes in the big, stainless steel sink. Her slender body was rigid and her face pale, her beauty marred by lines of strain.

The whole damn world was falling apart. A man had been murdered in cold blood on his land, and he was a suspect. Someone was killing his cattle, cutting his fences, and vandalizing his equipment, and Stella was leaving. He swallowed back the acid taste in his mouth.

She didn't belong there. He'd known that from the second he laid eyes on her. Talk about a fish out of water. But in spite of his misgivings, he'd relented and let her into his life. That was his first mistake. But then he'd gone and fallen for her and made a bad situation worse. Deirdre was devastated Stella was leaving. The poor kid had cried herself to sleep. And he—

Alf rushed into the kitchen, frantic and wild-eyed. "Dee's gone."

"What?" Stella's gasp was like an icy blast.

"Gone?" Dawson shot to his feet, knocking his chair over. It crashed on the floor with a loud bang.

"What do you mean, gone?"

"She's not in her room. Her bed's been slept in, but she's not there. I—" Alf paused for breath, worry lines carved deep into his forehead. "—I checked the rest of the house. I can't find her anywhere." His Adam's apple bobbed in his scrawny neck, and he tugged a faded handkerchief from his pants pocket and wiped at the sweat beading his brow.

"Are you sure she's not in the house?" A chill radiated through Dawson and settled deep in his bones. "You know how she likes to play games."

"I looked everywhere." Alf mopped his gleaming brow again.

"I'll check the barn and outbuildings." Dawson pinned Stella with a sharp look. "Keep searching the house. You know all the places she might hide."

Her face was ashen, but she nodded and ran out of the room.

He swallowed back the cold lump of fear blocking his throat. Dee was in the barn. Yes, that's where she was…playing with Daisey's new litter of kittens. His reasoning didn't calm the furious beating of his heart.

The kitchen door burst open, and Jim barged into the room. "Caspar's missing."

Icy tendrils gripped the pit of his stomach. "Caspar? Are you sure?"

"I put him in his stall last night." The livid scar on his cheek was a jagged red slash on his drawn face.

Dawson swung to Alf. "Do you think Deirdre took the horse?"

"More'n likely."

He staggered and grabbed the table for support. "Are you telling me she ran away?"

Alf didn't answer, but the truth was written across his pale, craggy face.

"Why would she run away? She's only five." An immobilizing fear settled over him as the devastating truth exploded like a bomb. Deirdre was upset. She'd burst into tears when he'd told her Stella was returning to Vancouver. She hadn't stopped crying until hours later, when she'd finally fallen asleep.

Why hadn't he checked on her like he did every morning? Why hadn't he made sure she was snuggled safely in her bed? A sour taste filled his mouth. Because that morning he'd been too damned wrapped up in the implications of finding a dead man on his land and the impending arrival of the RCMP. Stella, and all the unsettling emotions her leaving evoked, was the icing on the cake. He bit back a groan. Self-recriminations wouldn't bring back his daughter. He met Jim's worried gaze. "How long do you think she's been gone?"

Jim shook his grizzled head. "I'm not sure. Alphonse checked on Maybelle's calf around three this mornin'. He's pretty sure Caspar was in his stall then."

His heart raced. Bears, cougars, wolves, hell, any number of dangers awaited a small child in the wilderness. And he couldn't forget the dead man, shot in the back and left to rot. What if Deirdre ran into the killer?

He stared out the window at the encircling forest, and the menacing gloom lurking in the dark, impenetrable depths. The thought of his child, *his baby*, wandering the woods alone terrified him. Struggling to break free of the wave of panic threatening to engulf him, he met Alf's worried gaze. "She can't have ridden far. Get the men out searching."

"I'll help you look." Constable Pearson tugged on his coat and donned his cap.

Stella ran into the room. "I can't find her anywhere." Her face was pale, the whites of her eyes streaked with red.

"Stay here in case she returns," he said. "I'm going to ride out and look for her."

"This is my fault." Her voice was hoarse, and she swiped the back of her hand across her tear-filled eyes. "She was so upset. I should have known she'd do something like this. I should have known."

Her remorse chipped at the block of ice encasing his heart. He fought the urge to take her in his arms and ease her guilt. "You couldn't have known she'd run away. If anyone's to blame, it's me."

"I should have checked on her. I should have—" Her voice broke on a sob.

"We'll find her." He jammed on his hat and shrugged into his coat. He prayed to God he told the truth. He'd find his daughter. He had to.

Stella wiped her streaming face and nodded.

"Bring her back safe, Dawson," Alf choked out. His love for Dee was written in the deep grooves carved across his ravaged face and the haunted shadows in his eyes.

Dawson nodded at his friend. After Anna's death, Dawson had been a mess. He didn't know what would have happened if Alf hadn't shown up one day and torn the whiskey bottle out of his hand and poured its contents down the sink. The old man had dragged him kicking and screaming out of his self-pity and made him see how his actions were affecting Deirdre. Alf had convinced him to return to the Chilcotin and take over the running of the Circle 5. He'd forced Dawson to live, if not for himself, then for his daughter.

He flung open the door and sprinted across the yard to the barn. *We'll find her. We'll find her.* The words, part prayer, part heartfelt oath, reverberated through his head like a mantra.

We'll find her.

Chapter 13

"Come on, boy." He prodded the exhausted horse with his boot heels. He'd lost track of how many hours he'd scoured the dense forest and grassy meadows. The sun was making its final descent behind the mountains in the west. Streaks of vivid pinks and orange flamed across the sky like a glimpse into the fiery gates of Hell.

He was a good tracker—a skill he'd learned as a kid from Henry Rivers and honed during the many hours he'd hunted wild game—but so far, he hadn't seen any signs of Deirdre's passing—no broken branches, no hoofprints in the dirt, no disturbed ground, nothing.

Where is she?

The question beat a frantic refrain through his brain, becoming more strident with each passing hour. *Where the hell is she?* How far could a five-year-old ride in a few hours?

He urged Rocky up the last few feet of loose scree and shale to the summit of Tor's Ridge, hoping against hope she'd gone there. He cupped his hands around his mouth. "Dee." His cry rebounded off the surrounding hills. "Dee."

Swallowing over the lump clogging his throat, he dismounted and led his tired horse to the stream. While Rocky drank, he strode to the edge of the cliff and scanned the valley hoping, in spite of the fading light, to see some sign of Deirdre, a movement, a flash of color, anything.

His daughter was his entire world. Ever since Anna passed, his one reason for living had been the precious life she'd entrusted to him. He couldn't bear it if something happened to Dee. Losing one person he loved had nearly killed him. He wouldn't survive another loss.

He stared at the kilometers of unbroken forest and brooded over the pain in Stella's haunted blue eyes when she'd told him the heart-wrenching details of the death of her child. He was getting a glimpse into the hell she suffered. Tears filled his eyes, and he collapsed to his knees as the urge to do something he hadn't done in years overwhelmed him. He bowed his head and prayed.

The sun had set, and his muscles were stiff and cramped by the time he raised his head. Squinting through the deepening dusk, he made out the wheat-colored shape of Rocky as he grazed on the lush grass bordering the stream.

The horse's regal head drooped.

Dawson had pushed him hard. He hated demanding more from the big stallion, but he had one more place to check. Maybe she'd ridden to Henry's cabin. She'd feel safe there. Dawson had taken Dee with him just a couple of weeks ago when he'd brought Henry the mail he'd picked up on his last trip to Hosten. Henry had made hot chocolate and taught Dee checkers. They'd played for hours until Dawson had dragged a protesting Deirdre home.

With fresh determination, he leaped on his horse and spurred the animal into a canter.

Rocky slipped and slid over the loose rocks. He broke into a gallop once they descended into the grassy plains of the valley bottom.

Henry's cabin was dark, an air of desolation hanging over the weathered, old shack.

He dismounted, tied Rocky to the hitching rail, and ran up the steps and flung open the cabin door. "Dee?" His voice cracked.

As he'd feared, the cabin was empty. His knees buckled, and he stumbled out of the cabin.

A bulky, dark shape emerged out of the forest shadows. "Hey, Dawson."

He scrubbed the tears from his eyes and peered at Henry. "I didn't think you were home. I'm looking for Dee. I…I hoped she was here."

The whites of Henry's eyes gleamed under the cold light of the rising moon. "I was out hunting." A deer carcass was slung over his broad back. He lowered the dead animal to the ground. "You'd better tell me why you're out here in the dead of night looking for your little girl."

"She's missing, Henry." Dawson's gut clenched at the stink of fresh blood and entrails. "She…she took Caspar and ran away." He bit his bottom lip to stop the trembling.

"What? Why would she do that?"

"It's complicated." Dawson rubbed the back of his neck.

Henry's eyes narrowed. "I'll bet. Does it have something to do with your new nanny?"

"You know about her?"

Henry's mouth hardened, and he ignored Dawson's question. "I'll help you search." He gripped Dawson's arm. "Don't worry. I'll find her." Without another word, he strode back into the forest, disappearing into the night as silently as he'd appeared.

Dawson untied Rocky's reins and climbed back on the saddle. If anyone could find Dee, the old trapper could. Henry knew every inch of this land. Spurring his horse into a gallop, he headed back to the ranch.

He breathed a silent prayer when he spotted the lights of the ranch house. *Please let Deirdre be home safe. Please.* With hope in his heart, he spurred Rocky's sides and urged him toward home.

His heart sank when he rode into the clearing.

Jim, Bob, and Alphonse stood on the front porch. Their glum faces said it all. They hadn't found her.

Fresh pain stabbed him, and it was all he could do to hang onto the saddle. Still, he had to ask. "Any luck?"

Jim shuffled his feet and scuffed his boots on the wooden boards, his hands jammed in the front pockets of his faded jeans. He spat a stream of tobacco juice over the railing. "We searched everywhere, Dawson, but there's no sign of her. I called the men back in when it got too dark to see. We'll head out again once that moon gets over the hills."

He swallowed past the thickening in his throat. "Thank you. I know you did the best you could."

Jim cleared his throat, and Dawson's gut twisted with the certainty that more bad news was on its way.

"We found Caspar over by Simm's Butte. The poor horse was pretty frightened. Looks like something spooked him, and he bucked off little Dee."

Fear knifed into Dawson's soul at this devastating news. As long as Dee was with Caspar, he had hope of finding her. Rocky would scent his stable mate and lead Dawson to the white horse and his daughter. But if she'd been bucked off... A hundred scenarios, each more nightmarish than the one before, rocketed through him.

The back door of the house opened, spilling yellow light across the yard, and Alf stepped onto the porch. His gaze flew to Dawson with a silent, desperate question.

Dawson shook his head, and Alf sagged, clutching the railing.

Dawson climbed off his horse and with heavy steps led Rocky toward the barn.

"Where're you going?" Alf called from across the clearing.

"Rocky's done. I'm saddling another horse and heading back out."

"You've got to eat something first."

He kept walking. One goal ruled his mind—find Deirdre. A hand grasped his arm. He spun around and glared at Alf. "Get out of my way, old man."

Even though he towered over Alf and outweighed the older man by a good hundred pounds, Alf held his ground. "You're not going anywhere until you eat something. You won't do that child a damn bit of good if you keel over."

He shoved Alf's hand away. "I'm not stopping until I find her."

"We all want to find her. You're not the only one who loves her."

Dawson rubbed the grit from his eyes. Every muscle in his body ached. He didn't think he'd ever been more exhausted. But he couldn't stop. Not now, not with Dee lost in the wilderness, alone, cold, frightened, maybe injured.

"You haven't eaten anything since breakfast, and by my reckoning, you didn't eat more than a mouthful then." Alf snatched the stallion's reins from Dawson's hand. "Go on in and eat something. I'll look after Rocky. I'll get Jean-Luc to saddle Midnight. After you eat, you can ride out." The fierce light in the old man's eyes made it clear arguing would be useless.

Dawson blew out a long breath. "All right." He trudged with heavy steps out of the barn and across the clearing to the house. He'd have a quick bite and ride out again. He wouldn't rest until Deirdre was home safe and sound.

****

The door slammed.

Stella's hand jerked and coffee spilled onto the table. She spun around.

Dawson's rugged face was pale and wan. Deep lines bracketed his mouth, and dark circles underscored his bloodshot eyes. His broad shoulders drooped with exhaustion.

She didn't have to ask the question burning on the tip of her tongue. The haunted hollows of his eyes confirmed her worst fear. He hadn't found Deirdre. Blinking back a fresh sting of tears, she rose from the table and walked over to the stove and filled a cup with strong, dark coffee. She handed him the mug. "Drink."

He stared into his cup, swirling the coffee as if the answer to where his missing daughter was, lay in the steaming liquid.

"Come and eat. I made sandwiches." She touched his arm.

His eyes remained disconnected and vague.

She tightened her grip and tugged. "Dawson, you need to eat."

He heaved a heavy sigh and relented, and allowed her to lead him to his seat at the table.

"Drink," she urged again. Once he obeyed and sipped some coffee, she hurried over to the fridge and removed a platter of sandwiches. She placed a plate before him and piled it with sandwiches. "I made chicken, roast beef, ham, and egg salad. I didn't know what anyone would like, so I made everything I could find." She was babbling, but she couldn't stop the unceasing flow of words. His zombie-like behavior frightened her.

He sat rigid, staring into his cup.

"Dawson, you have to eat. Please."

He blinked and met her gaze.

She sucked in a ragged breath at the despair in his dark depths. "She'll be okay." She forced a bright smile. "She's a smart girl. She'll come riding back on Caspar, wondering what all the fuss is about. Just you wait."

"The men found Caspar."

"What? Then where's Dee? Why isn't she here?"

He rubbed his forehead with the pads of his fingers. "Dee wasn't with him."

She opened her mouth to ask more questions, but the bleak emptiness in his eyes silenced her.

"She's afraid of the dark. Did you know that? She'd never stay out this long, not at night. Not unless there's a reason she can't come home." A sob shook his broad shoulders. "I can't erase the image of her alone and hurt and crying for her daddy." He scrubbed his palms over his eyes. "She's all I've got. I don't know what I'd do if I lost her."

His words tore off the scab covering her own grief. All too well she recalled her devastating pain and guilt when Keegan died. It was as if her heart had been ripped out. But this wasn't about Keegan. Dee was alive. Hope wasn't lost. They'd find her. They had to. She placed her hands on his shoulders and squeezed, massaging the rigid stiffness of his knotted muscles.

He closed his eyes and released a long breath. His body relaxed, and he leaned his head against her breasts. His breathing slowed.

The clock ticked a steady beat. Five minutes passed, ten minutes…as her fingers continued their steady pressure, easing and soothing.

He heaved a sigh, opened his eyes, and sat up. A smile tugged the corners of his mouth. "Thanks."

"Better eat something before you head out again."

He tossed back the remainder of his coffee and grabbed a sandwich and wolfed it down in a few quick bites. Snagging another from the platter, he stood and strode toward the back door.

"Dawson."

He paused and turned back.

"You'll find her. I know you will."

He met her gaze and nodded, flung open the door, and was gone.

She sank on a chair and buried her face in her hands. *He'll find her.* The fervent prayer resonated through her head. *He'll find her.*

He had to. She couldn't live with her guilt if he didn't.

****

Hours later, as the morning sun shone through the big kitchen windows, Stella collapsed on a chair, folded her arms on the table, and rested her head on her arms. All night long, a steady stream of exhausted and hungry men had stopped by to fill their bellies with food and mugs of strong coffee before heading out again to continue the search.

She and Alf made plate after plate of thick sandwiches, pots of filling soup, and coffee…gallons of coffee. As the hours ticked by with no sign of Deirdre, hope diminished, and the ranch hands' faces grew more and more somber.

Just before dawn, she'd convinced Alf to get some much-needed rest. One look at his sunken, red-rimmed eyes, confirmed her worst fears. He was on the verge of collapse. He hadn't gone willingly, but eventually, he'd untied his apron and limped out of the kitchen. She hoped he was in his room resting.

Earlier, she'd overheard Sergeant Murphy and Corporal Pearson discussing the dangers Deirdre faced. She shuddered as she recalled their conversation. Hypothermia was the greatest threat. Even though the night was mild for the time of year, a strong wind blew, and it wouldn't take long before the child's internal temperature dropped and exposure set in.

She'd worked hard to block out their words, but now in the kitchen's empty silence they echoed hollowly. "No." She raised her voice to be heard over the rising doubt. "No way. Dawson will find her." Too tired to cry, she rubbed her aching eyes. Her eyelids were heavy, and she closed them, intending to rest for just a second until another searcher arrived looking for nourishment.

Loud, excited voices woke her. She opened her eyes and blinked. Lifting her head from the table, she rubbed her stiff neck and smoothed back her tangled hair.

The voices grew louder, buzzing with excitement.

Jumping up, she raced to the door and flung it open. She caught her breath and clutched the doorframe, her hand covering her mouth.

A mountain of a man dressed in a dirty, olive-green parka and a tattered gray wool toque pulled low over greasy strands of long graying hair strode across the porch carrying a motionless Deirdre.

Dawson rushed across the yard and bounded up the steps. "You found her! Thank the Lord. Where…where was she, Henry?"

"Out by Jack Pine Creek." The big man held Deirdre's still form cradled in his muscular arms like she was a newborn infant. "Looks like her horse threw her. She was lying under some trees. I almost passed her by, but luckily, I caught sight of her pink shirt."

Dawson's hand trembled as he brushed his palm against Deirdre's damp hair and trailed a finger along her pale cheek. Unshed tears glistened in his dark eyes. "What—" His throat worked. "—what's wrong with her? Why isn't she awake?"

Henry pressed Deirdre into Dawson's arms. "Looks like she hit her head when Caspar bucked her off. Poor little mite's got a lump the size of a tennis ball on the back of her head."

Cuddling Deirdre in his arms, Dawson sagged against the porch railing. "Thank you, Henry. Thank you for bringing back my little girl. How can I ever repay you?"

Under the glow of light streaming from the kitchen the big man's bearded cheeks flushed red. He sniffed and wiped his nose with his sleeve. "Shit, Dawson, I love Dee. You know that." His voice was gruff. "I'd do anything for her."

Tears filmed her eyes as Stella watched the emotional scene. So this was Henry Rivers. The man whose cabin she and Dawson had sought refuge in from the rainstorm. Somehow the reclusive trapper had found Deirdre. She studied Dee's pale face, and her heart lodged in her throat. The usually energetic dynamo lay unmoving like a rag doll in her father's arms.

Her breath hitched in her throat. The room wavered, and she clutched the doorframe for support. All of a sudden, she was back in Keegan's bedroom clasping his still body to her breasts, staring with dawning terror at his sightless eyes, and feeling the unnatural coldness of his flesh.

But this wasn't Keegan. This was Dee, and she was alive. She forced the heartrending memories away and focused on Dawson and the precious bundle in his arms. "What…what can I do to help?"

Dawson's anguished gaze met hers. "Tell Alf to call for help. Deirdre needs a doctor." He strode into the house. The door slammed shut after him.

She studied the circle of silent, watching men. Elbowing through the crowd, she grabbed Jean-Luc's arm. "Where's Alf?" Her voice was a thin squeak over the lump of fear threatening to choke her.

Rubbing his hands over dark stubble, he slipped off his stained cap and scrubbed his thick mop of dark hair. A deep furrow ran between his heavy, dark brows. His eyes were red rimmed and puffy. "I don't know. Last I saw the old man, he was in the barn saddling Kermit. Said he was gonna ride out and look for Dee." He patted her shoulder. "Don't you worry. I'll make the call." Shouldering through the men, he wrenched open the door and hurried into the kitchen.

The other men nodded good night and headed down the steps and into the night.

She turned to go back into the house, but Henry Rivers' big, burly body blocked the door.

He leaned so close his warm, stale breath washed over her. "I know the truth."

She stumbled back from the malice sparking in his heavy-lidded eyes. "What are you talking about? What truth?" She shot a look over her shoulder seeking help, but the porch was deserted. The exhausted searchers had slipped away to their beds. The porch was painted with dark shadows, but streaks of soft light leaked through the kitchen windows. "Please. Let me pass. I want to see Deirdre."

The icy glint in his eyes softened. "You love her, don't you?"

"I do." She swallowed over a sudden lump in her throat. Maybe she'd overreacted, and in the dark she'd mistaken his anger for concern over Dee. "Thank you for finding her. I don't"—another swallow—"know what Dawson would do if he lost Dee."

"That little girl and this ranch are his whole life. He wouldn't survive if someone hurt either one. You best remember that." He moved aside and lumbered across the porch and tromped down the steps and vanished into the shadows.

Inhaling a steadying breath, she brushed aside his enigmatic comment and yanked open the door and hurried through the kitchen and up the stairs. The hall was eerily quiet. She paused outside Deirdre's bedroom door. Squaring her shoulders, she tapped on the door and eased it open.

A heavy pall hung in the air. Dawson perched on the edge of the bed, his gaze fixed on his daughter's tiny form.

Shas lay on the floor at the foot of the bed. He raised his head and whined, his dark, liquid eyes shining when she entered the room. His tail thumped the floor.

Deirdre was motionless, her skin pale and waxen, her lips colorless. The smattering of freckles across her nose and cheeks stood out in sharp contrast to the stark whiteness of her skin. Her red hair was a snarled tangle, littered with twigs and dried leaves. Her thin chest rose and fell; her breathing was so shallow, the movement barely disturbed the quilt covering her small body.

Stella's heart pounded as she inched closer. "How is she?"

"I don't know. She won't wake up." Dawson's broad, tanned hand shook as he brushed a lock of flaming hair from Deirdre's dirt-smudged forehead. He looked like a man caught in the throes of a nightmare. His face was haggard. New lines bracketed his mouth and grooved between his dark brows. "I can't lose her, Stella. She's all I have."

Pain lanced through her at his all-too-familiar agony, but there was a huge difference—Deirdre was alive. As long as the child breathed, hope existed. She squeezed his shoulder. "She's strong, she'll get through this. The important thing is Henry found her, and you have her back."

His hand sought hers, and their fingers threaded, squeezing, as if drawing strength from her warmth.

She studied their joined hands...his large and tanned, scarred from working on the ranch...hers pale and small, more suited to an office than hard, physical labor. For some reason the stark contrast shot a bolt of heat straight to her center.

"I just heard. Is she okay?" Alf rushed into the room. His gray hair was mussed, and trail dust coated his weathered cheeks.

Dawson shook his head. "I don't know yet."

Alf ran his hands over his face, the rasp of his beard loud. "The investigators have arrived. The medical examiner's with them. I'll go see if he'll take a look at her." He spun around and hurried away.

Shas laid his big head on the end of the bed and whined.

Dawson's grip on her hand tightened.

Deirdre lay still, pale, and silent, so at odds from her usual boundless energy.

They both jumped when a tall, lean man with thinning blond hair swept back from a high forehead and wearing a pair of thick, dark-framed glasses, pushed open the door and stepped into the room. "I hear you have an injured little girl. I'm Dr. Peter Stavely. I'm a provincial medical examiner, but I assure you, I'm fully trained as a medical doctor." He shifted closer to the bed and studied Deirdre. "Do you mind if I take a look?"

Dawson released his grip on Stella's hand and stood. "I don't know what's wrong with her. She won't wake up."

"Let's take a look." The doctor rolled up his

sleeves, and in an efficient, methodical manner examined Deirdre.

Stella studied his every gesture, trying to read his diagnosis from his expression. She slid a glance at Dawson.

His face was a frozen mask out of which his eyes burned with a tortured light.

The doctor poked and prodded Deirdre's still body. Using a stethoscope he tugged from a worn leather bag, he lifted her shirt, rubbed the end of the stethoscope between his hands to warm the metal, and placed the end on Dee's slender chest. He listened for several long seconds before he smoothed down her top and covered her with the quilt. "She'll be fine."

Stella blew out a breath she wasn't aware she'd been holding.

"Why isn't she waking up?" Dawson's voice cracked.

"She's got a nasty bump on the back of her skull. It looks like she fell and hit her head. She should regain consciousness soon."

"She has a concussion?"

The doctor nodded. "Normally, I'd recommend she spend the night in the hospital under observation, maybe have a CAT scan, but..." His voice trailed off and he shrugged, his meaning clear. The nearest hospital was in Hosten or Bethany Springs. Both centers were several hours away by plane or helicopter.

Dawson's gaze flitted from his daughter's tiny form to the doctor. "Are you sure she'll be okay?"

"She'll have a headache for a few days, but she's young and healthy. She'll be running around causing trouble in no time."

Deirdre groaned, and her eyelids flickered and opened. "Daddy?"

Dawson stroked her cheek, his hand shaking. "I'm here, Dee. Daddy's here." A tear slid down his unshaven cheek and dripped off his chin onto the quilt.

Feeling like an intruder witnessing the intimate scene, Stella slipped out of the room. She halted in the hall, her legs weak as relief surged through her. Collapsing against the wall, she covered her face with her hands.

"Are you all right?" Doctor Stavely stood in front of her, a look of concern on his compassionate face.

"I'm just…I…I was so worried."

"She's a fortunate little girl."

"Wha…what about hypothermia? She was out in the cold all night."

"I didn't detect any evidence of hypothermia."

"Thank goodness." She exhaled a shaky breath.

"She'll need to be monitored for the next twenty-four hours."

"Of course. What should I look for?"

He explained Deirdre's care, and she listened with rapt attention, determined to do whatever she could to ensure the little girl made as quick a recovery as possible.

Alf shuffled down the hall, his craggy face filled with concern.

"She's okay, Alf, but she has a concussion," she said.

His gaze flew to the man beside her. "Doctor Stavely?"

"Go and see for yourself."

Alf's face lit up, and he looked as if he lost ten

years in a single heartbeat. With a joyous yelp, he opened the bedroom door and stepped into the room.

"Well, I'd better get going." The doctor unrolled the sleeves of his shirt. "I have a crime scene to examine."

Her hand flew to her chest. In all the worry about finding Deirdre, she'd forgotten the corpse in the meadow. "Is what the police think true? Was that poor man murdered?"

"From what the investigating officers told me, he was shot in the back, but whether it's murder, I don't know. I'll have to examine the body and the crime scene before I'll know for sure." He turned to leave.

"Doctor?"

His blond brows arched.

"Who—" She swallowed over the sudden dryness in her mouth. "—who was he?"

His eyes narrowed, and he stared at her as if trying to decide how much to reveal. "The victim's name was Hank Morrison. He was an employee of Imperial Monarch Resources. Now, if you'll excuse me, I have work to do." He strode down the hall to the stairs.

Chapter 14

Stella opened the door to Deirdre's room and peeked inside. A lamp bathed the room in a warm, golden glow.

Dawson hadn't moved from his vigil by his daughter's side. He slouched in a chair, his head slumped, resting his chin on his chest. His eyes were closed, and a low rattle of snores escaped his open mouth.

The regular rise and fall of the blankets covering Deirdre was reassuring. Her complexion was a healthier color, and the bruising circles rimming her eyes had faded.

Tiptoeing over to the bed, Stella perched on the edge and trailed her fingers across Deirdre's soft, warm cheek. Her heart swelled as she scanned the small, dear face, taking in the strong cheekbones and firm chin so like those of her father. They'd come close to losing this precious child. Too close. She hiccupped a sob and slapped her hand over her mouth to cover the sound.

Deirdre stirred. Her eyes opened, and her pale lips parted in a smile. "Stella, you're here."

A rush of warmth swept her. "Yes, Dee, I'm here."

"But you said you were leaving." Deirdre's lower lip trembled. "I don't want you to go." Tears filled her eyes and clung to her lashes. "Everyone leaves me. Mommy left. I don't want you to go, too. That's why I ran away. I don't want to be here without you."

Stella sniffed and blinked back tears. How could she break this dear child's heart? "Don't worry, honey. I'm not going anywhere, at least not for a long time." As soon as she uttered the words, she prayed they were true. Somehow she had to convince Dawson to allow her to stay.

Deirdre beamed, tears forgotten. "Really? You'll stay?"

Stella stroked the child's matted hair. "Really."

"Yes!" Deirdre's smile faded, and she yawned. "I'm so tired." She yawned again and winced. "Why does my head hurt?"

"You bumped your head when you fell off Caspar, but the doctor says you'll be fine in a few days. Go back to sleep. You need your rest."

A frown creased Dee's forehead. "Will you be here when I wake up?"

A lump formed in Stella's throat. She nodded.

"You promise?"

Tears blurred Stella's vision. "I promise."

Dee's lips curved in a smile. "I love you, Stella." Her eyes drifted closed. "I love you the bestest."

"I love you, too." As soon as she said the words, the truth hit her like a slap to the head. She loved Dee as if the precious child were her own flesh and blood.

"How is she?"

She swung toward Dawson.

He was awake, an inscrutable expression on his handsome face.

"She's tired and has a headache, but she seems fine."

"Why are you here?" He pinned her with a probing

look.

"I…I wanted to check on Dee. Make sure she's all right."

"Why do you care? You're leaving in a few days."

Her stomach twisted. "It's my fault she ran away."

"Your fault? You're not the one who told her that her new best friend was leaving." He rubbed his red-rimmed eyes. "I don't know what I would have done if I'd lost her. She's everything I have." Expelling a deep breath, he looked at her, his eyes bleak, riddled with guilt.

"You couldn't have known she'd run away."

"Don't you get it? I should have known. I should have been there. I'm her father. It's my job to protect her." Self-disgust coated his voice. "I let Anna down. Now Dee."

The weight of his guilt grounded her to the bed. She struggled to think how to ease his pain. Words were ineffective. She knew that all too well. No matter how many times she was told Keegan's death wasn't her fault, she didn't believe it. Her guilt over his senseless death lived inside her like a condemning specter, castigating with every beat of her heart.

"Will you stay on at the ranch like you promised her?"

Dawson's whiskey-rough voice broke into her thoughts.

"Please. Will you stay? She loves you." He swiped the back of his hand over his eyes. "I know we've had our…er…our difficulties, but, I'd like you to stay." A second ticked by. "For Dee."

For Dee.

His quiet plea pierced her heart like a fusillade of

arrows. Was that the only reason he wanted her to stay? For his daughter? She opened her mouth to tell him she was leaving anyway, but remembered her promise to the little girl. "Okay."

"Okay?" His breath expelled in a rush. "That's good. Real good. Thank you."

The gold band on the ring finger of his left hand glimmered in the lamplight, adding fresh pain. "I'll stay, but only until I figure out how to explain to her why I'm returning to Vancouver."

He studied her for a heartbeat. "I guess I don't have a choice. I'll have to be happy with that, but I have one request."

"What's that?" She braced for his next words.

"What do you say we start fresh, put aside our mistakes and begin again?"

"Mistakes?"

"Look, I don't know what this *thing* is between us. It's complicated, and it's clear that neither of us wants complications. Not now. Not with all the trouble going on around here." He propped his ankle on his opposite knee and jiggled his foot. "We have to forget what happened at Henry's cabin and again in the kitchen yesterday morning and move on. It's the only way this situation will work."

She sucked in a breath. Was he serious? Did he really expect her to ignore their passionate kisses? He might be able to forget, but she sure couldn't. Just imagining kissing him made her blood heat and her body tremble. But if that's what he wanted. "I agree. We can't allow Deirdre to be hurt by our foolish mistakes."

His mouth pursed as if he tasted something sour.

"You can be assured our *foolish* mistakes won't happen again."

The fixed smile on her face wobbled, but she soldiered on. "You can't imagine how relieved I am to hear that—" The roar of a helicopter filled the air and cut off the rest of her snide comment. She shot him a startled look.

His brows knit together in a frown. "Looks like more police have arrived."

"More police? What's going on?"

"I don't know, but whatever it is, it can't be good." He heaved to his feet and ran a hand over his rumpled hair. "Stay here with Dee. I'll go see what's up." Without waiting for her agreement, he strode out of the room.

She stumbled over to the chair he'd vacated and sank onto the hard surface.

The piercing roar of the helicopter swelled to a screaming crescendo, damping down to a rumble as the helicopter landed in the yard outside. The engine quit, and the silence that followed was deafening.

Deirdre slept on, undisturbed by the noise, her blue-veined eyelids fluttering as she dreamed.

Stella laid her hand on the soft wool blanket. The warmth from Deirdre's small body seeped into her palm. Being near Dee, seeing her so happy, healthy, and alive had ripped the scab off Stella's wounded heart. Before she'd come to the Circle 5, grief was her constant companion. All she thought of was Keegan and what could have been. But then, Dee burst into her life, and each day she woke up excited to spend the day with the energetic child. The pain of losing Keegan, though still a seeping wound, eased. She brushed her lips over Dee's smooth forehead.

"Stella." Alf hustled into the room. "They want to see you downstairs."

"Me? The police want to see me?"

His gaze didn't meet hers. "Go on. I'll watch Dee."

She rose from the chair and headed toward the door. "Call me if she wakes. I promised her I'd be here when she woke up." With a last, lingering glance at Deirdre, she shuffled down the hall. At the top of the stairs, she paused.

Loud, male voices rose from below. A door slammed, muting the heated conversation.

Something was definitely going on. Heart hammering, she descended the stairs and followed the voices to Dawson's office. She knocked, opened the door, and stepped inside. The small room was crowded and ripe with the odor of male sweat. Conversation ceased, and her skin prickled as all gazes fixed on her.

A man standing with his back to the door turned, a grin wreathing his fleshy face. "Hello, Stella. It's been a long time."

Staggering, she grabbed onto the back of a chair and held on. Her fingers dug into the soft leather. "Nicholas." His name rushed out in a squeak.

"You look good, Stel." He pried her hand off the chair back and clasped it between his large, soft, moist ones. "The great outdoors must agree with you."

She choked on a breath. He wasn't a mirage. The man standing before her was indeed her ex-husband, Nicholas King. A man whose last words to her had been bitter accusations blaming her for their son's death. She snatched back her hand, resisting the urge to wipe her palm on her pants. "What...what are you doing here?"

He frowned, but held his smile. "I missed you."

She snorted. They'd been divorced for almost a year, and in all that time their sole communication was through emails and texts. Even those short missives focused on business, and only when absolutely necessary. Since she'd been granted her leave of absence from Imperial Monarch Resources, she hadn't heard from him. She peered into his golden-brown eyes. As usual, they were shuttered. "You can do better than that, Nicholas. Why are you really here?"

He smoothed his hand over his gelled hair. "One of my employees was murdered. Another one's missing. I came to find out what the hell's going on. Imagine my shock when I heard you were here."

His words broke through the fog. "Someone's missing? One of our—" She broke off, all too aware the men crammed in the room watched with avid interest. "A man is missing? Are you sure? But how can that be? This whole ranch was searched just yesterday when we looked for Deirdre."

His mouth tightened. "Of course, I'm sure. I'm the one who assigned him the job." He edged a step closer. "The question is—why are *you* here?"

"That's a good question, Stella. Answer the man. Why *are* you here?" Dawson's face was like stone, but his eyes blazed.

She opened her mouth to say something, anything, but no words escaped. What could she say? How could she explain?

"Yeah, I thought so." His voice was filled with disgust. "You're one of them, aren't you? You work for that damn mining company."

"Work for them?" Nicholas snorted. "She's the senior legal counsel at Imperial Monarch Resources. Didn't she tell you?"

A heavy silence filled the room as Nicolas's words reverberated like gunshots.

"Dawson...I...I..." He turned his back, and the words died in her throat.

Sergeant Murphy elbowed to the front of the men facing her like an accusing tribunal. "Ms. King, it seems you've been withholding vital information and impeding this investigation." He jerked a thumb at Nicholas. "Is what your husband says true? Do you work for Imperial Monarch?"

Terrified of meeting his accusing eyes, she couldn't look at him, but she bobbed her head, admitting the damning truth.

Dawson's curse blasted the stuffy air.

"Why did you keep this information from me when I questioned you?" Murphy's thick brows bristled. "Never mind." He blew out a puff of air. "We'll discuss this later. For now, we have more important issues."

He nodded at Nicholas. "Mr. King informs us the gunshot victim wasn't working alone. Another geologist was with him. It's urgent we locate the missing man. He could be a witness or worse, he might be injured. Either way, it's essential we find him as soon as possible." He pointed at two uniformed officers. "Constables Perry and Johnson, take Mr. Wheeler's ATV and check the upper pasture again. You're looking for tire tracks, footprints, whatever, but find that man."

The officers nodded and brushed past Stella on their way out the door.

"I want to help." Nicholas's voice, filled with the ring of authority, boomed through the room. He was used to being in control and having others bend to his will.

"I'm sorry, but no." Sergeant Murphy's scrutiny was hardened steel. "We can't have amateurs stumbling around a potential crime scene."

"It's my company. These are my employees." High color flushed Nicholas's face. "I'll be damned if I'll sit here and do nothing." He shoved Murphy aside and stomped to the door.

"I'm going too. I know this ranch better than anyone," Dawson said and followed Nicholas.

Sergeant Murphy nodded to a uniformed officer.

The constable, a broad-shouldered, muscular man, who towered over the other men, stepped in front of the door and crossed his arms over his massive chest, blocking Dawson and Nicholas's charge out of the room.

Nicholas spun to the sergeant, his eyes shooting angry sparks. "Tell him to get the hell out of my way."

Murphy held up his hand. "You're not going anywhere. This is a murder investigation. *My* murder investigation." Anger coated his voice. "Both of you are suspects."

"Suspect?" Nicholas burst out. "Me? Are you kidding? I just got here. Before that, I was in meetings in Toronto. There's no way I could have done this. Besides, why would I?" His gaze skittered around the room, settling on Dawson. He pointed his finger. "There's your suspect, Sergeant. Dawson Wheeler has made no secret he doesn't want my employees on his land. Hell, two of my people filed complaints against him three weeks ago." His face was fierce. "He threatened to kill them if he found them on his property again. Have you asked him about that? Have you?"

Stella bit back a gasp.

Dawson's rugged face paled, and a thin white line rimmed his mouth.

"Look at him," Nicholas continued. "He can't even defend himself." He marched over to Dawson, his large, well-padded body bristling. "And what the hell are you doing with my ex-wife?" He grabbed Dawson's arm. "Do you think if you screw her, she'll convince the company's board members to halt this project?"

Dawson's eyes spit fire. "You're an ass, King." He threw off Nicholas's hold. His hands bunched into fists.

Sergeant Murphy stepped between the two men. "Enough! This isn't helping. I've got enough to do without playing referee between you two cock-of-the-walk roosters." He called to a uniformed policeman who stood in the corner by the window, "Keep an eye on these two. I'm going up in the helicopter to help with the search. Maybe we'll get lucky and spot something."

"Let me go with you, Sergeant," Dawson pleaded. "My men and I scoured most of the ranch looking for my daughter, and we didn't find any sign of this missing man. I can tell you the areas where we've already looked. That should refine the search parameters."

Murphy stared at Dawson and nodded. "Okay. Come on. That man's been out there for almost a week. We need to find him before this becomes a recovery mission rather than a rescue."

Dawson grabbed his hat from the desktop and

jammed it on his head, then glanced at Stella.

She shuddered at the anger smoldering in his eyes.

His mouth tightened and he stomped out of the room.

The remaining police officer looked from Stella to Nicholas. "I'll be outside." He followed the men out and closed the door behind him.

The room was empty…too empty. She released her grip on the chair and grasped the doorknob. She didn't want to be alone with Nicholas.

"Running away again?"

She shook her head. "I…I—"

"Look, this isn't getting us anywhere." He slouched against the desk. "We need to talk."

She kept her hand on the door handle. "You've said more than enough."

"I'm sorry. This murder has me on edge. Hank Morrison was a good employee. He didn't deserve to die like that. He was just doing his job and some wacko killed him. Shot him in the back, for God's sake." He swiped a hand over his face. "Do you have any idea what it's like to tell a woman she's a widow? I just hope to God we find his partner alive."

She searched his eyes. The golden brown had darkened under the sheen of tears. "You really care, don't you?"

"I guess I deserve that." He blew out a gust of air. "I imagine you hate me."

She studied his face. Lines etched across his forehead and grooved between his well-tweezed brows, lines that hadn't existed a year ago.

"I said some terrible things, and acted like an ass, but you weren't to blame for Keegan's death. I knew that then, but I hurt so much, I wanted you to hurt too." His voice cracked. "You loved him as much as I did." He pushed away from the desk and crossed the room. "I know it's months late in coming, probably too late, but I want you to know I'm sorry." He clasped her hand and his thumb caressed the back of her hand as he stared into her eyes. "Can you find it in your heart to forgive me?"

She chewed the inside of her cheek. This man had turned on her in her darkest moments, attacked when she was her most vulnerable. She'd hated him, but the grief etched across his face dulled some of her anger. She, better than anyone, knew how losing a child shattered a person and turned you into someone who uttered cruel words you never believed possible. "I...I don't know what to say."

"Say you forgive me, please." His fervent gaze fixed on her. "Let's take this first step toward healing. For Keegan."

Keegan.

The sound of his name sliced through her like a knife, and she flinched, grabbing her stomach to ease the familiar stab of pain. Tears filmed her eyes, matching the moisture in his.

"Please, Stel."

Her mouth opened and closed as she struggled for words. Forgive him? She didn't know if she could. He'd shattered her soul. But they had to move on. Maybe forgiveness was the first step toward healing.

The door burst open, and the stern-faced, muscular, uniformed police officer stood in the doorway. "They found him! They found the missing man."

Chapter 15

Dawson rubbed the grit from his burning eyes and sank onto the leather recliner. The house was quiet, a world apart from the chaos of the past hours. One man was dead, another critically injured. On his ranch! He raised his glass and gulped a mouthful of scotch, relishing the burn as the liquor worked its way down his throat and into his gut, dissolving the block of ice.

The RCMP had found the missing geologist bleeding from a bullet wound to his shoulder and huddled under a tree where he'd crawled after his ATV had crashed into a rock and slid down a bank into a creek. He'd broken his leg and was suffering from exposure and dehydration. The police had airlifted the injured man to the hospital trauma unit in Hosten, and he'd undergone emergency surgery. He hadn't regained consciousness, but hopes were high he would, and when he did, he'd be able to identify his attacker.

He took a long pull of his drink. Warm tendrils of alcohol seeped through his body, loosening the strained tightness in his back, his shoulders, and his neck. He slumped deeper into the chair, his legs splayed.

Sergeant Murphy had questioned everyone on the ranch again, but he hadn't hidden the fact that the focus of his interrogations was Dawson. They'd been sequestered in Dawson's office for over two hours while the stern-faced policeman had asked him who else was against the proposed mine. He grimaced. Murphy would have better luck figuring out who was in support of the damn development.

Dawson rubbed the back of his neck. Of course he was the prime suspect. He'd threatened the mining people. And why not? They wanted to destroy his ranch, to dig a giant pit and spew thousands of tons of poison into his watershed. What man who cared for his land would stand back and allow such devastation without doing everything in his power to stop it?

He rubbed his jaw and grimaced at the loud rasp of beard. He hadn't shaved in days. Hell, he hadn't slept or eaten in God knew how long either. Over the past three months, one disaster after another had befallen the Circle 5. And the bad only got worse with the arrival of Stella King. He slugged back another swallow.

Mrs. King.

He sneered. Chief legal counsel at Imperial Monarch Resources. *Married* to the owner of the damn mining company. All this time he'd known she was hiding something, but he'd never suspected her secret was something so vile. She knew how he felt about the proposed mine development; yet, she hadn't said a word. Not one damn word.

As if called forth by his thoughts, the tread of light footsteps sounded down the hall and Stella appeared at the bottom of the stairs, her arms filled with folded laundry.

His chair was in the shadows, and by the relaxed expression on her face, it was obvious she didn't know he was watching. In spite of her betrayal, he couldn't look away. He licked his dry lips and drank his fill. Her hair was a golden halo around her beautiful face, her lips pink and moist.

He winced at the familiar kick in his gut. Even now he wanted to kiss her and hold her, and feel her soft warm body crushed to his. What the hell was wrong with him? He cursed and banged his glass on the table.

Her body stiffened, and she spun toward him. The laundry fell to the floor. "Dawson. I...I didn't see you."

He fought to control his racing heart. *She lied to you. She's been lying since the moment she arrived.* The condemning words rang through him, cooling his ardor like a dousing of ice water. "Where's your husband?"

Her face flamed. "Nicholas is my ex-husband. We divorced months ago."

Ex-husband.

A tiny spurt of—relief? happiness?—filled him. But then he remembered her betrayal. "What's it like to work for a major mining corporation? Do you get a kick out of digging holes in pristine land, fouling streams, and cutting down forests for profit?" Once started, he couldn't halt the acid stream of vitriol. "Tell me the truth. Is it fun to destroy wildlife habitats, pollute the ground, ruin people's lives? Do you enjoy that?"

He smirked. "I bet you do. You only care about your high-priced salary so you can shop in fancy boutiques and eat in exclusive restaurants. Yup, you're all about the money, aren't you?" Panting as if he'd run a kilometer, he grabbed his glass, and ignoring the tremor in his hand, drained the last of his drink.

She stood frozen under the force of his vicious attack, her azure-blue eyes wide and unblinking.

A door slammed somewhere upstairs. The wind buffeted the large glass window as a storm brewed. A log shifted in the fireplace.

She marched closer, not stopping until she stood over him, her eyes blazing. Two red patches on her cheeks stained her creamy skin. "You have no right to talk to me like that. What I did before I came here is none of your business." She bit off each word as if it were a separate sliver of ice. "I may work for you, but you don't own me."

"No, I don't, but that damn mining company sure does." He forced a laugh, but the sound was harsh and false. He wanted another drink more than he wanted his next breath of air, but he couldn't get up without bumping into her. "You came into my house, lady, *my* house. You lied to me. I have a right to know why."

Some of the fire drained from her body, and she stumbled back a step. Her upper teeth worked her lower lip. "I'm sorry I didn't tell you of my connection to Imperial Monarch."

"Connection? You're their goddamned lawyer."

"You never would have hired me if you knew."

"Damn straight I wouldn't." He surged to his feet, brushed past her, and strode over to the shelf where he'd left the bottle of scotch. He fought to hide his shaking hands as he filled his glass to the brim.

"I haven't worked at Imperial Monarch for over a year. Ever since Keegan—" She paused as if the words were too painful. "—ever since he was born, I've been on a leave of absence."

"So? What difference does that make? You're married to the damn owner." He sounded like a petulant boy, but her betrayal was too painful, and he couldn't halt his attack.

"*Was* married. Nicholas and I have been divorced

for almost a year." She inhaled a deep breath. The movement tightened her sweater, revealing the fullness of her breasts.

And just like that his anger fled, and a searing wave of heat washed over him. He reeled as if he'd been struck. Was he disloyal to Anna by desiring another woman, drooling over the swell of her hips, the endless length of her slim legs, wanting her with every cell of his being?

He bit back a groan. His fingers clamped like a vise around the drink in his hand until he feared he'd shatter the glass. He wheeled around and fled to the fireplace, desperate to put distance between them before he did something really stupid like kiss her.

"When we divorced, I signed over my shares in the business." She ran a hand over her hair. "I'm no longer connected in any way to Imperial Monarch."

He lost focus for a heartbeat as he stared at the rippling strands of gold. Distance wasn't helping. Sweat broke out under his armpits, but his mouth was bone dry.

She inhaled another breath. "I'm sorry. I should have told you, but I didn't know Imperial Monarch had anything to do with your ranch, not at first."

"I'm supposed to believe you?"

"It's the truth."

Again, silence stretched between them. The house creaked in a sudden blast of wind. Rain pelted the window, sounding like tiny fingernails scratching the glass.

"Why did you want to work at the Circle 5?" He asked the question that had eaten at his gut since her ex-husband arrived, and Dawson learned the shocking truth. "You don't need the money. You're way overqualified. Why would someone like you come all the way out here to look after a little girl?"

"I…I needed a…a change."

"A change? That's why you came?" He waved his hands at the rustic view of the white-capped lake and distant mountains visible through the large rain-streaked window. "This isn't a change from the city, lady; it's another planet."

"After…after Keegan died, I couldn't stand to be in my house. The empty rooms and the choking silence reminded me of what I'd lost." She tugged at a lock of hair and twirled the golden strand around her fingers. "I sold the house and bought a condo, but that didn't help.

"I extended my leave of absence from work, but it still wasn't enough. Finally, I went to a grief counselor. She convinced me I needed a complete change, to go somewhere no one knew of my loss, and bitter memories weren't lurking around every corner." Her chest heaved, and she glared as if daring him to comment.

He stared. Hell, he couldn't look away, even though the raw pain on her face staggered him, almost dragging him to his knees. The air between them percolated with a well of heated emotions—anger, grief, loss, guilt—all exposed like bedrock. His hand shook as he set his glass on the mantel and crossed the room. He drew her stiff body into his arms. "I'm so very sorry."

Her muscles loosened, and she sagged into his embrace and gave in to tears.

He crooned soothing words and stroked her long fall of silken hair like he did for Deirdre when she hurt.

Her tears dampened his shirt, but he nestled her closer, wanting to ease her pain, yet knowing nothing he said or did would bring back her son.

The light streaming in the windows was dim, and the fire had almost burned out when she stopped shaking.

Heat from her soft body burned through his clothes, and in a nanosecond, desire raged through him like a wildfire. He bit back a groan. Her familiar scent reminded him of wild roses and clover in June, and he swallowed, his throat dry. "Stella." Her name was a croak, filled with a different sort of pain—the agony of wanting her; the certainty he didn't deserve her; the knowledge he couldn't have her.

The tip of her tongue peeked out and swiped her bottom lip, and his good intentions vanished like a mist.

Kiss her.

The urgent demand screamed through him.

Kiss her!

She must have read the intent in his eyes because her mouth tightened, and her eyes shuttered. Shoving off his arms, she backed away. "Don't you think it'll be crowded in your bed with you, me, and your wife's ghost?"

He flinched as though she'd slapped him. "Stella, no—"

She shook her head and ran out of the room.

He staggered across the room and fumbled for the glass on the carved wooden mantel. His wedding ring caught the light and blazed like a neon sign. Guilt swamped him. He slammed the glass back down and covered his face with his hands.

****

"Look at this, Stella. Look what I can do." Deirdre's high-pitched cry echoed in the cavernous barn.

Stella stopped brushing Caspar's gleaming white coat.

Deirdre was standing on top of a large bale of hay, jumping and spinning in circles as she tossed clumps of straw in the air. "Whee!"

"Careful. You don't want to fall. Remember what the doctor said. You're to take it easy for the next few days." In spite of her concern, she smiled at the child's antics. The hit on her head and the time spent alone in the forest hadn't slowed her exuberance. She'd recovered unscathed, and it was all Stella could do to rein in Dee's boundless energy. She set the brush on the shelf. "Let's go inside and read a story. It's time you rested."

"Awww." Dee stuck out her lower lip in a pout. "Do I have to? Can't we stay and play a little longer?"

Stella bit back a sigh and stretched her aching shoulders. She hadn't had a moment's rest since Deirdre had awakened her at first light, eager to get on with the day's activities. Normally, she could handle anything Dee threw at her, but not that day, not when Stella had spent the night tossing and turning, reliving every second of her upsetting conversation with Dawson.

If she closed her eyes, images of his heated gaze paraded before her, his pupils dark pools of desire, his arms warm where they held her close. The intoxicating weight of his lean length and hard muscles pressed against her curves.

He'd been going to kiss her.

C. B. Clark

She'd wanted him to, but with the flash of gold at the corner of her eye, her desire died, doused by the sight of his wedding band. Her anger flared, and she'd wielded it like a shield against her desire.

"Whoohoo! Look, Stella, I'm flying."

Stella jerked out of her dark thoughts.

Deirdre was clinging to a rope extending from the loft, swinging back and forth over the barn floor in wide arcs.

"Get down this minute," she ordered, her heart in her throat. The doctor had explained the importance of Deirdre resting. Swinging from a rope like Tarzan was probably not his idea of rest.

"Watch, Stella. Watch me do it again."

"Deirdre Wheeler, get down from there this minute." She jammed her hands on her hips and marched over to where Dee hung from the rope.

Deirdre let go of the rope, screeching as she fell, landing with a thump on a bale of hay.

"Are you all right?" Stella ran her hands over Dee's body checking for injuries, and finding none, lifted her in her arms and hugged her.

"That was fun." An impish grin lit Dee's freckled face. "Can I do it again? Please?"

"No more playing Tarzan. Let's go in and read a story."

Dee's small face lit up, and she squirmed free of Stella's arms. "I love Tarzan. That's the bestest movie." She pounded her tiny fists against her chest, hooting the distinctive gorilla-like yell.

Stella made a show of covering her ears against the loud scream.

"Looks like you've got your hands full today,

194

Stella." Alf stood inside the barn, a wide grin wreathing his lined face. "Our Miss Dee is giving you a run for your money."

Stella blew a strand of hair off her damp face. "Her little escapade the other night doesn't seem to have affected her at all."

He stepped into the barn and clasped Deirdre's hand. "Let me take her. You look done in. Why don't you catch a nap while I read Dee a story?"

Alf's offer was tempting, but she shook her head. "Thanks, but I'm fine." He had enough on his plate. He carried his sixty-odd years well, but he wasn't a young man. Besides, looking after Deirdre was her job.

"No way, Stella. You're not ruining my fun. I haven't had much of a chance to spend time with this little monkey these past few days." He grinned at Deirdre. "What do you say, Dee?"

Deirdre leaped up and down and clapped her hands. "Yes, Alf. Please. I want one of your special stories." She tugged him toward the barn door. "Come on. Let's go."

Alf chuckled and called over his shoulder to Stella. "If you don't want to nap, why don't you take Caspar out for a ride. It's a mighty nice day. The fresh air would do you good." He stomped out of the barn, Deirdre skipping beside him.

She studied the sunlight streaming through the open barn door and glanced at Caspar.

The horse tossed his head and nickered.

Alf was right. It was a beautiful fall day. Escaping, if only for a brief time, the tension of being in the close confines of the ranch house with Dawson, was tempting. A ride in the fresh air would clear her head.

She'd come to the Circle 5 seeking a refuge from her grief. Her unbridled attraction for Dawson, a man still in love with his dead wife, was an entanglement she hadn't counted on.

The icing on the cake was Nicholas's unexpected arrival. Her ex-husband had spent the past days ensconced in a guest bedroom down the hall from her room. He'd tried to talk to her, but she'd brushed him off. She wasn't in the mood to hear more about the proposed mine. He'd finally tired of the rustic accommodations and her cold attitude and had arranged to leave that day.

Dust motes danced in the broad band of sunshine streaming through the open barn door. The day was too nice to be stuck inside. Her time at the ranch was limited. Soon she'd be back in the city. Why waste this gorgeous day?

She hesitated. The police hadn't caught the murderer. The killer could still be out there. She squashed the niggle of fear. Whoever had shot the geologists was long gone. Why would he hang around where the police were searching?

Caspar waited patiently while she grabbed the wool saddle pad and settled the thick red blanket on his back. She hefted the heavy saddle from the bench, staggered over to the horse, heaved the saddle over the pad, and cinched the straps. Next, she guided the bridle over his muzzle and slipped the bit between his teeth. She looped the reins over his head and lowered the stirrups. Placing the toe of her boot in the stirrup, she climbed onto the saddle. "Okay, boy. Let's do this."

Tightening her thighs, she kicked her heels against Caspar's flanks and urged the horse out of the barn and through the yard to the field beyond. As they loped across the open grassland, she breathed in the fresh scents of horse, pine trees, and sun-warmed grass.

She loved the rugged beauty of this land, the forested foothills, the endless acres of open grassland, the small, hidden aquamarine lakes, tumbling streams, and thick stands of mature pine trees. The air was so clear the distant mountains, gleaming under a mantle of fresh snow on their jagged peaks, looked close enough to touch.

A raven cawed from high atop a nearby pine, its croak echoing across the open meadow.

Geese honked as they flew in a vee across the clear blue sky heading south.

Winter was on its way, and she shivered at the bite in the air. The first snow had fallen three days ago, and temperatures had dipped to freezing, a foreshadowing of the icy blast to come. But that day a bright sun shone, warming the frigid ground and glistening on the melting patches of snow.

The sun was a warm caress on her back, and she slowed Caspar to a walk. The log ranch house and the white-capped, cobalt-blue waters of Checheko Lake were visible in the distance, but there on the hills above, the house and barn were tiny, like a child's toy structures, and her worries a world away. Inhaling a cleansing breath of brisk air, she relaxed as the weight of tension eased.

A sudden roar broke the peace of the day as a small plane circled overhead. Sunlight flashed off its twin metal pontoons as the plane banked and swung around, aligning with the lake. The small craft's engines blasted to a fever pitch as it swooped lower and lower.

Her light mood vanished.

More police. More questions. In the past few days, a steady stream of homicide detectives, crime scene investigators, and uniformed officers had descended on the ranch.

The thunder of the plane's engine dialed back to a roar as the plane landed on the water and taxied to the wharf. The pilot cut the engine.

In the sudden silence, a branch snapped like a gunshot.

Caspar's ears pricked and he nickered.

She scanned the dark shadows beneath the thick stand of trees.

More rustling. A clump of bushes swayed.

The skin on the back of her neck prickled. She peered through the tangle of evergreen boughs.

An enormous black bear wandered into the clearing. The creature's head was down, its large, brown snout nosing through the wild rose bushes and blueberry shrubs.

Adrenaline seared through her blood like a supernova. She couldn't breathe, couldn't move a single muscle, not even to scream. Every horror story she'd heard of bears attacking people ran through her brain. Alf had told her what to do if she encountered a bear. Don't run. Don't look the bear in the eyes. Wave your arms. Make yourself look big. Shout.

But the bear was too big and too close. She was terrified if she moved the animal would attack.

Caspar tossed his mane and nickered again and pranced backward.

The bear's head shot up, and the beast stared with small, dark, feral eyes.

Time slowed. Every sense intensified—the bear's musty, wet-dog smell; the wind soughing through the branches; the riot of ambers and bronzes of the leaves on the poplar trees. A single golden leaf spiraled through the air as if in slow motion.

The muscles on Caspar's sides rippled, and he jerked his head up, fighting to break free of the reins.

The bear grunted and rose on its hind legs, its big head bobbing.

A thin trickle of sweat dripped down the back of her neck.

Chapter 16

The huge black bear reared up on its hind legs, and from a hundred meters away, Dawson's heart stopped beating. He kicked Rocky into a gallop, slid his rifle out of the leather scabbard strapped to his saddle, and laid the gun across his lap.

He scanned the forest, but couldn't see a cub.

That's good.

The bear was curious and wanted a better look at the woman and horse.

Probably.

The animal turned at the pounding of hoofbeats, snorted, dropped on all fours, and lumbered into the forest.

Dawson reined in Rocky, and the big horse skidded to a stop, kicking up a hail of mud and grass. "What the hell do you think you're doing out here alone?" His fear of what could have happened made his voice harsher than he intended.

"Dawson. Thank God. I was so…so frightened—"

He cut her off. "What were you thinking? You shouldn't be riding alone."

"It's such a nice day. I…I wanted to get out…I never thought—"

"That's just it. You didn't think. You shouldn't be out here on your own. It's not safe." He jerked his thumb over his shoulder in the direction the bear had run. "That bear could just as easily have attacked you as run away. Bears are generally shy around people, but in the fall, they become more aggressive in their relentless quest for food." One thing he'd learned over his years in the wilderness, you couldn't predict what a wild animal would do, especially if it felt threatened. The thought of what could have happened made him shudder.

"I hardly think the bear would attack when I'm on Caspar."

"Lady, you should hear some of the stories the old timers tell about bear attacks. They'd have you running right back to that city you love so much."

She smoothed her hand over Caspar's neck, soothing the nervous horse. "I...I guess we were lucky."

"Have you forgotten a murderer's on the loose? What the hell were you doing out here alone?"

"And who would go with me?" Her lip curled in a sneer. "You?"

Yes, me. The words blazed through him bursting to be spoken aloud, but self preservation rose to the fore, and he said instead, "I'm sure your husband would be happy to go with you."

"My *ex*-husband."

"You could have asked him to ride with you."

"Nicholas doesn't ride. Besides, he's leaving today."

"You must be sad. I'm sure you'll miss him." The tightening of her mouth made it clear his efforts to hide his fake sincerity failed.

"Nicholas and I—" She cleared her throat. "—well, we're not close. We've hardly spoken since Keegan died."

She and her ex weren't close. His heart skipped a beat. That was good. Real good. He slid the rifle into the case and studied her.

Her fair skin glowed from the fresh air. Her golden hair, tangled from her ride, caressed her shoulders. The moist softness of her full lips reminded him of kissing her and how sweet she tasted.

Without pausing to think of the consequences, he nudged Rocky closer to her mount, grasped Caspar's reins, and held the horse steady. Gaze locked on Stella, he leaned over and captured her mouth with his.

The second their lips touched, the truth hit him like a bolt of lightning. He was wrong, her lips tasted sweeter than he remembered, so much sweeter. With a groan, he deepened the kiss, urging her mouth open.

The pungent scents of horse, autumn leaves, and Stella washed over him.

Her tongue stroked his, igniting a rush of fiery heat.

His knees weakened, and it was all he could do not to fall off the saddle. Needing more, so much more, he swung her from her saddle and settled her on his lap. He cupped her bottom and snuggled her softness between his thighs.

Even through the thickness of their coats, the enticing fullness of her breasts stirred his senses. Ignoring the warning sirens clamoring in his head, he slipped his hands under her jacket and caressed her silken skin, following the soft indentations of her ribs.

Rocky snorted and pranced in a tight circle, but the desire raging through Dawson was too fierce to stop. His fingers found the peaks of her swelling breasts. All fear of wild animals and murderers on the loose vanished as desire cascaded over him.

Rocky's fear-filled neigh acted like a splash of cold water.

Dawson pulled free of Stella's embrace, and chest heaving he searched the clearing. Something was up. Had the bear returned?

Caspar grazed a few feet away, munching on dried grass.

Birds flitted in the trees. A breeze rustled the golden, dried leaves.

A flock of sandhill cranes flew overhead, filling the air with their loud, rattling, bugle calls.

No bear.

No threat he could see.

He patted Rocky's sweaty neck. "Easy boy. Settle down. Nothing to worry about." He turned his attention back to the beautiful woman in his arms. "Now, where were we?"

"What's that?" She stiffened.

Focused on a single golden curl, admiring its silken softness, he murmured, "Don't worry. The bear's long gone. Rocky's just jumpy."

"I saw something—" She pointed behind him. "—up there, on the ridge."

He followed the direction of her gaze. Tall trees swayed in the rising wind, and swallows swept and dove in the warm air currents. "I don't see anything."

"I don't either. Not anymore, but I was sure—"

"Come here." He tilted her face to his. Their lips met. She threaded her fingers through the hair at the nape of his neck, igniting a thousand fires.

He tightened his arms, drawing her closer in spite

of the tight confines of the saddle. He wanted more, so much more, but he couldn't get close enough. Not on the damn horse.

She mewed a protest and tugged his shirt free of his jeans and slipped her soft hands under the tail of his shirt and over his stomach.

Her touch detonated a barrage of sensations.

Rocky snorted, his powerful muscles tensing beneath Dawson's thighs.

A trill of alarm filtered through the sensual haze fogging his brain. Digging deep, using super-human strength, he tore his mouth free and studied the meadow.

Caspar had stopped grazing, and his ears twitched. His tail was clamped tight between his back legs. Something had him spooked.

Dawson's unease skyrocketed. Was that a flicker of movement on the top of the bluff? He narrowed his eyes and squinted into the sun.

A person. Silhouetted on the ridge. Watching them.

Dawson's heart skipped a beat.

The man's bearded face was shadowed by a dark cowboy hat.

Who was he? One of the ranch hands? A trespasser? The murderer? Dawson's unease ratcheted to the next level, but before he could warn Stella, the man raised a rifle, settled the weapon into his shoulder, and sighted along the long barrel, pointing the deadly weapon at them.

Adrenaline kicked in like a boot to the gut. Dawson leaped off the saddle, dragging Stella with him. "Get down!" Shoving her behind a small outcropping of rock, he dove in behind her.

The ground where they'd been standing exploded in a cloud of dirt and mud. A loud crack resonated across the valley.

Rocky neighed and reared onto his hind legs, his eyes rolling, nostrils flaring.

Caspar tossed his head and galloped into the trees, Rocky hot on his heels.

"What was that?" Stella's voice was laced with fear. She craned her head and peered around the rock.

"Stay down." He flattened his body on top of hers.

Another loud crack echoed over the narrow valley, and the trunk of a nearby pine tree shattered.

He had to do something. They were sitting ducks. The rocks didn't provide enough cover. It was only a matter of minutes before one of the bullets found its mark. Jamming his hat on his head, he shifted to a crouch. "Stay here and don't move." He crawled from behind the protection of the rock and crept through the sea of tall grasses and shrubs, keeping his head low.

Body braced for the impact of a bullet, he covered the distance to the thick stand of trees in seconds. Once in the concealing shadows, he surged to his feet and ran through the trees, heading at an angle to the bluff. If he reached the base of the hill undetected, he could sneak up the backside and surprise the shooter.

Maybe.

Heart pounding, breath rasping, he raced up the bluff. Sweat dampened his forehead, and trickles of moisture leaked from under his arms as he clambered over the final jumble of boulders. He crouched behind a rocky outcrop, fighting for breath.

The clump of willows where the shooter had stood was deserted. Flattened grass and scuffmarks marred the rocky ground. Two empty, brass shell casings shone in the sun. The bastard must have heard Dawson's approach and taken off.

He placed his hand over his brow, blocking the afternoon sun's glare. Where was the man? He couldn't have gone far. He studied the rippling waves of grass and stands of pine trees. Was the intruder skulking in one of the gullies carved into the land by passing glaciers eons ago, biding his time, waiting to take his next shot?

Nothing stirred. No sign of the shooter. It was as if he'd vanished in a puff of air.

Dawson blew out a breath and peered over the edge of the bluff. His heart stuttered, and a chill threaded along his spine. Stella's red jacket shone like a flag from behind the rock where she crouched.

The shooter hadn't wanted to kill them. They'd be dead if that were the case. He'd had a clear shot. The intention had been to frighten them.

Dawson wiped his damp forehead with the sleeve of his coat and skidded down the hill in a hail of rocks and dirt. The hairs on the back of his neck prickled with the certainty he was being watched. The sooner they left the exposed meadow, the better.

The second Stella spotted him, she ran into his arms.

Her terror-filled sobs wrenched his soul. He tightened his embrace. "It's okay. We're safe. He's gone." He studied the surrounding hills praying he was telling the truth, but he couldn't shake the twitch centered in the middle of his back and the certainty they were too damned exposed. "Let's get out of here."

"How?" Her voice was frantic. "The horses ran

off."

He placed two fingers in his mouth and whistled.

An answering neigh echoed from within the woods.

He whistled again, and the crackle and snap of horse hooves on the forest floor grew louder.

Rocky emerged from the trees followed by Caspar. Both horses were skittish and rolled their eyes, their ears pricked upright, nostrils flaring, their long tails tucked between their legs.

"Easy, boy." Dawson dug out a sugar cube from his pants pocket and held out his hand, palm up. "Easy. That a boy. Good boy."

Rocky's ears flattened, his big head bobbing and weaving, but he didn't run. He nuzzled Dawson's palm and chewed the sugar cube.

Dawson held the reins and rubbed the horse's soft snout. "Good boy."

Caspar bumped the back of Dawson's neck, warm moist air gusting in fragrant waves, wanting some sugar.

Dawson fished in his pocket for another cube and offered it to Caspar. He rubbed the horses' sweaty necks, thanking the good Lord the frightened animals hadn't run off. He'd taken them on hunting trips plenty of times so the sound of gunshots weren't unfamiliar, but animals smelled fear, and he'd been pretty damn frightened.

He held Caspar steady and motioned to Stella. "Come on. Let's saddle up."

Her face was ashen as she placed her boot in the stirrup and climbed onto the saddle.

He leaped onto Rocky's back, then leaned over and

unclipped the covering to the rifle strapped to the side of the saddle. If anyone shot at them, he sure as hell was shooting back.

****

She was never so glad to see something as she was to see the metal roof of the old log barn glistening in the sun. Holding tight to Caspar's reins, she urged him into a trot and followed Dawson and his horse into the open corral.

Dawson dismounted Rocky and grasped Caspar's reins. His dark gaze met hers. "You okay?"

She nodded, though she was anything but okay. She doubted she'd ever be okay again. *Someone had tried to kill them.* The terrifying truth had echoed through her as they galloped back to the ranch house. She clambered off Caspar, her knees wobbling as a sudden weakness overwhelmed her.

Dawson caught her in his arms as she crumpled. "Hey, you're safe now."

She burrowed into his warmth. "Was it—" Her throat worked as she swallowed. "—was it the same man who shot the geologists?"

"Probably."

Beneath her cheek, the timbre of his voice rumbled deep in his chest. His comforting, familiar masculine scent surrounded her. "I was terrified when you went after that man. I…" She sucked in a breath. "You could have been killed."

He loosened his embrace and eased back so he could see her face. "You were pretty brave yourself."

She studied him through the blur of tears. "Really?"

"You bet. You faced down the bear, and you held it

together when the bullets were flying. That's gutsy any way you look at it."

Her mouth trembled in a smile. "So I'm not just a city slicker?"

"No way." He chuckled, the sound rich and warm. "You're a gal after my own heart...a real cowgirl."

A gal after my own heart.

The sweet words blossomed and filled the space between them. In the next breath, he cupped the back of her head, tilted her face to his, and kissed her. Not just any kiss, but a deep, probing, curl-your-toes kind of kiss.

She melted against him.

"Well, well, well. Isn't this cute. I guess it's true what they say about buckle bunnies. They'll kiss any man in a cowboy hat."

Nicolas's sardonic voice broke through the passionate haze heating her blood. She backed out of Dawson's arms. "Nicholas. What...what are you doing here? I thought you were leaving."

Nicholas's legs were stuffed into designer jeans. Gleaming, high-heeled alligator-skin cowboy boots covered his feet. His stomach strained against the pearl buttons on his silk shirt. A leather belt with a large shiny buckle completed his urban cowboy ensemble.

"Last I checked, I'm here because one of my employees was killed and another gravely wounded." His dark brows arched. "Your employees too, I might add. Or have you forgotten?"

She staggered back from the anger radiating off him. "Of course I haven't forgotten. Dawson and I were just—"

"I know exactly what you were doing, and I can't

say I'm impressed. Jesus, Stella, a man is dead, murdered in cold blood, and this guy—" He pointed an accusing finger at Dawson. "—is the prime suspect."

She opened her mouth to explain she and Dawson were just…just what? If Nicholas hadn't appeared, who knew where their kisses would have led. "Nicholas—"

"I don't give a damn if you want to play *house* with the cowboy." His scathing gaze raked Dawson. "What I do care about is my company and the people who work for me. You used to care, too." He jerked a thumb over his shoulder. "The police are waiting for you in the house. They have more questions. Come on." He grasped her arm and started towing her behind him.

Dawson stepped forward, his face a thunderous cloud, his eyes spitting fire. "Get your hands off her."

Nicholas dropped her arm like he'd been scalded.

She shivered at the fury coloring Dawson's handsome face.

His hands were clenched at his sides, his muscles bunched, ready to strike.

"It's okay, Dawson. I'll be all right." She forced a calmness she didn't feel to her voice. "Why don't you go in and tell Sergeant Murphy about the man who shot at us? I want to talk to Nicholas."

"Someone shot at you?" Nicholas's face blanched. "Jesus Christ, Stella. Why didn't you tell me? You could have been killed."

She ignored his outburst and focused on Dawson. "Go on. I'll see you inside in a few minutes."

He hesitated, his reluctance to leave her alone with Nicholas clear.

"Please?" After everything that had happened, she couldn't bear any more drama. Her stomach still cramped at the memory of being a target for a murderer.

With a shrug, Dawson spun and strode across the corral, through the gate, and over to the house. The screen door slammed.

Nicholas clasped her shoulder. "Stel, talk to me. Tell me what happened. Did someone really shoot at you? My God. Are you okay? Did you see the shooter?"

She shrugged off his hand. "Please don't touch me."

He held up both hands, palms out. "I'm sorry. It's just that I'm worried about you. You could have been killed."

His earnest gaze met hers, his apology deflating her anger. She offered him a weak smile. "I'm fine. You don't need to worry."

"You know, no matter what you think, I still care. That's why I decided not to leave today. It's not safe here." He ran his hands over his face. "I was hoping I'd be able to talk you into leaving with me."

Suddenly she was exhausted, almost too tired to stand. It had been a hell of a long day, and the police with all their questions awaited. "Look, I appreciate your concern, but let's not do this now."

"Okay. Whatever you want, but please think about what I said. There's a murderer hanging around this place, and he doesn't seem to care who he shoots." He kicked at a loose mound of straw. Dust filled the air, and he sneezed. He yanked a handkerchief out of his back pocket and sneezed again. "Damn allergies."

"I'll talk to you later." As if she were crossing a hundred kilometers rather than twenty meters, she trudged out of the corral and across the yard to the house.

Chapter 17

"Are you okay? You're shaking like a leaf." Alf clucked like a mother hen and handed her a steaming mug of coffee the second she stepped into the crowded kitchen. "Dawson told us what happened. Poor girl. You must have been terrified."

She sipped the welcome brew, and an instant jolt of heat and caffeine punched her bloodstream like a hit of cocaine.

Sergeant Murphy sat at the table beside two serious-looking men who wore attire more suited for the city than the rugged ranch. With their matching light-brown hair buzzed in a military-style, their identical, hard, penetrating gazes, and their stern, all-business bearing, they were clones of each other.

A uniformed RCMP officer wearing a bulletproof vest over his gray shirt and regulation cap stood at attention by the door.

Dawson leaned against the wall, his arms crossed in front of his broad chest. His face was a thunderous dark cloud.

Sneakers lay at his feet. The dog's ears pricked up at the sight of her, and his tail thumped the floor.

Swallowing another gulp of the high-test coffee, she stumbled to an empty chair before her legs gave out. She sank onto the hard-backed chair and folded her freezing hands around the warm mug.

Murphy pointed to a chair. "You too, Dawson. We need to hear from both of you exactly what happened."

Dawson pushed away from the wall, stepped over the dog, and settled at the table.

Murphy gestured at the two new arrivals. "Detectives Samuelson and Francis are on loan from the Vancouver Homicide Investigation Unit. I asked them to come out here and take a look at the situation."

The investigators nodded acknowledgment, but didn't speak.

Silence reigned, thickening and expanding with each passing second. The fire hissed, and a log shifted with a shower of sparks. Sneakers whined.

Alf bustled over refilling mugs. He stopped and stared. "You're as pale as a ghost, Stella. No wonder, you poor thing." He tugged off his cap and mopped his forehead with a red-checkered, cloth handkerchief he'd tugged from his back pocket. "I can't believe someone shot at you and Dawson. How terrifying. You must be a bundle of nerves."

She swallowed, her mouth dry in spite of the coffee. Her tongue was thick, and she couldn't seem to form words as the full horror of what happened hit her.

Dawson kneaded the back of his neck. "The bastard used a high-powered rifle."

Murphy stiffened, and his eyes narrowed. "Are you sure?"

"I found the shell casings. They're from the same type of rifle you said the killer used to shoot those geologists. The same one used to kill my cattle." He fished in the front pocket of his jeans and hauled out two shiny brass bullet casings. "I should have left these where I found them, but I was afraid the shooter would come back and take them." He dropped the casings on the table. They landed with an ominous clunk.

She stared at the gleaming brass casings and shivered. They looked benign, almost pretty, not something with the power to maim and kill.

Detective Samuelson—or was it Detective Francis?—tugged a pair of nitrile gloves from the inside pocket of his suit coat. Slipping the gloves over his hands, he picked up the bullet casings, examined them, and slipped them in a small paper envelope Detective Francis handed him. "I'll have the lab look at these, but you're right. They're not your typical hunter's ammunition."

Sergeant Murphy turned to Dawson. "Tell us again what happened."

While Dawson described the chilling events in the meadow, she shuddered. An image of the corpse she'd found rose before her. That could just as easily have been her and Dawson. They could be lying bloodied and dead, food for the eagles and crows.

Her stomach heaved. She fought back the waves of nausea, but bile surged up her throat. Slapping a hand over her mouth, she bolted to her feet and raced for the kitchen door, elbowing past the burly policeman. *Bathroom. Now.*

"Stella, are you okay?" Alf's worried voice followed her into the hall.

She bounded up the stairs and rushed into her bedroom, flung open the door to the adjoining bathroom, and fell to her knees, spewing vomit into the toilet.

When the spasms eased, she sank back on her heels and wiped the back of her hand over her mouth. Sweat beaded her upper lip, and she closed her eyes and focused on deep breathing. The sour stink of half-digested food permeated the air.

She rose on shaky legs. Clutching the edge of the sink, she turned on the tap and splashed her face. The cold water was invigorating, and after rinsing her mouth, she felt almost human again. She tottered to the bedroom and sank on the edge of the bed.

"Stella?" Deirdre peeked around the half-open bedroom door.

Stella forced a smile. "Hey, Dee."

"Are you okay?" She crept into the room. "You don't look so good." Dee spoke in an exaggerated whisper.

Stella's mouth twisted. Trust a child to state the obvious. "Why are you whispering?"

"Daddy made me promise I wouldn't bug you." The child's blue-eyed gaze scoured Stella's face.

In spite of her turmoil, Stella smiled. "So, if your father told you not to disturb me, why are you in here?"

A flush suffused Deirdre's cheeks. "I missed you." She plopped on the bed, bouncing on the mattress, before settling her warm body against Stella.

Stella's heart swelled. How was she going to leave this child? Where would she find the strength?

"You're not mad, are you?" Dee twisted a red curl around her finger.

Stella hugged her. "Of course not. I missed you too."

"Why are those policemen here?" Dee twisted her thin hands in a knot. "They scare me."

Stella sucked in a breath. How to explain the events of the past days to a five-year-old? She couldn't tell Deirdre about the murder or the man who'd shot at her and Dawson today. The poor child would have nightmares. She grasped Deirdre's hands, halting the nervous twisting. "You shouldn't be frightened of them. They're here to help."

Dee's blue eyes studied Stella. Her lower lip trembled. "Is Daddy in trouble?"

"Of course not." Her face heated at the lie. Dawson was the number-one suspect, but surely not after today, not after someone shot at them.

Shas padded into the room, his tail wagging like a metronome, and leaped on the bed. Tongue lolling, he licked Deirdre's face.

She giggled. "Shas, stop."

The dog gave a few more licks and settled with a groan beside Deirdre.

Deirdre petted the dog as she swung her legs on the edge of the bed. "I don't like your friend."

"My friend?"

A tiny furrow appeared between Dee's red-gold brows. "He told me he was taking you home. Are you going to go with him?" Her luminous blue eyes studied Stella. "Are you going to leave me and Daddy?"

She was saved from having to answer by a knock on the door.

Deirdre jumped off the bed and ran to the door and flung it open.

Nicholas stood in the doorway. He brushed past Deirdre and strode into the room as if it were something he did every day. "Hi, Stel."

Shas raised his shaggy head and growled.

Nicholas stilled and eyed the dog warily. "Have you thought about what I said? Are you coming with

217

me?"

She frowned and nodded toward the listening Deirdre, trying to get Nicholas to shut up, but it was too late.

Deirdre jumped off the bed, her hands on her hips and glared at Nicholas. "She's not going anywhere. Not with you. She promised she'd stay. Good people don't break promises. Right, Stella? You promised."

"Oh, Dee." Stella reached for the little girl, but she backed away. "You don't have to worry. I'm not leaving."

"But he said—"

"I'm not leaving, Dee. At least, not for a long time." She clasped the girl in a quick hug. Her gaze met Nicholas's over the child's head.

Nicholas mouthed a silent apology, but instead of leaving the room, he perched on the edge of the bed as far from Shas's low, rumbling growl as possible. "We need to talk, Stella. Alone." He shot a piercing glance at Deirdre. "It's important."

She was too tired to deal with him now, but the determined expression on his face was all too familiar. Once his mind was set on something, he wouldn't be deterred. With a sinking sensation, knowing she wasn't going to like what he had to say, she turned to Deirdre. "Why don't you see if you can find the game you were telling me about this morning? You know, the one with the hippos? We'll play as soon as Nicholas and I are finished talking."

Deirdre's face lit up. "Promise?"

"I promise." Stella crossed her finger over her heart in an X.

Deirdre shot Nicholas a fierce glare and skipped

out of the room, making a big point of leaving the door wide open.

With a final growl, Shas jumped off the bed and loped after the little girl.

Stella smiled at the child and dog's protectiveness.

"So, that's the kid you came all this way to look after." His mouth tightened. "She seems a handful."

A wave of fierce protectiveness washed over her. "What are you talking about? Dee's a great kid." She dragged in a deep breath. "I'm tired, Nicholas. What did you want to discuss?"

He rose and strolled to the window and looked out. "My God, Stella, how do you stand it? I get why you needed some time off from work after"—his voice cracked—"our son died. That's why I encouraged the Board to grant your extended leave." He faced her. "But this—" He waved his arm at the scene outside the window. "—this is the back of beyond."

"I like it here. The Circle 5 is beautiful. You should see the acres of grasslands, the thick forests, the snow-covered mountains, the crystalline lakes…" His eyes glazed over, and she trailed off. He was a man more comfortable golfing on the manicured greens at his exclusive country club than walking through a stand of old growth pine trees.

"You do realize our company is hoping to develop a mine here, don't you? A very *unpopular* mine. Dawson Wheeler hasn't hidden the fact he'll do anything to stop the mine from proceeding."

"I didn't know anything about that when I took the job." She chewed on the inside of her cheek. "I just needed to get away for awhile."

"Well, you picked a poor time to find your inner

zen. Whoever shot our geologists has made it clear he doesn't like Imperial Monarch employees. Your name's still on the company website. That's probably why someone shot at you today. Did you consider that? Have you thought of the danger you're in? I sure as hell have. I can't stop worrying about you." He stuffed his hands in the front pockets of his designer jeans. "Pack your bags. You're leaving with me."

"I'm not going anywhere."

He returned to the bed and plopped down beside her. "Of course you are. A murderer's skulking around your little Garden of Eden. For God's sake, Stella, you were almost killed today." He grasped her hand. "Look, I don't want to argue. Come with me. Please." He pinned her with a fervent gaze. "It's time you went back to work. The company misses you. *I* miss you. Keegan's been gone more than a year. Time for you to move on with your life."

Anger burned like a live coal in her gut. She yanked her hand free. "Are you serious? Move on with my life? How can you say that? How can you even think of moving on?" Tears burned her eyes, but she blinked them back. "We lost our son. Our *baby*. I'll never get over his death. Ever."

His brown eyes glistened with unshed tears. "You don't own the rights to grief, Stella. I miss him as much as you." His voice was low and thick. "He was my son, too."

She wiped her eyes with her sleeve and swallowed over the lump in her throat. "I know you loved Keegan."

He sniffed, tugged out a monogrammed silk handkerchief, and blew his nose. "When Keegan—"

His Adam's apple bobbed up and down in his throat as he swallowed. "—when he died…I…I was angry at everyone." His voice thickened. "How could my vibrant little boy be gone? How could he be dead? I wanted to blame someone, anyone."

Tears streamed down his smooth cheeks. "I chose you. You were an easy target. You were there." He sniffed. "I'm not proud of myself. Hell, I know it wasn't your fault. I knew it then too, but I was so devastated by grief, I struck out at you and said things, terrible things." His red, swollen eyes stared out of his blotchy face. "I…I'm so sorry. I've wanted to apologize for a long time. I just didn't know how."

The anger she'd carried like a burden all these months dissolved in the face of his genuine remorse. She leaned into him and wrapped her arms around him and clung to his familiar body, finding comfort in their shared grief.

He drew back and inhaled a wobbly breath. "Look, this isn't how I planned to tell you, but I…ah…I met someone." His eyes were sheepish and wary. "We're getting married."

She swallowed her surprise. Somehow she'd never expected him to remarry. Affairs? Yes, but not the permanence of marriage. "That's great. I'm happy for you." And she was. The anger and resentment she'd borne him all those months was gone. She wanted him to be happy, to move on with life. Even if she couldn't.

He flashed his famous one-hundred-watt grin. "Wait until you meet her. You'll like her." His smile faltered, and he squeezed her hand. "We want children."

"Then you should have them. You were a

wonderful father to Keegan." Again, she blinked back the sting of tears.

His face lit like a beacon, and he smiled. The lines of grief eased, and for the first time in many months, he resembled the man she'd married. He pressed his lips to her damp cheek. "Thank you, Stel. Thank you for everything."

A loud cough broke the intimate moment, and she sprang away.

Dawson stood in the doorway. A scowl marred his rugged good looks, and his dark eyes blazed. "Deirdre was worried about you, Stella. She asked me to check on you, but I see you're fine. You're both fine."

The venom in his voice struck her dumb.

His lips curled in a sneer. "When you two are finished doing whatever it is you're doing, Sergeant Murphy would like to see both of you in the kitchen." With a last scathing smirk, he stormed out of the room and stomped down the hall, his boots pounding a staccato rhythm on the hardwood floors.

"Sorry, Stel. Seems I got you in trouble with your employer."

Stella's body vibrated with fury. How dare Dawson imply she and Nicholas were doing something inappropriate? Who was he to judge her? "It's not your fault. He has no right to be angry."

"He seems to think he does." He clasped her hand again, forcing her to look at him. "Is something going on between you and the backwoods farmer? Something I should know?"

She jerked her hand free. "Of course not."

"I hope you're right. He could be a killer. You'd best remember that." He toyed with the tasseled trim on the bedspread. "What I have to tell you isn't going to help the situation." His gaze swung away from hers. "I just heard we received the okay on our proposal. Looks like the mine's a go."

"What?" Her heart skipped a beat. "How did that happen so quickly? These projects usually take years to get approved."

He shrugged. "Who knows? One of our people greased the right wheels, whispered in the right ears, climbed into bed with the right person. What do I care? Just so long as Imperial Monarch can push ahead with the next step."

"Where's the mine going to be located?"

"Over near Munson Lake. We're planning to use the lake for our tailings pond if we can get environmental approval." He brushed a speck of dirt off his pant leg. "I have the plans in my room if you want to look at them."

She huffed out a breath. Munson Lake was a few short kilometers from the ranch house. She and Dawson had ridden by the small, pristine lake on their way to Tor's Ridge. "You're going to develop a copper mine on the Circle 5 Ranch?"

"Yep." He wouldn't look at her.

"But Dawson and his family live here."

"He'll be fully compensated. You know that. He'll make a fortune." He met her gaze, and one eyebrow arched. "What's the big deal? Why are you so upset? It's just one more mine in an area no one gives a shit about."

She shook her head. How could he not understand? "People live here. This land is their home."

"Yeah, and with the money they'll make on this

deal, they can make their home somewhere else."

"You can't do this! I won't let you."

His eyes narrowed. "Why do you care? We've done the same thing dozens of times. You know the drill. Why are you so upset about this mine?" A light dawned in his eyes. "You care for him, don't you?" He frowned. "You've fallen in love with this cowpoke." He gripped her arm. "You can't be serious. He's trouble. Even I can see that." His grip tightened. "Even if he isn't guilty of murder, the man has issues, serious issues. You don't need that in your life, Stel."

She shoved off his hand and sprang to her feet. "You don't know what you're talking about. I'm not in love with Dawson." She forced a laugh, but the brittle sound stuck in her throat. "I know how much this land means to him, and I don't want him to get hurt. That's all this is. Simple, human compassion."

"Whatever you say, Stel, but your *boyfriend's* going to have to accept the fact a copper mine will be developed on his property." He patted her arm. "Progress." He stood and smoothed his shirt over his bulging belly. "As soon as Sergeant Murphy and his men find the maniac who attacked our geologists and shot at you, we'll shift into phase one of development plans."

We'll see about that.

The fervent words reared with shocking intensity, and in that moment, she vowed, no matter what happened between her and Dawson, she'd do her level best, employ whatever power she wielded, call in favors due, whatever it entailed, to stop the mine development from destroying the Circle 5.

Chapter 18

Dawson raised the ax over his head and slammed the blade down on the stump. The resounding whack boomed and echoed across the lake and surrounding hills. Once more he smashed down, cleaving the knotty wood in half. Sweat dripped off his brow and into his eyes. His hands and arms were numb from pounding the ax again and again into one hunk of wood after another.

With every swing, he pictured Nicholas King's smarmy face on the block of wood. As the wood split, he experienced a momentary satisfaction that vanished as soon it appeared. How he'd love to smash his fist into the creep's face. Who did he think he was? Putting his hands all over Stella. Kissing her!

From the second he laid eyes on King, he'd taken a dislike to the man. Not only was he head of Imperial Monarch Resources and determined to destroy Dawson's land, but he didn't bother to the hide the fact he looked down upon those who lived and worked outside the city.

And then there were his clothes.

Where the hell had King found those jeans? With their designer logo and skintight fit, it was a miracle the man could walk without squeaking. And his boots? How many alligators had been killed so King could prance around in fancy, thousand-dollar footwear?

He swung the ax again, shattering the log into a dozen jagged chunks. Wiping the sweat from his brow with the sleeve of his shirt, he stared off into the surrounding forest. He'd been angry when he found King and Stella together. Hell, he was still fuming.

He'd stormed away from her room, his fury pounding. One force drove him—the visceral need to smash something. Hard.

Alf had been waiting in the hall, watching him with those all-knowing eyes.

He swung the ax, grunting with the bone-jarring impact as the blade buried deep in the block of wood.

Their conversation still burned.

"Get out of my way, Alf." Dawson glowered at the old man.

Alf held his ground. "Not until I shake some sense into that thick head of yours."

Dawson could shove his friend aside. Hell, he outweighed him by a good hundred pounds, but past experience had taught him avoiding the coming confrontation would be futile. Alf was like a terrier after a badger. He wouldn't leave Dawson alone until he had his say. He sucked in a deep breath and fought to rein in his anger. "Okay, go ahead. What horrible crime have I committed?"

"You're a damn fool."

Dawson gave a half shrug. "What's new?"

Alf shook his head. "I know you miss Anna, son. I know that. But it's time to stop wearing that ring and walking around like you died, too. You deserve a chance at happiness. It's not your fault Anna did what she did. You've got to forgive yourself and start living again. You hear me? It's time."

226

Dawson stared at his left hand. His wedding ring shone in the hall light as if imbued with a life of its own. He squeezed his hand into a fist and faced Alf. "You have no idea what you're talking about. You don't know what it's like—"

Alf slammed his hands on his hips and thrust out his chest. "You're dumber than I thought. You really don't know, do you?"

"Know what?"

"Have you stopped to ask yourself why you're so angry Stella's husband is here?"

"Ex-husband!"

"Exactly." With that oblique comment, Alf twisted around and sauntered down the hall with his bandy-legged stride.

Alf's words didn't make any more sense now. Of course Dawson was furious that Nicholas King was at the Circle 5. Why wouldn't he be? The arrogant SOB was the goddamned president of the goddamned mining company that was determined to destroy his land. His outrage had nothing to do with Stella and King having a history together.

Nothing at all.

He raised the ax over his shoulder and crashed the blade down, grunting at the impact of steel on wood. Groaning, he rubbed his shoulder and stretched his aching back.

He glanced at the pile of split wood. Jean-Luc would be happy. The ranch hand was responsible for supplying the ranch with firewood. In the past two hours Dawson had chopped enough wood to last them a month, even in the coldest of winters. Exhaustion washed over him, and he sank on the ground and leaned back against the chopping block. He closed his eyes.

"I was told I'd find you out here."

He squinted into the glare of the afternoon sun.

Sergeant Murphy stood beside the jumbled pile of split wood, his legs apart, hands clasped behind his back. His badge glinted in the warm sunshine.

Dawson's gut clenched.

"Let's talk." Murphy shifted out of the sun's glare and settled on a stump. The lines on his craggy face were carved deep, his mouth tight. "Dan Turner, the wounded geologist, regained consciousness."

A wave of relief washed over Dawson. One death on his property was more than enough. "That's great. How's he doing?"

Murphy shrugged. "About as well as can be expected for a man who took a bullet and hid out in the wilderness for several days. He lost a hell of a lot of blood." He picked up a twig and twisted it around his fingers. "He remembers some of the events surrounding the attack."

Dawson sat upright. "Did he see who shot him?"

The policeman's sharp gaze pinned Dawson. "His memories of the incident are vague, as you'd expect, and the shooter was a good distance away, but Turner says he got a good look." The stick in his hand snapped with a loud crack. He tossed the pieces on the ground. "He says the shooter was you."

The air in Dawson's lungs expelled in a burst. "What?"

"Turner says he's pretty certain you shot him and his partner." Murphy's gaze never left his face.

"Me? Why the hell would I shoot them?" He sagged against the woodpile. Stupid question. By his own admission, he was on record as having made threats against the mining company's employees who trespassed on his land.

"Turner said the man who shot him and his partner was tall like you, and he wore a dark-brown cowboy hat." He nodded at the hat perched on Dawson's head.

Dawson ripped off his hat and stared at the brown-felt cowboy hat. He tossed it toward Murphy. "Lots of men wear hats like this. Hell, they sell them in Hosten." He surged to his feet. "I lost my hat last week over by Henry Rivers' cabin when we had that bad storm. Anyone could have found the hat." He picked up his hat and smacked the wide brim on his thigh. "This is an old one I've had for years. I have another one just like it in the barn." He kicked a hunk of wood, sending it flying across the yard.

Murphy's knees cracked as he stood. "All the same, Dawson, this doesn't look good."

"You think I'm the killer? The man who shot at me and Stella had a dark beard. Did Turner say anything about a beard?" The throbbing in the back of his neck escalated to a screaming pitch.

Murphy shook his head. "The killer's face was shadowed by the hat brim."

"There, see? It could have been anyone." He huffed out a breath. "Do you really believe I killed one man and wounded another?" His entire body bristled with outrage. "And I shot my own cattle?"

"If I did, you'd be in handcuffs, and I'd be hauling you into Hosten for interrogation."

Some of the clamping tension in his neck eased. "So you don't think I did it?"

"I didn't say that." Murphy's face hardened.

"There's not enough evidence to be certain. Not yet, anyway."

"Your men have been searching for days. Have they found any sign of this guy? Any evidence of where he's hiding out?"

"The men followed his tracks on the bluff, but they lost the signs on the rocky scree."

"I'll find the bastard. He can't hide on my ranch. Not for long." Dawson snagged his hat from the ground and jammed it on his head. "I'll track him down and haul his ass in."

"No, you won't. You're not going anywhere."

He spun back to Murphy. "Look, I know this country better than anyone. Your men haven't found this guy. My crew and I will."

Murphy's face remained impassive. "We've been friends for a long time, Dawson, and I appreciate your offer of help, but it's best if you stay out of the investigation and remain at the ranch house."

"To hell with that." He turned toward the barn, his mind already on saddling Rocky and heading out on the search.

Murphy's commanding voice stopped him cold. "Don't force my hand. If you leave the ranch house area, I'll have my men restrain you."

"You're kidding, right?" But the steel in the other man's eyes told Dawson better than words that Murphy hadn't offered an empty threat. He spit out a stream of curses. "Okay. You win, I'll stick around, but I'm not happy about it, not one damn bit."

"One more thing. Call a lawyer. You might need one." The sergeant nodded and strode across the yard and up the steps to the porch and into the house.

Dawson stormed back to the woodpile and yanked the ax from the cutting block. The heavy blade sliced through the air with a gratifying whoosh and embedded deep in the log.

****

She downed the last dregs of the cold coffee in her cup, and grimaced at the bitter taste. Her stomach roiled in protest. How many cups of Alf's high-octane coffee had she drunk that morning? Three? Four?

Once again, she hadn't been able to sleep and had tossed and turned through the long night. Nicholas's news that the mine had passed the first stages of development and was going to be built on Dawson's ranch had shaken her to her core. Somehow she had to stop the process. She had to save the Circle 5. If not for Dawson, then for Dee.

As if conjured by her thoughts, Nicholas strode into the kitchen wearing a red-and-black-checked flannel shirt under a quilted down vest, jeans, and heavy work boots. He looked like an advertisement from an outdoor adventure catalogue. "There you are, Stel. I was looking for you." He nodded at her cup. "Any more coffee?"

She pointed at the large pot simmering on the stove. "Help yourself."

He strode over to the stove and filled a cup with steaming coffee. "Want some?"

Her stomach spasmed, and she shook her head. Another cup of coffee was the last thing she needed. Already her nerves buzzed, and her hands trembled.

Pulling out a chair, he sat across the table from her and sipped his coffee. "Ahhh. This hits the spot. That cranky little guy makes damn good coffee." Silence settled over them, broken only by the steady ticking of the clock and the crackle and pop of the fire. "I suppose you heard."

She curled her fingers around her empty cup and squeezed. "Heard what?"

"Dan Turner regained consciousness and identified Wheeler as the shooter."

Her mouth opened and closed, her words stuck in her throat.

He slurped more coffee. "If you ask me, they should arrest him and be done with it."

"But that's—" She swallowed and tried again. "—that's not possible. Dawson was with me when we were attacked yesterday. That had to be the same person who shot the geologists. You heard the investigators. The shooter used the same ammo. Dawson couldn't have done it. He couldn't be in two places at once."

"Wheeler's threatened my men in the past. It's not a stretch to believe that when these two guys wouldn't leave, he tried to kill them." He shuddered. "I wish the cops would arrest him like I asked. No one's safe as long as that man's walking around free."

"Dawson's innocent."

"Don't you think it's pretty damn convenient that just when it looks like Wheeler's the number-one suspect, he suddenly spots this guy toting a rifle?" His lip curled. "And when the police go searching, they can't find hide nor hair of this mystery man? Come on, Stel, the guy's playing you."

"Someone shot at us. Believe me, I was there. Those bullets were real."

"Did you see the shooter?"

"I saw someone, but he was a long ways away. I'm

not sure who it was."

He smiled smugly as if she'd proven his point. "The man's the boss. He could have arranged for one of his men to stand up on that ridge and take potshots at you." He leaned closer. "Did any of those bullets come close to hitting you?"

Her grip on the cup handle tightened so much she feared the handle would break. Every time she closed her eyes the ear-splitting crack of the bullets striking the tree and rocks sickened her. Whoever was shooting meant business. "You're wrong. Dawson wouldn't do that, and none of his men would either."

He captured her hand in his. "Look, Stel, I know you like the guy."

She opened her mouth to protest, but he cut her off.

"Come on. It's obvious he's worked a number on you. But you need to think with your head, not your heart." He tightened his grip. "Wheeler's made no secret of the fact he'll stop at nothing to prevent a mine going in on his property. He's threatened my men— y*our* men too, for that matter. One of the victims identified him, for God's sake." He released her hand and sat back and crossed his arms over his chest. "The guy's guilty. What more proof do you need?"

She stared at the sprinkling of coffee grounds in the bottom of her empty mug. Nicholas was only saying what the police believed. Dawson had told her he'd do whatever it took to prevent the mine development. But that was his anger talking. He wouldn't go this far. He wouldn't kill anyone. And what about the previous day? Someone *had* shot at them, and it wasn't Dawson, or any of his men. She'd swear to that.

The table creaked as Nicholas leaned his elbows on

the top. "Look, Stel, I don't want you staying here. You're not safe." His fervent gaze bore into hers. "I'm going to check out the proposed mine site this morning, and then I'm flying back to Vancouver. Come with me."

Her breath hitched in her throat. Leave the Circle 5? Leave Dawson? She struggled to swallow. What about Deirdre? The last time she'd said she was leaving, the little girl had run away. She shook her head. "I...I can't, not yet."

He expelled a gust of air. "What do you think will happen once Wheeler learns about the mine? How do you think he'll react? Who will he blame? Do you want to be here when his hold on reality snaps, and he explodes? The man's a minefield."

"What's all this?" Dawson barked from the doorway. His eyes were burning coals as he glared at first Nicholas and then zeroed in on her. "Are you talking about me?"

Her mouth dried, and her stomach twisted.

He marched into the room and stood, legs wide, hands braced on his narrow hips. "Well? Are you going to tell me what you two are conspiring about?"

Nicholas shot her a look.

She hung her head, unable to meet Dawson's steel-glazed gaze.

A chair scraped across the floor and Nicholas stood. He faced Dawson. "I might as well tell you. You're going to know soon enough, Wheeler. Yesterday, Imperial Monarch received the okay from the provincial government to go forward with stage two of the development of a copper mine."

A thin white line rimmed Dawson's tight mouth. A

pulse beat in his clenched jaw. "Where is this mine going to be located?" Banked rage lurked behind his quiet tone.

"About three kilometers from here, near Munson Lake."

Dawson didn't flinch. The only evidence he'd heard Nicholas was the dilation of his pupils turning his eyes into bleak, dark holes.

Nicholas fell back a step as if he were afraid Dawson would lunge across the table and attack.

Dawson's accusing gaze settled on her. "How long have you known?"

She opened her mouth, but the words stuck in her throat.

"Don't blame her. Stella isn't part of this," Nicholas blustered. "She's no longer involved in the direct running of the company."

"I didn't ask you, King." Dawson's gaze didn't waver. "I asked *her*."

She squirmed on her chair, wishing with the essence of her soul to be anywhere but there. "I...I—"

His hand shot up, silencing her. "Yeah. That's what I figured." His words were laced with disgust.

"Dawson, I...I'm so sorry. I know this isn't what you wanted to hear."

A harsh, painful laugh burst from his lips. "You people are all the same. You have no damn idea how much this ranch means to me, to Alf, to Deirdre. All you see when you look at the Circle 5 is how much money you can make from raping the land."

Nicholas rushed to her side and draped his arm protectively around her shoulders. "You have no right to talk to her like that, Wheeler."

Dawson's gaze never left hers. "I want to hear you say it, Stella. I want you to tell me you don't give a shit about the Circle 5. How you don't care that your damn mine will ruin this land. How it'll destroy me and Deirdre."

She clapped her hands over her ears, refusing to listen to any more of his vitriol.

"That's it," Nicholas said. "I'm getting Sergeant Murphy." He lifted his arm, grabbed her hand and tugged her across the kitchen to the door leading to the hall.

His words roused her out of her stupor, and she dug in her heels. "Nicholas, stop." She breathed in a lung full of air. "I...I want to answer his question." Her mouth was so dry her tongue wouldn't work, but finally she forced out the words. "You're wrong, Dawson. I do care for this land. Maybe I didn't before, but I do now." She pointed out the kitchen window at the view of distant snow-covered mountains and verdant, forested hills. "I don't want a mine development in this area any more than you do."

He snorted.

She ignored his disbelief. "I promise you, I'll do whatever I can to stop this from happening. The mine isn't a done deal. Imperial Monarch has to complete an archaeological impact assessment and an environmental review. If that doesn't stop the mine, you can appeal to the government. Appeals take years to work their way through the courts." She held out her hands. "I'll help you. We'll stall this mine until it's no longer feasible to develop."

A minute, two minutes, three minutes ticked by, each one lasting an eternity.

Dawson chuckled, the sound false and chilling. "I just bet you will."

"She's leaving, Wheeler," Nicholas said. "She's flying out with me this afternoon."

"Why am I not surprised?" Dawson's lip curled in sneer. He spun around and stomped out of the room. The door slammed shut with a reverberating bang.

Chapter 19

"This man's in bad shape. We need help here!"

"Call Sergeant Murphy!"

"Hurry."

Dawson raised his head at the babble of frantic voices penetrating the thick log walls from outside the house. *What the hell's happened now?* He slammed the tumbler of scotch on the desk.

The thunder of feet pounded down the stairs and raced to the back door.

Shit.

He grabbed the glass again and drained the contents. He was going to need the fortitude to face this new calamity. Pushing to his feet, he strode out of his office and down the hall to the kitchen.

All four of the remaining police investigators, Sergeant Murphy, and Alf huddled around a man's motionless body lying on the kitchen table.

Sweat beaded his upper lip as he plodded on leaden feet toward the table, terrified of what he'd see.

The men shifted.

Blood, there was so much blood. My God, Nicholas King! Dread bubbled like acid in his stomach. "What happened?"

"He's been shot," Alf said.

Shot? He stared at the wounded man, stunned into inaction.

King's face was a ghastly shade of gray, his eyes sunken, his lips pale and bloodless. But there *was* blood. Lots of blood. A bright red stream seeped from a gaping wound in the unconscious man's chest and pooled on the table.

He tore his gaze from the gore. His head swam in a fog as he fought to take in the frantic scene.

One of the policemen climbed onto the table and crouched over King, wedged a compress to the wound, and pressed, stanching the flow of blood.

Another uniformed officer grasped the injured man's thick wrist and measured his pulse.

Stella rushed into the room. Her face blanched, and her anguished cry rent the air. "Nicholas!" She lunged toward the wounded man.

"Let these men look after him. They know what they're doing." Dawson wrapped his arms around her and rested her head against his chest, preventing her from witnessing the shocking sight of her ex-husband lying in a pool of blood. He lowered his voice and spoke in her ear. "He's alive, Stella. He's still breathing. He's alive."

She fought his restraint, but he held her tight until her struggles eased, and she sagged in his arms. Her hair hung in damp tendrils down her back. He breathed in the scent of soap and wild roses. She must have been in the shower when the alarm was raised.

Her blouse was buttoned wrong, and her feet were bare. Tears flowed down her face.

He fished in the back pocket of his jeans and removed his cloth handkerchief and dabbed at her tears.

"How...how is he?" Her voice was a hoarse croak.

Sergeant Murphy glanced over his shoulder. "He's

lost a lot of blood, Mrs. King, and he needs immediate medical attention. The medevac team has been called, but they're busy with another call right now. As soon as they're done, they'll send the helicopter, and we'll fly your husband to the trauma center in Hosten."

Alf cleared his throat. "Weather forecast says a bad storm's brewing. By the time they get the helicopter in the air, it could be too late."

Murphy's mouth tightened.

"I'll fly him." Dawson spoke through the rising tension. "I can have my plane ready to fly in fifteen minutes."

Murphy turned to the man holding pressure on the wounded man's chest. "How's he doing?"

The officer shook his head.

Stella moaned. "Nicholas."

"Come on, Sergeant. We're wasting time," said Dawson. "Let me fly him to Hosten."

Murphy tugged on his mustache, his indecision all too clear. "I can't let you do this."

"Why? Because I'm a suspect." Dawson pointed at the bleeding man. "That's bullshit and you know it. I didn't shoot King. I was here in the house." He slid a glance at Stella. The anguish in her eyes struck him like a mule kick to the gut. She'd already lost so much. He wouldn't let her lose someone else she loved. "I'm your best bet. If we don't get this man to the hospital, you're going to have another murder on your hands."

Murphy blew out a ragged breath. He turned to the men hovering by the table. "Okay. Let's do this." He swiped his gleaming forehead. "I want him ready for transport in fifteen minutes." He met Dawson's gaze. "Get that plane of yours ready."

Dawson nodded, and with a last reassuring squeeze, moved away from Stella. Striding toward the back door, his mind raced with the hundreds of details he needed to accomplish before the plane was ready for takeoff. If the weather coming at them was as bad as Alf said, the next hours were going to be a challenge. He'd flown in blizzards before, but he wasn't a fool. He knew all too well the unpredictability of the weather conditions in the Chilcotin and the risks involved.

With a last glance at Stella's pale, distraught face, he flung open the door and hurried outside. He'd risk the fires of hell if his actions saved her more grief.

****

Stella stood alone amid the flurry of activity. Her breath hitched on a broken sob, and she jammed her fist over her mouth. *Nicholas had been shot. Someone had tried to kill him.* The unbelievable words ran through her brain in an endless, unfathomable refrain.

On wobbly legs, she tottered over to his side and clasped his cold hand. Tears leaked in a steady flow from her eyes, running down her face and dripping onto her shirt. "Come on, Nicholas," she pleaded. "Be strong. You're going to be okay. Just hang on. We'll have you at the hospital in no time."

Jim burst through the kitchen door in a rush of cold air. His freckled face was red from the wind, his wisps of hair a wild tangle. "Plane's all set. Safety check's complete, but you'll have to move quick." He blew on his bare hands to warm their reddened knuckles. "Storm's already on the way. They're expecting freezing temperatures and snow. If you're gonna get this man to hospital, you'd best get a move on."

His words caused a frenzy of activity. In minutes,

Alf and two of the Mounties returned carrying a collapsible stretcher from the first aid supply closet.

The other two policemen slid Nicholas onto the stretcher and covered him with a gray woolen blanket. Straps on his thighs and across his shoulders secured him to the stretcher.

She tightened her death-like grip on his motionless hand.

Sergeant Murphy eyed the surrounding men. "All set?"

They nodded, and on a count of three, lifted the stretcher and headed toward the kitchen door.

She stumbled along beside them, clinging to Nicholas's hand.

Alf placed his hand on her shoulder, stopping her, and Nicholas's limp hand slipped from her grasp.

"Let him go, Stella."

"No!" She shook him off and ran after the stretcher. "I'm going with him."

Alf grabbed her arm. "You can't, Stella."

She fought him, twisting and turning in a wild frenzy, her fists striking his chest and his arms.

"Stella, listen to me. You're not helping. There's no room for you. The plane's full."

His raised voice penetrated her anguish, and she stopped fighting and stared after the departing stretcher through a blur of tears.

The kitchen door slammed closed behind the men.

She turned to Alf. "I have to go with him. Please, Alf. I have to make sure he's okay."

"Dawson's a good pilot. He'll get him to the hospital. They have expert doctors in Hosten. They'll take good care of him. Don't you worry." He patted her arm. "The best thing you can do for him is stay here and pray."

She stared into his eyes, desperate to believe him. "I want to be with him. Don't you see? I want to be at the hospital."

"I know you do, gal." He blew out a ragged breath. "Now, come on and sit down. I'll make you my special drink. It'll have you feeling better in no time."

Too tired to fight, she stumbled over to the chair by the crackling fire and rubbed the stab of pain throbbing in her right temple.

When the kettle boiled, Alf fussed about, adding ingredients to two cups. He handed her one steaming cup, and kept one for himself as they sat by the fire in silence and sipped the hot brew.

The house creaked and groaned under the force of the approaching storm and sinking temperatures.

The high-pitched roar of a floatplane taking off from the lake rattled the kitchen windows. She tightened her grip on her cup and listened as the roar settled into a steady throb and faded away.

A log rolled onto the hearth, and Alf grabbed the poker and shoved the burning log back into the flames. "Those doctors at the trauma center know what they're doing. They'll take good care of him. Don't you worry none."

"I hope so." She sipped the hot drink. The liquid warmth slid down her throat, thawing the block of ice in the pit of her stomach. *Please let Nicholas be okay. Don't let him die. Please.* She wasn't sure to whom she was praying. She wasn't even sure she believed in God. Not anymore. Not after Keegan's death. What sort of just god allowed an innocent baby to die? But still the prayer played through her mind. *Let him be okay.*

"Do you love him?"

She choked on a swallow of tea. "Wha…what?"

"Do you love your ex-husband?"

"Not in the way you're thinking." She stared into her cup. "He was the father of my child. Because of Keegan, we have a special bond. We'll always have that." She wrapped her cold hands around her mug. "He's getting married."

"And you're okay with that?"

"I'm happy for him. He deserves a life."

"But you don't."

"What do you mean?"

"You're in love with Dawson, but you won't admit it, not even to yourself."

She sat up. "What are you talking about? That's not true. Not at all."

"Believe what you want, but the light in your eyes when you look at him tells a different story. A woman doesn't look at a man like that unless she loves him."

She opened her mouth to refute his absurd comment, but he held up his hand, stopping her.

"He's in love with you, too."

Now she knew the old man was crazy. "Dawson can't wait for me to leave the Circle 5. The only reason I'm still here is because of the police investigation."

"Why do you think he's willing to brave a snowstorm to fly your ex-husband to the hospital?" Alf poked at the burning logs, igniting a shower of sparks. "You've got to understand Dawson and what made him the man he is today."

"He told me about his wife."

"Anna was a good woman, but she had her

demons." He stared into the flames. "Her death damn near killed Dawson."

"The death of a loved one's hard to bear." She swallowed over the lump clogging her throat.

"You know all about grieving, don't you? How it changes a person." He sipped tea. "Something died inside Dawson when Anna killed herself. I've known him since he was a boy, and I barely recognized him." Digging in his back pocket, he yanked out a faded handkerchief and blew his nose. "Watching that boy suffer was downright awful, but running this ranch gave him a reason to get up every morning. That, and little Deirdre.

"He drove himself hard, working 'round the clock, trying to make a go of the ranch." Alf's knees cracked as he rose and stalked to a cupboard and jerked out a bottle of whiskey. He held up the bottle. "Want some?"

"No thanks, but you go ahead." As much as the thought of alcohol oblivion beckoned, she needed a clear head if she was going to make it through the next hours.

"Don't mind if I do." He filled a tumbler with the amber liquor and guzzled a hefty swallow. His eyes watered, and he coughed and sputtered. He swiped the back of his hand over his mouth. "Dawson blames himself for Anna's death."

"He couldn't have known she'd kill herself. She must have suffered from severe depression. Maybe she had postpartum depression." Her heart ached for Dawson's pain. His guilt was all too familiar. For months she'd blamed herself for Keegan's death. Still did. Probably always would.

"You know that and I know that, but Dawson

doesn't believe he wasn't at fault. Guilt has a funny way of settling in and not letting go." He drained another long swallow from the tumbler of whiskey. "That's why he hides out on this ranch. And that's why he's terrified of loving again. He doesn't feel he deserves happiness."

She met his shadowed blue eyes. "Why are you telling me this?"

"So's you'll give him a chance. Look under his prickly hide and see the man he used to be, the man he can be again." He drained his glass in one large gulp. Grabbing the empty glass in one hand and the bottle in the other, he limped toward the door. "I need an afternoon nap."

She stared after his retreating back. No matter how often she was told Sudden Infant Death Syndrome was an unexplained and inexplicable cause of death for hundreds of infants every year, she couldn't help the certainty she could have prevented Keegan's death.

If she'd checked on him sooner, or let him sleep in the same room with her and Nicholas, or stayed home that night, or... She shook her head. The what-ifs weighed her down and kept her awake at night. How else to explain the sudden death of a perfectly healthy baby, if not for some sort of neglect on the part of the parent?

She rubbed her burning eyes. Blame over Keegan's death was a burden she'd carry the rest of her life. Guilt was something she'd almost grown used to...an unwelcome, but all-too-familiar companion haunting her every waking moment. Knowing Dawson shared the same remorse explained the kinship she'd felt from their first meeting.

Was Alf right? Was she in love with Dawson?

Maybe. Possibly.

Her stomach flip-flopped.

Probably.

All the more reason to leave the ranch before he broke her heart.

Reeling as if she'd aged a hundred years in the past two hours, she plodded down the hall to Deirdre's room and peeked her head around the half-open door. "Can I come in, Dee?"

Dee looked up from the game she was playing on a small laptop computer. "Wanna watch me play? I'm kicking butt."

Stella walked over to the bed, sat down beside Shas, who was stretched out across the quilt, and patted the spot beside her. "Come and sit down, Dee. I have something to tell you."

"Wait. Not right now." She shook her head, red curls bouncing around her face. "I've got two more lives left."

"Please."

Deirdre looked up from her game. Her face fell. "You're leaving." Her sky-blue eyes met Stella's. Tears shimmered in their depths. "You promised you wouldn't."

Stella formulated a hundred explanations for her sudden departure, but not one of them would ease Deirdre's pain, and none would be the truth. "I have to go, Dee. I'm sorry, but I have to."

"But you promised. You said you'd stay."

"I know." Pain tightened her gut. "I'm sorry. You must believe I wouldn't do this if I didn't have to."

"You lied." Deirdre stamped her foot. "You're a

liar."

Shas lifted his big head, and his ears pricked.

Unable to speak over the thick lump stuck in her throat, Stella shook her head, but Deirdre was right. She had lied. She'd promised she'd stay. And now she wasn't.

"Stella?" Dee's voice was a whisper, her misery clear. "Are you leaving because you don't love me?"

"Of course not." She opened her arms, but Deirdre backed away.

"If you loved me you'd stay." Deirdre thrust out her bottom lip.

Again, Stella patted the bed. "Come here. Let's talk."

Indecision was written across Deirdre's pale, freckled face.

"Please."

As if walking toward her doom, Deirdre shuffled to the bed and plopped down. She set the laptop computer on the bed beside her.

Stella blew out a ragged breath. "You remember my friend Nicholas?"

Dee nodded.

"Well, he was hurt this morning, and your daddy's flying him to the hospital in Hosten." She blocked out an image of Nicholas's pasty face and seeping chest wound. "Nicholas is my friend, and I want to be with him while he's in the hospital to make sure he gets better. As soon as your daddy returns, I'm going to get him to fly me to Hosten."

A thin line formed between Deirdre's brows. "I don't like that man. Daddy doesn't like him either. No one does. Alphonse said he wants to ruin the ranch."

She patted the girl's leg. "You have friends you care for, right? You'd want to help them if they were hurt."

"You and Alf are my friends."

Fresh tears stung her eyes at this sign of the child's isolation. Dee had few friends. Now that Stella was leaving, she'd have one less. Maybe after Nicholas was out of danger, she'd come back. Maybe she'd stay…for awhile…maybe.

"Why don't you marry Daddy? Then you wouldn't have to leave. You could stay. For always." Dee's eyes lit up. "You'd be my mommy."

Marry Daddy? She gulped. "It doesn't work that way, honey."

"Why not?" Dee jumped off the bed. "I heard Alf and Daddy talking. Alf told Daddy he was a fool if he didn't marry you. My daddy's not a fool. He's smart. He'll marry you." She sat back on her heels and picked up the laptop, a smug expression on her face. "Just you wait and see."

Stella hated to dash her dream, but she wouldn't lie to the girl, not again. "Your daddy's not going to marry me, Dee." No matter what Alf said, and no matter how much Deirdre wished it were true, Stella was certain of one thing—Dawson did not love her.

Dee was shaking her head before Stella finished speaking. "Daddy loves you." Her lower lip trembled. "*I* love you."

Stella rose from the bed and bent and hugged Dee. "You're such a special little girl."

Deirdre fought free of Stella's embrace. "I don't want you to go." Her eyes pooled with tears. "Please don't leave."

Breaking the child's heart chipped away a piece of Stella's soul. "I'm sorry, Dee. I have to." She forced brightness into her voice. "But we can email each other every day, if you'd like. And video chat."

Deirdre's small face crumpled. "I hate you." Her anguished shout filled the room and echoed from wall to wall. "I hate you." She tossed her computer on the floor and raced from the room. The door slammed with a bang.

Shas whined and stared at Stella, his dark eyes accusing.

She sagged on the bed. Dee's parting words blazed through her mind, scorching the air. *I hate you.* Eyes swollen and gritty, she slipped off the bed and trudged down the hall to her own room and into the bathroom. Leaning both hands against the sink, she stared into the mirror, hardly recognizing the woman facing her. Her eyes were red and swollen, her skin blotchy, her face haggard.

That's what you get for breaking a child's heart.

The house creaked and groaned under the strong gusts of wind buffeting the sturdy log structure. She wandered out of the bathroom over to the bedroom window and peered through the frost-glazed glass. A blizzard raged, and an inch of fresh snow blanketed the ground.

If everything went well, the plane carrying Nicholas should have landed an hour ago in Hosten. Alf had told her that in spite of the weather, once Dawson dropped off Nicholas, he planned to return to the ranch.

Pellets of ice peppered the window like handfuls of tiny pebbles, and a chill settled deep in her bones. Surely Dawson would stay the night in Hosten. He wouldn't fly in this mess. It was too risky. She couldn't bear it if anything happened to him, not when he'd risked his life to save Nicholas.

She blew out a shaky breath and headed out of the room and down the stairs in search of Deirdre. The last thing they needed was for the distraught little girl to run away again.

The yeasty aroma of fresh baked bread filled the kitchen, and her stomach heaved. Just the thought of food was enough to make her retch.

Using a pair of oversized oven mitts, Alf lifted a pan of perfectly browned buns from the oven. He wiped his shiny forehead with a handkerchief, studied her, and scowled. "You don't look so good."

"Have you seen Dee? She's pretty upset. I told her I'm leaving."

"You've made a decision then."

She spread her hands wide in a pleading gesture. "I don't have a choice."

"I didn't figure you for a coward." He heaved a sigh and dropped the oven mitts on the counter. "Last I looked, Jean-Luc and Dee were in the living room playing checkers."

"It's been a tough day." She huffed out a breath. "I wonder how Nicholas is doing?"

"You can relax. Sergeant Murphy called on the radiophone. King is holding his own. The bullet went clean through, missing his heart and lungs. He's expected to make a full recovery."

Her knees wobbled, and she gripped the back of a chair to hold steady as a wave of relief washed over her. "That's good. That's really good. Will Dawson be able to make it back tonight?" She nodded toward the snow pelting the windows. Her heart lurched. "Is it safe to fly?"

"The weatherman's predicting the temperature will drop below zero before morning. To say nothing of the foot of snow sure to follow." He clomped over and patted her shoulder. "Don't worry. Dawson'll hunker down in Hosten and wait out the storm. He'll be back in a few days once things warm up." He handed her a large spoon. "Supper's almost ready. I made a real nice stew. Why don't you dish up while I call everyone?"

Gorge filled her throat. "I'm not hungry."

"Nonsense. You have to eat." He hobbled over to the stove and poured a cup of steaming coffee and set it before her. Picking up the walkie-talkie hanging on a hook by the hutch, he pressed a button on its side, and hollered, "Supper's on." He rang a brass bell. The loud clanging resounded through the large room.

Within minutes, the kitchen was filled with people as the ranch workers and the two remaining RCMP constables filed in, brushing snow from their coats and warming their hands before the crackling fire.

Jean-Luc marched into the kitchen towing a reluctant Deirdre.

Her red hair was ablaze and tangled around her tearstained face. Mouth set in a stubborn line, she kept her back to Stella and flopped on her chair.

Stella heaped plates with mounds of mashed potatoes and stew, and set the laden plates on the table. A basket of homemade buns sat in the middle of the large table beside a dish of butter.

The men dug into their food like starving dogs.

"Dee tells me you're leaving the Circle 5, Stella," Jean-Luc said. "Sorry to hear that."

The men stopped chewing, their forks halting in midair as all gazes riveted on her.

"You're leaving us?" Jim asked. He scratched his freckled scalp. "But you've only been here a few weeks. Are you tired of our company already?"

She studied their rough, leathery faces. She'd miss their corny jokes, friendly teasing, and kindness. "Not at all. You've made me feel welcome, like part of the family. Thank you for that."

"So why are you going?" Brett's dark brows rose.

"I have to leave. I…" What could she say? How to explain to these good, honest men that she was afraid, terrified of her growing feelings for their boss?

They watched her for a long, silent minute, and then as if they'd choreographed their movements, each man returned his focus to his plate and began stuffing food in his mouth.

She sagged back on the chair, wishing she could twitch her nose like the witch from the old television show she'd watched when she was a child and vanish into the night. Lifting her fork, she stirred the hearty stew and gagged at the heady aroma of gravy and meat. The faint scent of bleach stung her nostrils. A few short hours ago, Nicholas had lain on this table, blood leaking from the wound in his chest. Alf must have scrubbed the table.

Jean-Luc wiped his mouth with his checkered, cloth napkin. "Dawson won't try and make it back tonight, will he?"

Bob snorted. "Not a chance. His plane ain't goin' nowhere, leastwise, not 'til spring. With all the snow the weatherman's predicting, he'll have to borrow someone's snowmobile and ride back on the winter trail."

Alf's cough shook the walls, and Bob's face flushed red. He slid a glance at Stella. "Don't you worry, Stella," he mumbled. "I...I could be wrong. Maybe the weather will warm up tonight, and he'll be able to fly in tomorrow. The weather does that here sometimes. Freezing one minute, baking hot the next."

"You'll be able to head home soon," Alphonse chimed in. "I'll bet you miss the shopping malls. Nothing like that around these parts."

A high-pitched cry and a chair slamming into the wall and crashing to the floor halted conversation. Dee raced out of the room, her sobs echoing behind her.

The silence at the table was deafening.

Stella pushed her chair back from the table and stood. "I'll go and talk to her."

Alf shook his head. "You've done more than enough. I'll see to her." He stomped out of the kitchen.

The sound of his boots clomping up the stairs was like bullets striking her. "I...I guess I'll clean up."

All seven ranch hands leaped to their feet.

Jim picked up a plate. "We'll help you, Stella."

She stared at the ring of rough-hewn men. Warmth washed over her. "Thank you, but I'm fine. You guys worked hard today. I'll finish up in here."

They hesitated, but at Bob's nod, they said their goodnights, donned their heavy coats and toques, and departed for the bunkhouse and their evening round of cards and television.

The uniformed policemen mumbled good nights and returned to their watch. They'd been left behind to keep an eye on the ranch and its inhabitants. No one had forgotten a murderer was on the loose.

An hour later as she dried the last dish and put it away in the cupboard, Alf limped into the kitchen.

His face was drawn and haggard. "Well, that wasn't easy." He blew out a breath. "Poor little mite. I think her heart's about to break."

Her own heart twisted as if clenched by a fist. "I don't mean to hurt her."

Striding to the stove, he lit the flame under the big kettle. "I guess a person's gotta do what a person's gotta do, no matter the consequences."

Chapter 20

Stella stood at the kitchen window. The barn was a dim outline through the raging blizzard. Tree branches sagged under the coating of heavy, wet snow. Deep drifts piled against the front porch.

"This storm's something, isn't it?" Alf stood at the counter kneading a mound of dough. His shirtsleeves were rolled above his elbows, and flour dusted the front of his apron.

"Dawson will be okay, won't he?"

A frown shadowed the old man's face. "I've seen him fly in worse."

"Why didn't he wait in Hosten? Why fly back in this storm?"

"You're mighty concerned for someone who doesn't care for the man." He stopped kneading and studied her with sharp eyes.

"He's Dee's father. Of course, I'm worried about him." She glanced at the tempest raging outside and shuddered. How could anyone fly in that weather?

"Worrying isn't going to make one bit of difference. Nothing we can do about it. Dawson made the call, and now it's up to him and the good Lord." He returned to kneading, his hands punching and rolling the dough.

Her shoulders sagged. He was right. They had no choice but to pray for Dawson's safe return. In the meantime, she needed to drag Deirdre out of her room where she'd sequestered herself since she'd learned Stella was planning to leave. She'd tried to convince the angry little girl to play a board game with her or watch a movie, but Dee kept her gaze fixed on the computer game she was playing and didn't look up or acknowledge Stella was speaking.

The tense situation had gone on too long. Bad enough Dawson was out in the storm somewhere struggling to get home. She didn't need his daughter stomping around, her tiny face a thundercloud, her eyes flashing wounded pain. Something had to be done.

Stella thrust back her shoulders, inhaled a deep, fortifying breath, and walked off in search of Deirdre. Somehow, someway, she'd soften the hurt child's stubborn resistance and convince her to leave her room, and if not forgive Stella for her betrayal, to at least be civil.

The morning dragged with painstaking slowness. The storm's fury intensified. Snowdrifts piled high against the foundations, but inside the cozy house, fires blazed. The lights were on to ward off the unsettling darkness.

With the promise of Alf's fresh baked chocolate chip cookies, she'd managed to convince Deirdre to put down her computer, leave her bedroom, and play a board game with her. When Stella let Dee win, some of the child's tension and resentment eased, and the little girl begged for another game, and another one after that.

The long afternoon wore on. As if sensing the adults' worry about Dawson's delayed return, Dee grew progressively cantankerous until Stella's patience wore thin, and after an early dinner, she sent the child to her bedroom with the promise she could watch a movie on her computer before bed.

Stella sat in the rocking chair by the fireplace in the kitchen staring into the flames.

Alf rocked beside her as he sipped a steaming cup of tea.

Neither spoke their worries aloud, but the air between them was thick with all the words they didn't say.

The distant roar of an airplane sounded over the storm's clamor.

She plunked down her cup and leaped from her chair and ran to the window. Her breath fogged the glass, and she used her sleeve to rub away the moisture. Snow swirled in thick clouds and pelted the window, making it impossible to see more than a dozen feet. Frustrated, she grabbed her coat from the hook by the door and slipped on her boots.

"Where do you think you're going? It's not safe out there."

Ignoring Alf, she opened the door and stepped onto the porch. The wind caught the door and slammed it shut, leaving her engulfed in a swirl of snow and cold. Huddled in her coat, shivering in the fierce wind, she squinted against the sting of snow.

The rumble of an approaching plane penetrated the storm. The noise of the engine increased to a screaming wail as the plane settled on the lake and taxied to the wharf.

A wave of relief washed over her. Somehow the foolish man had managed to navigate through the raging blizzard and find his way home. Joy flooded her heart, and she ran down the steps and plunged into knee-high drifts.

Slipping and sliding, she slogged through the thick blanket of white. Her heart thundered as the lake, the ranch house, and the world were erased, her disorientation total. Flakes swirled in a vortex, and she narrowed her eyes against the sting of driven snow. It pelted her face and clung to her eyelashes and hair. Her feet were numb, her exposed fingers burning with cold.

Her instinct was to keep moving, searching for a familiar landmark, but she stayed where she was. The farther she strayed from the house, the less likely anyone would find her. She blew on her frozen fingers and stamped her feet in an effort to keep warm. The relentless wind whipped her, and she clutched the collar of her coat tighter, shivering.

"Stella!" Dawson's voice lanced through the icy air.

"Dawson!" The breath whooshed out of her lungs in a cloud of vapor. "Dawson, I'm here. Over here."

A murky shape appeared out of the swirling snow, resolving into the figure of a man. Dawson, his dark hair coated in a dusting of snow, his cheeks ruddy from the cold, extended his gloved hand.

Wind swirled and snow pelleted her face like icy needle pricks. "You found me."

"You little fool. What are you doing out here?" His warm breath washed over her. "You're freezing. Let's go inside." Wrapping his arm around her, protecting her from the worst of the wind, he guided her through the snow, step by laborious step.

The welcoming lights of the house blazed through the storm.

She stumbled the last few steps onto the porch.

The door opened and light and warmth spilled out. "Where the hell have you two been? You damn near gave me a heart attack. Come on. Get in here." Alf held the door open as they staggered inside.

Inhaling the warm air, redolent of wood smoke, fresh baked bread, and brewing coffee, she shook snow off her coat and hair.

Large, fluffy white flakes clung to Dawson's dark hair and eyelashes. He shrugged out of his coat, and his gaze lasered into hers.

Heat flashed between them, and she lost herself in the compelling depths of his eyes.

"'Bout time you got here."

Dawson swung to Alf, severing the intense connection. "You weren't worried about me, were you, old man?"

Alf snorted. "I've got better things to do than worry about you. Besides you're too ornery to crash." In spite of his harsh words, the sheen of tears shone in Alf's faded blue eyes.

Dawson grinned. "I missed you too, Alf." He looked around the kitchen "Where's Dee?"

"In her room," Stella said. "She was driving us nuts, so I sent her to bed. Do you want me to wake her?"

He shook his head and droplets of melting snow sprayed from his wet hair. "Let her sleep. I'll see her in the morning." He focused on Stella. "Could I talk to you in my office?"

"Now?"

He nodded.

Her heart sank at the steel in his eyes. She slid a

glance at Alf.

He shrugged and arched his bushy gray eyebrows.

With heavy steps, she followed Dawson out of the kitchen to his office. This was it. Her time at the Circle 5 was over. In spite of the storm, he'd arranged some way of getting her back to the bus stop. She should be thrilled. She was getting exactly what she wanted. She was leaving him, Deirdre, the Circle 5, everything.

So why was her stomach twisted in knots? And why were tears burning her eyes? Her knees shook as she sat on the leather couch.

"Want something?" Without waiting for her answer, he opened a cupboard behind his desk, removed a bottle of liquor, and filled two glasses with amber liquid. He handed her a glass.

Their fingers brushed, and she huffed out a shaky breath at the instant tingle of awareness.

He must have felt the jolt too, because he jerked his hand away as if he'd been burned. "I imagine you're wondering how your—" He tightened his jaw. "—how King is doing." Gulping his drink, he drained half the contents before he glanced up. "When I left the hospital, he'd just gotten out of surgery. His doctor told me he was doing as well as could be expected for a man who'd been shot, and he'd likely make a full recovery."

A weight lifted off her shoulders at this welcome news. "Thank you for flying him to the hospital. He wouldn't have made it if we'd had to wait for the medevac helicopter. The storm hit less than half an hour after you left."

"I know how important he is to you." He swallowed the remainder of his drink and set down his empty glass. "I guess I should congratulate you."

"Congratulate me? Why?"

"You're getting what you wanted."

"What do you mean?"

He held up a finger. "You and your husband are back together"—another finger joined the first—"you're returning to your life in Vancouver"—another finger—"and your mine development is going ahead." His lip curled in a sneer. "You must be very happy."

She lurched up, the back of her legs braced against the couch. "Nicholas and I aren't getting back together. Where'd you get that idea?"

He shrugged and poured another drink. His hand was unsteady and liquor slopped, forming a puddle around the base of his glass. "I just assumed. I mean, you two seemed close, and you were pretty upset when he was hurt."

"Of course I was upset. He'd been shot. I didn't know if he was going to live or die." She swiped a lock of hair out of her eyes. "Not that's it any of your business, but Nicholas is in love. He's getting married…to someone else."

His eyes widened. "Really?"

She nodded.

"You're not getting back together?"

She shook her head.

The corners of his mouth twitched. "That's good." He smoothed his hand over his hair and grinned. "I mean that's great."

Why was he so happy? If she didn't know better, she'd think—

Before she finished the thought, he moved closer until the toes of his boots brushed her shoes. The intriguing scents of crisp air, leather, and scotch filled the air between them.

His gaze dipped to her lips and lingered.

She read the hunger in his eyes. Every cell in her body pinged, and she leaned toward him as if drawn by an irresistible force.

He raised his hand and the glint of gold on the ring finger of his left hand caught the light.

Warning bells clanged. *Danger! Broken-heart alert! Danger.* She tensed, but memories of him shielding her with his body when the bullets flew and risking his life to fly through a blizzard to take the man he thought she loved to the hospital kept her locked in place.

She was afraid, terrified what would happen if they took this next step, but he was a good man. An honest man. And God help her, she loved him. She wanted to touch his cheek, shadowed with dark stubble, and press her mouth to his. Her breath whooshed out, and her knees trembled. Her heart pounded so loud she was certain he heard.

Still focused on her mouth, he stroked her cheek. "You're so damn beautiful."

The soft rasp of his callused thumb against her skin and his sweet words ignited a raging wildfire spreading from her cheek through her entire body and leaving her quivering with the certainty he was going to kiss her. If he didn't, she sure as hell was going to kiss him.

His fingers tangled in her hair as he lowered his head and kissed her. His hands slid down her back, following the dip of her waist and the flare of her hips.

Emboldened by her raging desire, she broke free of his kiss, backed away a step, and without daring to think of the consequences, peeled off her sweater, unclasped her bra, and let the straps slip over her shoulders and down her arms. She unbuttoned her jeans and tugged them over her hips. They pooled at her feet, and she stepped out of them and kicked them away. Her panties were next. She tossed the scrap of black lace on top of her discarded jeans and stood before him naked and vulnerable. "Your turn." Her voice was a husky whisper.

His hands flew as he tore at the buttons and shrugged out of his shirt. He tugged his white cotton T-shirt over his head. His sun-bronzed skin gleamed in the glow of the desk lamp.

She couldn't stop staring, drinking him in. Her mouth watered at his wide shoulders, defined pecs, and flat abdomen with a dusting of dark hair arrowing in an intriguing line below the waistband of his low-slung jeans. His chest expanded and contracted with each labored breath.

She closed the distance between them and smoothed her fingers over his skin, following the indentations of his ribs, the flat plane of his stomach, and the hollows of his hipbones. She paused, her fingers playing with the snap on his jeans and met his gaze. "Yes?"

He swallowed, his throat working, and nodded. "Yes." The single word ground out in a groan.

"Okay. If you're sure."

"Lady, if you stop now, I'll—"

His breath caught and his voice died as with a deft twist, she freed the snap on his jeans and inched down the zipper. She slid his jeans over his lean hips and down his muscular thighs.

No underwear.

She gulped.

He scooped her in his arms and carried her across the room. Kicking open the door, he strode out of the cozy den into the cool of the hall to his bedroom. He booted the door closed behind him, crossed the dark room, and laid her on the soft surface of a massive bed.

Light flared and she blinked in the soft glow of a bedside lamp.

The bed dipped as he sat beside her. His hair-roughened thigh brushed hers.

Silence coiled between them, broken by the rasp of his heavy breathing and the creak of the log building as the temperature outside dropped, and the wind buffeted the foundations.

"Stella, are you sure this is what you want?"

She opened her arms. "Come here, cowboy."

****

With a throaty groan, he leaned on his elbows and nuzzled her neck, inhaling the scents of wild roses and sweet clover. She reminded him of rolling grasslands stretching into the horizon, wildflowers blooming in June, forests heating under a summer sun…home.

Her gaze, bright with desire, locked on his. Her cheeks flushed.

His brain stopped working, and he focused on the warm and willing woman in his arms. He caressed her breasts, cupping them in the palms of his hands, teasing the sensitive tips until she writhed beneath him, begging for more.

He wanted her, right then, right that very second, but he held back. This had to be good—he needed it to be incredible—for her. He kissed her breasts, laving them with long, slow strokes, suckling until she squirmed. He slid his hands lower, caressing the satiny soft skin on her flat stomach, fondling, touching, teasing. His lips followed, burning a fiery path across her lithe body.

She lifted her hips, arching beneath him, and his good intentions vanished, replaced with a desperate need. He slipped inside her, but froze after the first thrust. If he kept moving, kept loving her, he'd explode. Biting hard on his bottom lip, the muscles in his arms taut, he fought for control.

"Don't stop. Please." Her thighs quivered, and she gripped his hips and pulled, urging him deeper and deeper still.

He plunged into her wet and welcoming heat, and in the next breath, blew apart into a hundred thousand pieces.

She moaned and clutched his biceps, her nails digging into his skin. Crying out, she tensed as her release flooded through her, and she expelled a shaky breath.

Chest heaving, he held her close, the rapid beating of her heart matching the frantic pace of his.

She curled into his sweat-dampened chest, resting her head against his shoulder.

He smoothed her hair from her damp face. A well of emotion overwhelmed him, a feeling that all was right in the world. She fit against his body as if she were made for him. He tightened his embrace and succumbed to the heavy weight of lethargy stealing through his body.

Sometime in the night, he awakened. She was snuggled in his arms, her breasts against his chest, her hips nestled against his.

Stripes of bright moonlight streaked the bed. He raised his head and peered out the window. The storm was over, though snowdrifts piled against the trunks of trees and covered the ground in a thick blanket. The next day would be bitterly cold, but the animals needed feeding and watering, paths cleared of snow, the roof shoveled. He ran the palm of his hand over the silken strands of Stella's hair and tugged her warm body closer and breathed in the musty smell of sex.

Tomorrow she'd be on her way to Vancouver.

Tomorrow his heart would break as he returned to darkness.

But she was there now. He brushed a gentle kiss on her forehead.

She stirred, lifted her head, and smiled, a lazy, satisfied smile.

His heart lurched. "Hey." His voice was a hoarse croak, thick with unshed tears.

She shifted until their bodies meshed together, until he couldn't tell where her body ended and his began. Her mouth found his, and her hands explored his shoulders and slid over his back.

Thrusting aside thoughts of tomorrow, he succumbed to the raging fire only she could quench.

Chapter 21

She opened her eyes and blinked in the bright glare. Shoving her tangled hair off her face, she sat up. The bed beside her was empty, the bedroom deserted.

She studied the room in the light of day. Aside from the king-size bed, a tall, six-drawer bureau, an upholstered leather chair, and matching bedside tables crafted in rich golden pine filled the large room. Flames popped and crackled in a river-stone fireplace. A large window took up most of one wall and revealed a blinding scene of clear, robin's-egg-blue skies and brilliant sunshine. The snow sparkled as if infused with thousands of tiny diamonds.

She stretched and her muscles ached in places she hadn't thought of in a very long time, but she was rested. For the first time in months, she'd slept without waking to nightmare dreams. A pile of folded clothing lay on the foot of the bed. Tugging the sheet over her breasts, she smiled. Someone…Dawson…had retrieved her clothes from the den.

Her face heated as images of the previous night swept over her. One minute she was determined to leave him and the Circle 5, and the next she was in his bed practically begging him to make love. What had she been thinking? Flopping back on the pillow, she expelled a frustrated breath. That's just it, she wasn't thinking, not with her brain. Dawson had regarded her with his soulful dark eyes, and her heart had been only too happy to take over.

A memory of his caresses, the passion glazing his eyes, and the tenderness of his touch rose before her. He'd wanted her, and she'd wanted him. Heck, she still wanted him. But then she remembered the flash of gold on his left hand, and her desire vanished.

The past night hadn't changed anything. He was a man with all the needs and desires of a healthy young male. He'd wanted her for the physical release. She was available, and she'd made her willingness clear when she ripped off her clothes.

He didn't love her. She was a fool if she thought he did. He was in love with his dead wife. The gold ring on his left hand was proof of his devotion. He'd always love a ghost. Is that what she wanted? To stay at the Circle 5 and have an affair with a man who didn't love her, who *couldn't* love her?

In spite of all the walls she'd erected around her heart, somehow he'd broken through and stolen her heart. And now she'd fallen in love with him. How could she leave him and return to her bleak, empty life in the city? A life without Dawson Wheeler.

Maybe she didn't have to. Maybe she could stay at the ranch.

Her stomach clenched. Was she willing to stay with him, even though he was in love with his dead wife? Would she be happy with that? Could she live with him and make love to him knowing he didn't love her, not fully, not one hundred per cent, not with all his heart?

The thought of leaving brought her to her knees, and head spinning, she climbed out of the bed and dressed. She ran her hands through her tangled hair and opened the bedroom door and stepped into the hall.

"There you are. I've been looking all over for you." Deirdre's button-bright eyes pinned her to the spot. "What were you doing in Daddy's bedroom?"

Heat engulfed Stella like a furnace, creeping up her neck and flooding her face. "I…I was…I was looking for him."

"He's not in his room, silly. He's in the barn."

"Oh. Then I'll—" She waved her hand in a vague gesture. "—I'll have a shower and look for him later." Desperate to escape, she pivoted to flee up the stairs.

"I guess you need to pack."

The sadness in Dee's voice stopped her in her tracks. She slowly twisted around. "I…I'm not sure." Was she still leaving?

"Daddy said it's supposed to warm up tomorrow, and he should be able to fly you to the bus stop."

"He…he said that?"

Dee nodded, her red curls bouncing around her elfin face.

Anger began a slow burn. "Where's your dad?"

"I told you. He's in the barn."

Stella spun away from Deirdre and stormed toward the kitchen.

Deirdre hurried behind her. "Wait for me. I wanna come."

"Stay here, Dee." Her voice brooked no argument. Grabbing her coat from the hook by the back door, she shrugged into the heavy parka and yanked up the zipper.

"Better put on a toque and mitts. It's bitter out there this morning." Alf rocked in his favorite chair by the fire, a book open on his lap.

The cat wound around his feet, rubbing against his legs.

Shas and Snickers were curled before the fire.

She jammed a wool toque on her head and tugged on leather gloves. Tingling under the weight of Alf's gaze, she snapped, "If you have something you want to say, spit it out."

"Whatever Dawson did to make your pretty face look like a thundercloud, I'm thinking it might be better if you waited until you cooled down a mite before you have it out with him."

Deirdre stood by the table, munching on a cookie, watching the two adults, listening to their conversation.

Stella bit her lip, stopping the rush of angry words. "I need to talk to him...now."

"Just talk?" His brows arched, his meaning more than clear.

Her face flamed. Last night she and Dawson hadn't done much talking...plenty of other things, but talking hadn't been high on the agenda. She shrugged off the heated images. They were going to talk now. Damn straight. They'd settle this thing between them if she had to hogtie him with a rope and strap him to the hitching rail. She clapped a hand over her mouth. Dear God. Now she was thinking like an old cowpoke. She nodded at Alf. "Keep Deirdre here. This won't take long."

Alf's chuckle followed her out the door and onto the front porch. Someone had shoveled the snow off the steps and cleared a path through the knee-deep snow to the barn. The frosty air stung her face, and she hunched into her coat. She squinted against the bright glare of sun and dazzling snow. Her boots crunched through the snow as she slipped and slid on the frozen ground. Fueled by anger, her breath puffing out in billowing clouds, she marched through the corral and flung open the barn door.

The interior of the barn was gloomy after the brightness of the clear day. Dust motes danced in a streak of light filtering through a crack in one of the logs forming the frosted walls. The barn was cold, and the air was rank with the musty tang of manure, hay, and horse sweat. A soft nicker and the clop of hooves on wooden boards echoed from the horse stalls.

She strode past straw bales piled in neat stacks, and edged around a wooden-rung, narrow ladder leading to the loft.

Dawson was in the second stall from the end. One of Rocky's massive hoofs rested on his jean-clad knee as he worked with a metal tool, scraping debris out of the horse's hoof. His hair was a riot of curls, his whiskers a dark shadow on his lean cheeks. Focused on his task, he manipulated the tool with deft skill. It was obvious he hadn't heard her approach.

Those hands had touched her with such tenderness.

Cutting the thought dead in the water before her resolve weakened, she cleared her throat.

He glanced up. The crinkles beside his eyes deepened, and a grin wreathed his handsome face. His teeth flashed white against the tan of his skin, his dimples dancing. "Stella."

****

His breath whooshed out. She looked so damn good. Her hair was mussed, her clothes wrinkled from lying in a crumpled heap on the floor all night until he'd picked them up, smoothed them, and folded them on the foot of his bed. Her lips were red and swollen from his kisses, and her cheeks were flushed pink from the cold.

His first instinct was to take her in his arms and kiss her sweet lips, but 'hands off' vibrated from her like a red neon sign. He gripped Rocky's hoof tighter to stop from reaching for her. "Good morning."

Her blue eyes flashed fire.

And just like that, before she even uttered a word, his gut plummeted like he was on a roller coaster ride. He released Rocky's hoof and stood, stretching his back. "That bad, huh?"

Her frown deepened. "What happened last night?"

"You were there. You know what happened. We made love." He couldn't help a satisfied grin slipping out. "Twice."

"Did we? Did we *make love*? Or was it just sex?" She picked up a clump of hay and crumbled the dried stalks to dust. "Tell me the truth. Did it happen because I'm the only woman in a hundred kilometers, and you were horny?"

"What are you talking about? It wasn't like that. You know that. You were there with me every step of the way. You wanted it as much as I did." He might have imagined it, but he was pretty certain steam rose from her head.

"What about *that*?" She jabbed her finger at him.

"What are you talking about?" He studied his dirty work jeans, but saw nothing other than dried clumps of manure and some sprigs of straw. What was with her? The previous night she'd been warm and welcoming. She'd wanted him as much as he'd wanted her. Hell, he still wanted her. And now she was pissed they'd made love? What the hell had happened? His own anger smoldered to life. "What are you talking about?"

She stomped closer, grabbed his hand, and held it up. She poked her finger at the gold band. "This. This is what I'm talking about."

He snatched his hand back and rubbed the smooth gold, twisting the ring around his finger. A chill settled over him. "What about it?"

"You're still in love with *her*!" Her accusation filled the barn, echoing in the rafters.

"What's my…my wife got to do with us?"

Her face tightened. She crossed her arms over her chest. "Are you kidding me? Are you actually asking me that?"

Her body bristled with anger, and she stared at him like he was a particularly nasty bug she'd like to squash. What happened to the warm, loving woman he'd held in his arms last night, the woman who'd set his senses on fire and rocked his world?

He blew out a frustrated breath and stepped closer and enfolded her in his arms, but his heart chilled when she stiffened and backed away. "Come on, Stella, don't do this. Please." He swallowed over a lump the size of a boulder.

She chewed on her bottom lip, the lip he'd kissed a few short hours ago. Her anger evaporated, and her eyes turned bleak and cold.

His heart sank. He preferred the anger. At least then he knew she felt something.

"I can't do this, Dawson. Not anymore. I thought—" She hung her head and her fall of golden hair covered her face. "—maybe it would work, but…"

274

He grasped at the straw of hope. "It can work. *We* can work. Don't you see? We're good together." He rubbed his jaw. "Last night was…it was pretty special."

"I'd like to leave as soon as possible."

"Leave? Now?" Was she serious? After the night before? *Especially* after that night?

"As soon as your plane can fly."

"But—"

She cut off his protest. "Last night was a mistake. You're still in love with your wife. Admit it. I know it. Alf knows it. Heck, everyone knows." She huffed out a blast of air. "There's no room for three of us in your bed."

Last night was a mistake. Mistake? Sleeping with her wasn't just a mistake…it was one hell of a catastrophe.

Her words rattled through him, cutting deeper into his soul with each reverberation. *A mistake.* Then her last words struck home, and he reeled as if she'd stabbed him. *There's no room for three of us in your bed.* "Come on, Stella. Don't do this."

She shook her head and rushed out of the barn.

Go after her. Stop her.

But he couldn't. Not when everything she'd said was true. He stared at the burnished gold ring—his wedding ring. Tears filmed his eyes. He'd loved Anna, still loved her. How could he not? Every time he looked into his daughter's vivid blue eyes, he saw Anna. Every time Dee laughed, he heard his wife's laughter. And every single time, a deep ache settled in the pit of his gut, and he grieved anew at the unbearable loss. He'd give anything, do anything, to have his wife back.

He stared at the open barn door, his heart heavy.

Stella was right. She had to leave the Circle 5. Not for his sake. Hell, he'd miss her with every fiber of his being, relive every moment they'd shared, lie awake at night missing her, wanting her like an addict craved his next hit.

If it were up to him, he'd beg her to stay. But she'd had her heart broken when her son died and again when she and her husband split. She didn't need him making promises he wasn't sure he could keep. He'd hurt her enough. He refused to cause her any more suffering. He'd do this one thing for her—he'd let her go—even if it killed him.

****

Deirdre tossed the die, and the white game cube tumbled and skittered across the table. "Yes!" She shifted a small, purple plastic horse six spaces ahead on the game board. "Your turn." She grinned, exposing a missing tooth, and sat back on the rug and crossed her coltish legs under her.

Stella fought back a yawn. The intense cold had kept them cooped up inside for two long days playing endless board and card games and watching videos. She didn't know how much more she could stand.

The tension between her and Dawson had settled over the house like a dark weight, setting everyone on edge.

The ranch hands tiptoed around, their faces glum, laughter stilled.

Alf glowered at her every chance he got.

And Dawson—she gulped and swallowed back tears—well, she didn't even want to think about the smoldering anger suffusing his face. The only person who seemed oblivious to the swirling undercurrents was Deirdre.

Alf strode into the living room and placed two more chunks of wood on the fire in the big stone fireplace. "You gals warm enough in here?"

"Guess what, Alf? I'm beating Stella again. That's the third time today." Dee clapped her hands. "This is the bestest game in the whole world." She flopped on her stomach beside Sneakers and ruffled his thick black hair.

The big dog's tail thumped on the floor like a bass drum.

"Time you worked on your school lessons, Dee," Alf said.

Stella studied her watch. "I hadn't realized the time." She picked up game pieces and set them in the box. "Why don't you head up and start, Dee? I'll be along as soon as I clean up this mess." Two mugs with the dregs of hot chocolate rimming the sides, a plate scattered with crumbs from Alf's famous chocolate chip cookies, and pieces of the current board game were scattered across the table.

"Awww. Do I have to?"

Alf made a fierce face. "You know you do, young lady. Now get a move on before I tan your hide."

Dee giggled, not threatened in the slightest by his ferocious scowl. She leaped up and ran for the staircase, skipping past Alf's half-hearted swat. Her small feet thudded up the stairs.

Stella sat back on her heels. "What's up? Why did you want her out of the room? Her lessons don't start for another hour."

He sank onto the couch. "Sergeant Murphy called."

She nodded, waiting for more. In the past two days,

Alf had been unusually quiet. It was obvious he knew what had happened between her and Dawson, and he wasn't happy. But he hadn't said anything and neither had she, both preferring to ignore the elephant in the room.

He cleared his throat. "The police talked to your ex-husband. He didn't see who shot him." He rubbed his grizzled face. "The bullet they dug out of his chest was the same caliber as the casings Dawson found on the ridge when someone shot at you guys."

A draft wafted through the room, and she wrapped her arms across her chest. A murderer lurked on the Circle 5 killing people. The land's stark natural beauty, and the horror of murder were polar opposites. "Are they certain the shootings weren't hunting accidents?"

His mouth tightened. "Not a chance in hell."

"What's this about hell?" Dawson strolled into the room. His hair was rumpled, his face pale. Dark circles underscored his eyes. His red plaid shirt was untucked, and the top two buttons were undone, revealing a tuft of dark hair. He looked like he hadn't slept in days.

The temperature in the room plummeted ten degrees, and her stomach knotted. She'd done her best the past days to avoid him. She left the room when he entered, gave him a wide berth if they passed in the hall, even carried her meals up to her room to eat, using the excuse that she was exhausted.

The weight of his gaze was like a hand crushing her, and she wanted to run upstairs and hide, but if she fled, he'd know she was afraid, know he'd broken her heart. She bit down on her bottom lip, and held firm.

"I was just telling Stella what Sergeant Murphy told me," Alf said. His sharp-eyed gaze slid between her and Dawson and back again.

"The police spotters in the helicopter Sergeant Murphy sent up haven't found any sign of the shooter." Dawson crossed the room and stood with his back to the fire.

She focused on the orange ball of the setting sun gilding the drifts of snow in the front yard.

"How can that be?" Alf sounded rattled. "He has to be hiding out somewhere."

"Exactly."

The grimness in Dawson's voice unsettled her, and in spite of her determination to avoid his gaze, she looked at him. "You think he's still in the area? Surely with all the police and the snowstorm, he's long gone."

"The killer's in the same boat we are. When the storm hit, he was stuck. Any tracks he made in the snow would be all too visible. He'd have to hole up somewhere and wait out the weather."

"Have the cops checked with Henry?" Alf asked.

Dawson nodded. "He hasn't seen anything unusual."

"This character's been hanging around the ranch for days. He's killed our cattle, cut our fences, and shot people. You'd think someone would have seen his tracks or some evidence of this bastard's presence." Alf paced to the window and jammed his hands on his hips. "How come nobody's seen this guy? Answer me that. Is he a damn ghost?"

Dawson threaded his hands through his hair. "I've had the men out searching. They've checked all the outbuildings, and they've snowmobiled out to the line shacks, but they haven't found any signs of a trespasser."

Alf shot Dawson a hard look. "He's gotta be here somewhere."

A chill prickled along her spine like tiny fingernails scratching. "If you're so certain this killer is still on the Circle 5, what are we doing about it? How are we protecting ourselves?"

"*We?*" Dawson asked. "All of a sudden we're a *we*? I thought you couldn't wait to get away from here."

Her hackles rose at the sarcasm in his voice, but Alf spoke before she snapped.

"You don't have to worry, Stella. Dawson'll keep us safe. He's ordered the men to take turns patrolling the areas around the ranch house and barn." He placed another log on the fire and stoked the coals with the poker until the flames roared, and a blast of heat filled the room.

Dawson will keep us safe.

Alf's words pierced her heart like he'd struck her with a bayonet. Too late. Dawson had already hurt her more than any crazed gunman. If she didn't get away from him and this ranch soon, she feared what would happen. Something had to break, probably her heart.

And then what?

She shivered. Yes, and then what?

"I should check on Deirdre." And with that, she fled like the hounds of hell were after her.

Chapter 22

Stella sat up and rubbed her scratchy eyes. Another sleepless night wasted agonizing over the mistakes she'd made. Falling in love with Dawson took top billing. Sleeping with him ran a close second. How much longer could she endure the stress without going crazy?

Tossing off the tangle of blankets, she sat up on the edge of the bed. Her bags were packed, and she was ready to leave as soon as the weather warmed enough to melt the layer of ice covering the lake and Dawson's plane could take off. Alf assured her a chinook was on its way, and warm, drying winds would flow through the valley, melting the snow and ice. A last reprieve before winter settled in for good.

She'd talked to Nicholas on the radiophone the day before, and he was making a good recovery. He worried he'd left her at the ranch with the killer still at large, but she assured him she was fine, and she'd be leaving any day.

She crossed to the window. Blowing warm air on the ice-glazed glass, she rubbed the moisture droplets with the sleeve of her nightgown and peered through the small, clear circle. The world outside, encased in a blanket of snow and ice, was a frozen wonderland. Stars twinkled in the clear night sky, and the moon was bright and full. Millions of tiny ice crystals sparkled in the snowy yard. Icicles hung from the eaves trough above her window.

She peered closer, and her heart skipped a beat. Had she imagined it? No, there it was again—a tiny, jewel-like drop of melting ice. For the first time in days, her spirits lifted. The chinook was on the way. Alf told her that once the warm winds hit, the snow and ice would melt, and temperatures could rise as much as twenty degrees in mere hours.

She hadn't eaten the previous day, or the day before. Why bother when food tasted like paper? But now she was hungry, ravenously hungry. Grabbing her robe from the back of the chair, she shrugged it on and tiptoed along the hall and down the stairs to the kitchen.

Bright moonlight streamed through the windows lighting the large room, and she didn't bother turning on the light. She removed a platter of leftover roast beef from the refrigerator and rummaged in a cupboard for a loaf of Alf's homemade, sauerkraut-and-rye bread. Opening jars of mustard and horseradish, she spread a thick layer of each condiment on a piece of bread. Piling thin slices of rare roast beef on top, she finished with another slab of bread. Her mouth watered as she admired her creation. Talk about a sandwich.

The house creaked, and she stiffened and peered over her shoulder. The last time she'd ventured into the kitchen in the middle of the night, Dawson had been sitting in the rocking chair by the fire, but this time the room was deserted. Relief washed over her.

Placing the sandwich on a plate, she tidied up, and with sandwich in hand, she slipped out of the kitchen and crept down the hall to the stairs. A stream of light spilled from the open door of Dawson's office.

She started up the stairs, but hesitated. What was he doing awake in the middle of the night? Was he okay? She frowned. Why did she care? She climbed another step, but the light beckoned, and with a heavy sigh, she retraced her steps, set the plate on the hall table, and tiptoed down the hall. Her heart beat like a trip-hammer, and she peered around the edge of the door.

Dawson was slumped in his chair, his long legs stretched in front of him, a glass clasped in his hand. A half-empty whiskey bottle was on the table beside his chair. In the muted glow of the lamplight, his rugged features were softened. His hair was mussed from his habit of running his fingers through the dark strands, and several curls hung over his forehead, shadowing his eyes.

He set down his glass and stood and lifted the large photograph of Deirdre and her mother from the wall. Even from across the room, his grief was palpable as he stared into the smiling face of his dead wife. The lines at the corners of his mouth deepened. A tormented moan like that of a wounded animal slipped from his mouth.

Wincing as if she'd been kicked in the gut, she backed away and scooted down the hall and up the stairs, the roast beef sandwich forgotten. If she needed to be reminded of Dawson's anguish over the loss of his wife, she'd just witnessed his raw, gut-wrenching grief firsthand.

She sat on the edge of her bed and stared at the wall, her mind churning. If Dawson couldn't fly her out in the morning, she'd find some other way to leave. She couldn't remain at the ranch. Each time she passed him in the hall or sat across from him at the dinner table, another piece of her heart shattered.

A tap at her door startled her. Was the entire household awake? She threaded her fingers through her hair in a futile attempt to smooth out the tangles. "Come in."

Dawson opened the door and stepped inside. His broad-shouldered frame and virile masculinity overpowered the small room. He held out the plate with the roast beef sandwich. His gaze, hot as laser points, burned into hers. All traces of the grief she'd witnessed earlier had vanished. "You forgot this."

She stared at the incriminating sandwich, but didn't reach for it. Heat flared onto her cheeks. Did he know she'd witnessed his emotional breakdown?

He set the plate on the dresser. "The weather's warming. Once a chinook hits, the temperature rises fast. We should be able to leave in a couple of days."

"Good."

He cleared his throat. "Deirdre's going to miss you."

"She's young. She'll get over it." Her voice sounded wooden even to her own ears.

His gaze was dark and brooding.

Why didn't he leave? Why was he making this so difficult? "Was there something else?"

He opened his mouth to speak, but stopped and tilted his head as if listening to something. His body tensed, the furrow between his dark brows deepening.

"What is it? What's wrong?"

"I thought I heard something. It's probably nothing, but I'd better check." He wheeled around and strode out of the room.

****

Dawson hurried down the stairs, taking the steps two at a time. He'd heard something…a thump? Probably nothing, but his gut pinged a warning. With the killer on the loose, he'd been on edge. Hell, he'd locked and bolted the doors and checked that the windows were all locked, something he'd never done before. Never had to do. But then there'd never been a murder on the Circle 5 either.

Fifteen minutes later, he stood in the kitchen. He'd searched all the downstairs rooms. Nothing seemed out of place. The house was quiet.

Snickers was in Dee's room sound asleep, and Shas was with Stella.

The cat slept on Alf's chair by the fire.

All seemed peaceful, but he couldn't dispel the uneasy tingle deep in his gut. He strode to the door, slid back the bolt, and opened the door. A blast of cold air hit him as he stepped onto the porch.

The vivid sky of early dawn was streaked with shades of red and charcoal gray. The weather was changing. A warm front was on the way. Even the air smelled different. The icicles hanging from the eaves dripped in the warming air.

A small pool of light bobbed and weaved by the barn.

He walked down the porch steps and clomped through the melting snow. "Everything okay, Jim?"

Jim stepped out of the shadows cast by the barn and flicked off his flashlight. "Quiet as a mouse." He spit out a brown stream of tobacco juice. "You're up early, Dawson."

"Thought I heard something."

"Nothing out here as far as I can tell."

"You've been patrolling the perimeter like I asked?"

"Like clockwork." Another gob of spittle hit the snow. "If you ask me, this is all a waste of time. The shooter's long gone."

Dawson nodded. Jim was probably right. He'd had his men searching the ranch for the past two days, and they hadn't found any signs of a stranger. If they were lucky, the murderer had frozen to death in the storm, and they'd find his rotting body in the spring thaw. He patted the foreman on the arm. "Keep up the good work. Who's on shift after you?"

"Bob. If he remembers to get up. That old guy sleeps like the dead."

Dawson chuckled. Bob's ability to sleep through any commotion was legendary. Last year a bear had ransacked the shed behind the bunkhouse. They'd had to shoot off the bear banger to scare the beast away, but Bob had slept through the entire debacle.

The man liked his sleep, but Dawson wasn't worried he wouldn't show up for his shift. He trusted his men. "I'll leave you to it. Good night." He studied the color-soaked sky. "Or I guess I should say, good morning."

"Dawson?"

"What is it?"

"Is Stella really leaving?"

He frowned at the disappointment shining in Jim's dark eyes. Another one of Stella's conquests. *Join the club, buddy.* "As soon as the ice is off the lake, and it's safe to fly, I'm taking her to Hosten."

Jim hawked up another mouthful of tobacco juice.

"The boys will be disappointed. It's been nice having her around."

A cold, hard lump formed in Dawson's stomach. "Yeah, well, she's leaving. Better get used to it." He wheeled around and stomped back to the porch, already regretting his harshness. It wasn't Jim's fault Stella was leaving. The blame for her imminent departure lay squarely on Dawson's shoulders. He'd driven her away. By lowering his guard and falling in love with her, he'd made her leaving inevitable.

"Hey, Dawson." The husky whisper seeped like a breath of air from the deep shadows under the eaves of the house.

He stilled and peered into the dark. "Henry? Is that you?"

Henry stepped out of the darkness. "Can I come in for a spell?"

Dawson eyed the rifle hanging by a strap over Henry's broad shoulder. His gut tightened. "What's going on, Henry? Why are you here at this time of night?"

"Can't a man ask a neighbor for a cup of coffee on a cold night?"

"A cup of coffee?" His gut screamed a warning, but he squashed his unease. He'd known Henry almost his entire life. The trapper was like family. Sure, he didn't care for people much, but his reclusiveness wasn't unusual. Lots of antisocial characters inhabited the remote river valleys and hills in the Chilcotin. Henry was just...well, Henry.

The alarm bells in his gut continued to clang, but inhabitants in the backcountry lived by a code. You didn't turn someone away from your door. Not ever.

The shootings had put him on edge, and he was seeing danger even in old friends. He smiled. "Sure, come on in. I'll put a fresh pot on for you."

Henry nodded. "Thanks."

Dawson opened the door and stepped into the kitchen's warmth and light.

Henry shuffled in after him, closed the door, and slid the bolt.

Dawson spun at the sound of metal locking in place. "What are you doing?"

"Making sure we're not disturbed."

The warnings clanging through him coalesced into an ear-piercing screech. "What's going on, Henry?"

Henry's gaze flitted around the room, his eyes wild. "We need to talk." The big man's bulky body was tense, his hands twitching. Sweat beaded his brow.

"Sure, Henry. Let's talk, but first, why don't you put the gun down?" An icy block of fear clogged his throat. Deirdre was asleep upstairs.

The grizzled mountain man scowled at the rifle as if he'd forgotten he had it, but he didn't set the gun down. He tugged off his gray wool toque and tossed it on the counter. Unzipping his parka, he revealed a stained and tattered plaid shirt. His heavy wool pants bagged on his burly frame. His feet were encased in knee-high, fleece-lined, leather boots. A hunting knife was in a sheath strapped to a leather belt around his waist.

Fear coiled like a serpent in Dawson's gut at the wild light shining in Henry's gray eyes, and his jerky, almost robotic mannerisms. He struggled to remain calm. His five-year-old daughter slept upstairs. Stella was awake and could appear at any moment. He had to get the rifle away from Henry and defuse the situation before anyone got hurt.

"Let me make some coffee. It's pretty cold out there tonight." Each pump of his heart seemed to be in slow motion. "I figured you'd be hunkered down in your cabin waiting until the chinook hit. What made you come to the ranch house?" Henry didn't own a horse or a snowmobile. It would have taken him hours to walk from his cabin to the house.

"I already told you. We need to talk."

Dawson affected a laugh. "That's right. You did." He faked a yawn. "Guess I'm just tired. It's been a long few days." As he poured coffee grounds into the pot and added water, he watched Henry out of the corner of his eye.

The older man's face was tanned and creased from years of living outdoors. His shaggy beard had more gray in it than Dawson remembered, and his wild tangle of brown hair was sprinkled with gray.

Henry shuffled over to the rocking chair by the fire and sat down. He unstrapped the long rifle and laid the gun across his lap. Leaning closer to the fire, he rubbed his big, rawboned hands together. "This weather's a bitch. Can't remember the last time we had a snowstorm hit so early in the season. Can you?"

The coffee pot perked, and the rich aroma of fresh coffee filled the warm kitchen.

Dawson didn't reply. Henry hadn't walked five kilometers to talk about the weather. Something more was going on. The pinging in his gut transformed to a high-pitched scream.

The cat awoke and jumped off the chair and strolled over to Henry and rubbed against his legs. Loud purring resonated.

Henry patted the cat, rubbing his thick fingers under the cat's chin.

The purring intensified.

Dawson huffed out a breath. Maybe he'd read the situation wrong. Maybe everything was okay. The strain of the past days had taken their toll, and he was jumping at every little thing, expecting the worse. How could he be worried about Henry? Henry was a family friend, a harmless old man. He cleared his throat. "So what did you want to talk about? It must be pretty important to get you out on a night like this."

Henry stopped stroking the cat and looked up and met Dawson's gaze. "I don't like change. Never have."

Dawson nodded, but he had no idea where this conversation was going. "Things change. That's a fact of life."

"The police and their helicopters have been flying all over the ranch for days. The damn machines are scaring away the game." He licked his cracked lips. "A man can't get a moment's peace and quiet anymore. I want you to tell them to leave."

"I can't do that. A man was murdered. Two others were shot. The asshole even shot at me and Stella. The police have to find this guy before he hurts someone else."

"Stella's the woman you hired to be Deirdre's nanny, isn't she? I met her the night I brought Dee home." The trapper stared at the flickering flames. "She's not who you think she is."

Dawson pulled two mugs from the cupboard and poured steaming coffee into each cup. "What do you mean?"

Henry lurched to his feet, his dark eyes blazing, the rifle clenched in his hands. "You don't understand. I checked her out. I went into Hosten and used a computer at the town library, and I ran her name. Guess what I found?"

Dawson opened his mouth to tell Henry he already knew what the Internet search revealed, but Henry cut him off.

"She works for the damn mining company. Did you know that? She's the head lawyer for Imperial Monarch Resources. She's the person who ties up the mining contracts with a bunch of bullshit legal mumbo jumbo that fools the government into granting permission for her company to go ahead with their mines." Henry's big body vibrated with agitation as he spit out his outrage.

A trill of alarm raced down Dawson's spine along with a sickening realization. "You're the one, aren't you? You killed that geologist and wounded his partner. You shot my cattle." He sucked in a quick breath. Henry Rivers was a cold-blooded murderer. "You shot at me and Stella. You tried to kill us. Why? Why would you do that? I thought we were friends."

An even more terrifying thought reared its head. He'd let a murderer in the house! Stella was awake. How long before she came downstairs? And what of Dee? The thought of something happening to his daughter was enough to turn his bowels to water. With an explosive burst, he lunged for the gun.

Henry jerked up the rifle and pointed the deadly weapon at Dawson.

Dawson froze at the menacing sound of the click of the trigger. The moisture in his mouth dried. A trickle of sweat ran down the back of his neck as he stared down the long barrel at certain death.

"What the hell do you think you're doing?" demanded Henry.

"Trying to stop you from doing something stupid."

"Stupid? You call protecting this land *stupid*?" His eyes flashed fire. "You, of all people? Hell, Dawson, it's your land they want to destroy." He shook his head. "If those mine people have their way, they'll turn the Circle 5 into a toxic dump. That's why I did what I did. I thought if your cattle turned up dead and some of your fences were cut, you'd call in the cops, and they'd blame the mining company, and that would halt any further intrusions while they defended themselves."

He blew out a gust of air. "When that didn't stop them, I had to ramp things up to the next level and shoot those geologists. They were trespassing on Circle 5 land, digging up the soil with their damn machines, and staking out patches of ground. I had to do something." His finger played with the trigger. Twin red patches heated his bearded cheeks. "I'm not about to let anything happen to the Circle 5. Not on my watch. No damn way."

Ice settled deep in Dawson's gut as Henry revealed the shocking truth. He wanted to stop the mine. That's why he'd killed the geologist and wounded the other man, and why he'd shot Nicholas King. "I understand you're upset about the mine. We all are, but this isn't the way to stop it. Murdering that man didn't change anything, and killing me won't change anything either."

"Shit, man, I don't want to hurt you. Your dad gave me a place to stay and never bothered me. You've been good to me, too."

"So why—" Dawson nodded at the rifle. "—are you holding that damn rifle pointed at me? Why did you shoot at me and Stella the other day? None of this makes any sense." His mind raced. Time was ticking. Stella could come down to the kitchen at any minute. Or Dee could wake up and come looking for a glass of water. And how long before Alf started breakfast?

"I wasn't shooting at you. I was shooting at that woman."

"Stella? You were trying to kill *Stella*?" His stomach heaved. "Is that why you're here? To kill her?"

"No, it wasn't like that. If I wanted her dead, she'd be dead. I had her in my rifle sight. It would have been an easy shot." The corners of his mouth tightened. "I didn't want to kill her, just wound her and let her know she and her damn company aren't welcome here."

Footsteps creaked in the hall. "You'll be happy to know I'm all packed and ready to go."

A pang of dread zinged through Dawson like a bolt of lightning as the nightmare turned real, and Stella strode into the room, Shas at her heels.

She stopped and stared. Her gaze swiveled between Dawson and Henry and back to Dawson. "Dawson?" Her voice was a thin squeak. "What's going on?"

Chapter 23

Shas's low growl sent a chill whispering up her back.

"Dawson?" She stared at the tall, bear of a man holding a long, menacing-looking gun pointed at Dawson.

Henry's weathered face was almost obscured by a thick, salt-and-pepper beard. His hair hung in dark, greasy strands. He grinned, exposing a row of startling white teeth. "Well, well, well. We were just talking about you." His smile widened, but his eyes were cold and feral. "Come on in and sit down, Mrs. King."

She shot a glance at Dawson. "Dawson? What's going on? Why is he pointing a gun at you?"

Dawson's face was ashen, his jaw squared in anger. He gave a subtle warning shake of his head. "Do what he says, Stella."

"Sit down." The bearded man gestured with the gun toward a chair by the large oak table.

She was too terrified to move. Her knees were locked in place, her feet glued to the floor.

Shas growled. The hackles on the back of his neck rose, and his tail swished back and forth.

"Shut that dog up, or I'll kill it." Henry swung the rifle toward the big black dog.

"Don't shoot him. Please." She gripped Shas's collar, holding the dog to her side. "It…it's okay, boy.

It's okay." Patting the dog's velvety head, she ordered, "Sit."

The dog growled again, his gaze fixed on the intruder. He tugged at her restraint, but she held tight. "Sit," she repeated, forcing a calm authority into her quavering voice. If he killed Shas, the noise of the rifle shot would wake Deirdre, and the little girl would come to investigate. Her heart stuttered. Whatever it took, she had to stop that from happening. She jerked on Shas's collar. "Sit!"

The big dog whined and licked her hand. His hackles were a darker stripe down his spine, but he obeyed and sat on his haunches.

"Good boy." Her voice cracked. "Stay." Knees shaking, she stumbled over to the chair and sat down. She clasped her hands on her lap to hide their trembling.

Henry nodded at Dawson. "You too, Dawson."

"Think about what you're doing, Henry. If you kill us, the police will hunt you down and lock you in a jail cell. You'll never get out." Dawson's voice was cool and unruffled as he reasoned with the man. "You hate being confined. You wouldn't survive a week in an eight-foot by eight-foot cell."

He held his hands out in a pleading gesture. "Put the rifle down, and we'll talk about this. Stella's a lawyer. She knows the legal system. She'll convince Imperial Monarch to halt their plans for the mine. She'll stop the development. Just give her a chance."

Henry grabbed the back of a chair and hauled it out and kicked it toward Dawson. "Sit down. Now." He pointed the barrel. "Or I kill her. Your choice."

Dawson, his eyes spitting venom, moved over to

the chair and sat. "What now, Henry? Are you going to kill both of us? Because that's what you're going to have to do. I won't let you shoot Stella. You'll have to kill me as well. Is that what you want?"

"Awww, Dawson, don't do that." Henry scratched the back of his neck. "This isn't about you. I told you that." His eyes narrowed, and he glared at her. "It's about *her*."

She sucked in a breath, stunned by his hatred. "I…I don't understand. What did I ever do to you?"

"You and your damn company don't care who you hurt or what you destroy in your endless quest for wealth."

Her heart pounded so loud in her chest his vitriol was silenced, but she'd heard enough. She ached to rub her throbbing temples, but she was terrified he'd shoot if she so much as twitched. He'd killed and wounded all those people because he didn't want Imperial Monarch to develop a mine on the Circle 5. And he blamed her for the development. A block of ice congealed in her gut.

Dawson jumped to his feet. "Stop this, Henry, now, before it's too late. You don't want to hurt anyone else. You're a good man. I know you are." He held out his hand. "Give me the gun."

"I can't do that, Dawson." Henry wiped sweat from his gleaming brow with the back of his stained coat sleeve. "Someone has to stand up to these people. Someone has to show them we won't lie down and let them trample our land."

"So let's do that. We'll go to the government ministry together. We'll fight the mine. We'll stop it. I promise you. Just put the gun down."

"It's too late. You know it is. I've gone too far to stop." Henry seized her arm and hauled her out of the chair. "She's coming with me."

She yelped and fought him, twisting and kicking, but his grip was too strong. Her stomach heaved at the stink of sour sweat of his unwashed body. His arm tightened across her chest, crushing her against him and cutting off her breath. Spots danced before her eyes. She stopped fighting and focused on sucking in oxygen.

Dawson charged, but froze when Henry yanked out a vicious-looking knife from a leather scabbard on his belt and jammed the blade against her throat.

Terror blasted her bloodstream as the sharp blade sliced her skin. A burning sensation, and then a warm trickle of blood slid down her neck.

"Don't make a mistake you'll regret, Dawson. I'll kill her if I have to." Henry slung the rifle over his shoulder on a canvas strap. Holding the knife against her throat, he dragged her with him as he backed across the kitchen to the outside door.

The blade pressed against her skin chilled her to the bone even though she was crushed against Henry's hard, sweating body.

Do something!

The frantic order blazed through her, but her fear was overpowering. What if Henry shot Dawson? The thought alone was enough to turn her legs to jelly. She sought Dawson's gaze, willing him not to do anything rash.

His hands were squeezed into fists at his sides, and his body visibly vibrated with his supreme effort to stand still and do nothing.

Henry lowered the knife, unbolted the door, and

yanked it open.

"This is crazy, Henry." Dawson's voice was raw. "Leave Stella. You don't need her. I won't tell anyone you were here. You can escape. You know this country better than anyone. You can disappear. The cops'll never find you."

Yes, leave me. The plea filled her mind. *Leave this house and go.* Her heart thundered in her chest, and her breath rasped in and out like a steam engine. She twisted in the tight confines of his arm and slid a glance at her captor's face. Her blood chilled.

Insanity gleamed in Henry's wild, bloodshot eyes. "Tell your friends at Imperial Monarch if they want to see their lawyer alive, they'd better stop their plans for the mine." He slid the knife into the scabbard, and with both hands free, he half-carried, half-dragged her onto the back porch, his grip like iron. "I'll be in touch."

Relief that they were outside the house, and the razor-sharp blade was no longer digging into her skin washed over her. She opened her mouth to scream, hoping one of the men patrolling the ranch house would hear her cry for help.

As if reading her mind, Henry slapped his big, callused palm over her mouth. "Shut up, or I'll kill Dawson." His growl was fierce, making it clear he wouldn't hesitate to follow through on his threat.

She gagged, struggling to breathe through his clamped palm.

The back door slammed open, and Dawson burst onto the porch, his eyes blazing. "If you hurt her, you're a dead man." His voice was steel.

"Stay back." Henry yanked her closer, drew out his gun, and pointed the barrel at Dawson. "I'm doing this for you, Dawson. You and little Dee. The Circle 5 is your legacy. I won't let Imperial Monarch destroy the ranch your grandfather built from nothing." He hauled her down the steps and away from the shoveled path and into the gloom of the snow-shrouded trees.

She struggled, but his grip around her body was too strong. Wishing she were wearing boots instead of her fuzzy, soft-soled slippers, she scrabbled to keep her feet under her as they headed deeper into the forest, thrashing through drifts of knee-high snow.

When they were well away from the lights of the ranch house, her captor removed his hand from her mouth, but his death-like hold on her arm never weakened.

"Please. Let me go." Her pleas fell on deaf ears as he dragged her behind him, his pace steady.

The cold and damp seeped through her sweater, and she shivered. Her pants were soaked. Clumps of melting snow clung to the soft fabric. One slipper had fallen off, lost in a snowdrift. Her bare foot was numb, feeling like a block of solid ice.

Tears streamed down her cheeks, blinding her. Henry was going to kill her. He already faced murder and attempted murder charges and a lifetime in prison. What was one more life? His goal was to stop the mine. In his crazed state he thought she had that power. She hiccupped a sob. If only he knew the truth. She didn't have any say in the company. Not anymore.

Nicholas had softened this past year, but the company came first. It always had. If she needed proof, she'd only to consider the past few days. One of his employees had been murdered, another lay wounded in the hospital, and Nicholas himself was recovering from a bullet wound. And yet, he never considered shutting down the mine deal. Too much money was at stake, and money was what Nicholas was all about.

Even if he wanted to agree to the demands of her kidnapper, the company's shareholders would pressure him to move forward with the mine development. Due to their numerous mining ventures in foreign countries, the company had a strict policy of not being swayed by kidnappers or extortionists. Another sob shuddered through her. She should know. She'd written the policy.

Dawson would raise the alarm, and the men would start searching. They'd follow their tracks. But what if they didn't find her in time? What if Henry killed her before help arrived? She had to do something. She had to save herself.

Filling her lungs, she released a bellow of anger and outrage and struck. Her fist connected with his cheek with a resounding smack.

"You little bitch," he hissed and grabbed her hands and jerked her palms together in front of her. Holding her wrists with one dirt-encrusted hand, he dug in his coat pocket and tugged out a thin nylon rope. Ignoring her thrashing, he wrapped the rope around her wrists.

She mewed in panic as the rope dug into her flesh, but the more she struggled, the tighter the rope squeezed.

He drew out another, longer piece of rope and tied it to the rope binding her hands. "Now shut up and follow like a good girl." He towed her behind him like she was a dog on a leash.

Slipping and sliding on the icy ground, she stumbled over unseen roots and loose rocks. Each time she fell, he yanked on the rope and hauled her to her feet. The rope rubbed the skin on her wrists raw, and warm blood dripped onto the melting snow. Her hands and feet were numb. The early morning cold seeped through her thin sweater, and her teeth chattered so loud she feared she'd crack a molar.

The sun was rising in the sky when he stopped and tied the rope tethering her to a tree. Without a word, he wiped sweat from his broad brow and trudged into the forest.

She tore against the rope, terrified he'd return; terrified he'd left her to freeze to death. As the minutes ticked by, she stared at the dense stand of trees and jumble of snow-covered rocks. She'd die there…alone.

An image of the geologist's bloated corpse torn apart by the crows and coyotes flashed before her, and she moaned. "No, no, no." The anguished wail ended on a whimper, and she sagged against the tree trunk, tears streaming down her face.

A shadow in the shape of a man moved out of the trees. Relief soared through her. Help had arrived. She was safe. Dawson had found her. "Help." Her voice was weak, barely a whisper. She moistened her lips and tried again. "Help me, please." She blinked at the approaching figure through her streaming tears. A weight settled over her, and she sagged on her knees as she recognized the burly mountain man.

Henry, packing a shovel he'd found somewhere, tromped over to a pile of large boulders and scooped snow and branches away, revealing a small opening in the jumble of rocks. Stone-faced and silent, he set down the shovel and untied the rope binding her to the tree. Grunting with the effort, he half carried and half towed her up the hill toward the opening. "Get in." Not giving her the chance to resist, he slammed his hands on her back and shoved her through the narrow opening.

She yelped and thrust out her arms to stop from falling face-first on the rocky ground, but her bound hands were useless. Her head struck something hard. An explosion of stars danced before her eyes. A swirl of darkness swooped down, and she fell into emptiness.

****

Her eyes watered at the unceasing, painful throbbing. Wincing, she lifted her bound hands and explored the lump on her forehead. Dried blood crusted the wound. She licked her lips, grimacing at the brackish taste on her furred tongue. How long had she been unconscious?

Henry's big body seemed to fill the cramped, dark cave. He sat on the ground with his legs crossed before a small, smoldering fire, watching her with hooded eyes.

She scrunched against the cold rock wall, struggling to get as far from him as possible. Her hands were still tied together, and her fingers were numb.

He added twigs to the fire.

Smoke billowed in a noxious cloud and stung her eyes. Her teeth chattered, adding to the throbbing pain in her head. Judging by the steady drip of what must be snow melting off the trees, the temperature outside was above zero, but the air inside the cave was dank and freezing.

"You're cold." Frowning, he shrugged off his coat, rose to his knees, and draped the heavy coat over her shoulders.

Her nostrils flared at the pungent stink of rancid sweat. The animal fur trimming the hood reeked, but desperate for warmth, she swallowed back bile and huddled into the coat.

Tugging a nylon sack from the back of the dugout, he opened the bag and removed a small plastic bottle of water. He unscrewed the cap and placed the water on the ground by her feet. "Drink."

Her parched throat closed tight at the sight of the life-saving liquid. Thirst reared up like a beast, and she leaned forward and grasped the bottle, but it slipped through her nerveless fingers and fell. Water spilled onto the ground.

He grabbed the water bottle and raised it to her lips. "Drink."

Refusing to accept anything from him, she shook her head, but he prodded her lips until she opened her mouth. Cold water drizzled down her throat, soothing the aching tightness. Unable to resist, she gulped and swallowed, and gulped again.

When the bottle was empty, he tossed it into the corner and once again foraged in his pack. He pulled out an energy bar, and some strips of what looked like dried meat.

Her stomach rumbled at the smoky, meat smell.

"Eat." He tossed a strip of jerky on the ground.

She held up her bound hands. "I can't eat with my hands tied. Untie me. Please."

He shook his head.

She bit back her frustration. What was he afraid of…if her hands were free, she'd somehow slip by him and escape? He was blocking the entrance. She'd have to climb over him to get out.

Large slabs of rough, gray, granite-like rock formed the back and three sides of the small shelter.

The low roof, constructed of interlaced fir branches and dried moss, allowed just enough room to sit. Shafts of sunlight seeped through gaps in the roof, and melting snow dripped onto the dirt floor, creating tiny mud puddles.

Henry snapped more sticks and set them on the fire. The light from the flames highlighted the network of deep lines radiating from his hooded, gray eyes. Deeper grooves furrowed between his thick, bristly eyebrows.

"They'll find us, you know. Dawson will follow our tracks, and he'll find us." Her voice was a rough husk.

He folded his arms over his chest. "It snowed while you were asleep. Our tracks are buried. No one will find us. Not unless I want them to."

She sucked in a breath. Those were the most frightening words he'd spoken since he'd dragged her out of the ranch house. *No one will find us.* But Dawson would. Of course he would. He was a hunter. He'd follow their tracks no matter how much it had snowed. She clung to the thin thread of hope. "What are you going to do with me? Are you going to kill me like you did that geologist?"

Silence.

"Murder is a major crime. You don't want to spend the rest of your life in jail. Let me go. I won't tell them where you are." She licked her cracked lips. "I promise."

Another beat of silence.

She tried again. "Look, I agree with you. The mine would ruin the Circle 5, but you have to understand, I'm on a leave of absence from Imperial Monarch. I haven't worked there for almost a year. I don't have any say in the company. Not anymore."

"You're married to the owner."

"*Was*. I *was* married to him. We're divorced." Her heart beat a trip-hammer in her chest as she fought to reason with the maniac. "We're in the middle of nowhere. How are you going to inform the company of your demands?" She pointed at the smoldering fire. "Are you planning to use smoke signals?"

"Dawson will tell them what I want." He fished in the nylon sack and pulled out a satellite phone. "If not, I'll use this." He patted the black plastic case and smirked. "With this gizmo I can communicate with the world."

She tried another tack. "Dawson will have called the Mounties. They'll bring in their search teams, helicopters, planes, maybe even dogs. Either way, they'll find us. You know they will."

He shrugged. "Maybe. Maybe not."

"How long are you going to keep me here?"

"Until this thing is settled." He stuffed the phone back in the pack and added more wood to the fire.

Until this thing is settled.

How long would that be? Days? Weeks? Never?

She wanted to yell, to demand he let her go, but her throat sealed closed, and only a tiny squeak emerged. *Calm down. Help's on the way.* The second Henry hauled her out of the house Dawson would have called the police. They'd send out search parties. The manhunt would be massive. A murderer was on the loose.

Murderer.

The terrifying word leaped out, and she swallowed back bile.

"I don't want to hurt you."

Henry's deep, gravel-filled voice jerked her out of her frightening thoughts. "Let me go, then."

"I can't. Not yet."

"Look at my wrists." She held out her bound hands, revealing the bloody wounds. "Untie me. I won't run away. I promise." She bit her bottom lip hoping he didn't hear the lie in her words. The second he turned his back she was out of there. Even if she had to knock him over the head with the damn satellite phone, she was getting the hell out of the cramped cave.

The flickering firelight revealed his unrelenting gaze.

She shivered with the sinking certainty he knew exactly what she was thinking. Eying his broad shoulders and thick, muscled body, she sagged on the hard ground in defeat. No way could she overpower him. Not in her wildest dreams. "What—" She struggled to swallow. "—what are you planning to do with me?"

"I told you. Hold you for ransom. If the mine proposal is cancelled, I'll let you go. If it isn't revoked, no one will see you again."

His words, spoken in a tone someone would use to discuss the weather, chilled her to the bone. She'd die in this cave. Dawson would never know how much she loved him. Deirdre would lose another person she cared for. She slumped against the cold, unforgiving rock slab and gave in to silent tears.

Chapter 24

The high-octane fuel of rage and fear kept Dawson plowing through the heavy, melting snowdrifts as he headed deeper into the forest. His body screamed for rest, but he trudged on, one step after another, refusing to stop until Stella was safe.

Time was running out. The longer Henry held her captive, the more chance she'd be harmed. Or worse. His breath caught in his throat, and he stumbled, grabbing onto a tree trunk to stop his fall.

Bob plodded behind, his harsh breathing loud in the silent forest. "Dawson, let's take a break. The men can't go on like this. They need food and rest." He grabbed Dawson's coat sleeve and dragged him to a halt. "Just for a few hours, and then we'll start again."

Dawson studied the deep lines of exhaustion aging Bob's face, and guilt flooded him. He'd pushed his men hard. Maybe too hard. But from the second Henry dragged Stella out of the house he'd been out of his mind with fear. He'd raised the alarm, grabbed a few supplies, and headed after them. In all the hours since, he hadn't stopped searching, even though his breath rasped in and out of his chest in painful gusts, and each step took a monumental effort.

Stella's life was in danger.

Henry was unstable.

He'd seen the light of madness in the trapper's

eyes. He was determined to stop the mine, and he'd do anything to achieve his goal. He'd already murdered one man and wounded two others. Killing Stella wouldn't faze him.

His gut clenched at the certainty this nightmare was his fault. He should have suspected Henry was behind the shootings. Dawson had given the man a brown-felt cowboy hat last Christmas, just like the one the injured geologist had seen on the man who'd shot him.

Henry was an excellent marksman and owned several guns. His past was a mystery, but Dawson's dad had told him Henry had served in the US military Special Forces in Afghanistan. He'd come to the Chilcotin a broken man. That was why his father had let Henry stay on the ranch.

Dawson ground his teeth. How could he have been so stupid? He'd allowed a murderer into his house. Hell, he'd welcomed him with open arms. That's what angered him the most. In spite of his misgivings, he'd let a killer inside the house where his daughter slept. If he'd acted on the pinging in his gut, if he'd called for Jean-Luc's help, none of this horror would have happened. He swiped a hand over his eyes, surprised at the moisture.

"Dawson. Did you hear me? The men need a break."

He regarded Bob's drawn face and nodded. "Call them back."

Bob didn't budge. "What about you? You need rest too."

"I have to find her." He tore his arm free of Bob's grip and trudged onward.

Bob's exasperated sigh echoed through the trees, followed by his plodding footsteps as he retreated, and the crackling static of the walkie-talkie as he called off the men.

He was on his own. But it didn't matter. He'd find her. No other option existed. He'd lost one woman he loved. He wouldn't lose another, not as long he breathed, and his heart beat in his chest.

A team of armed officers dressed in full combat gear and two search helicopters had arrived. The helicopters had flown over the ranch all day, scouring the rugged hills and valleys. The three inches of fresh snow that had fallen the previous night covered any tracks. A couple of hours past, one of the ground searchers had found Stella's slipper buried under the snow. There'd been nothing since that discovery.

He wasn't surprised. Henry knew this land, all the crevices, bear dens, and rocky overhangs. If he'd stockpiled supplies, he could hide out for months without being detected.

Grunting with the effort, he climbed out of the valley and trudged along the escarpment to the rocky ridge. He frowned at the fading light. The hard-packed ground hid its secrets well. There were no tracks to follow, no indication of which way Henry and his captive had gone. Dawson was going on instinct alone, letting his gut lead.

He studied the jumble of rocks. Would Henry find shelter there? Maybe, but hauling an unwilling hostage up the steep slope would be a challenge. It made more sense he'd stick to the low ground where the going was easier.

The distant rumble of a helicopter filled the valley,

and a dot appeared in the darkening sky as one of the search helicopters made a final sweep before heading to the ranch house for the night.

A bone-deep tiredness washed over Dawson, and it was all he could do to put one foot in front of the other. The weight of despondency added to his exhaustion. He shifted the nylon straps of the heavy pack on his back. He'd only packed the essentials, but at this time of year with unpredictable weather, he needed a tarp, a small shovel, food, water, a headlamp, and a down sleeping bag. He also carried his hunting rifle slung on a canvas-webbing strap over his right shoulder and a walkie-talkie strapped to his belt.

He inhaled a deep breath of frigid air. Long, dark shadows covered the ground, masking the dips and hollows. A half hour more, and he'd have to find shelter for the night. He couldn't risk stumbling around in the dark. He'd begin his search again at first light.

As if to prove his point, he slipped on a patch of ice and crashed on the ground, landing on his left knee. A sharp jolt of pain ricocheted up his leg. Damn. The last thing he needed was an injury. He couldn't find her if he was lying there like a beached whale.

Wincing, he struggled to stand. His leg wobbled, and he slipped again, but he grabbed onto a rock and stopped his fall. He tested his knee, putting more weight on the bruised joint. Sore, but he could walk.

Limping across the rocky scree, he studied the ground, searching for signs they'd passed this way. The hairs on the back of his neck bristled, and he halted. He sniffed, inhaling a lungful of crisp air and a hint of woodsmoke. His heart raced, and all his senses fired on high alert.

He'd found her!

He shrugged off his backpack, fished out his headlamp, and undid the straps of the leather case holding the rifle. Hefting the heavy rifle onto his shoulder, he squinted through the spotting scope into the gloom, searching for a spiral of smoke. No smoke was visible in the fading light, but the distinctive acrid stench of burning pine tainted the brisk air.

Following his nose, he climbed up the ridge, clambering over massive sheets of rock and slipping and sliding down the other sides. The going was easier without the heavy pack, and he made good time.

The scent of smoke grew stronger.

Slowing his steps, he placed one foot after another on the hard ground, careful not to make any sound. Stealth was essential. Henry was an experienced outdoorsman, and he'd be on high alert, attuned to approaching footsteps. The crunch of snow, skitter of rocks, even Dawson's heavy breathing was a danger to detection.

The daylight faded, and darkness settled like a shroud over the land.

A faint glow appeared in the jumble of rocks ahead. Tiny tendrils of smoke settled like a gray mist in the low hollows. The overhanging rocks concealed the smoke and light and would be impossible to detect from a helicopter hovering overhead.

But Dawson was there, on the ground, just outside Henry's lair.

His heart thundered. He crouched, tightened his grip on the rifle, and ignoring the searing pain in his injured knee, crawled on his belly, inching toward the flickering light.

A voice. Her voice. A rough croak, but *her* voice, filtered through the opening.

Relief washed over him, and for a moment he couldn't breathe.

She was alive!

With renewed determination, he edged closer.

The glimmer of light vanished as a large figure filled the cave opening.

Someone was coming out.

Steadying his breath, he raised the rifle to his shoulder and squinted into the scope, fixing the cave opening in the crosshairs. His index finger rested on the trigger. He didn't want to kill Henry. Hell, he didn't want to hurt anyone, but he sure as hell would if the mountain man refused to release Stella.

Henry's shaggy head appeared, followed by the rest of his body as the big man crawled on his hands and knees through the narrow opening. He stood, placed both of his hands on the small of his back and stretched. The rifle hung from a strap across his shoulder. His body stiffened, and he stared into the dark. Unstrapping his rifle, he held the weapon clutched in his hands.

Dawson plastered his body to the frozen ground. Raising his gun, he sighted on Henry again. He didn't breathe, didn't flinch. His one thought was to get off a shot before Henry shot him.

Henry's body filled the viewer, marked by the crosshairs.

Dawson's finger tightened on the trigger. His gut knotted. He'd hunted plenty of deer and moose, but shooting a man, killing a human being in cold blood, was different. A slew of memories of the countless times he'd played chess with Henry, and the warm summer afternoons when the old trapper had taught him to track wild animals flooded him. Henry had always been kind to Dawson. As far as he knew he'd never harmed anyone.

Until now.

Now he was a murderer. He'd killed one man and wounded two others. And he had Stella.

A chill inched along his spine. Focus. He inhaled and sighted in again.

"I know you're out there, Dawson." Henry's deep baritone filled the night.

Dawson swore under his breath and wiped a trickle of sweat from his eye. *Do it. Do it now.* The command screamed through his brain. His hands shook.

"Are you going to pull the trigger?" Henry stood unmoving, silhouetted against the glow from the fire.

A perfect target.

Dawson blew out a ragged breath, and with a defeated sigh, lowered the rifle to the ground, and rose to his feet, unarmed. "No, Henry, I'm not gonna kill you." Holding his hands out to his sides, he moved toward the big man. "But I am going to take the woman."

Henry barked out a laugh. "You've got balls. I'll give you that."

Dawson edged closer. If he could tackle Henry and take him down, he could end this without anyone else getting killed. But Henry was strong, his powerful muscles honed by a lifetime spent chopping wood, trapping, and hunting in this rugged land. His only hope was surprise. Somehow he had to distract him and then attack.

Another step.

"Let her go. She's not part of this."

And another.

Almost there.

Henry's face tightened with anger. "Why are you doing this? Why do you care? She's with the damn mining company." Spittle flew. "She didn't tell you that when you hired her, did she? She lied to you. She lied to all of us." In the encroaching darkness, the gleam of insanity shone in Henry's wild eyes.

A shimmer of fear raced up Dawson's spine.

Henry grunted, and his eyes widened as he lurched. The rifle fell from his hands as he flung out his arms and pitched forward. He landed on the rocky ground with a loud oomph.

Dawson gaped at the sprawled body. What the hell?

Stella's slight form appeared in the cave opening, a fierce expression on her beautiful face.

He blinked. She'd done that. She'd pushed Henry.

Henry groaned and shook his head as if he too was confused, but in the next moment, he sprang to his feet and faced Dawson, his eyes fierce.

Dawson's immobility vanished, and with a roar he lunged, tackling Henry around his knees. The big man fell like a felled oak tree and landed with a resounding thud on the unforgiving ground.

They grappled, rolling over and over in rocks, mud, and snow.

Henry's fingers dug like claws into Dawson's windpipe, cutting off his breath.

Dawson heaved and bucked, his legs kicking, fighting for leverage. *Air! He needed air.* Lungs burning, he drew up his leg, and as spots filled his fading vision, he rammed his knee into his attacker's crotch.

Henry yowled and released his death grip on Dawson's throat. He hunched over, writhing on the ground, his hands cupping between his legs.

Dawson scrabbled away, his throat on fire as he drew in great gulps of air.

Stella stumbled forward and grabbed a large rock, hefted it in both hands, and smashed it down on Henry's head.

The trapper stopped moving. His hands clutching his testicles fell to his sides. He stared at Dawson, blinked, and collapsed face-first on the ground.

Dawson's chest heaved. Sweat soaked his shirt, drenched his hair, and dripped into his eyes.

"Dawson!"

He blinked away the stinging sweat.

Stella's hands were tied in front of her, and she slipped and slid across the uneven ground.

He opened his arms and she fell into them. Her body molded to his. His stomach flipped upside down and turned inside out as a fierce protectiveness flooded him.

She placed her mouth on his, and all thought vanished under the delicious onslaught of the sensations rioting through him.

****

"Well, I sure as hell don't understand why you're letting her go without a fight." Alf slammed a cupboard door closed.

Dawson winced at the loud bang and ignored the old man's glower. That burr had been up Alf's ass ever since Stella informed them the previous night that she was still leaving the Circle 5. The last thing he needed was Alf riding his case. He had enough regrets for the both of them. He rubbed the crick in the back of his neck. Every inch of his body ached from his fight with Henry. His knee was swollen and bruised, and he had a black eye.

Stella was set on leaving. Their passionate embrace in the cold and snow outside the cave had meant nothing. The stubborn set to her mouth when she made her announcement told him better than her words that she was determined to leave him and Dee and the Circle 5. He'd tossed and turned all night, reliving her painful edict, the taste of impending loss bitter in his mouth.

After she knocked Henry out cold, he'd hauled Henry's unconscious body into the cave and trussed him like a hog-tied calf. He'd built up the smoldering fire to ensure the big man survived the next hours until the police picked him up in the morning.

Even with Henry's coat, Stella's thin clothing was unsuitable for the cold. Her feet were bruised and frozen, and her wrists raw and bleeding where Henry had bound her hands. She needed medical help. She couldn't wait until morning. If they walked back to the ranch, even in the dark, they'd be quicker than if they waited at the cave for the cops to arrive in the morning. Besides, she was desperate to get away from the cave and Henry.

He'd fished out an extra pair of wool socks from his packsack and slipped them over her freezing feet. Clinging to each other, he'd half-carried, half-dragged her as they'd fought through the snow and the dark to the ranch house.

At first, she'd burrowed into his embrace, but the closer they came to the ranch house, the quieter she became, and by the time they staggered into the clearing, she'd stiffened and transformed into a different woman.

He'd tried to explain, to apologize for letting Henry kidnap her, to finally confess how he felt, but before he could get the heartfelt words out, she cut him off. And then it was too late. She was swept away in a crowd of people, her wounds treated, her preliminary statement given, and then she limped off to bed, exhaustion staining her pale face.

That morning the police had taken Henry into custody and flown him to Hosten in the police helicopter. Sergeant Murphy stayed behind to take more detailed statements from both Dawson and Stella, but now he too had left, and the ranch was quiet.

Another cupboard door banged shut.

Or at least the ranch had been quiet until Alf got his dander up.

As if to prove a point, Alf slammed a large metal pot on the stove. The resounding clang rattled the windows.

Get in line, old man.

Dawson was in the doghouse around the ranch. No one was happy with him. Deirdre stomped around with a thundercloud over her head and a pout on her lips. The men were angry. Hell, *he* was furious with himself. Ever since Stella had arrived at the ranch, he'd done his best to get her to leave. Now that she was actually going, he wanted more than anything for her to stay.

He held out his hand and studied the gold band on his finger. A familiar lump filled his throat. An image of Anna, young and beautiful in her white wedding gown, eyes filled with love as she slid the ring over his knuckle and repeated the minister's words of love and devotion joining them together, flashed before him.

When he thought back to that day, he hardly recognized himself. He'd been so happy, so naive, unaware of the looming tragedy. He'd thought the future was secure, and he and the woman he loved would raise a family, have grandchildren, grow old together—the whole nine yards.

Wrong.

Anna changed after Deirdre was born. She transformed from the sweet, good-natured, funny woman he'd married into a bitter, angry person who spent her days sleeping, ignoring the squalling, red-faced infant.

Like a fool he'd thought she'd get over it. He made excuses for her behavior. Hundreds of them. She was exhausted from Deirdre's difficult birth. She needed time to adjust to caring for a newborn infant. She was just having a few down days.

Instead of calling the doctor and getting her help, he'd let her stay huddled under the blankets in their bed in the dark bedroom and sleep. At her request, he'd moved his things to the guest bedroom and taken on the feeding and comforting of their new baby.

As the weeks and months passed, Anna seemed to get better. She took an interest in Deirdre and cradled her for hours, singing sweet lullabies to the sleeping infant. He moved back into the master bedroom and into their marital bed. Life was good again.

But he'd been wrong, so terribly wrong.

He'd driven to the store to pick up diapers, a task

he'd undertaken hundreds of times. In the half hour he was gone—thirty lousy minutes—his life transformed into a nightmare.

He'd come home, a box of diapers under his arm, a bouquet of red roses clutched in his hand, and found her in the bathtub, her lifeless body half submerged in the bloody water. Deirdre was squalling from her crib in the nursery as if she too sensed the unspeakable tragedy.

A sob caught in his throat. He'd expected to die of a shattered heart that day, had wanted to die, but life was cruel, and his heart continued to beat and his lungs to draw in air. Besides, Deirdre needed him. It was as simple and as complicated as that.

In the days that followed, he'd stumbled through each minute of every day as if in a trance. It was all he could do to feed Dee and change her diapers. Who knows what would have happened if Alf hadn't come back into his life as if sent by an angel.

With the hard work of keeping the ranch a viable and profitable business, Dawson had gone through the motions of living. As one year followed the next, he'd existed, but that was all.

It wasn't until Stella arrived, and he saw himself through her eyes, that he realized how shallow his life was. He was a mere husk of a man. Alf was right. He might as well have been buried inside the casket with Anna. He'd wanted to burrow into his cocoon of grief, but now, for the first time in years, the darkness had lifted and light returned.

He twisted his wedding ring around his finger and tugged. The band was tight, and a callus had built up on his skin behind the ring. He'd never taken it off, not to bathe, shoe a horse, nor brand a calf. Once, a few years back, Alf had asked him why he didn't remove his wedding ring, but he'd snapped at the poor man and told him to mind his own damn business. Alf hadn't mentioned the ring again.

He tugged harder on the gold band, trying to yank it over his knuckle, but after six years, the ring seemed molded to his flesh, and refused to be dislodged. He gave another tug, pulling so hard the ring scraped off skin as it slid over his knuckle.

He held the gold band in the palm of his hand. The ring glowed with a ghostly luminescence in the dim light from the flickering fire as if it were imbued with a life of its own. His left hand felt naked, exposed. Shuddering, he shoved the ring back on his finger. The creak of a floorboard startled him, and he jerked his head up.

Alf was watching, a frown fixed on his leathery face.

Irritation, mixed with a hefty dose of guilt, flooded him. "What are you staring at, old man?"

"A damn fool."

Biting back a sharp retort, Dawson stormed out of the kitchen and limped down the hall to his office. He slammed the door as hard as he could. The walls shook, and the portrait of Anna and Deirdre fell and landed with a crash on the hardwood floor. The sound of breaking glass sickened him.

He fell to his knees, ignoring the jolt of pain in his injured knee, and lifted the photograph. Broken glass spidered across the faces of his loved ones. A low moan escaped his mouth. His hands shook when he picked up the glass shards. Pain lanced his palm as a sharp sliver of glass stabbed into his skin. Blood oozed from the cut and dripped in red splotches on Anna's smiling face.

He stared in horror at what he'd done. A shuddering sob worked its way up his throat and broke free, followed by another, and another as he dissolved in tears.

Chapter 25

Stella froze at the bottom of the stairs. The hairs on the back of her neck prickled as a low moan echoed from down the dark hall. Alf had gone to his room in the bunkhouse an hour ago. When she'd peeked in Deirdre's room before she headed downstairs for a glass of milk, the child had been sound asleep. The unsettling sound was coming from Dawson's office.

A thin stream of light shone beneath the closed door. She tiptoed closer and pressed her ear to the wood. The anguished keening was louder. *Walk away. This is none of your business. Not anymore. Not since you decided to leave.* She wheeled around, but stopped.

He sounded like he was in pain. Her breath caught in her throat. An image of Dawson lying injured on the floor rose before her, and before she stopped herself, she turned the knob and opened the door.

Dawson sat on the couch, his face buried in his hands, his shoulders shaking with wracking sobs. A half-empty bottle of scotch was on the floor beside the couch. A glass lay on its side, a pool of amber liquid staining the floor.

She wrinkled her nose at the overpowering, sickly sweet stench of alcohol. "Dawson? What's wrong? Are you okay?" She bit down on her lip. What was she thinking? He wasn't okay; he wasn't anywhere near okay.

The terrible sobbing ceased, and his shoulders stiffened, but he kept his face covered.

She edged closer, glass crunching under her shoes.

The large photograph from the wall behind the couch lay on the floor. Dark spatters—blood?—smudged the faces of the happy mother and child.

Dawson's breath hitched in a broken sob, and she ignored the fallen photograph and sat beside him and touched his shoulder.

"Go away." He shrugged off her hand. "If you know what's good for you, you'll get the hell out of here."

His words stung. He didn't want her help. He didn't want *her*, period. She stood and turned to go, but once again she stopped. She couldn't leave. She loved him. He was in pain. Whether he knew it or not, he needed her. "I'm not going anywhere."

He lowered his hands.

His eyes were swollen and red, his face haggard. Tears stained his rugged cheeks. The utter desolation in the dark depths of his eyes chilled her to the bottom of her soul.

He wiped his face with his sleeve. "I told you to leave."

"I heard you."

His lip curled in a sneer. "What's with you? Huh? For weeks you've been bound and determined to leave the ranch, but now you won't leave me alone?" His words were slurred. "What is this, a pity move? You feel sorry for me? Is that it?"

"You're drunk."

"Not nearly drunk enough." He grabbed the bottle of scotch, lifted it to his lips, and swallowed a big gulp.

Spots of dried blood covered his hands.

She sucked in a breath. "You're hurt."

He lowered the bottle and studied his hand. "It's nothing."

Kneeling before him, she took the bottle and set it on the floor, and grasped his injured hand.

This time he didn't resist, though the muscles in his arm tensed.

A small shard of glass was lodged deep in his palm. The wound had stopped bleeding, but the piece of glass needed to be removed before infection set in. "Wait here." She rose and hurried out of the den and down the hall to the first aid closet and retrieved antiseptic wipes, gauze, tweezers, ointment, and medical tape.

He was drinking more liquor when she strode back into the office. "Don't you think you've had enough?"

"What do you care? You're not my wife." The words, made all the more cruel because of the stark truth, blasted the small den like an explosion. His face paled. "Damn. I'm sorry. I didn't—"

"Don't speak." She stopped his halting apology. "You've said more than enough." His words stung. She wasn't his wife, and never would be. She hid her hurt, and with surprisingly steady hands, tended to his wound. Using the tweezers, she removed the glass, wiped antiseptic on the wound, dabbed ointment, and wrapped strips of sterile gauze around his hand.

"I love you."

She spluttered and met his bleary gaze. "Wha...what did you say?"

"Please don't leave me. I love you." The words, spoken in a clear, lucid voice, were unmistakable.

Her heart soared as the full meaning of what he said struck her, but just as quickly, disappointment hit like a cold, wet blanket as the bottle slipped from his hand, and he sagged on the couch and closed his eyes.

His mouth opened and a snore emerged.

He was drunk, and he thought he was talking to his dead wife. Desolation, like a lethal poison, flowed through her veins and deadened her heart. A black mist settled over her soul.

He didn't love her. How could he? He was in love with his wife, a woman who'd been dead for five years.

How could she compete with a dead woman?

****

He cracked open an eyelid and winced as bright morning sunlight stabbed like a needle into his tired brain. He snapped his lid closed. His mouth tasted like a herd of cattle had spent the night. An incessant throbbing pain spiked behind his eyeballs.

He struggled to think, but his brain was fuzzy, his thoughts a confusing kaleidoscope of images. He opened both eyes, squinting against the light. Rubbing his temples, he sat up. The room swayed. Nausea roiled in his belly, but he swallowed back the sour taste of bile.

He was lying on the couch in his office. A blanket covered him and a pillow rested beneath his aching head. He had a hangover all right, a doozy. He lifted his hand to scrub his whiskers, but stopped. A gauze bandage was wrapped around his right hand. He flexed his fingers, and memories filtered in with the pain.

He jerked up. The portrait was hanging on the wall where it always was, but the glass covering the photograph was gone.

Now he remembered...slamming the door, the picture falling, smashing on the floor...broken glass...blood...Stella.

He moaned and leaned forward with his forearms on his thighs. The room swirled, and he closed his eyes and sucked in deep, steadying breaths until the sickening sensation passed and the room stilled.

Stella.

Even though he'd been a drunken ass and ordered her to leave, she'd stayed and tended his wound. He shook his head at her stubbornness and grimaced as the throbbing behind his eyes escalated to an explosion of pain. After he'd passed out, she must have picked up the shattered pieces of glass, hung the photograph on the wall, and covered him with the blanket and placed the pillow under his head.

He dug the pads of his fingers into his temples. His memory was a blur. Other than getting shitfaced and making a damn fool of himself, had he done or said anything stupid? Was she mad at him? He snorted. How could she not be? If he'd wanted to drive her away, last night's drunken debacle sealed the deal.

He'd never known anyone like her. From the very beginning she'd surprised him with her gentle loving of his daughter, her easy affability with the ranch hands, and her fierce loyalty toward Alf. Each and every day she'd been on the ranch, she'd proven how he'd misjudged her.

She was the most courageous person he'd ever met. For her to leave her familiar life in the city behind and travel halfway across the province to work at an isolated ranch with a bunch of strangers took amazing strength of will. The fact she'd survived the loss of her only child was further proof of her strength. She'd not only survived Keegan's tragic death, she'd set her grief behind her and showered Dee with her unselfish caring and love.

Deirdre was the one perfect thing he'd created. He treasured his daughter above all else, but he'd been blind to her desperate need for companionship. He'd been too wrapped up in his work on the ranch and his drive to make the business a success, and he'd ignored his daughter's needs. Hell, he'd fought Alf tooth and nail until the old codger had worn him down, and he'd agreed to hire a nanny.

Deirdre was a different child since Stella arrived. Dee's boundless energy and enthusiasm for life had found a focus. For the first time in a very long time, she was happy, really happy. And all because of Stella King.

And how had he repaid Stella? By clinging to a memory of the past. He stared at the ring on his finger.

It was time.

Past time.

He tugged the ring from his finger, surprised at how easily the band of gold slid off this time, and clutched it in his injured palm. A stab of pain shot through him, but he held tight. The ring wasn't Anna. Removing it wasn't a betrayal of their love. After more than four long years of grieving, he was finally ready to move on. Finally ready to live.

Opening his hand, he stared at the symbol of the past. He'd never forget Anna. He'd always treasure the love they shared. Life moved on, and in spite of his determination to remain in the shadows of the past, his heart led him along a different path.

He pushed to his feet, stumbled over to the desk, and set the ring on the surface. His hand looked naked. A circle of pale skin marked where the gold band had rested for so many years. A sense of peace settled over him with the certainty that this was right. Somewhere far away, Anna watched and gave her silent approval.

Lightness filled his soul, and he smiled through his tears. He wheeled around, wrenched open the door, and raced out of the office. One goal in mind—find Stella and convince her to stay.

****

"What do you mean she's gone?"

Alf wiped a pot with a dishtowel and set the heavy cast iron pan on the stove. "She left this morning with Alphonse. He's taking her to Spirit Falls on his snowmobile."

Dawson sagged against the wall. "Snowmobile?" he parroted, unable to digest Alf's words. "What the hell are you talking about? That's a hundred and fifty kilometers of open country."

"Alphonse knows his way around this territory. She'll be fine."

He gripped the back of a chair, his nails scoring the wood. Stella was gone. She'd left while he was passed out in a drunken stupor. She hadn't bothered with goodbye. So desperate to leave, she hadn't waited for him to take her. Instead, she'd chosen to ride for hours on the back of a snowmobile over mountainous terrain to escape. He swallowed back the thickening lump in his throat. "What…what about Dee? Does she know?"

Alf nodded. "She's in her room crying her little heart out."

Dawson's heart cracked. All too well he identified

with Deirdre's pain. They both loved Stella. But she didn't love them. Not enough to stay.

Alf cleared his throat. "You're a damn fool. Drinking yourself to death isn't going to help anything. You realize that, don't you?"

"I know. I made a mistake. I...I didn't plan to drink, but the photograph fell, and the next thing I knew the bottle was in my hand, and I was gulping scotch like it was a life-saving elixir." He scrubbed his fingers over his unshaven face. "I lost her, Alf. I...I thought she'd at least say goodbye." The lump in his throat thickened.

"You need help, boy. More help than I can give you."

"I know."

Alf met his gaze. "You've said that before."

"I know, but I mean it this time. I called Hosten this morning. I'm seeing someone next week."

Alf's faded blue eyes shimmered as he blinked rapidly. "You'll be okay. Just give it time. You won't be alone. I'll be here to help every step of the way." He hung the dishtowel on the rack.

"Thanks, Alf. What would I do without you?"

"You'd be in a pickle all right." Alf sniffled and grinned.

The cat wandered into the kitchen and threaded his plump, furry body through Alf's legs. His purring filled the silence in the warm room.

Alf tugged out a cloth handkerchief from his pants pocket and blew his nose. "Oh, I forgot. Nicholas King called."

"What did he want?" Not that he cared. Not now. Not when his life was falling apart.

"Imperial Monarch Resources is withdrawing the

mine proposal. Seems the appeal you launched worked."

"What? I didn't launch an appeal. I thought about it, but events have been too crazy around here." He'd been busy dealing with the stark reality of a murderer on the loose on his ranch and fending off suspicion he was the one responsible. To say nothing of rescuing Stella from Henry's clutches and dealing with his broken heart.

Alf harrumphed. "Well, someone sure did. What's wrong? I'd have thought you'd be happy. You've been fighting this mine development for months, but now you're acting like you don't give a damn."

Dawson frowned. Alf was right. He should be ecstatic an open-pit copper mine wasn't going to destroy his ranch, but he didn't care. Not now. Imperial Monarch could rip up the whole ranch, and he wouldn't give a damn.

Stella was gone.

He couldn't think of anything else. Later, when his heart wasn't lying on the floor, shattered in a hundred pieces, he'd celebrate, but not now. And probably not tomorrow, or the next day, or the day after that.

Alf tromped closer. His eyes narrowed. "Where's your wedding ring?"

"What?"

"Your ring." He nodded at Dawson's bare left hand. "You're not wearing your wedding band."

"I took it off."

Shas whined and twitched in his dreams where he lay on the mat before the crackling fire.

The cat meowed and strolled over to her dish and crunched on the hard food pellets.

Sunlight streamed through the window and streaked the floor.

"They left a couple of hours ago." Alf's voice broke the heavy silence. "You can catch them if you hurry."

He stared at Alf, his heart leaping at his friend's suggestion.

Alf placed his hand on Dawson's shoulder. "If you love her as much as I think you do, you'll go after her."

"But she doesn't want to stay. She doesn't want me."

Alf chuckled. "I thought you were smarter than that." He patted Dawson's shoulder as if he were a child. "Now make us all happy. Get your ass in gear and go after the damn woman."

Dawson held still another heartbeat, until a burst of adrenaline coursed through him, and he sprang into action. He flew across the room, shrugged on his coat, tugged on his boots, and pulled on a pair of warm gloves.

"I had Jean-Luc bring your snow machine and your helmet up to the house." Alf handed Dawson a small canvas sack. "Here's some food and a thermos of hot coffee."

"Thank you." He blinked back the sting of tears. "Thank you for everything."

Alf's eyes gleamed with moisture. "Go get her, son."

Dawson nodded and flung open the door and hurried outside. Leaping down the steps, he sprinted across the yard to the snowmobile. He strapped on his helmet, slung the small packsack over his shoulders, and straddled the seat. The powerful machine started with a roar. He squeezed the throttle, and the snowmobile leaped forward like an unleashed beast and flew across the clearing onto the path through the trees.

Chapter 26

Dawson's heart raced as he followed the tracks of Alphonse's snowmobile through the forest, across snow-covered grasslands, and over the hills. He was two hours behind Alphonse and Stella, but his machine was newer than Alphonse's, and it wasn't slowed by the weight of two people. With luck and daring, he should catch up to them.

He paused on the ridge and studied the frozen lake below. Sunlight shone on a thin layer of melt water covering the gray ice. Crossing the lake would save a good thirty minutes of travel time, but the warm winds of the chinook over the past few days had weakened the ice.

Crossing the lake was a gamble. If the ice cracked under him, both he and the snowmobile would end up in the lake. He wouldn't survive long in the freezing water. No one would find his body, and Dee would never know what happened to her father.

Another tragedy in her young life.

He chewed on his bottom lip. If he made it across the lake, he'd catch up to Alphonse and Stella. If he followed the safe route around the lake, he might not find them before they reached Spirit Falls. By then, Stella would be on the bus back to Hosten. Could he live with himself knowing he hadn't done everything in his power to convince her to stay?

Setting his jaw, he tightened the strap on his helmet, lowered his visor, patted the engine hood for good luck, and gunned the throttle. Motor screaming, the snowmobile surged ahead and sped down the hill. He kept the engine roaring, his hand tight on the accelerator, not daring to slow.

The skis flew over the snow and slammed onto the frozen lake and splashed through a thin layer of melt water, skidding on the slick ice. Gouts of slush sprayed in the snowmobile's wake as it skimmed across the lake.

"Come on. Come on." He muttered the words, focused on the distant shoreline.

Halfway.

He could do this.

His heart pounded in time with the frantic pulsing of the engine.

Almost there.

The snow-covered rocky shore loomed ahead. Each second the snow machine stayed above the dark, freezing water was another meter closer to success.

A loud crack resounded across the lake.

Adrenaline coursed through him, and he goosed the gas.

Another retort like the blast of a rifle boomed above the roar of the machine. A narrow crack spidered across the ice. The fissure widened. Dark water lapped over the jagged edges.

The snowmobile tilted on the breaking ice, but he didn't reduce his speed. To slow down was certain death. His hand was numb from squeezing the throttle, yet he tightened his grip. The machine's back end dipped, sinking into the slushy water.

He rose on one knee and leaned forward, shifting his weight to the front of the snowmobile. His breath caught in his throat.

Close, so close.

"Yes!" His shout was lost in the roar of engine as the powerful machine leaped onto shore, and the skids hit solid ground. He released his breath and glanced over his shoulder. Long cracks fractured the lake surface. Open water lapped over the blocks of shattered ice. Ignoring his cramping hand, he kept the gas on hard and raced through a copse of trees and up a hill.

A snowmobile blazed across the snow not more than two hundred meters ahead on the flat ground beside the river.

He'd found them!

Beads of sweat pooled under his arms and dripped down his sides under his coat. What if his Hail Mary didn't work? Stella had made her feelings clear. She wanted to leave the ranch, to get away from him. And here he was stalking her. What was he planning to do once he caught up to her and Alphonse? Beg her to stay?

Damn straight.

He'd do whatever it took to convince her she was making a mistake. Hell, he'd risked his life crossing a lake covered with a few, thin inches of candled ice to confront her. Confessing his love couldn't be any more frightening. Swallowing his trepidation, he gunned his machine and raced down the hill.

They didn't hear him approaching over the roar of their own snowmobile, and he raced up beside them and waved.

Stella shifted on her seat and stared. She nudged

Alphonse.

The other man turned and peered through his visor and released his grip on the gas. The snowmobile slowed and stopped.

Dawson steered beside them. He unsnapped his chinstrap and flipped off his helmet, and set it on the machine's padded bench seat.

"Dawson?" Alphonse's surprise would have been funny if the situation were different, if Dawson's whole life wasn't at stake. "What's going on? Is everything okay?"

Dawson couldn't take his gaze off Stella. Her arms were still wrapped around Alphonse's waist, her chest pressed to his back. A spurt of jealousy struck him, but he quashed it and focused on why he was there.

In the rush to catch them, he hadn't planned what he'd say, how he'd convince her to stay. And now, when he needed them the most, words failed him. He stared at her, tongue-tied like a heartsick teenager.

****

"What are you doing here?" She released her grip on Alphonse, climbed off the snowmobile, unhooked her helmet, and slipped it off. A sliver of fear gelled in her stomach. "Is Dee okay? Is that why you're here? Has she run away again?" When she'd said goodbye to the little girl that morning, Dee had collapsed in tears. She'd refused to talk to Stella and closed herself in her room. Alf said he'd keep an eye on her, but what if Deirdre had run after her? She studied the rugged, snow-covered wilderness and shuddered. A child wouldn't have a chance of surviving, not for long, not in the winter.

Dawson watched her, his face flushed from the

cold, his eyes fierce.

"Please tell me, is Dee okay?"

He nodded.

A surge of relief washed over her.

"Did we forget something?" Alphonse asked.

Dawson nodded again.

Stella bit her bottom lip in frustration. What was wrong with him? Couldn't the man speak?

"Dawson, are you all right?" Alphonse's deep voice was filled with concern.

Dawson inhaled a deep, shuddering breath. "No, I'm not all right, not at all." His fervid gaze fixed on her. "Why are you leaving?"

She blew out a breath. "We've been through this."

"Alf told me your company's decided against building the mine on the Circle 5. Someone launched an appeal, and the government accepted it." His gaze narrowed. "That was you, wasn't it? You sent in the paperwork."

She tucked a lock of hair behind her ear. Attempting to stop the mine development was her gift to him and Deirdre, but she hadn't wanted him to know she was responsible for setting the appeal process in motion.

When Nicholas told her Imperial Monarch Resources was planning on developing a mine on the Circle 5, she contacted a friend who worked for an environmental lobby group. He'd always been a thorn in her side, but he was an expert in the environmental appeal process, and he knew how to stall mine developments for years in the legal hinterland.

He was good. Very good. She would know, from past standoffs, but Dawson's news didn't make sense.

A decision on the mine proposal for the Circle 5 had happened too quickly. Way too quickly. Appeals took months, sometimes years, to be resolved.

Nicholas had done this. He'd halted Imperial Monarch's plans. Somehow he'd convinced the board members to dismiss the project. She released a long breath. He'd done this for her. His way of atoning for how he'd treated her after Keegan's death.

"Thank you for doing that. The mine would have destroyed the Circle 5," Dawson said.

Her nerves hummed with disappointment. So this was why he'd chased after her—to thank her for saving his precious ranch. "You should be thanking Nicholas. He's the one who made the decision to halt the mine development."

He picked up a clump of snow, wadded it into a ball, and tossed the snowball into the trees. His eyes were raw when he turned back. "I love you."

Her legs wobbled, and she collapsed onto the snowmobile seat. "Wha...what?"

"You heard me."

Alphonse coughed and shuffled his feet. "Um, I'll, um, I'll just be over there having a smoke." Striding to a stand of trees well out of earshot, he fished a cigarette out of his coat pocket, and lit the end with a flaming match. He slipped the cigarette between his lips and blew out a plume of smoke.

She shot to her feet and faced Dawson. "I don't believe you." He'd said those same three words the previous night when he was drunk. Anna's ghost had hovered between them in the small office, and Stella knew with a sickening certainty that he wasn't talking to her, but affirming his love for his wife. That was why she'd asked Alphonse for help. She couldn't bear one more minute of watching the man she loved devote his life and his heart to a ghost.

Like a wolf stalking its prey, a fierce light gleamed in his dark eyes, and he moved closer.

Her breath caught in her throat. She edged back until her hips bumped the snowmobile, and there was no more room for escape. Licking her dry lips, she struggled to swallow over the stone in her throat.

He halted a breath away, towering over her. Grasping her chin with gentle fingers, he raised her face to meet his burning gaze. "I love you, Stella King. You. Just you." He released his grip on her chin and trailed his leather-clad fingers along her cheek. "Hear me out before you say anything. Please."

He released her and lowered his gloved hands to his sides. "After my wife…after Anna…died, the pain was so immense I was afraid to love again." He blew out a ragged breath. "But then you came into my life, and…and you turned my world upside down. I fell in love with you, and I was terrified. Terrified I'd lose you."

She wanted to leap into his arms and kiss him, but stopped. This was too important. Her heart was at stake. She had to be certain. "I don't understand."

The air stilled, and the tree branches stopped rattling in the wind.

She held her breath. So much depended on his next words.

He tugged off his leather gloves, tossed them on the snow, and held his left hand before her.

"Your wedding ring…it's gone." She blinked. "You took off your wedding ring." As the full impact of what he'd done struck her, she sank onto the snowmobile seat again. "Why?"

His gaze met hers, direct and unflinching. "It was time."

"Are...are you sure?" His words found soft, tillable soil in her heart. Warmth unfurled within her and blossomed until liquid heat flowed through her veins and melted the block of ice deep in her belly, but she held back. She couldn't risk the agonizing pain of losing another person she loved. "What about your wife? What about Anna? Are you still in love with her?"

His dark eyes glistened with moisture. "I'll always love Anna. I'll never get over losing her. She was my first love. Our love created Dee.

"After...after Anna died, I couldn't think beyond surviving the next second."

His strong, tanned throat worked, and he met her gaze.

"For a long time, my life passed in solitary, gray moments. Then I met you, and now I see days, months, and years. I see a future filled with joy...filled with you." He tapped his left hand over his heart. "Whether my heart beats one more day or a hundred years, it's yours and only yours."

The sun arched high against a cloudless blue sky. It gilded the snow-frosted, razor-backed, distant mountain peaks with showers of gold.

She inhaled a deep breath, filling her lungs with the smell of pine, fresh air, and for the first time since she lost Keegan—hope.

This was the love she'd waited a lifetime to find. Amazingly, in this isolated, rugged wilderness, thousands of kilometers from everything she'd ever known, she'd found salvation. A warm glow swelled low in her belly, expanding and enveloping her with joy. Standing on wobbly legs, she drew his face to hers and kissed him, trying to express the strength of her love in the single, tender touch. She deepened the kiss, feeling it all the way to her toes. "I love you too, Dawson."

His face lit up as if a light shone from within, and he drew her closer, resting his beard-roughened cheek against her hair. The strong, steady beat of his heart matched hers.

She burrowed into his warmth, melding her body with his. His familiar masculine scent surrounded her, and she heaved a sigh of contentment.

In the next breath he released her. He clasped her hands in his and knelt before her on the snow. "Stella King, will you marry me? Will you be my wife?"

"About time you asked." She threw herself into his arms, and they collapsed in a tangle of limbs on the snow. Their mouths fused, heart to heart, soul to soul.

The roar of a snowmobile starting up broke through her elation.

Alphonse, helmet on, straddled his snow machine. He grinned and gestured with his thumb up and raced off in a spray of snow in the direction of the Circle 5.

Dawson grinned. "Was it something we said?"

She chuckled, joy bubbling up in her heart and spilling over.

He stood, gripped her hands, and helped her to her feet. His heated expression dialed up her heart rate. "Does this mean you're staying?"

"Damn straight." She stifled a giggle.

"Deirdre will be happy. And of course, there's an upside." He grinned. "I won't have to pay a nanny."

She faked a fierce frown and slugged his arm.

"Ouch." He rubbed his biceps. "Okay, okay. You can have Caspar. Consider him part of the deal."

"Great. Just what I want—a horse who bucks me off. I want Rocky."

"Whatever you want. He's yours. Just say the word."

She laughed as happiness radiated through her. No one knew what the future held, but one thing was certain, life with this man would never be dull. No matter what fate had in store, she wouldn't face the future alone.

She glanced up at an overhanging branch. The gnarled limb, frosted with clumps of wet snow and thick with pine needles, curved over her and Dawson like a protective canopy.

Another smile broke out as she recalled Dee's rainbow trees. The little girl's wish had come true. She was getting the mother she'd always wanted.

She closed her eyes and whispered a fervent wish that the strength of their love would be enough. They'd be a family.

A new family.

She couldn't wait to share her news with Dee.

A word about the author...

C.B. Clark has always loved reading, especially romances, but it wasn't until she lost her voice for a year that she considered writing her own romantic suspense stories. She grew up in Canada's Northwest Territories and Yukon. Graduating with a degree in Archaeology, she has worked as an archaeologist and an educator. She enjoys hiking, canoeing, and snowshoeing with her husband and dog near her home in the wilderness of central British Columbia.

Thank you for purchasing
this publication of The Wild Rose Press, Inc.

For questions or more information
contact us at
info@thewildrosepress.com.

The Wild Rose Press, Inc.
www.thewildrosepress.com